PENGUIN

THE SOUL OF MAN UNDER SOCIALISM
AND SELECTED CRITICAL PROSE

OSCAR FINGAL O'FLAHERTIE WILLS WILDE was born in Dublin in 1854, his father an eminent eye-surgeon and his mother a nationalist poet who wrote under the pseudonym 'Speranza'. He went to Trinity College, Dublin, and then to Magdalen College, Oxford, where he began to propagandize the new Aesthetic (or 'Art for Art's Sake') Movement. Despite winning a first and the Newdigate Prize for Poetry, Wilde failed to obtain an Oxford fellowship, and was forced to earn a living by public lecturing and writing for periodicals. He published a largely unsuccessful volume of poems in 1881 and in the next year undertook a lecture tour of the United States in order to promote the D'Oyly Carte production of Gilbert and Sullivan's comic opera *Patience*. After his marriage to Constance Lloyd in 1884, he tried to establish himself as a writer, but with little initial success. However, his three volumes of short fiction, *The Happy Prince* (1888), *Lord Arthur Savile's Crime* (1891) and *A House of Pomegranates* (1891), together with his only novel, *The Picture of Dorian Gray* (1891), gradually won him a reputation, confirmed and enhanced by the phenomenal success of his society comedies – *Lady Windermere's Fan*, *A Woman of No Importance*, *An Ideal Husband* and *The Importance of Being Earnest*, all performed on the West End stage between 1892 and 1895.

Success, however, was short-lived. In 1891 Wilde had met and fallen extravagantly in love with Lord Alfred Douglas. In 1895, when his success as a dramatist was at its height, Wilde brought an unsuccessful libel action against Douglas's father, the Marquess of Queensberry. Wilde lost the case and two trials later was sentenced to two years' imprisonment for acts of gross indecency. As a result of this experience he wrote *The Ballad of Reading Gaol*. He was released from prison in 1897 and went into an immediate self-imposed exile on the Continent. He died in Paris in ignominy in 1900.

LINDA DOWLING has written a number of books about Victorian literature in the 1890s, including *Language and Decadence in the Victorian Fin de Siècle* (1986), *Hellenism and Homosexuality in Victorian Oxford* (1994) and *The*

Vulgarization of Art: The Victorians and Aesthetic Democracy (1996). She has held Alexander von Humboldt, Rockefeller and Guggenheim fellowships, and is a past fellow of the Rutgers Center for Historical Analysis. She lives in Princeton, New Jersey.

OSCAR WILDE

The Soul of Man under Socialism and Selected Critical Prose

Edited with an introduction and explanatory notes by
LINDA DOWLING

PENGUIN BOOKS

PENGUIN BOOKS

Published by the Penguin Group
Penguin Books Ltd, 80 Strand, London WC2R 0RL, England
Penguin Putnam Inc., 375 Hudson Street, New York, New York 10014, USA
Penguin Books Australia Ltd, 250 Camberwell Road, Camberwell, Victoria 3124, Australia
Penguin Books Canada Ltd, 10 Alcorn Avenue, Toronto, Ontario, Canada M4V 3B2
Penguin Books India (P) Ltd, 11 Community Centre, Panchsheel Park, New Delhi – 110 017, India
Penguin Books (NZ) Ltd, Cnr Rosedale and Airborne Roads, Albany, Auckland, New Zealand
Penguin Books (South Africa) (Pty) Ltd, 24 Sturdee Avenue, Rosebank 2196, South Africa

Penguin Books Ltd, Registered Offices: 80 Strand, London WC2R 0RL, England

www.penguin.com

First published 2001

033

Set in 10/12.5 pt Monotype Baskerville
Typeset by Rowland Phototypesetting Ltd, Bury St Edmunds, Suffolk
Printed and bound in Great Britain by Clays Ltd, Elcograf S.p.A.

www.greenpenguin.co.uk

MIX
Paper from
responsible sources
FSC
www.fsc.org   FSC® C018179

Penguin Books is committed to a sustainable
future for our business, our readers and our planet.
This book is made from Forest Stewardship
Council™ certified paper.

CONTENTS

INTRODUCTION

'I was a man,' Oscar Wilde famously declared, 'who stood in symbolic relations to the art and culture of my age.' He made the remark in a long letter written during the final months of a prison sentence served for committing 'acts of gross indecency with other male persons'. When part of the letter was published in 1905 under the title of *De Profundis*, Wilde's claim seemed to many readers to be at once grandiose and pathetic – symptomatic of the manic egotism that had seemingly driven Wilde, then a brilliantly successful playwright, author and wit, on his mad course to prison: first publicly courting Lord Alfred Douglas, the beautiful but forbidden son of the Marquess of Queensberry, then suing Queensberry for libel, at a time when Wilde's own life, with its reckless forays into the underworld of homosexual prostitutes, could hardly bear the scrutiny of a public proceeding. Even many decades later, in 1962 when the full text of the *De Profundis* letter was published for the first time, Wilde's statement seemed to many to be excessive and overweening – tragic proof of a deterioration of mind and character under the savage conditions of late Victorian prison life.

Today the claim reads as the simple statement of an obvious truth. Wilde's rehabilitation has been complete, exceeding anything his most loyal defenders could have imagined when he first went to prison. In 1995, one hundred years after his conviction, a memorial to Wilde would be dedicated in Westminster Abbey. In recent years, Wilde's plays have been continuously revived on the stage and successfully translated into films. His tragic plunge from the height of success to the depths of social ruin has been depicted in everything from lavishly illustrated coffee-table books to an acclaimed twentieth-century literary biography, Richard Ellmann's *Oscar Wilde* (1987). With his distinctive image reproduced on T-shirts and coffee mugs and his witty apothegms repeated everywhere, Wilde now seems more our contemporary than he ever was the Victorians'.

Most twenty-first-century audiences seeing Wilde's society plays or reading *The Picture of Dorian Gray* or his fairy tales and stories find them immediately attractive. This response has been matched by the tendency of modern literary and cultural critics to take Wilde as a spokesman for our own contemporary concerns. He has been portrayed as a critic of commodity capitalism, as a professional writer struggling to overcome the gritty material conditions imposed by Grub Street, and as an early postmodern exponent of irony, plagiarism and pastiche. Perhaps most remarkably, Wilde has been made into a major figure in our contemporary preoccupation with homosexual identity and gay rights, whether as a theorist of the gay transgressive aesthetic or as an example of gay self-hatred. So it has come about that Wilde, more, perhaps, than any other Victorian, has been made to stand in a symbolic relation at least to our own age.

The critical prose brought together in the following pages, on the other hand, gives us a Wilde not so easily made over in the image of our contemporary concerns. Readers expecting to find in the critical prose of *Intentions* or *The Soul of Man under Socialism* pronouncements on consumer capitalism or hints about the secret life of Victorian homosexuality will discover instead Wilde's deep imaginative engagement with great literary works, his long preoccupation with the theory and practice of criticism, and bravura passages bristling with learned references to artists and artworks, many of them wholly unfamiliar to modern readers. Readers who turn to *The Portrait of Mr W. H.* hoping to see Wilde wholly engrossed in questions of boy-love or the ambiguity of the sexes will find him unaccountably absorbed, to no less degree, in such matters as Elizabethan stage costume and the transmigration of souls. In short, instead of hearing Wilde as a voice of modern or postmodernist ideas, the reader will find him to be absorbed in issues we now tend to think of as remote from contemporary concerns – beauty, aesthetic form, the contemplative life, the moral imperatives underlying the slogan of Art for Art's Sake.

The twenty-first century, it may be, will mark the period during which we begin to grasp Wilde's importance as a philosophical spokesman for the autonomy of art. For our current preoccupation with Wilde as a witty and languid poseur tends to obscure the Wilde who was, at the same time, a deep and serious reader of literature and philosophy, a brilliant student of languages and an original thinker about the complex relations between art and society. Yet this is in a real sense the essential or fundamental Wilde, a Wilde needed to explain, for instance, an awed remark by Thomas Martin, his prison warder during the last seven months in Reading Gaol. 'He was so unlike other men,' Martin recalled. 'Just a bundle of brains – and that is all.' For Martin had seen a Wilde *in extremis*, all poses and defences cut away. After two years' imprisonment, with its hard labour, solitary confinement, racking illness and constant threat of insanity – penned within what the prisoner himself called 'this tomb for those who are not yet dead' – what finally remained to Wilde, as this sympathetic warder saw, was his intellect.

Wilde was born in Dublin in 1854, the second son of two energetic and strikingly intelligent parents. His father was an innovative eye and ear physician later given a knighthood in recognition of his services to medicine. Sir William Wilde founded an eye and ear hospital in Dublin, wrote what became the earliest textbooks in the British Isles on aural surgery and epidemic ophthalmia and compiled the first systematic statistics on the incidence of deafness and blindness in Ireland. Wilde's mother, a dashing bohemian and bluestocking who wrote fiery patriotic poetry under the pen-name of 'Speranza', conducted the most celebrated salon in Dublin, no mean accomplishment in that city of brilliant talkers. Both parents were committed Irish nationalists, devoting much time to preserving the rich oral tradition of folklore still precariously surviving in the west of Ireland.

From 1864 to 1871 Wilde attended Portora Royal School in Enniskillen, where his brother Willie was also a student. Once there, as Richard Ellmann tells us, Wilde began to overtake Willie, who was two years older and until then considered to be the cleverer boy. Oscar became famous for a prodigious memory and ability to read at great speed. In what came to be regarded as a sort of parlour trick, he would offer to read a three-volume novel in thirty minutes, mastering both plot and characters in the allotted time. After sixty minutes, Wilde could recount even the minor scenes and recite whole stretches of dialogue. Such abilities were to prove especially useful later, in the 1880s, when Wilde would become a book reviewer perennially under deadline. But it is vital to see that beneath the parlour trick lay magnificent powers of intellect and judgement. In 'The Critic as Artist', Wilde's protagonist Gilbert declares that no reviewer should ever read works through, because, as he puts it, 'to know the vintage and quality of a wine one need not drink the whole cask'. Thus does Wilde echo Samuel Johnson's famously incredulous question, 'Sir, do you read books *through*?' in a manner that unexpectedly emphasizes certain deep similarities between the two men. For Wilde and Johnson alike possessed a lightning quickness of apprehension, a firmness of memory and an aptness of citation that their friends regarded as nothing less than astonishing. This, not least, is something that would be obscured by the tragic fate that was to leave Wilde to die in disgrace with only a few friends remaining to testify to what one of them, Robert Ross, called 'the sumptuous endowment of his intellect'.

Although Wilde won some early prizes at Portora, the extraordinary range of his intellectual talent would pass unremarked there until he began to read classical literature. Then, translating Thucydides, Plato, Virgil – and especially Aeschylus' *Agamemnon* – he caught fire. The intellectual awakening came to a young man already keenly sensitive to aesthetic stimuli, and growing up in a Victorian world recently and urgently made to attend to the importance of colour, pattern and form. For from 1843 onwards, pre-eminently in *Modern Painters* and *The Stones of Venice*, John Ruskin had been presiding over an 'education of the eye' among British readers, his exquisitely sensitive prose giving a voice to what had been hitherto invisible or inexpressible, his marvellous eloquence teaching an entire generation to see. At Oxford, where Ruskin was in residence as the Slade Professor of Art, Wilde would seek him out, attend his lectures and even volunteer to fill wheelbarrows with dirt as part of Ruskin's famously quixotic project of building a road to Ferry Hinksey. Above all, Wilde was moved by what Gilbert in 'The Critic as Artist' would call Ruskin's 'mighty and majestic prose', 'so fervid and so fiery-coloured', when, especially, Ruskin was writing about colour. For colour had always entranced Wilde. At thirteen, he was already wearing what he contentedly described as 'quite scarlet' shirts. From boyhood on, he would declare in *De Profundis*, there had not been 'a single colour hidden away in the chalice of a flower, or the curve of a shell, to which, by some subtle sympathy with the very soul of things, my nature does not answer'.

To be sure, an intense response to the visible world, and especially an acute delight in colour, would become the universal passport of the nineteenth-century aesthete: Edgar Allan Poe, Walter Pater, William Morris, Marcel Proust – sooner or later, in varying accents, all of them can be overheard murmuring with Théophile Gautier, 'Je suis un homme pour qui le monde visible existe' ('I am a man for whom the visible world exists'). But for Wilde, colour was also intensely metaphysical, the visible signature of the 'undying beauty of things that fade and die', and therefore part of the mystery of consciousness. When Wilde read Pater's *Studies in the History of the Renaissance* during his first term at Oxford, he took that strange and beautiful book to have presented him with nothing less than a demand to choose between metaphysics and aesthetic experience. For, reacting against the bodiless Neoplatonism of Shelley and the abstract aesthetic theorizing of Friedrich Schiller – both of whom he thought had reduced the beauty and poignancy of human life to ghostly paradigms – Pater had insisted that 'we must renounce metaphysics if we would mould our lives to artistic perfection'.

Yet Wilde also saw, and it is no small part of his originality to have seen, that no simple or peremptory rejection of metaphysics in favour of sensory experience was possible. For surely the intuition of a poet like Shelley that the actual world disclosed the existence of an ideal realm also contained an important truth, confirming as it did his own sense that colour was no exterior paint or hue but the visible manifestation of an inward 'soul of things'. 'Surely he who sees in colour no mere delightful quality of natural things but a spirit dwelling in things,' said Wilde of his own position, struggling to answer Pater in the pages of his Oxford commonplace book, 'is in a way a metaphysician.' Metaphysics would somehow have to be reconciled with aesthetics at a higher level. The central endeavour of Wilde's criticism would be to express this indwelling 'spirit', without either encumbering it with the dross of actuality or rarifying it out of all tangible existence. In the same way, his critical theory would constantly strive to acknowledge the metaphysical essence of works of art while at the same time refusing to reduce any given novel or poem or picture to the ghostly or spectral status of an 'aesthetic object'.

Just as he had discovered a metaphysics of the unseen world in colour, Wilde would always hear overtones of the metaphysical in the rhythm, sonority and verbal texture of words. Wilde's exquisite sensitivity to the sensuous power of language is already to be glimpsed in his early response to the *Agamemnon*, a work to which he would turn throughout his career as a touchstone of literary or imaginative greatness. For Helen's fatal beauty, thought Wilde, is invoked by Aeschylus in the very syllables of her name, with Greek Ἑλένη, 'Helen', treated throughout as if derived from ἑλεῖν, 'to destroy'. In the same spirit, Wilde would maintain in an unpublished Oxford essay on Greek heroines that Helen was rightly called Helen because she was 'a hell to ships, a hell to men, a hell to cities'. Such aural elements seem to have operated upon Wilde with the power of sensory experience, as vividly present to him as the touch of ice or fire. In one of his later fairy tales, he would thus locate the nest of the nightingale – against all natural history – in a holm-oak tree, simply to bring into his story the haunting assonance of 'holm' and 'oak'. So Wilde, everywhere in his prose and verse, is to be found incessantly plucking the lute strings of alliteration. Yet we penetrate to the source of Wilde's originality as an aesthetic theorist only when we have seen that what might seem like a superficial entrancement with mere sound is in reality something else, an endless fascination with the power of language to create reality, with language, as Gilbert will say, 'the parent, and not the child, of thought'. For Wilde possessed a sense of Language as autonomous power not to be equalled, perhaps, until Vladimir Nabokov's brilliant wordplay and punning in the mid twentieth century. 'Words, mere words!' Wilde will make Dorian Gray exclaim. 'Was there anything so real as words?'

Wilde's early absorption in the *Agamemnon* would become the type for his experience of literature: reading such a work was not merely an accomplishment or a stage in some career of self-culture. To read the *Agamemnon* was, for Wilde, to enter and apprehend the work as a world, an organizing structure within which one's own experience became intelligible. Wilde's encounter with Aeschylus must thus be viewed as one of his earliest experiences of literature's power to, as the narrator of *The Portrait of Mr W. H.* will later say, give 'form and substance to what is within us'. Mere words, as Dorian Gray will marvel, can 'give a plastic form to formless things', can create inside us 'a new world'. Wilde's sense of literature as a separate and indispensable reality would expand outwards in every direction from this paradigmatic schoolboy encounter with the *Agamemnon*, as classical, English, French, German, Italian and American literatures all became living possessions to him. But within his vast reading, he would always seek the same experience of an incandescence at once aesthetic and intellectual. Here is the reason, one suspects, that Pater's *Renaissance* would so powerfully move Wilde when he came to read it at Oxford and afterwards. For Pater had seized upon just this same moment of aesthetic and cognitive incandescence as the crucial event in the existence of a wholly sentient being. 'To burn always with this hard, gem-like flame,' declared the famous 'Conclusion' to the *Renaissance*, 'is success in life.' 'The demand of the intellect,' Pater had similarly said in his chapter on Winckelmann, 'is to feel itself alive.' Wilde's Gilbert will later appropriate this very sentence in 'The Critic as Artist'. And Wilde himself would echo it in his letter to the Home Secretary from Reading Gaol after he had been totally deprived of books. Literature was for him, he would repeat with a poignant desperation, the mode 'by which, and by which alone, the intellect could feel itself alive'.

At Trinity College, Dublin, where he attended from 1871 to 1874, Wilde quickly established the pattern that would mark his later career: intense short bursts of hard work and triumphant achievement alternating with long periods of indolence, extravagance and what he himself called 'utter vacancy of employment'. His solid classical preparation at Portora and conscientious work at Trinity, Ellmann tells us, earned Wilde the highest standing at the end of his initial year: he was first of the first class. A period of backsliding followed, but Wilde none the less managed to finish with laurels, winning one of ten foundation scholarships and carrying off the Berkeley Gold Medal for Greek. When he went up to Oxford in the autumn of 1874 – a move he famously considered, with prison, 'one of the two great turning points of my life' – the pattern of high achievement alternating with indolence would continue. Although in June Wilde had won a demyship or scholarship in classics to Magdalen College, breezing through with the highest marks among those competing, by November he had managed to fail the preliminary examination called Responsions. In his second-year examinations, failing divinity by way of signalling his indifference to the subject, Wilde none the less won a first in the examination in classical languages and literatures known as Honour Moderations. In March of 1877, rousing himself from the labour of collecting blue china, decorating his rooms and 'scribbling sonnets', Wilde competed for the Ireland Scholarship, only to lose out to the zealous 'reading men' who had been doing nothing else except preparing for the competition. Vowing 'to reform and read hard if possible' in the next year for the final examination in classical philosophy and history called Greats, Wilde astonished the Oxford dons – and perhaps even himself – by winning the Newdigate Prize in Poetry for 'Ravenna' and then capturing the best first of 1878. Imagine, he wrote to a friend with evident and immense satisfaction, 'the Bad Boy doing so well in the end!'

Wilde's success in the rigorous honours curriculum of *Literae Humaniores* came at a time when Greats was the most intellectually demanding and prestigious course of study at Oxford. For the rest of his life, he would speak dismissively of mediocre or untalented persons as mere 'passmen' – people who shunned the effort of distinction involved in reading for honours, being willing merely to get by. The gift of the Greats curriculum to its successful candidates was, Wilde thought, what he called the 'Oxford temper', by which he did not mean anything resembling the attitude of *nil admirari* conventionally associated with Oxford men: a manner 'arid, aloof, incurious, unthinking' and 'unthanking', as Rudyard Kipling trenchantly described it in 'The Islanders'. What Wilde meant by the term was a specifically intellectual bearing in the world, a disposition to play with ideas, to show truth and falsehood as 'merely forms of intellectual existence', to treat the universe 'as if'. Writing to congratulate Rennell Rodd on winning a second in *Literae Humaniores* in the December of 1880, Wilde declared, 'Greats is the only fine school at Oxford, the only sphere of thought where one can be, *simultaneously*, brilliant and unreasonable, speculative and well-informed, creative as well as critical, and write with all the passion of youth about the truths which belong to the august serenity of old age.' This is the notion of 'serious play' exemplified in Wilde's critical dialogues already being described ten years before the publication of *Intentions*. Not only was there no conflict between intellect and play, Wilde would always insist: intellect at its best *was* play. The dandiacal heroes of his later fiction and drama are simply imaginative realizations of this principle, as with Lord Henry Wotton in *The Picture of Dorian Gray*, who 'played with the idea, and grew wilful; tossed it into the air and transformed it; let it escape and recaptured it; made it iridescent with fancy, and winged it with paradox'. Or Lord Illingworth in *A Woman of No Importance*, insouciantly remarking that the 'intellect is not a serious thing, and never has been. It is an instrument on which one plays, that is all'.

For Wilde, the companionship of ideas meant not only books but talk. His extraordinary powers as a conversationalist, which were later to command the admiration of distinguished listeners in London and Paris, originated too in the Greats conception of intellect as 'free play'. When a fellow Greats candidate and friend left Oxford in 1877, Wilde wrote to the young man, complaining that now 'there is no *intellectual friction to rouse me up to talk or think*, as I used when with you'. The modern tendency of Freudian and post-Freudian commentators to regard Wilde's conversation as either a mode of aggression – dominating the dining-rooms of London, or of sexual sublimation – seducing listeners instead of lovers, amounts to little more than prurient gossip when measured against the actual energy, volume and brilliancy of Wilde's talk. If the dimensions of seduction and aggression are to be sensed, it is because Wilde would always imagine conversation in terms of Plato's *Symposium*, with its glowing picture of artworks and ideas as immortal offspring begotten of a spiritual intercourse – or, as Wilde glossed this passage in his commonplace book, art and ideas satisfying 'one's desire of immortality by providing for one's mental continuity'. Plato's concept of ἔρως – 'love', Wilde insisted in this same passage, included both 'the impassioned search after truth' and 'the romantic side of that friendship so necessary for philosophy because *discussion* was the primitive method'.

In *De Profundis*, the *Symposium* ideal provides the golden standard against which the companionship of Lord Alfred Douglas would be found so dismally to fail. For Douglas, whose mind ultimately proved incapable of rising to the level of ideas, could provide only 'an unintellectual friendship', a bond which became, Wilde bitterly confesses, 'intellectually degrading to me'. From his prison cell in Reading Gaol, Wilde would remember that 'the first and best of my critical dialogues' – he meant 'The Decay of Lying' – had come to him over a simple café supper with Robert Ross. In a single conversation he had hit upon 'idea, title, treatment, mode, everything'. This vivid evening he would contrast with the food- and drink-sodden nights spent in the company of Douglas, whose conversation kept monotonously circling back to the topic of physical gratification. 'You did not realize,' Wilde would tell the incurious, thoughtless, thankless young man in *De Profundis*, 'that an artist, and especially such an artist as I am, ... requires for the development of his art the companionship of ideas, and intellectual atmosphere.' It would become his bitterest reproach.

Wilde had first met the 'Oxford temper' in his attentive reading of Matthew Arnold. For Arnold's notions of 'Hellenism' and 'criticism' stressed the importance to cultural vitality of an intellectual 'atmosphere' – the importance of what he simply and grandly called 'ideas'. Hellenism, as Arnold defined it, was a 'spontaneity of consciousness', a 'play of thought' upon stock notions and fixed opinions. Echoing Arnold in an unpublished essay written at Oxford in 1877, Wilde approvingly described the Hellenism of the ancient Greeks as 'a one-sided enthusiasm for ideas', a passion for enlightenment which extended over 'a multitude of peoples'. For Arnold, the point was to get this intellectual light to penetrate the British middle classes. Arnold became for Wilde the first great extramural apostle of the Oxford temper in the public sphere – Arnold's suavely amusing attacks upon Philistinism in his lectures, essays, reviews and letters to the editor becoming an important, if only temporary, model for Wilde. Thus the reader of this volume will hear Arnold's characteristic tone, for instance, in Wilde's early review of Roden Noel's essays, calling in an Arnoldian vein for more sanity of judgement and less crudity of statement. Noel's book fails as criticism, Wilde declares, because, 'It is simply a record of the mood of a man of letters, and its criticisms merely reveal the critic without illuminating what he would criticize for us'.

The emergence of Wilde as a genuinely original thinker about art and culture may be marked, therefore, from the moment he drops this Arnoldian mask, enunciating a precisely contrary position. By the time he publishes 'The Critic as Artist', we will hear Gilbert declaring to Ernest that the critic's 'sole aim' is to chronicle his own impressions, 'the spiritual moods and imaginative passions of the mind', because perfect criticism 'seeks to reveal its own secret and not the secret of another'. Yet this apparent rejection of Arnold is itself Arnoldian, the latest development in a thoroughly Arnoldian 'play of thought', with criticism breaking up the 'fixed ideas' of criticism itself. For Wilde, the truth of criticism – like the truth of art famously defined in his essay 'The Truth of Masks' – becomes a proposition 'whose contradictory is also true'.

As important to Wilde's development as a critic was Arnold's stress on literary criticism as the chosen medium of what he called Hellenism, with Hellenism always being the best hope for Victorian civilization. Indeed, so closely does Arnold identify criticism with Hellenism, and both together with 'ideas' and the 'play of thought' and 'creating an intellectual atmosphere', that the two notions are not always readily distinguishable in his writing. Only a Hellenism made available as commentary on literature, Arnold thought, could rescue Britain from a steadily encroaching mediocrity from intellectual stagnation and the grinding worship of money. This had long been Arnold's great message to the modern Philistines, from his early warnings in 'On the Modern Element in Literature' of 1857 through the brilliantly marshalled attack in *Culture and Anarchy* of 1869. Presenting his message with sparkling wit, Arnold contrived at the same time to endow it with a grand significance. 'The future of poetry is immense,' he declared, and, 'Hellenism is the master-impulse even now of the life of our nation and of humanity.' Such pronouncements powerfully attracted a younger generation grown cynical about socially earnest good works and socially graceless reformers. With an ironic elegance and unfailing lightness of touch, Arnold mobilized the utopian ardours of the young in an altogether new way by making it clear that in London the fashionable West End required reforming quite as much as the impoverished East End, and by suggesting that reform was much more a matter of sympathetic, inward becoming than of outward and busily self-important doing.

To understand Wilde's subsequent importance as a theorist of art and culture, we must always remember that he began to read for an honours degree in *Literae Humaniores* at Oxford at precisely the moment when the Greats curriculum and Oxford Hellenism were being re-imagined as powerful new agencies for regenerating national life. In the course of establishing a far more open and competitive system during the university reform movement of the 1850s, Oxford academic liberals had brought about two epochal changes to *Literae Humaniores*, shifting its curricular bias from Latin authors to Greek, and changing its pedagogical emphasis from a grammatical deciphering to a deeply historical and philosophical mode of reading and interpretation. The chief architect of these changes was Benjamin Jowett, Master of Balliol College and Regius Professor of Greek. Strongly influenced by Hegel and by German biblical criticism, Jowett had become convinced that the irresistible tide of modern thought was away from conventional religious orthodoxy and towards a more plenary understanding of the mind as a means of perfection no less worthy than the soul. Jowett undertook to present Plato's works to Oxford undergraduates as the 'greatest *uninspired* writings' because, first of all, Plato portrayed through Socrates an archetypal account of what mental illumination could mean to human life, and secondly, because Plato so clearly anticipated Hegel. Jowett promoted Plato's writings as a secular scripture by producing widely influential translations of the *Dialogues*, complete with long introductions so solemn as to suggest biblical commentary and exegesis. Nor did his efforts on behalf of Plato stop at the university walls, for Jowett was able to ensure that Greek and Latin studies would count for more points on the competitive civil service exams than other subjects. Exerting an enormous influence both inside and outside the university, Jowett would use Greek studies to introduce progressive Continental thought within Oxford, while deploying the Greats machinery – tutorials, examinations, ranked degrees – to induct the most successful Oxford graduates into the civic élite of Britain. Though he was never Jowett's pupil, Wilde as a Double First in *Literae Humaniores* was in an important sense his foster son.

Recently, the impassioned Hellenism among Wilde's Victorian generation has been read primarily in terms of homosexual apologetics. But at the time, both Hellenism and the 'Renaissance', understood specifically as a rebirth of Greek art and ideas, were invested with politically liberal, even utopian hopes. Thus Pater and John Addington Symonds, for instance, following the lead of Jules Michelet and Jacob Burckhardt, would write histories of the Italian Renaissance in hopes of achieving among the Victorians what the Renaissance had achieved through its own revival of ancient Greece. The object was what Pater usually called 'liberty of the intellect' and 'liberty of the heart', an unconstrained scope for intellectual discovery, for expansion of the mind and spirit and only then, more covertly, for sensuous – including sexual – expressiveness. To the Oxford Hellenists, an intermittent rediscovery of Greek liberty had been something running just beneath the surface of European cultural history from the Middle Ages to the present. First erupting in twelfth-century France, it had reappeared in fifteenth-century Italy and Elizabethan England, and still later in eighteenth-century Germany. With each recovery had come nothing less than a transformation of consciousness, begetting in turn a cultural revolution: first Abelard's Paris, then Pico della Mirandola's Florence and Shakespeare's London, then Goethe's Weimar. The 'renaissance' of Hellenism, Pater insisted, was always taking place – *then why not here and now?* This was the electrifying question which Wilde understood Arnold, Pater and Symonds all to have posed to him at Oxford, as he was reading virtually everything written by each. Their question would come to occupy the centre of his thought and writing. At first, it would animate the most ambitious of his art lectures – 'The English Renaissance of Art' – during his 1882 lecture tour through North America. Later it would impel the work that Wilde, according to his friend Ross, at the end of his life considered his best, his literary criticism. Indeed, in the most brilliant of these critical writings, Wilde's protagonist Gilbert will say, 'There is no reason why in future years this strange Renaissance should not become almost as mighty in its way as was that new birth of Art that woke many centuries ago in the cities of Italy.'

The intellectual ferment generated by Oxford Hellenism may be glimpsed in all its vitality in two notebooks Wilde kept while at Oxford – a commonplace book he seems to have used to prepare for Greats and a second notebook he used to gather material for the essay he submitted for the Chancellor's Prize in 1879. (His entry, 'The Rise of Historical Criticism', was Arnoldian but disorganized. The judges elected to award no prize that year.) Reading these notebooks today, we may witness at first hand just that breaking up of 'stock notions' under the pressure of 'fresh streams of thought' that Arnold had called for. In them too one sees at work the 'dephlegmaticizing' of existence – rousing and startling it into 'a life of constant attention' – that Pater had urged in his *Renaissance*. This Socratic pursuit of open-ended inquiry was precisely the cultural work imagined for the Greats course specifically, and philosophical study more generally, by such Oxford liberals as Jowett and Mark Pattison, Pater and Thomas Hill Green. 'Philosophy serves culture,' Pater had declared in his chapter on Winckelmann, 'not by the fancied gift of absolute or transcendental knowledge, but by suggesting questions which help one to detect the passion, and strangeness, and dramatic contrasts of life.' Wilde copied the sentence into his commonplace book. It would become one of the central themes of his later career. Thought is itself among the sensations. In the highest thought, the mind remains undivorced from the body. 'Nothing refines,' as Lord Illingworth will later say, 'but the intellect.'

Wilde's Oxford notebooks, as their editors Philip E. Smith and Michael S. Helfand have pointed out, bring into view the two major influences that would mould Wilde's later criticism – philosophical idealism and evolutionary science. Plato and Darwin, Hegel and Herbert Spencer – these are constant points of reference in the notebooks. A few years after leaving Oxford, Wilde would be able to dismiss J. S. Mill as a thinker specifically because Mill 'knew nothing of Plato and Darwin'. Such a mind, he declared, 'gives me very little'. If we are today likely to see Plato and Darwin as an odd combination of influences, it is only because the late Victorian ethos in which Wilde was speaking has become to us a lost world of thought. Its key figure is Hegel, for from 1865 to 1900 Oxford was the centre of a vigorous English neo-Hegelianism. Emerging in sudden and emphatic opposition to the dominant British empiricist tradition of Locke and Hume, Bentham and Mill, the Hegelian strain would just as abruptly vanish with the reconquest of British philosophy by twentieth-century logical positivism. Yet Oxford Hegelianism, today regarded as a curiosity associated with the work of such figures as Thomas Hill Green, Edward Caird, Bernard Bosanquet and F. H. Bradley, had a very broad impact on Victorian intellectual culture, being continuously channelled to such brilliant undergraduates as Wilde through the institutional machinery of Greats – its tutorials, reading lists and examinations. During the 1870s, moreover, such popularizers of Hegel as Jowett and William Wallace were attempting to neutralize the dark threat of materialism and random selection implicit in Darwin by interpreting the theory of evolution in terms of Hegel's account of the evolution of *Geist* or pure Mind.

As Smith and Helfand have also demonstrated, Wilde assiduously studied Wallace's book *The Logic of Hegel* (1873), consisting of a translation of the 'Logic' section of Hegel's *Encyclopedia* to which Wallace then added 'Prolegomena' (both translation and 'Prolegomena' remain valuable to this day). The material and mental transformations in history, Wallace's 'Prolegomena' taught Wilde to believe, were in fact two aspects of an identical evolutionary process. For the genetic and adaptational changes occurring at the biological level in amoebae and beans, Wallace suggested, demanded explanation in terms of the thesis, antithesis and synthesis of the Hegelian dialectic. In the same way, the alternations of scepticism and positive belief throughout the history of philosophy, Wallace argued, operate according to something very like natural selection. Science and philosophy, no less than morals and art, obeyed a law of rational progress which was itself identical with the constantly unfolding development of pure Idea or Mind. The gravitational pull of this half-submerged Hegelianism explains, for instance, why Wilde sometimes seems to be taking a strangely Lamarckian view of evolution, writing as if acquired characteristics could be genetically inherited, as when in *The Soul of Man under Socialism* he defines individualism as a 'differentiation towards which all organisms grow'. In the same way, readers of the present volume will hear Wilde declaring in a review of Pater's *Appreciations* that the 'legacies of heredity may make us alter our views of moral responsibility, but they cannot but intensify our sense of the value of Criticism; for the true critic is he who bears within himself the dreams and ideas and feelings of myriad generations, and to whom no form of thought is alien, no emotional impulse obscure'.

Recent commentary on Wilde has wanted to see in the heightened sublimity of such passages a deliberately seductive code meant to appeal to a secret group of readers. Yet the philosophical reverberations of Wilde's grand and unembarrassed sublimity would have been picked up by any educated reader of Wilde's own generation. The 'dreams and ideas of myriad generations' borne within the true critic, like the 'something within us that knew nothing of sequence or extension' invoked by Wilde's narrator in *The Portrait of Mr W. H.*, declares by its verbal sublimity that its voice is ultimately that of the Hegelian World-Spirit. 'The Critical Spirit,' as Gilbert declares with serene conviction towards the end of 'The Critic as Artist', 'and the World-Spirit are one.' Wilde's criticism summons such entities as 'dreams' and 'soul' and 'spirit' precisely because these are the notions – contemptuously dismissed by British utilitarians as rank fictions or trivial epiphenomena – that a triumphant neo-Hegelianism had taught him to see as belonging to the very dynamics of human progress.

Here too we see Jowett's influence on Wilde. For Jowett's introductions to Plato's *Dialogues* had continually emphasized the purely critical power of Hegelian philosophy. Philosophers in the British empiricist tradition, blinded by 'facts' and 'experience', Jowett believed, had failed to recognize that such elements themselves implied an unacknowledged metaphysics. 'We do not consider,' Jowett remarked urbanely in his introduction to the *Theaetetus*, 'how much metaphysics are required to place us above metaphysics.' Wilde promptly copied the remark into his commonplace book, adding, 'We talk about facts when we are really resting on ideas,' and elsewhere remarking that, 'Metaphysics seems to me the one science which has a future.' When in 'The Decay of Lying' Wilde opposes Zola in France and writers of naturalistic novels in England, his recurrent point is that their world is simply not credible, being metaphysically grounded in nothing more persuasive than 'facts'. During Wilde's tour of America, similarly, travelling through the wild Dakota territory, he would report that the red-shirted and yellow-bearded miners he met in Sioux City were 'almost as real as Bret Harte's miners, and quite as pleasant'.

Even as they display Wilde's wide-ranging intellectual curiosity and his intellectual influences, the Oxford notebooks permit us to glimpse the origins of his critical style. Throughout, we see Wilde experimenting with the tactics of presentation and argument later so visible in the critical dialogues. For Wilde's procedure in the notebooks is always relentlessly dialogic, operating in insouciant disregard of both chronology and the standard continuities of intellectual history, as when one typical entry treats a passage by Bacon as having been written 'against Hegel's Philosophy of History'. Entered under some identifying term or name, the quoted passages without quotation marks, Wilde's notebook entries operate as dramatic enactments of ideas and points of view, or what Wilde would later call 'standpoints' or 'masks' of thought. Nowhere is the influence of Wilde's study of the dialogues of Plato, that secular bible of liberal Oxford, more marked than in his unremitting allegiance to what his protagonist Gilbert once calls the 'wonderful literary form of the dialogue'.

The point of dialogic form for Wilde is that it alone is able to embody the mysterious truth that genuine thinking inescapably involves experiencing oneself, in Paul Ricoeur's phrase, as another. 'To arrive at what one really believes,' Wilde's Gilbert will say, 'one must speak through lips different from one's own.' The truth that Plato illustrated by writing philosophy in dialogic form is thus the same truth that lies at the centre of Hegel's philosophical project. Only dialogue enables the thinker to break through the constraints of his own subjectivity to grasp his idea from alternative points of view. Like a sculptor working in the round, declares Gilbert, the thinker pursues his thought through each new standpoint, 'gaining in this manner all the richness and reality of effect that comes from those side issues that are suddenly suggested by the central idea in its progress'. What Gilbert means by progress is at the level of individual thought a reflection of the much vaster progress of the Hegelian *Geist* or Mind, that progressive unfolding in which Hegel himself would see the ultimate goal as the development of greater differentiation, complexity and freedom. Thus self-consciousness, far from representing the symptom of moral solipsism so dreaded by many Victorians, becomes in Wilde's criticism the mark of a growth in human consciousness, as momentous and unmistakable an evidence of evolutionary progress as the step from the amoeba to multicellular organism or from creeping lizard to soaring bird.

The key move in Wilde's criticism, also anticipated in his Oxford notebooks, is a mode of daring transposition in which the metaphysical or ethical arguments of Plato or Aristotle, for instance, are transposed from their own discourse into another, applying them to modern aesthetic questions, and transforming while in a sense retaining their original meaning. Thus Wilde notes in his commonplace book Aristotle's opinion that the philosophic life need have no aim or consequence beyond itself. Contemplative life 'is good says Aristotle for it's own sake', with the odd punctuation of Wilde's paraphrase making the point punningly in English, 'because it is an "ἀρετή ['excellence'] of the soul": the fact of it's existence is the reason for its existence.' Transposed from ethics to aesthetics, Aristotle's dictum will later reappear in 'The Critic as Artist' as the controlling principle of Wilde's criticism, Gilbert telling Ernest that criticism 'has least reference to any standard external to itself, and is, in fact, its own reason for existing'.

The Greats examination system encouraged this tendency to arrive at new truth through a transposition of established truths, as when, for instance, Wilde was called upon during his final viva or oral examination to say what Aristotle would have thought of Walt Whitman. This is why the centrality of Plato in the Greats curriculum means so much for an understanding of Wilde's critical writings. By transposing Plato's metaphysics into the key of modern aesthetics, Wilde was able to endow the local insights of such writers as Théophile Gautier and Algernon Swinburne with an unexpected philosophical weight. Repeatedly invoking Plato's image of the philosopher in *The Republic* as 'the spectator of all time and of all existence' – he would do so in 'The Rise of the Historical Criticism', in 'The English Renaissance of Art', in *The Portrait of Mr W. H.*, in 'The Critic as Artist' – Wilde would come to regard it as the model for the separate reality of art as glimpsed by the artist and critic, a realm eternal and illimitable, operating in accordance with its own logic and laws of coherence.

The transposition of Plato's vision to art is the essential move. For Plato's metaphysics, gazing always towards a realm of colourless, formless, intangible Being, have in themselves nothing to offer the modern age. Were contemporary men and women to try to enter Plato's heaven, they would, Wilde will have Gilbert say, 'starve amidst the chill mathematics of thought'. 'But,' Gilbert continues – it is the key moment in Wilde's critical thought – 'transfer them to the sphere of art' and 'you will find that they are still vital and full of meaning'. This is Plato as read through Hegel: jettisoning such alien elements of Plato's metaphysics as their abstraction, bodilessness and colourlessness, the Wildean critic glimpses an ideal realm of art and beauty in which timelessness has been bestowed, in a movement culminating in something very like Hegelian synthesis, even on concreteness, colour, variety and change – a new aesthetic world of 'things beautiful and immortal and ever-changing'.

The centrality of Hegelian becoming to Wilde's thought serves to explain why his critical protagonists are so often heard speaking in 'poetic' prose. Nothing has worn less well with modern-day readers, perhaps, than this sort of elaborate writing. Nor is this solely a modern response: Victorian satirists began to parody it almost as soon as they had done lampooning Wilde's 'Aesthetic' knee-breeches and love of lilies in the 1880s. Reading such ornate, highly cadenced prose passages today, one hears a distant chorus of Wilde's satirists and imitators murmuring, 'Quite too, too utterly *intense*.' Yet the point of such passages in their original context is always clear: they are evidence of the global change that may be wrought in individual consciousness by imaginative art. The critic speaks differently because the world has become different to him. His heightened language reveals, or to speak more precisely, enacts, the heightened consciousness produced in him by high aesthetic experience. Hector, Patroclus, Achilles – in 'The Critic as Artist' Gilbert does not describe the warriors of Homer's *Iliad* so much as voice the response of someone who has just seen them: 'Phantoms, are they? Heroes of mist and mountain? Shadows in a song? No: they are real.'

'It may be as a critic of Beauty that Plato is destined to live,' says Gilbert in 'The Critic as Artist', 'and that by altering the name of the sphere of his speculation we shall find a new philosophy.' Gilbert's tentativeness is as significant as the thought to which he gives expression, for in it we hear the awareness of the late-nineteenth-century Hegelian that the evolution of *Geist* must ultimately remain a mystery. Wilde himself seems to have understood his own greatest innovation in critical thought only in retrospect. Years after publishing 'The Critic as Artist', looking back at his life from his prison cell in Reading Gaol, Wilde would write as if he had suddenly come to understand the dynamic which had been motivating his aesthetic theory from the first. He recalled having once made a remark in the early 1890s to André Gide in Paris, a generalization he now saw was 'as profound as it was novel'. It was this: that there was nothing Plato had ever said about metaphysics that 'could not be transferred immediately into the sphere of Art, and there find its complete fulfil-ment'. Fragmentary and approximate as this insight would ultimately prove to be, due to the turmoil and tragic disruption of Wilde's later life, it would none the less provide the metaphysical ground for the intuition he had first had when reading the *Agamemnon* as a schoolboy: Helen of Troy inhabited a world more real than the hand that turned the page, her world would live when hand and page were dust. 'Every day,' Gilbert tells Ernest, 'the swan-like daughter of Leda comes out

xxvi

on the battlements, and looks down at the tide of war.' Is Helen a mere shadow in a song? No: she is real.

The world will always remember of Wilde, that the life which began to be such a brilliant success in the decisive moment when, as he said in *De Profundis*, 'my father sent me to Oxford', turned into an irretrievable failure 'when Society sent me to prison'. Bankrupt, disgraced, recurrently ill and in pain, Wilde survived two years of prison life at hard labour in part by keeping a notebook of his reading, much as he had done long ago in his other life at Oxford. 'I cling to my notebook,' he wrote to a friend from prison. 'It helps me: before I had it my brain was going in very evil circles.' Upon his release, Wilde found that intellectual and artistic work on the old terms had become impossible, and aside from *The Ballad of Reading Gaol* and two letters on prison reform, he published nothing more. He led a wandering, bohemian existence in France and Italy, borrowing money, writing amusing letters to his friends and under the pseudonym of 'Sebastian Melmoth' haunting the places where he had once been Oscar Wilde. 'At times, being morbid, I am bored by the lack of intellect,' he wrote to one friend in December 1898. 'But that is a grave fault: I attribute it to Oxford.' He died in Paris on 30 November 1900.

NOTE ON THE TEXTS

The absence of a scholarly edition of Wilde's works has long been felt. It will at last be rectified by the *Complete Works of Oscar Wilde*, soon to appear under the general editorship of Russell Jackson and Ian Small in the Oxford English Texts series. In the meantime, I have taken the texts of Wilde's early reviews, *The Soul of Man under Socialism* and the four essays of *Intentions* from Robert Ross's 1908 edition of Wilde's works. The text of the expanded version of *The Portrait of Mr W. H.* is based on Vyvyan Holland's Methuen edition of the work published in 1958. The texts of Wilde's letters relating to *The Picture of Dorian Gray* have been taken from Rupert Hart-Davis's *The Letters of Oscar Wilde* of 1962. I have silently corrected minor printer's errors throughout.

Eight Reviews (1885–90)

1. Mr Whistler's Ten o'Clock

Last night, at Prince's Hall, Mr Whistler[1] made his first public appearance as a lecturer on art, and spoke for more than an hour with really marvellous eloquence on the absolute uselessness of all lectures of the kind. Mr Whistler began his lecture with a very pretty *aria* on prehistoric history, describing how in earlier times hunter and warrior would go forth to chase and foray, while the artist sat at home making cup and bowl for their service. Rude imitations of nature they were first, like the gourd bottle, till the sense of beauty and form developed, and, in all its exquisite proportions, the first vase was fashioned. Then came a higher civilization of architecture and arm chairs, and with exquisite design, and dainty diaper,[2] the useful things of life were made lovely; and the hunter and the warrior lay on the couch when they were tired, and, when they were thirsty, drank from the bowl, and never cared to lose the exquisite proportion of the one, or the delightful ornament of the other; and this attitude of the primitive anthropophagous[3] Philistine formed the text of the lecture, and was the attitude which Mr Whistler entreated his audience to adopt towards art. Remembering, no doubt, many charming invitations to wonderful private views,[4] this fashionable assemblage seemed somewhat aghast, and not a little amused, at being told that the slightest appearance among a civilized people of any joy in beautiful things is a grave impertinence to all painters; but Mr Whistler was relentless, and with charming ease, and much grace of manner, explained to the public that the only thing they should cultivate was ugliness, and that on their permanent stupidity rested all the hopes of art in the future.

The scene was in every way delightful; he stood there, a miniature Mephistopheles[5] mocking the majority! He was like a brilliant surgeon lecturing to a class composed of subjects destined ultimately for dissection, and solemnly assuring them how valuable to science their

3

maladies were, and how absolutely uninteresting the slightest symptoms of health on their part would be. In fairness to the audience, however, I must say that they seemed extremely gratified at being rid of the dreadful responsibility of admiring anything, and nothing could have exceeded their enthusiasm when they were told by Mr Whistler that no matter how vulgar their dresses were, or how hideous their surroundings at home, still it was possible that a great painter, if there was such a thing, could, by contemplating them in the twilight, and half closing his eyes, see them under really picturesque conditions, and produce a picture which they were not to attempt to understand, much less dare to enjoy. Then there were some arrows, barbed and brilliant, shot off, with all the speed and splendour of fireworks, at the archaeologists, who spend their lives in verifying the birthplaces of nobodies, and estimate the value of a work of art by its date or its decay; at the art critics who always treat a picture as if it were a novel, and try and find out the plot; at dilettanti in general, and amateurs in particular, and (*O mea culpa!*) at dress reformers[6] most of all. 'Did not Velásquez[7] paint crinolines? what more do you want?'

Having thus made a holocaust of humanity, Mr Whistler turned to Nature, and in a few moments convicted her of the Crystal Palace,[8] Bank holidays, and a general overcrowding of detail, both in omnibuses and in landscapes, and then, in a passage of singular beauty, not unlike one that occurs in Corot's[9] letters, spoke of the artistic value of dim dawns and dusks, when the mean facts of life are lost in exquisite and evanescent effects, when common things are touched with mystery and transfigured with beauty, when the warehouses become as palaces, and the tall chimneys of the factory seem like campaniles in the silver air.

Finally, after making a strong protest against anybody but a painter judging of painting, and a pathetic appeal to the audience not to be lured by the aesthetic movement into having beautiful things about them, Mr Whistler concluded his lecture with a pretty passage about Fusiyama[10] on a fan, and made his bow to an audience which he had succeeded in completely fascinating by his wit, his brilliant paradoxes, and, at times, his real eloquence. Of course, with regard to the value of beautiful surroundings I differ entirely from Mr Whistler. An artist

4

is not an isolated fact, he is the resultant of a certain milieu and a certain entourage, and can no more be born of a nation that is devoid of any sense of beauty than a fig can grow from a thorn or a rose blossom from a thistle. That an artist will find beauty in ugliness, *le beau dans l'horrible*, is now a commonplace of the schools, the argot of the atelier, but I strongly deny that charming people should be condemned to live with magenta ottomans and Albert blue[11] curtains in their rooms in order that some painter may observe the side lights on the one and the values of the other. Nor do I accept the dictum that only a painter is a judge of painting. I say that only an artist is a judge of art; there is a wide difference. As long as a painter is a painter merely, he should not be allowed to talk of anything but mediums and megilp,[12] and on those subjects should be compelled to hold his tongue; it is only when he becomes an artist that the secret laws of artistic creation are revealed to him. For there are not many arts, but one art merely – poem, picture, and Parthenon, sonnet and statue – all are in their essence the same, and he who knows one, knows all. But the poet is the supreme artist, for he is the master of colour and of form, and the real musician besides, and is lord over all life and all arts; and so to the poet beyond all others are these mysteries known; to Edgar Allan Poe and to Baudelaire, not to Benjamin West and Paul Delaroche.[13] However, I would not enjoy anybody else's lectures unless in a few points I disagreed with them, and Mr Whistler's lecture last night was, like everything that he does, a masterpiece. Not merely for its clever satire and amusing jests will it be remembered, but for the pure and perfect beauty of many of its passages – passages delivered with an earnestness which seemed to amaze those who had looked on Mr Whistler as a master of persiflage merely, and had not known him, as we do, as a master of painting also. For that he is indeed one of the very greatest masters of painting, is my opinion. And I may add that in this opinion Mr Whistler himself entirely concurs.

2. The Relation of Dress to Art

'How can you possibly paint these ugly three-cornered hats?' asked a reckless art critic once of Sir Joshua Reynolds.[1] 'I see light and shade in them,' answered the artist. 'Les grands coloristes,' says Baudelaire, in a charming article on the artistic value of frock coats, 'les grands coloristes savent faire de la couleur avec un habit noir, une cravate blanche, et un fond gris.'[2]

'Art seeks and finds the beautiful in all times, as did her high priest Rembrandt, when he saw the picturesque grandeur of the Jews' quarter of Amsterdam, and lamented not that its inhabitants were not Greeks,' were the fine and simple words used by Mr Whistler in one of the most valuable passages of his lecture. The most valuable, that is, to the painter: for there is nothing of which the ordinary English painter needs more to be reminded than that the true artist does not wait for life to be made picturesque for him, but sees life under picturesque conditions always – under conditions, that is to say, which are at once new and delightful. But between the attitude of the painter towards the public, and the attitude of a people towards art, there is a wide difference. That, under certain conditions of light and shade, what is ugly in fact may, in its effect, become beautiful, is true; and this, indeed, is the real *modernité* of art; but these conditions are exactly what we cannot be always sure of, as we stroll down Piccadilly[3] in the glaring vulgarity of the noonday, or lounge in the park with a foolish sunset as a background. Were we able to carry our *chiaroscuro*[4] about with us, as we do our umbrellas, all would be well; but, this being impossible, I hardly think that pretty and delightful people will continue to wear a style of dress as ugly as it is useless and as meaningless as it is monstrous, even on the chance of such a master as Mr Whistler spiritualizing them into a symphony, or refining them into a mist. For the arts are made for life, and not life for the arts.

Nor do I feel quite sure that Mr Whistler has been himself always true to the dogma he seems to lay down, that a painter should paint only the dress of his age and of his actual surroundings; far be it from me to burden a butterfly[5] with the heavy responsibility of its past: I have always been of opinion that consistency is the last refuge of the unimaginative: but have we not all seen, and most of us admired, a picture from his hand of exquisite English girls strolling by an opal sea in the fantastic dresses of Japan? Has not Tite-street[6] been thrilled with the tidings that the models of Chelsea were posing to the master, in peplums, for pastels?[7]

Whatever comes from Mr Whistler's brush is far too perfect in loveliness, to stand or fall by any intellectual dogmas on art, even his own: for Beauty is justified by all her children, and cares nothing for explanations; but it is impossible to look through any collection of modern pictures in London, from Burlington House to the Grosvenor Gallery,[8] without feeling that the professional model is ruining painting, and reducing it to a condition of mere pose and *pastiche*.

Are we not all weary of him, that venerable impostor, fresh from the steps of the Piazza di Spagna,[9] who, in the leisure moments that he can spare from his customary organ, makes the round of the studios, and is waited for in Holland Park?[10] Do we not all recognize him, when, with the gay *insouciance* of his nation, he reappears on the walls of our summer exhibitions, as everything that he is not, and as nothing that he is, glaring at us here as a patriarch of Canaan, here beaming as a brigand from the Abruzzi?[11] Popular is he, this poor peripatetic professor of posing, with those whose joy it is to paint the posthumous portrait of the last philanthropist who, in his lifetime, had neglected to be photographed – yet, he is the sign of the decadence, the symbol of decay.

For all costumes are caricatures. The basis of Art is not the Fancy Ball. Where there is loveliness of dress, there is no dressing up. And so, were our national attire delightful in colour, and in construction simple and sincere; were dress the expression of the loveliness that it shields, and of the swiftness and motion that it does not impede; did its lines break from the shoulder, instead of bulging from the waist; did the inverted wineglass cease to be the ideal of form: were these things brought about, as brought about they will be, then would painting be no longer an artificial reaction against the ugliness of life, but become, as it should be, the natural expression of life's beauty. Nor would painting merely, but all the other arts also, be the gainers by a change such as that which I propose; the gainers, I mean, through the increased atmosphere of Beauty by which the artists would be surrounded, and in which they would grow up. For Art is not to be taught in Academies. It is what one looks at, not what one listens to, that makes the artist. The real schools should be the streets. There is not, for instance, a single delicate line, or delightful proportion in the dress of the Greeks, which is not echoed exquisitely in their architecture. A nation arrayed in stove-pipe hats, and dress improvers, might have built the Pantechnicon,[12] possibly, but the Parthenon, never. And, finally, there is this to be said: art, it is true, can never have any other aim but her own perfection, and, it may be, that the artist, desiring merely to contemplate and to create, is wise in not busying himself about change in others; yet wisdom is not always the best; there are times when she sinks to the level of common sense; and from the passionate folly of those, and there are many, who desire that Beauty shall be confined no longer to the *bric-à-brac* of the collector, and the dust of the museum, but shall be, as it should be, the natural and national inheritance of all – from this noble unwisdom, I say, who knows what new loveliness shall be given to life, and, under these more exquisite conditions, what perfect artist born? *Le milieu se renouvelant, l'art se renouvelle.*[13]

Speaking however from his own passionless pedestal, Mr Whistler in pointing out that the power of the painter is to be found in his power of vision, not in his cleverness of hand, has expressed a truth which needed expression, and which, coming from the lord of form and colour, cannot fail to have its influence. His lecture, the Apocrypha[14] though it be for the people, yet remains from this time as the Bible for the painter, the masterpiece of masterpieces, the song of songs. It is true he has pronounced the panegyric of the Philistine,[15] but I can fancy Ariel praising Caliban[16] for a jest: and, in that he has read the Commination Service[17] over the critics, let all men thank him, the critics themselves indeed most of all, for he has now relieved them from the necessity of a tedious existence. Considered, again, merely as an orator, Mr Whistler seems to me to stand almost alone.

Indeed, among all our public speakers, I know but few who can combine, so felicitously as he does, the mirth and malice of Puck,[18] with the style of the major prophets.

3. A Sentimental Journey through Literature

This is undoubtedly an interesting book, not merely through its eloquence and earnestness, but also through the wonderful catholicity of taste that it displays. Mr Noel has a passion for panegyric. His eulogy on Keats is closely followed by a eulogy on Whitman, and his praise of Lord Tennyson is equalled only by his praise of Mr Robert Buchanan.[1] Sometimes, we admit, we would like a little more fineness of discrimination, a little more delicacy of perception. Sincerity of utterance is valuable in a critic, but sanity of judgement is more valuable still, and Mr Noel's judgements are not always distinguished by their sobriety. Many of the essays, however, are well worth reading. The best is certainly that on 'The Poetic Interpretation of Nature', in which Mr Noel claims that what is called by Mr Ruskin the 'pathetic fallacy of literature'[2] is in reality a vital emotional truth; but the essays on Hugo[3] and Mr Browning are good also; the little paper entitled 'Rambles by the Cornish Seas' is a real marvel of delightful description, and the monograph on Chatterton[4] has a good deal of merit, though we must protest very strongly against Mr Noel's idea that Chatterton must be modernized before he can be appreciated. Mr Noel has absolutely no right whatsoever to alter Chatterton's 'yonge damoyselles' and '*anlace* fell'[5] into 'youthful damsels' and '*weapon* fell', for Chatterton's archaisms were an essential part of his inspiration and his method. Mr Noel in one of his essays speaks with much severity of those who prefer sound to sense in poetry and, no doubt, this is a very wicked thing to do; but he himself is guilty of a much graver sin against art when, in his desire to emphasize the meaning of Chatterton, he destroys Chatterton's music. In the modernized version he gives of the wonderful 'Songe to Ælla', he mars by his corrections the poem's metrical beauty, ruins the rhymes and robs the music of its echo. Nineteenth-century restorations[6] have done quite enough harm to English architecture without English poetry being treated in the same manner, and we hope that when Mr Noel writes again about Chatterton he will quote from the poet's verse, not from a publisher's version.

This, however, is not by any means the chief blot on Mr Noel's book. The fault of his book is that it tells us far more about his own personal feelings than it does about the qualities of the various works of art that are criticized. It is in fact a diary of the emotions suggested by literature, rather than any real addition to literary criticism, and we fancy that many of the poets about whom he writes so eloquently would be not a little surprised at the qualities he finds in their work. Byron, for instance, who spoke with such contempt of what he called 'twaddling about trees and babbling o' green fields'; Byron who cried, 'Away with this cant about nature! A good poet can imbue a pack of cards with more poetry than inhabits the forests of America,' is claimed by Mr Noel as a true nature-worshipper and Pantheist along with Wordsworth and Shelley; and we wonder what Keats would have thought of a critic who gravely suggests that *Endymion* is 'a parable of the development of the individual soul'. There are two ways of misunderstanding a poem. One is to misunderstand it and the other to praise it for qualities that it does not possess. The latter is Mr Noel's method, and in his anxiety to glorify the artist he often does so at the expense of the work of art.

Mr Noel also is constantly the victim of his own eloquence. So facile is his style that it constantly betrays him into crude and extravagant statements. Rhetoric and over-emphasis are the dangers that Mr Noel has not always succeeded in avoiding. It is extravagant, for instance, to say that all great poetry has been 'pictorial', or that Coleridge's 'Knight's Grave' is worth many 'Kubla Khans', or that Byron has 'the splendid imperfection of an Æschylus', or that we had lately 'one dramatist living in England, and only one, who could be compared to Hugo, and that was Richard Hengist Horne',[7] and that 'to find an English dramatist of the same order before him we must go back to Sheridan if not to Otway'.[8] Mr Noel, again, has a curious habit of classing together the most incongruous names and comparing the most incongruous works of art. What is gained by telling us that *Sardanapalus*[9] is perhaps hardly equal to 'Sheridan', that Lord Tennyson's ballad of 'The Revenge' and his 'Ode on the Death of the Duke of Wellington' are worthy of a place beside Thomson's 'Rule Britannia',[10] that Edgar Allan Poe, Disraeli and Mr Alfred Austin[11] are artists of note whom we may affiliate on Byron,[12] and that if Sappho[13] and Milton 'had not high genius, they would be justly reproached as sensational'? And surely it is a crude judgement that classes Baudelaire, of all poets, with Marini[14] and medieval troubadours, and a crude style that writes of 'Goethe, Shelley, Scott, and Wilson,[15] for a mortal should not thus intrude upon the immortals, even though he be guilty of holding with them that *Cain*[16] is 'one of the finest poems in the English language'. It is only fair, however, to add that Mr Noel subsequently makes more than ample amends for having opened Parnassus[17] to the public in this reckless manner, by calling Wilson an 'offal-feeder', on the ground that he once wrote a severe criticism of some of Lord Tennyson's early poems. For Mr Noel does not mince his words. On the contrary, he speaks with much scorn of all euphuism and delicacy of expression and, preferring the affectation of nature to the affectation of art, he thinks nothing of calling other people 'Laura Bridgmans',[18] 'Jackasses' and the like. This, we think, is to be regretted, especially in a writer so cultured as Mr Noel. For, though indignation may make a great poet, bad temper always makes a poor critic.

On the whole, Mr Noel's book has an emotional rather than an intellectual interest. It is simply a record of the moods of a man of letters, and its criticisms merely reveal the critic without illuminating what he would criticize for us. The best that we can say of it is that it is a Sentimental Journey through Literature,[19] the worst that any one could say of it is that it has all the merits of such an expedition.

4. Mr Pater's *Imaginary Portraits*

To convey ideas through the medium of images has always been the aim of those who are artists as well as thinkers in literature, and it is to a desire to give a sensuous environment to intellectual concepts that we owe Mr Pater's last volume. For these Imaginary or, as we should prefer to call them, Imaginative Portraits of his, form a series of philosophic studies in which the philosophy is tempered by personality, and the thought shown under varying conditions of mood and manner, the very permanence of each principle gaining something through the change and colour of the life through which it finds expression. The most fascinating of all these pictures is undoubtedly that of Sebastian Van Storck. The account of Watteau is perhaps a little too fanciful, and the description of him as one who was 'always a seeker after something in the world, that is there in no satisfying measure, or not at all', seems to us more applicable to him who saw Mona Lisa[1] sitting among the rocks than to the gay and debonair *peintre des fêtes galantes*.[2] But Sebastian, the grave young Dutch philosopher, is charmingly drawn. From the first glimpse we get of him, skating over the water-meadows with his plume of squirrel's tail and his fur muff, in all the modest pleasantness of boyhood, down to his strange death in the desolate house amid the sands of the Helder,[3] we seem to see him, to know him, almost to hear the low music of his voice. He is a dreamer, as the common phrase goes, and yet he is poetical in this sense, that his theorems shape life for him, directly. Early in youth he is stirred by a fine saying of Spinoza,[4] and sets himself to realize the ideal of an intellectual disinterestedness, separating himself more and more from the transient world of sensation, accident or even affection, till what is finite and relative becomes of no interest to him, and he feels that as nature is but a thought of his, so he himself is but a passing thought of God. This conception, of the power of a mere metaphysical abstraction over the mind of one so fortunately endowed for the reception of the sensible world, is exceedingly delightful, and Mr Pater has never written a more subtle psychological study, the fact that

Sebastian dies in an attempt to save the life of a little child giving to the whole story a touch of poignant pathos and sad irony.

Denys l'Auxerrois is suggested by a figure found, or said to be found, on some old tapestries in Auxerre, the figure of a 'flaxen and flowery creature, sometimes wellnigh naked among the vine-leaves, sometimes muffled in skins against the cold, sometimes in the dress of a monk, but always with a strong impress of real character and incident from the veritable streets' of the town itself. From this strange design Mr Pater has fashioned a curious medieval myth of the return of Dionysus[5] among men, a myth steeped in colour and passion and old romance, full of wonder and full of worship, Denys himself being half animal and half god, making the world mad with a new ecstasy of living, stirring the artists simply by his visible presence, drawing the marvel of music from reed and pipe, and slain at last in a stage-play by those who had loved him. In its rich affluence of imagery this story is like a picture by Mantegna,[6] and indeed Mantegna might have suggested the description of the pageant in which Denys rides upon a gaily-painted chariot, in soft silken raiment and, for head-dress, a strange elephant scalp with gilded tusks.

If *Denys l'Auxerrois* symbolizes the passion of the senses and *Sebastian Van Storck* the philosophic passion, as they certainly seem to do, though no mere formula or definition can adequately express the freedom and variety of the life that they portray, the passion for the imaginative world of art is the basis of the story of *Duke Carl of Rosenmold*. Duke Carl is not unlike the late King of Bavaria,[7] in his love of France, his admiration for the *Grand Monarque*[8] and his fantastic desire to amaze and to bewilder, but the resemblance is possibly only a chance one. In fact Mr Pater's young hero is the precursor of the *Aufklärung*[9] of the last century, the German precursor of Herder and Lessing and Goethe himself, and finds the forms of art ready to his hand without any national spirit to fill them or make them vital and responsive. He too dies, trampled to death by the soldiers of the country he so much admired, on the night of his marriage with a peasant girl, the very failure of his life lending him a certain melancholy grace and dramatic interest.

On the whole, then, this is a singularly attractive book. Mr Pater is an intellectual impressionist. He does not weary us with any definite doctrine or seek to suit life to any formal creed. He is always looking for exquisite moments and, when he has found them, he analyses them with delicate and delightful art and then passes on, often to the opposite pole of thought or feeling, knowing that every mood has its own quality and charm and is justified by its mere existence. He has taken the sensationalism of Greek philosophy and made it a new method of art criticism. As for his style, it is curiously ascetic. Now and then, we come across phrases with a strange sensuousness of expression, as when he tells us how Denys l'Auxerrois, on his return from a long journey, 'ate flesh for the first time, tearing the hot, red morsels with his delicate fingers in a kind of wild greed', but such passages are rare. Asceticism is the keynote of Mr Pater's prose; at times it is almost too severe in its self-control and makes us long for a little more freedom. For indeed, the danger of such prose as his is that it is apt to become somewhat laborious. Here and there, one is tempted to say of Mr Pater that he is 'a seeker after something in language, that is there in no satisfying measure, or not at all'. The continual preoccupation with phrase and epithet has its drawbacks as well as its virtues. And yet, when all is said, what wonderful prose it is, with its subtle preferences, its fastidious purity, its rejection of what is common or ordinary! Mr Pater has the true spirit of selection, the true tact of omission. If he be not among the greatest prose writers of our literature he is, at least, our greatest artist in prose; and though it may be admitted that the best style is that which seems an unconscious result rather than a conscious aim, still in these latter days when violent rhetoric does duty for eloquence and vulgarity usurps the name of nature, we should be grateful for a style that deliberately aims at perfection of form, that seeks to produce its effect by artistic means and sets before itself an ideal of grave and chastened beauty.

5. [The Actor as Critic]

Madame Ristori's[1] *Etudes et Souvenirs* is one of the most delightful books on the stage that has appeared since Lady Martin's[2] charming volume on the Shakespearean heroines. It is often said that actors leave nothing behind them but a barren name and a withered wreath; that they subsist simply upon the applause of the moment; that they are ultimately doomed to the oblivion of old play-bills; and that their art, in a word, dies with them, and shares their own mortality. 'Chippendale, the cabinet-maker,' says the clever author of *Obiter Dicta*,[3] 'is more potent than Garrick[4] the actor. The vivacity of the latter no longer charms (save in Boswell); the chairs of the former still render rest impossible in a hundred homes.' This view, however, seems to me to be exaggerated. It rests on the assumption that acting is simply a mimetic art, and takes no account of its imaginative and intellectual basis. It is quite true, of course, that the personality of the player passes away, and with it that pleasure-giving power by virtue of which the arts exist. Yet the artistic method of a great actor survives. It lives on in tradition, and becomes part of the science of a school. It has all the intellectual life of a principle. In England, at the present moment, the influence of Garrick on our actors is far stronger than that of Reynolds on our painters of portraits, and if we turn to France it is easy to discern the tradition of Talma,[5] but where is the tradition of David?[6]

Madame Ristori's memoirs, then, have not merely the charm that always attaches to the autobiography of a brilliant and beautiful woman, but have also a definite and distinct artistic value. Her analysis of the character of Lady Macbeth, for instance, is full of psychological interest, and shows us that the subtleties of Shakespearean criticism are not necessarily confined to those who have views on weak endings and rhyming tags, but may also be suggested by the art of acting itself. The author of *Obiter Dicta* seeks to deny to actors all critical insight and all literary appreciation. The actor, he tells us, is art's slave, not her child, and lives entirely outside literature, 'with its words for ever on his lips, and none of its truths engraven on his heart'. But this seems to me to be a harsh and reckless generalization. Indeed, so far from agreeing with it, I would be inclined to say that the mere artistic process of acting, the translation of literature back again into life, and the presentation of thought under the conditions of action, is in itself a critical method of a very high order; nor do I think that a study of the careers of our great English actors will really sustain the charge of want of literary appreciation. It may be true that actors pass too quickly away from the form, in order to get at the feeling that gives the form beauty and colour, and that, where the literary critic studies the language, the actor looks simply for the life; and yet, how well the great actors have appreciated that marvellous music of words which in Shakespeare, at any rate, is so vital an element of poetic power, if, indeed, it be not equally so in the case of all who have any claim to be regarded as true poets. 'The sensual life of verse,' says Keats, in a dramatic criticism published in the *Champion*, 'springs warm from the lips of Kean,[7] and to one learned in Shakespearean hieroglyphics, learned in the spiritual portion of those lines to which Kean adds a sensual grandeur, his tongue must seem to have robbed the Hybla bees[8] and left them honeyless.' This particular feeling, of which Keats speaks, is familiar to all who have heard Salvini,[9] Sarah Bernhardt,[10] Ristori, or any of the great artists of our day, and it is a feeling that one cannot, I think, gain merely by reading the passage to oneself. For my own part, I must confess that it was not until I heard Sarah Bernhardt in *Phèdre*[11] that I absolutely realized the sweetness of the music of Racine. As for Mr Birrell's statement that actors have the words of literature for ever on their lips, but none of its truths engraved on their hearts, all that one can say is that, if it be true, it is a defect which actors share with the majority of literary critics.

6. Poetical Socialists

Mr Stopford Brooke[1] said some time ago that Socialism and the socialistic spirit would give our poets nobler and loftier themes for song, would widen their sympathies and enlarge the horizon of their vision and would touch, with the fire and fervour of a new faith, lips that had else been silent, hearts that but for this fresh gospel had been cold. What Art gains from contemporary events is always a fascinating problem and a problem that is not easy to solve. It is, however, certain that Socialism starts well equipped. She has her poets and her painters, her art lecturers and her cunning designers, her powerful orators and her clever writers. If she fails it will not be for lack of expression. If she succeeds her triumph will not be a triumph of mere brute force. The first thing that strikes one, as one looks over the list of contributors to Mr Edward Carpenter's *Chants of Labour*, is the curious variety of their several occupations, the wide differences of social position that exist between them, and the strange medley of men whom a common passion has for the moment united. The editor is a 'Science lecturer'; he is followed by a draper and a porter; then we have two late Eton masters and then two boot-makers; and these are, in their turn, succeeded by an ex-Lord Mayor of Dublin, a bookbinder, a photographer, a steel-worker and an authoress. On one page we have a journalist, a draughtsman and a music-teacher, and on another a Civil servant, a machine fitter, a medical student, a cabinet-maker and a minister of the Church of Scotland. Certainly, it is no ordinary movement that can bind together in close brotherhood men of such dissimilar pursuits, and when we mention that Mr William Morris is one of the singers, and that Mr Walter Crane has designed the cover and frontispiece of the book, we cannot but feel that, as we pointed out before, Socialism starts well equipped.

As for the songs themselves, some of them, to quote from the editor's preface, are 'purely revolutionary, others are Christian in tone; there are some that might be called merely material in their tendency, while many are of a highly ideal and visionary character'. This is, on the whole, very promising. It shows that Socialism is not going to allow herself to be trammelled by any hard and fast creed or to be stereotyped into an iron formula. She welcomes many and multiform natures. She rejects none and has room for all. She has the attraction of a wonderful personality and touches the heart of one and the brain of another, and draws this man by his hatred of injustice, and his neighbour by his faith in the future, and a third, it may be, by his love of art or by his wild worship of a lost and buried past. And all of this is well. For, to make men Socialists is nothing, but to make Socialism human is a great thing.

They are not of any very high literary value, these poems that have been so dexterously set to music. They are meant to be sung, not to be read. They are rough, direct and vigorous, and the tunes are stirring and familiar. Indeed, almost any mob could warble them with ease. The transpositions that have been made are rather amusing. ' 'Twas in Trafalgar Square'[2] is set to the tune of ' 'Twas in Trafalgar's Bay'; 'Up, Ye People!' a very revolutionary song by Mr John Gregory, boot-maker, with a refrain of

> Up, ye People! or down into your graves!
> Cowards ever will be slaves!

is to be sung to the tune of 'Rule, Britannia!' the old melody of 'The Vicar of Bray'[3] is to accompany the new *Ballade of Law and Order* – which, however, is not a ballade at all – and to the air of 'Here's to the Maiden of Bashful Fifteen' the democracy of the future is to thunder forth one of Mr T. D. Sullivan's most powerful and pathetic lyrics. It is clear that the Socialists intend to carry on the musical education of the people simultaneously with their education in political science and, here as elsewhere, they seem to be entirely free from any narrow bias or formal prejudice. Mendelssohn is followed by Moody and Sankey;[4] the 'Wacht am Rhein' stands side by side with the *Marseillaise*;[5] 'Lillibulero', a chorus from *Norma*, 'John Brown' and an air from Beethoven's Ninth Symphony[6] are all equally delightful to them. They sing the National Anthem in Shelley's version and chant

William Morris's 'Voice of Toil' to the flowing numbers of 'Ye Banks and Braes of Bonny Doon'. Victor Hugo talks somewhere of the terrible cry of 'Le Tigre Populaire', but it is evident from Mr Carpenter's book that should the Revolution ever break out in England we shall have no inarticulate roar but, rather, pleasant glees and graceful part-songs. The change is certainly for the better. Nero fiddled while Rome was burning – at least, inaccurate historians say he did; but it is for the building up of an eternal city that the Socialists of our day are making music, and they have complete confidence in the art instincts of the people.

> They say that the people are brutal –
> That their instincts of beauty are dead –
> Were it so, shame on those who condemn them
> To the desperate struggle for bread.
> But they lie in their throats when they say it,
> For the people are tender at heart,
> And a wellspring of beauty lies hidden
> Beneath their life's fever and smart,

is a stanza from one of the poems in this volume, and the feeling expressed in these words is paramount everywhere. The Reformation gained much from the use of popular hymn-tunes, and the Socialists seem determined to gain by similar means a similar hold upon the people. However, they must not be too sanguine about the result. The walls of Thebes[7] rose up to the sound of music, and Thebes was a very dull city indeed.

7. Mr Swinburne's Last Volume

Mr Swinburne once set his age on fire by a volume of very perfect and very poisonous poetry.[1] Then he became revolutionary and pantheistic, and cried out against those who sit in high places both in heaven and on earth. Then he invented Marie Stuart, and laid upon us the heavy burden of *Bothwell.* Then he retired to the nursery, and wrote poems about children of a somewhat over-subtle character. He is now extremely patriotic, and manages to combine with his patriotism a strong affection for the Tory party. He has always been a great poet. But he has his limitations, the chief of which is, curiously enough, an entire lack of any sense of limit. His song is nearly always too loud for his subject. His magnificent rhetoric, nowhere more magnificent than in the volume that now lies before us, conceals rather than reveals. It has been said of him, and with truth, that he is a master of language, but with still greater truth it may be said that Language is his master. Words seem to dominate him. Alliteration tyrannizes over him. Mere sound often becomes his lord. He is so eloquent that whatever he touches becomes unreal.

Let us turn to the poem on the Armada:

> The wings of the south-west wind are widened; the breath of his fervent lips,
> More keen than a sword's edge fiercer than fire, falls full on the plunging ships.
> The pilot is he of their northward flight, their stay and their steersman he;
> A helmsman clothed with the tempest, and girdled with strength to constrain the sea.
> And the host of them trembles and quails, caught fast in his hand as a bird in the toils;
> For the wrath and joy that fulfil him are mightier than man's, whom he slays and spoils,
> And vainly, with heart divided in sunder, and labour of wavering will,

20

The lord of their host takes counsel with hope if haply their star shine
still.

Somehow, we seem to have heard all this before. Does it come from
the fact that of all poets who ever lived Mr Swinburne is the one who
is the most limited in imagery? It must be admitted that he is so. He
has wearied us with his monotony. 'Fire' and the 'Sea' are the two
words ever on his lips. We must confess also that this shrill singing –
marvellous as it is – leaves us out of breath. Here is a passage from a
poem called 'A Word with the Wind':

Be the sunshine bared or veiled, the sky superb or shrouded,
  Still the waters, lax and languid, chafed and foiled,
Keen and thwarted, pale and patient, clothed with fire or clouded
  Vex their heart in vain, or sleep like serpents coiled.
Thee they look for, blind and baffled, wan with wrath and weary
  Blown for ever back by winds that rock the bird:
Winds that seamews breast subdue the sea, and bid the dreary
  Waves be weak as hearts made sick with hope deferred.
Let the clarion sound from westward, let the south bear token
  How the glories of thy godhead sound and shine:
Bid the land rejoice to see the land-wind's broad back broken,
  Bid the sea take comfort, bid the world be thine.

Verse of this kind may be justly praised for the sustained strength
and vigour of its metrical scheme. Its purely technical excellence
is extraordinary. But is it more than an oratorical *tour-de-force*?
Does it really convey much? Does it charm? Could we return to it
again and again with renewed pleasure? We think not. It seems to us
empty.

Of course, we must not look to these poems for any revelation of
human life. To be at one with the elements seems to be Mr Swinburne's
aim. He seeks to speak with the breath of wind and wave. The roar of
the fire is ever in his ears. He puts his clarion to the lips of Spring and
bids her blow, and the Earth wakes from her dreams and tells him
her secret. He is the first lyric poet who has tried to make an absolute

surrender of his own personality, and he has succeeded. We hear the song, but we never know the singer. We never even get near to him. Out of the thunder and splendour of words he himself says nothing. We have often had man's interpretation of Nature; now we have Nature's interpretation of man, and she has curiously little to say. Force and Freedom form her vague message. She deafens us with her clangours.

But Mr Swinburne is not always riding the whirlwind, and calling out of the depths of the sea. Romantic ballads in Border dialect[2] have not lost their fascination for him, for this last volume contains some very splendid examples of this curious artificial kind of poetry. The amount of pleasure one gets out of dialect is a matter entirely of temperament. To say 'mither' instead of 'mother' seems to many the acme of romance. There are others who are not quite so ready to believe in the pathos of provincialisms. There is, however, no doubt of Mr Swinburne's mastery over the form, whether the form be quite legitimate or not. 'The Weary Wedding' has the concentration and colour of a great drama, and the quaintness of its style lends it something of the power of a grotesque. The ballad of 'The Witch-Mother', a medieval Medea who slays her children because her lord is faithless, is worth reading on account of its horrible simplicity. The 'Bride's Tragedy' with its strange refrain of

> In, in, out and in,
> Blaws the wind and whirls the whin:

The 'Jacobite's Exile',

> O lordly flow the Loire and Seine,
> And loud the dark Durance:
> But bonnier shine the braes of Tyne
> Than a' the fields of France;
> And the waves of Till that speak sae still
> Gleam goodlier where they glance:

'The Tyneside Widow', and 'A Reiver's Neck-verse', are all poems of fine imaginative power, and some of them are terrible in their fierce intensity of passion. There is no danger of English poetry narrowing itself to a form so limited as the romantic ballad in dialect. It is too vital a growth for that. So we may welcome Mr Swinburne's masterly experiments with the hope that things which are inimitable will not be imitated. The collection is completed by a few poems on children, some sonnets, a threnody on John William Inchbold, and a very lovely lyric entitled 'The Interpreters'.

> In human thought have all things habitation;
>> Our days
> Laugh, lower, and lighten past, and find no station
>> That stays.
>
> But thought and faith are mightier things than time
>> Can wrong,
> Made splendid once with speech, or made sublime
>> By song.
>
> Remembrance, though the tide of change that rolls
>> Wax hoary,
> Gives earth and heaven, for song's sake and the soul's,
>> Their glory.

Certainly 'for song's sake' we should love Mr Swinburne's work, cannot indeed help loving it, so marvellous a music-maker is he. But what of the soul? For the soul we must go elsewhere.

8. Mr Pater's Last Volume

When I first had the privilege – and I count it a very high one – of meeting Mr Walter Pater, he said to me, smiling, 'Why do you always write poetry? Why do you not write prose? Prose is so much more difficult.'

It was during my undergraduate days at Oxford; days of lyrical ardour and of studious sonnet-writing; days when one loved the exquisite intricacy and musical repetitions of the ballade, and the villanelle with its linked long-drawn echoes and its curious complete-ness; days when one solemnly sought to discover the proper temper in which a triolet[1] should be written; delightful days, in which, I am glad to say, there was far more rhyme than reason.

I may frankly confess now that at the time I did not quite compre-hend what Mr Pater really meant; and it was not till I had carefully studied his beautiful and suggestive essays on the Renaissance that I fully realized what a wonderful self-conscious art the art of English prose-writing really is, or may be made to be. Carlyle's stormy rhetoric, Ruskin's winged and passionate eloquence, had seemed to me to spring from enthusiasm rather than from art. I don't think I knew then that even prophets correct their proofs. As for Jacobean prose, I thought it too exuberant; and Queen Anne[2] prose appeared to me terribly bald, and irritatingly rational. But Mr Pater's essays became to me 'the golden book of spirit and sense, the holy writ of beauty'.[3] They are still this to me. It is possible, of course, that I may exaggerate about them. I certainly hope that I do; for where there is no exagger-ation there is no love, and where there is no love there is no understand-ing. It is only about things that do not interest one, that one can give a really unbiased opinion; and this is no doubt the reason why an unbiased opinion is always absolutely valueless.

But I must not allow this brief notice of Mr Pater's new volume to degenerate into an autobiography. I remember being told in America that whenever Margaret Fuller[4] wrote an essay upon Emerson the printers had always to send out to borrow some additional capital 'I's', and I feel it right to accept this transatlantic warning.

'Appreciations', in the fine Latin sense of the word,[5] is the title given by Mr Pater to his book, which is an exquisite collection of exquisite essays, of delicately wrought works of art – some of them being almost Greek in their purity of outline and perfection of form, others medieval in their strangeness of colour and passionate suggestion, and all of them absolutely modern, in the true meaning of the term modernity. For he to whom the present is the only thing that is present, knows nothing of the age in which he lives. To realize the nineteenth century,[6] one must realize every century that has preceded it, and that has contributed to its making. To know anything about oneself, one must know all about others. There must be no mood with which one cannot sympathize, no dead mode of life that one cannot make alive. The legacies of heredity may make us alter our views of moral responsibility, but they cannot but intensify our sense of the value of Criticism; for the true critic is he who bears within himself the dreams and ideas and feelings of myriad generations, and to whom no form of thought is alien, no emotional impulse obscure.

Perhaps the most interesting, and certainly the least successful, of the essays contained in the present volume is that on 'Style'. It is the most interesting because it is the work of one who speaks with the high authority that comes from the noble realization of things nobly conceived. It is the least successful, because the subject is too abstract. A true artist like Mr Pater is most felicitous when he deals with the concrete, whose very limitations give him finer freedom, while they necessitate more intense vision. And yet what a high ideal is contained in these few pages! How good it is for us, in these days of popular education and facile journalism, to be reminded of the real scholarship that is essential to the perfect writer, who, 'being a true lover of words for their own sake, a minute and constant observer of their physiognomy', will avoid what is mere rhetoric, or ostentatious orna-ment, or negligent misuse of terms, or ineffective surplusage, and will be known by his tact of omission, by his skilful economy of means, by his selection and self-restraint, and perhaps above all by that conscious artistic structure which is the expression of mind in style. I think I have been wrong in saying that the subject is too abstract. In Mr Pater's hands it becomes very real to us indeed, and he shows us how, behind the perfection of a man's style, must lie the passion of a man's soul.

As one passes to the rest of the volume, one finds essays on Wordsworth and on Coleridge, on Charles Lamb[7] and on Sir Thomas Brown,[8] on some of Shakespeare's plays and on the English kings that Shakespeare fashioned, on Dante Rossetti, and on William Morris. And that on Wordsworth seems to be Mr Pater's last work, so that on the singer of the 'Defence of Guenevere'[9] is certainly his earliest, or almost his earliest, and it is interesting to mark the change that has taken place in his style. This change is, perhaps, at first sight not very apparent. In 1868 we find Mr Pater writing with the same exquisite care for words, with the same studied music, with the same temper, and something of the same mode of treatment. But, as he goes on, the architecture of the style becomes richer and more complex, the epithet more precise and intellectual. Occasionally one may be inclined to think that there is, here and there, a sentence which is somewhat long, and possibly, if one may venture to say so, a little heavy and cumbersome in movement. But if this be so, it comes from those side-issues suddenly suggested by the idea in its progress, and really revealing the idea more perfectly; or from those felicitous afterthoughts that give a fuller completeness to the central scheme, and yet convey something of the charm of chance; or from a desire to suggest the secondary shades of meaning with all their accumulating effect, and to avoid, it may be, the violence and harshness of too definite and exclusive an opinion. For in matters of art, at any rate, thought is inevitably coloured by emotion, and so is fluid rather than fixed, and, recognizing its dependence upon moods and upon the passion of fine moments, will not accept the rigidity of a scientific formula or a theological dogma. The critical pleasure, too, that we receive from tracing, through what may seem the intricacies of a sentence, the working of the constructive intelligence, must not be overlooked. As soon as we have realized the design, everything appears clear and simple. After a time, these long sentences of Mr Pater's come to have the charm of an elaborate piece of music, and the unity of such music also.

I have suggested that the essay on Wordsworth is probably the most recent bit of work contained in this volume. If one might choose between so much that is good, I should be inclined to say it is the finest also. The essay on Lamb is curiously suggestive; suggestive, indeed, of a somewhat more tragic, more sombre figure, than men have been wont to think of in connection with the author of the *Essays of Elia*. It is an interesting aspect under which to regard Lamb, but perhaps he himself would have had some difficulty in recognizing the portrait given of him. He had, undoubtedly, great sorrows,[10] or motives for sorrow, but he could console himself at a moment's notice for the real tragedies of life by reading any one of the Elizabethan tragedies, provided it was in a folio edition. The essay on Sir Thomas Browne is delightful, and has the strange, personal, fanciful charm of the author of the *Religio Medici*, Mr Pater often catching the colour and accent and tone of whatever artist, or work of art, he deals with. That on Coleridge, with its insistence on the necessity of the cultivation of the relative, as opposed to the absolute spirit in philosophy and in ethics, and its high appreciation of the poet's true position in our literature, is in style and substance a very blameless work. Grace of expression, and delicate subtlety of thought and phrase, characterize the essays on Shakespeare. But the essay on Wordsworth has a spiritual beauty of its own. It appeals, not to the ordinary Wordsworthian with his uncritical temper, and his gross confusion of ethical with aesthetical problems, but rather to those who desire to separate the gold from the dross, and to reach at the true Wordsworth through the mass of tedious and prosaic work that bears his name, and that serves often to conceal him from us. The presence of an alien element in Wordsworth's art, is, of course, recognized by Mr Pater but he touches on it merely from the psychological point of view, pointing out how this quality of higher and lower moods gives the effect in his poetry 'of a power not altogether his own, or under his control'; a power which comes and goes when it wills, 'so that the old fancy which made the poet's art an enthusiasm, a form of divine possession, seems almost true of him'. Mr Pater's earlier essays had their *purpurei panni*,[11] so eminently suitable for quotation, such as the famous passage on Mona Lisa, and that other in which Botticelli's strange conception of the Virgin is so strangely set forth. From the present volume it is difficult to select any one passage in preference to another as specially characteristic of Mr Pater's treatment. This, however, is worth quoting at length. It contains a truth eminently suitable for our age:

That the end of life is not action but contemplation – *being* as distinct from *doing* – a certain disposition of the mind: is, in some shape or other, the principle of all the higher morality. In poetry, in art, if you enter into their true spirit at all, you touch this principle in a measure; these, by their sterility, are a type of beholding for the mere joy of beholding. To treat life in the spirit of art is to make life a thing in which means and ends are identified: to encourage such treatment, the true moral significance of art and poetry. Wordsworth, and other poets who have been like him in ancient or more recent times, are the masters, the experts, in this art of impassioned contemplation. Their work is not to teach lessons, or enforce rules, or even to stimulate us to noble ends, but to withdraw the thoughts for a while from the mere machinery of life, to fix them, with appropriate emotions, on the spectacle of those great facts in man's existence which no machinery affects, 'on the great and universal passions of men, the most general and interesting of their occupations, and the entire world of nature' – on 'the operations of the elements and the appearances of the visible universe, on storm and sunshine, on the revolutions of the seasons, on cold and heat, on loss of friends and kindred, on injuries and resentments, on gratitude and hope, on fear and sorrow'. To witness this spectacle with appropriate emotions is the aim of all culture; and of these emotions poetry like Wordsworth's is a great nourisher and stimulant. He sees nature full of sentiment and excitement; he sees men and women as parts of nature, passionate, excited, in strange grouping and connection with the grandeur and beauty of the natural world: images, in his own words, 'of man suffering, amid awful forms and powers'.

Certainly the real secret of Wordsworth has never been better expressed. After having read and re-read Mr Pater's essay – for it requires re-reading – one returns to the poet's work with a new sense of joy and wonder, and with something of eager and impassioned expectation. And perhaps this might be roughly taken as the test or touchstone of the finest criticism.

Finally, one cannot help noticing the delicate instinct that has gone to fashion the brief epilogue that ends this delightful volume. The difference between the classical and romantic spirits in art has often, and with much over-emphasis, been discussed. But with what a light sure touch does Mr Pater write of it! How subtle and certain are his distinctions! If imaginative prose be really the special art of this century, Mr Pater must rank amongst our century's most characteristic artists. In certain things he stands almost alone. The age has produced wonderful prose styles, turbid with individualism, and violent with excess of rhetoric. But in Mr Pater, as in Cardinal Newman,[12] we find the union of personality with perfection. He has no rival in his own sphere, and he has escaped disciples. And this, not because he has not been imitated, but because in art so fine as his there is something that, in its essence, is inimitable.

The Portrait of Mr W. H.
(expanded version 1889)

I had been dining with Erskine in his pretty little house in Birdcage Walk,[1] and we were sitting in the library over our coffee and cigarettes, when the question of literary forgeries happened to turn up in conversation. I cannot at present remember how it was that we struck upon this somewhat curious topic, as it was at that time, but I know we had a long discussion about Macpherson, Ireland, and Chatterton,[2] and that with regard to the last I insisted that his so-called forgeries were merely the result of an artistic desire for perfect representation; that we had no right to quarrel with an artist for the conditions under which he chooses to present his work; and that all Art being to a certain degree a mode of acting, an attempt to realize one's own personality on some imaginative plane out of reach of the trammelling accidents and limitations of real life, to censure an artist for a forgery was to confuse an ethical with an aesthetical problem.

Erskine, who was a good deal older than I was, and had been listening to me with the amused deference of a man of forty, suddenly put his hand upon my shoulder and said to me, 'What would you say about a young man who had a strange theory about a certain work of art, believed in his theory, and committed a forgery in order to prove it?'

'Ah! that is quite a different matter,' I answered.

Erskine remained silent for a few moments, looking at the thin grey threads of smoke that were rising from his cigarette. 'Yes,' he said, after a pause, 'quite different.'

There was something in the tone of his voice, a slight touch of bitterness perhaps, that excited my curiosity. 'Did you ever know anybody who did that?' I cried.

'Yes,' he answered, throwing his cigarette into the fire – 'a great friend of mine, Cyril Graham. He was very fascinating, and very foolish, and very heartless. However, he left me the only legacy I ever received in my life.'

'What was that?' I exclaimed laughing. Erskine rose from his seat, and going over to a tall inlaid cabinet that stood between the two windows, unlocked it, and came back to where I was sitting, carrying a small panel picture set in an old and somewhat tarnished Elizabethan frame.

It was a full-length portrait of a young man in late sixteenth-century costume, standing by a table, with his right hand resting on an open book. He seemed about seventeen years of age, and was of quite extraordinary personal beauty, though evidently somewhat effeminate. Indeed, had it not been for the dress and the closely cropped hair, one would have said that the face, with its dreamy, wistful eyes and its delicate scarlet lips, was the face of a girl. In manner, and especially in the treatment of the hands, the picture reminded one of François Clouet's[3] later work. The black velvet doublet with its fantastically gilded points, and the peacock-blue background against which it showed up so pleasantly, and from which it gained such luminous value of colour, were quite in Clouet's style; and the two masks of Tragedy and Comedy that hung somewhat formally from the marble pedestal had that hard severity of touch – so different from the facile grace of the Italians – which even at the Court of France the great Flemish master never completely lost, and which in itself has always been a characteristic of the northern temper.

'It is a charming thing,' I cried, 'but who is this wonderful young man whose beauty Art has so happily preserved for us?'

'This is the portrait of Mr W. H.,' said Erskine, with a sad smile. It might have been a chance effect of light, but it seemed to me that his eyes were swimming with tears.

'Mr W. H.!' I repeated; 'who was Mr W. H.?'

'Don't you remember?' he answered; 'look at the book on which his hand is resting.'

'I see there is some writing there, but I cannot make it out,' I replied.

'Take this magnifying-glass and try,' said Erskine, with the same sad smile still playing about his mouth.

I took the glass, and moving the lamp a little nearer, I began to spell out the crabbed sixteenth-century handwriting. 'To The Onlie Begetter Of These Insuing Sonnets.' . . . 'Good heavens!' I cried, 'is this Shakespeare's Mr W. H.?'

'Cyril Graham used to say so,' muttered Erskine.

'But it is not a bit like Lord Pembroke,'⁴ I rejoined. 'I know the Wilton portraits very well. I was staying near there a few weeks ago.'

'Do you really believe then that the Sonnets are addressed to Lord Pembroke?' he asked.

'I am sure of it,' I answered. 'Pembroke, Shakespeare, and Mrs Mary Fitton⁵ are the three personages of the Sonnets; there is no doubt at all about it.'

'Well, I agree with you,' said Erskine, 'but I did not always think so. I used to believe – well, I suppose I used to believe in Cyril Graham and his theory.'

'And what was that?' I asked, looking at the wonderful portrait, which had already begun to have a strange fascination for me.

'It is a long story,' he murmured, taking the picture away from me – rather abruptly I thought at the time – 'a very long story; but if you care to hear it, I will tell it to you.'

'I love theories about the Sonnets,' I cried; 'but I don't think I am likely to be converted to any new idea. The matter has ceased to be a mystery to any one. Indeed, I wonder that it ever was a mystery.'

'As I don't believe in the theory, I am not likely to convert you to it,' said Erskine, laughing; 'but it may interest you.'

'Tell it to me, of course,' I answered. 'If it is half as delightful as the picture, I shall be more than satisfied.'

'Well,' said Erskine, lighting a cigarette, 'I must begin by telling you about Cyril Graham himself. He and I were at the same house at Eton. I was a year or two older than he was, but we were immense friends, and did all our work and all our play together. There was, of course, a good deal more play than work, but I cannot say that I am sorry for that. It is always an advantage not to have received a sound commercial education, and what I learned in the playing fields at Eton has been quite as useful to me as anything I was taught at Cambridge. I should tell you that Cyril's father and mother were both dead. They had been drowned in a horrible yachting accident off the Isle of Wight.

His father had been in the diplomatic service, and had married a daughter, the only daughter, in fact, of old Lord Crediton, who became Cyril's guardian after the death of his parents. I don't think that Lord Crediton cared very much for Cyril. He had never really forgiven his daughter for marrying a man who had no title. He was an extraordinary old aristocrat, who swore like a costermonger,[6] and had the manners of a farmer. I remember seeing him once on Speech-day. He growled at me, gave me a sovereign, and told me not to grow up a "damned Radical" like my father. Cyril had very little affection for him, and was only too glad to spend most of his holidays with us in Scotland. They never really got on together at all. Cyril thought him a bear, and he thought Cyril effeminate. He was effeminate, I suppose, in some things, though he was a capital rider and a capital fencer. In fact he got the foils before he left Eton. But he was very languid in his manner, and not a little vain of his good looks, and had a strong objection to football, which he used to say was a game only suitable for the sons of the middle classes. The two things that really gave him pleasure were poetry and acting. At Eton he was always dressing up and reciting Shakespeare, and when we went up to Trinity he became a member of the A.D.C.[7] in his first term. I remember I was always very jealous of his acting. I was absurdly devoted to him; I suppose because we were so different in most things. I was a rather awkward, weakly lad, with huge feet, and horribly freckled. Freckles run in Scotch families just as gout does in English families. Cyril used to say that of the two he preferred the gout; but he always set an absurdly high value on personal appearance, and once read a paper before our Debating Society to prove that it was better to be good-looking than to be good. He certainly was wonderfully handsome. People who did not like him, philistines and college tutors, and young men reading for the Church, used to say that he was merely pretty; but there was a great deal more in his face than mere prettiness. I think he was the most splendid creature I ever saw, and nothing could exceed the grace of his movements, the charm of his manner. He fascinated everybody who was worth fascinating, and a great many people who were not. He was often wilful and petulant, and I used to think him dreadfully insincere. It was due, I think, chiefly to his inordinate desire to please. Poor Cyril! I told him once that he was contented with very cheap triumphs, but he only tossed his head, and smiled. He was horribly spoiled. All charming people, I fancy, are spoiled. It is the secret of their attraction.

'However, I must tell you about Cyril's acting. You know that no women are allowed to play at the A.D.C. At least they were not in my time. I don't know how it is now. Well, of course Cyril was always cast for the girls' parts, and when *As You Like It* was produced he played Rosalind. It was a marvellous performance. You will laugh at me, but I assure you that Cyril Graham was the only perfect Rosalind I have ever seen. It would be impossible to describe to you the beauty, the delicacy, the refinement of the whole thing. It made an immense sensation, and the horrid little theatre, as it was then, was crowded every night. Even now when I read the play I can't help thinking of Cyril; the part might have been written for him, he played it with such extraordinary grace and distinction. The next term he took his degree, and came to London to read for the Diplomatic.[8] But he never did any work. He spent his days in reading Shakespeare's Sonnets, and his evenings at the theatre. He was, of course, wild to go on the stage. It was all that Lord Crediton and I could do to prevent him. Perhaps, if he had gone on the stage he would be alive now. It is always a silly thing to give advice, but to give good advice is absolutely fatal. I hope you will never fall into that error. If you do, you will be sorry for it.

'Well, to come to the real point of the story, one afternoon I got a letter from Cyril asking me to come round to his rooms that evening. He had charming chambers in Piccadilly overlooking the Green Park, and as I used to go to see him almost every day, I was rather surprised at his taking the trouble to write. Of course I went, and when I arrived I found him in a state of great excitement. He told me that he had at last discovered the true secret of Shakespeare's Sonnets; that all the scholars and critics had been entirely on the wrong track; and that he was the first who, working purely by internal evidence, had found out who Mr W. H. really was. He was perfectly wild with delight, and for a long time would not tell me his theory. Finally, he produced a bundle of notes, took his copy of the Sonnets off the mantelpiece, and sat down and gave me a long lecture on the whole subject.

'He began by pointing out that the young man to whom Shakespeare addressed these strangely passionate poems must have been somebody who was a really vital factor in the development of his dramatic art, and that this could not be said of either Lord Pembroke or Lord Southampton.[9] Indeed, whoever he was, he could not have been anybody of high birth, as was shown very clearly by Sonnet XXV, in which Shakespeare contrasts himself with men who are "great princes' favourites"; says quite frankly –

> Let those who are in favour with their stars
> Of public honour and proud titles boast,
> Whilst I, whom fortune of such triumph bars,
> Unlooked for joy in that I honour most;

and ends the sonnet by congratulating himself on the mean state of him he so adored:

> Then happy I, that love and am beloved,
> Where I may not remove nor be removed.

This sonnet Cyril declared would be quite unintelligible if we fancied that it was addressed to either the Earl of Pembroke or the Earl of Southampton, both of whom were men of the highest position in England and fully entitled to be called "great princes"; and he in corroboration of his view read me Sonnets CXXIV and CXXV, in which Shakespeare tells us that his love is not "the child of the state", that it "suffers not in smiling pomp", but is "builded far from accident". I listened with a good deal of interest, for I don't think the point had ever been made before; but what followed was still more curious, and seemed to me at the time to dispose entirely of Pembroke's claim. We know from Meres[10] that the Sonnets had been written before 1598, and Sonnet CIV informs us that Shakespeare's friendship for Mr W. H. had been already in existence for three years. Now Lord Pembroke, who was born in 1580, did not come to London till he was eighteen years of age, that is to say till 1598, and Shakespeare's acquaintance with Mr W. H. must have begun in 1594, or at the latest in 1595.

Shakespeare, accordingly, could not have known Lord Pembroke until after the Sonnets had been written.

'Cyril pointed out also that Pembroke's father did not die until 1601; whereas it was evident from the line,

> You had a father, let your son say so,

that the father of Mr W. H. was dead in 1598; and laid great stress on the evidence afforded by the Wilton portraits which represent Lord Pembroke as a swarthy dark-haired man, while Mr W. H. was one whose hair was like spun gold, and whose face the meeting-place for the "lily's white" and the "deep vermilion in the rose"; being himself "fair", and "red", and "white and red", and of beautiful aspect. Besides it was absurd to imagine that any publisher of the time, and the preface is from the publisher's hand, would have dreamed of addressing William Herbert, Earl of Pembroke, as Mr W. H.; the case of Lord Buckhurst being spoken of as Mr Sackville being not really a parallel instance, as Lord Buckhurst, the first of that title, was plain Mr Sackville when he contributed to the "Mirror for Magistrates", while Pembroke, during his father's lifetime, was always known as Lord Herbert. So far for Lord Pembroke, whose supposed claims Cyril easily demolished while I sat by in wonder. With Lord Southampton Cyril had even less difficulty. Southampton became at a very early age the lover of Elizabeth Vernon, so he needed no entreaties to marry; he was not beautiful; he did not resemble his mother, as Mr W. H. did –

> Thou art thy mother's glass, and she in thee
> Calls back the lovely April of her prime;

and, above all, his Christian name was Henry, whereas the punning sonnets (CXXXV and CXLIII) show that the Christian name of Shakespeare's friend was the same as his own – *Will*.

'As for the other suggestions of unfortunate commentators, that Mr W. H. is a misprint for Mr W. S., meaning Mr William Shakespeare; that "Mr W. H. all" should be read "Mr W. Hall"; that Mr W. H. is

Mr William Hathaway; that Mr W. H. stands for Mr Henry Willobie, the young Oxford poet, with the initials of his name reversed; and that a full stop should be placed after "wisheth", making Mr W. H. the writer and not the subject of the dedication – Cyril got rid of them in a very short time; and it is not worth while to mention his reasons, though I remember he sent me off into a fit of laughter by reading to me, I am glad to say not in the original, some extracts from a German commentator called Barnstorff, who insisted that Mr W. H. was no less a person than "Mr William Himself". Nor would he allow for a moment that the Sonnets are mere satires on the work of Drayton and John Davies of Hereford.[11] To him, as indeed to me, they were poems of serious and tragic import, wrung out of the bitterness of Shakespeare's heart, and made sweet by the honey of his lips. Still less would he admit that they were merely a philosophical allegory, and that in them Shakespeare is addressing his Ideal Self, or Ideal Manhood, or the Spirit of Beauty, or the Reason, or the Divine Logos, or the Catholic Church. He felt, as indeed I think we all must feel, that the Sonnets are addressed to an individual – to a particular young man whose personality for some reason seems to have filled the soul of Shakespeare with terrible joy and no less terrible despair.

'Having in this manner cleared the way, as it were, Cyril asked me to dismiss from my mind any preconceived ideas I might have formed on the subject, and to give a fair and unbiased hearing to his own theory. The problem he pointed out was this: Who was that young man of Shakespeare's day who, without being of noble birth or even of noble nature, was addressed by him in terms of such passionate adoration that we can but wonder at the strange worship, and are almost afraid to turn the key that unlocks the mystery of the poet's heart? Who was he whose physical beauty was such that it became the very cornerstone of Shakespeare's art; the very source of Shakespeare's inspiration; the very incarnation of Shakespeare's dreams? To look upon him as simply the object of certain love-poems was to miss the whole meaning of the poems: for the art of which Shakespeare talks in the Sonnets is not the art of the Sonnets themselves, which indeed were to him but slight and secret things – it is the art of the dramatist to which he is always alluding; and he to whom Shakespeare said –

> Thou art all my art, and dost advance
> As high as learning my rude ignorance, –

he to whom he promised immortality,

> Where breath most breathes, even in the mouths of men, –

he who was to him the tenth "muse" and

> Ten times more in worth
> Than those old nine which rhymers invocate,

was surely none other than the boy-actor for whom he created Viola and Imogen, Juliet and Rosalind, Portia and Desdemona, and Cleopatra herself.'

'The boy-actor of Shakespeare's plays?' I cried.

'Yes,' said Erskine. 'This was Cyril Graham's theory, evolved as you see purely from the Sonnets themselves, and depending for its acceptance not so much on demonstrable proof of formal evidence, but on a kind of spiritual and artistic sense, by which alone he claimed could the true meaning of the poems be discerned. I remember his reading to me that fine sonnet –

> How can my Muse want subject to invent,
> While thou dost breathe, that pour'st into my verse
> Thine own sweet argument, too excellent
> For every vulgar paper to rehearse?
> O, give thyself the thanks, if aught in me
> Worthy perusal, stand against thy sight;
> For who's so dumb that cannot write to thee,
> When thou thyself dost give invention light?

– and pointing out how completely it corroborated his view; and indeed he went through all the Sonnets carefully, and showed, or fancied that he showed, that, according to his new explanation of their meaning, things that had seemed obscure, or evil, or exaggerated, became clear and rational, and of high artistic import, illustrating Shakespeare's conception of the true relations between the art of the actor and the art of the dramatist.

'It is of course evident that there must have been in Shakespeare's company some wonderful boy-actor of great beauty, to whom he intrusted the presentation of his noble heroines; for Shakespeare was a practical theatrical manager as well as an imaginative poet; and Cyril Graham had actually discovered the boy-actor's name. He was Will, or, as he preferred to call him, Willie Hughes. The Christian name he found of course in the punning sonnets, CXXXV and CXLIII; the surname was, according to him, hidden in the seventh line of Sonnet XX, where Mr W. H. is described as –

A man in hew, all *Hews* in his controwling.

'In the original edition of the Sonnets "*Hews*" is printed with a capital letter and in italics, and this, he claimed, showed clearly that a play on words was intended, his view receiving a good deal of corroboration from those sonnets in which curious puns are made on the words "use" and "usury", and from such lines as –

Thou art as fair in knowledge as in hew.

Of course I was converted at once, and Willie Hughes became to me as real a person as Shakespeare. The only objection I made to the theory was that the name of Willie Hughes does not occur in the list of the actors of Shakespeare's company as it is printed in the first folio. Cyril, however, pointed out that the absence of Willie Hughes's name from this list really corroborated the theory, as it was evident from Sonnet LXXXVI that he had abandoned Shakespeare's company to play at a rival theatre, probably in some of Chapman's[12] plays. It was in reference to this that in the great sonnet on Chapman Shakespeare said to Willie Hughes –

But when your countenance filled up his line,
Then lacked I matter; that enfeebled mine –

the expression "when your countenance filled up his line" referring clearly to the beauty of the young actor giving life and reality and added charm to Chapman's verse, the same idea being also put forward in Sonnet LXXIX:

> Whilst I alone did call upon thy aid,
> My verse alone had all thy gentle grace;
> But now my gracious numbers are decayed,
> And my sick Muse doth give another place;

and in the immediately preceding sonnet, where Shakespeare says,

> Every alien pen hath got my *use*,
> And under thee their poesy disperse,

the play upon words (use = Hughes) being of course obvious, and the phrase, "under thee their poesy disperse", meaning "by your assistance as an actor bring their play before the people".

'It was a wonderful evening, and we sat up almost till dawn reading and re-reading the Sonnets. After some time, however, I began to see that before the theory could be placed before the world in a really perfected form, it was necessary to get some independent evidence about the existence of this young actor, Willie Hughes. If this could be once established, there could be no possible doubt about his identity with Mr W. H.; but otherwise the theory would fall to the ground. I put this forward very strongly to Cyril, who was a good deal annoyed at what he called my philistine tone of mind, and indeed was rather bitter upon the subject. However, I made him promise that in his own interest he would not publish his discovery till he had put the whole matter beyond the reach of doubt; and for weeks and weeks we searched the registers of City churches, the Alleyn MSS.[13] at Dulwich, the Record Office, the books of the Lord Chamberlain[14] – everything, in fact, that we thought might contain some allusion to Willie Hughes. We discovered nothing, of course, and each day the existence of Willie Hughes seemed to me to become more problematical. Cyril was in a dreadful state, and used to go over the whole question again and again, entreating me to believe; but I saw the one flaw in the theory, and I refused to be convinced till the actual existence of Willie Hughes, a boy-actor of the Elizabethan stage, had been placed beyond the reach of doubt or cavil.

'One day Cyril left town to stay with his grandfather, I thought at the time, but I afterwards heard from Lord Crediton that this was not the case; and about a fortnight afterwards I received a telegram from him, handed in at Warwick, asking me to be sure to come and dine with him in his chambers, that evening at eight o'clock. When I arrived, he said to me, "The only apostle who did not deserve proof was St Thomas,[15] and St Thomas was the only apostle who got it." I asked him what he meant. He answered that he had been able not merely to establish the existence in the sixteenth century of a boy-actor of the name of Willie Hughes, but to prove by the most conclusive evidence that he was the Mr W. H. of the Sonnets. He would not tell me anything more at the time; but after dinner he solemnly produced the picture I showed you, and told me that he had discovered it by the merest chance nailed to the side of an old chest that he had bought at a farmhouse in Warwickshire. The chest itself, which was a very fine example of Elizabethan work, and thoroughly authentic, he had, of course, brought with him, and in the centre of the front panel the initials W. H. were undoubtedly carved. It was this monogram that had attracted his attention, and he told me that it was not till he had had the chest in his possession for several days that he had thought of making any careful examination of the inside. One morning, however, he saw that the right-hand side of the chest was much thicker than the other, and looking more closely, he discovered that a framed panel was clamped against it. On taking it out, he found it was the picture that is now lying on the sofa. It was very dirty, and covered with mould; but he managed to clean it, and, to his great joy, saw that he had fallen by mere chance on the one thing for which he had been looking. Here was an authentic portrait of Mr W. H. with his hand resting on the dedicatory page of the Sonnets, and on the corner of the picture could be faintly seen the name of the young man himself written in gold uncial letters on the faded *bleu de paon*[16] ground, "Master Will Hews".

'Well, what was I to say? It is quite clear from Sonnet XLVII that Shakespeare had a portrait of Mr W. H. in his possession, and it seemed to me more than probable that here we had the very "painted banquet" on which he invited his eye to feast; the actual picture that awoke his heart "to heart's and eye's delight". It never occurred to me for a moment that Cyril Graham was playing a trick on me, or that he was trying to prove his theory by means of a forgery.'

'But is it a forgery?' I asked.

'Of course it is,' said Erskine. 'It is a very good forgery; but it is a forgery none the less. I thought at the time that Cyril was rather calm about the whole matter; but I remember he kept telling me that he himself required no proof of the kind, and that he thought the theory complete without it. I laughed at him, and told him that without it the entire theory would fall to the ground, and I warmly congratulated him on his marvellous discovery. We then arranged that the picture should be etched or facsimiled, and placed as the frontispicce to Cyril's edition of the Sonnets; and for three months we did nothing but go over each poem line by line, till we had settled every difficulty of text or meaning. One unlucky day I was in a print-shop in Holborn, when I saw upon the counter some extremely beautiful drawings in silver-point. I was so attracted by them that I bought them; and the proprietor of the place, a man called Rawlings, told me that they were done by a young painter of the name of Edward Merton, who was very clever, but as poor as a church mouse. I went to see Merton some days afterwards, having got his address from the print-seller, and found a pale, interesting young man, with a rather common-looking wife – his model, as I subsequently learned. I told him how much I admired his drawings, at which he seemed very pleased, and I asked him if he would show me some of his other work. As we were looking over a portfolio, full of really very lovely things – for Merton had a most delicate and delightful touch – I suddenly caught sight of a drawing of the picture of Mr W. H. There was no doubt whatever about it. It was almost a facsimile – the only difference being that the two masks of Tragedy and Comedy were not suspended from the marble table as they are in the picture but were lying on the floor at the young man's feet. "Where on earth did you get that?" I asked. He grew rather confused, and said – "Oh, that is nothing. I did not know it was in this portfolio. It is not a thing of any value." "It is what you did for Mr Cyril Graham," exclaimed his wife; "and if this gentleman wishes to buy it, let him have it." "For Mr Cyril Graham?" I repeated. "Did you paint the picture of Mr W. H.?" "I don't understand what you mean," he answered growing very red. Well, the whole thing was quite dreadful. The wife let it all out. I gave her five pounds when I was going away. I can't bear to think of it, now; but of course I was furious. I went off at once to Cyril's chambers, waited there for three hours before he came in, with that horrid lie staring me in the face, and told him I had discovered his forgery. He grew very pale, and said – "I did it purely for your sake. You would not be convinced in any other way. It does not affect the truth of the theory." "The truth of the theory!" I exclaimed; "the less we talk about that the better. You never even believed in it yourself. If you had, you would not have committed a forgery to prove it." High words passed between us; we had a fearful quarrel. I daresay I was unjust, and the next morning he was dead.'

'Dead!' I cried.

'Yes, he shot himself with a revolver. By the time I arrived – his servant had sent for me at once – the police were already there. He had left a letter for me, evidently written in the greatest agitation and distress of mind.'

'What was in it?' I asked.

'Oh, that he believed absolutely in Willie Hughes; that the forgery of the picture had been done simply as a concession to me, and did not in the slightest degree invalidate the truth of the theory; and that in order to show me how firm and flawless his faith in the whole thing was, he was going to offer his life as a sacrifice to the secret of the Sonnets. It was a foolish, mad letter. I remember he ended by saying that he intrusted to me the Willie Hughes theory, and that it was for me to present it to the world, and to unlock the secret of Shakespeare's heart.'

'It is a most tragic story,' I cried, 'but why have you not carried out his wishes?'

Erskine shrugged his shoulders. 'Because it is a perfectly unsound theory from beginning to end,' he answered.

'My dear Erskine,' I exclaimed, getting up from my seat, 'you are entirely wrong about the whole matter. It is the only perfect key to Shakespeare's Sonnets that has ever been made. It is complete in every detail. I believe in Willie Hughes.'

'Don't say that,' said Erskine, gravely; 'I believe there is something fatal about the idea, and intellectually there is nothing to be said for it. I have gone into the whole matter, and I assure you the theory is entirely fallacious. It is plausible up to a certain point. Then it stops. For heaven's sake, my dear boy, don't take up the subject of Willie Hughes. You will break your heart over it.'

'Erskine,' I answered, 'it is your duty to give this theory to the world. If you will not do it, I will. By keeping it back you wrong the memory of Cyril Graham, the youngest and the most splendid of all the martyrs of literature. I entreat you to do him this bare act of justice. He died for this thing – don't let his death be in vain.'

Erskine looked at me in amazement. 'You are carried away by the sentiment of the whole story,' he said. 'You forget that a thing is not necessarily true because a man dies for it. I was devoted to Cyril Graham. His death was a horrible blow to me. I did not recover from it for years. I don't think I have ever recovered from it. But Willie Hughes! There is nothing in the idea of Willie Hughes. No such person ever existed. As for bringing the matter before the world – the world thinks that Cyril Graham shot himself by accident. The only proof of his suicide was contained in the letter to me, and of this letter the public never heard anything. To the present day Lord Crediton is under the impression that the whole thing was accidental.'

'Cyril Graham sacrificed his life to a great idea,' I answered; 'and if you will not tell of his martyrdom, tell at least of his faith.'

'His faith,' said Erskine, 'was fixed in a thing that was false, in a thing that was unsound, in a thing that no Shakespearean scholar would accept for a moment. The theory would be laughed at. Don't make a fool of yourself, and don't follow a trail that leads nowhere. You start by assuming the existence of the very person whose existence is the thing to be proved. Besides, everybody knows that the Sonnets were addressed to Lord Pembroke. The matter is settled once for all.'

'The matter is not settled,' I exclaimed. 'I will take up the theory where Cyril Graham left it, and I will prove to the world that he was right.'

'Silly boy!' said Erskine. 'Go home, it is after three, and don't think about Willie Hughes any more. I am sorry I told you anything about it, and very sorry indeed that I should have converted you to a thing in which I don't believe.'

'You have given me the key to the greatest mystery of modern literature,' I answered; 'and I will not rest till I have made you recognize, till I have made everybody recognize, that Cyril Graham was the most subtle Shakespearian critic of our day.'

I was about to leave the room when Erskine called me back. 'My dear fellow,' he said, 'let me advise you not to waste your time over the Sonnets. I am quite serious. After all, what do they tell us about Shakespeare? Simply that he was the slave of beauty.'

'Well, that is the condition of being an artist!' I replied.

There was a strange silence for a few moments. Then Erskine got up, and looking at me with half closed eyes, said, 'Ah! how you remind me of Cyril! He used to say just that sort of thing to me.' He tried to smile, but there was a note of poignant pathos in his voice that I remember to the present day, as one remembers the tone of a particular violin that has charmed one, the touch of a particular woman's hand. The great events of life often leave one unmoved; they pass out of consciousness, and, when one thinks of them, become unreal. Even the scarlet flowers of passion seem to grow in the same meadow as the poppies of oblivion. We reject the burden of their memory, and have anodynes against them. But the little things, the things of no moment, remain with us. In some tiny ivory cell the brain stores the most delicate, and the most fleeting impressions.

As I walked home through St James's Park, the dawn was just breaking over London. The swans were lying asleep on the smooth surface of the polished lake, like white feathers fallen upon a mirror of black steel. The gaunt Palace looked purple against the pale green sky, and in the garden of Stafford House the birds were just

beginning to sing. I thought of Cyril Graham, and my eyes filled with
tears.

II

It was past twelve o'clock when I awoke, and the sun was streaming
in through the curtains of my room in long dusty beams of tremulous
gold. I told my servant that I would not be at home to any one, and
after I had discussed a cup of chocolate and a *petit-pain*,[17] I took out of
the library my copy of Shakespeare's Sonnets, and Mr Tyler's[18] facsimile edition of the Quarto, and began to go carefully through them.
Each poem seemed to me to corroborate Cyril Graham's theory. I felt
as if I had my hand upon Shakespeare's heart, and was counting each
separate throb and pulse of passion. I thought of the wonderful
boy-actor, and saw his face in every line.

Previous to this, in my Lord Pembroke days, if I may so term
them, I must admit that it had always seemed to me very difficult to
understand how the creator of Hamlet and Lear and Othello could
have addressed in such extravagant terms of praise and passion one
who was merely an ordinary young nobleman of the day. Along with
most students of Shakespeare, I had found myself compelled to set the
Sonnets apart as things quite alien to Shakespeare's development as a
dramatist, as things possibly unworthy of the intellectual side of his
nature. But now that I began to realize the truth of Cyril Graham's
theory, I saw that the moods and passions they mirrored were absolutely essential to Shakespeare's perfection as an artist writing for the
Elizabethan stage, and that it was in the curious theatre conditions of
that stage that the poems themselves had their origin. I remember
what joy I had in feeling that these wonderful Sonnets,

> Subtle as Sphinx; as sweet and musical
> As bright Apollo's lute, strung with his hair,

were no longer isolated from the great aesthetic energies of Shakespeare's life, but were an essential part of his dramatic activity, and

revealed to us something of the secret of his method. To have discovered the true name of Mr W. H. was comparatively nothing: others might have done that, had perhaps done it: but to have discovered his profession was a revolution in criticism.

Two sonnets, I remember, struck me particularly. In the first of these (LIII) Shakespeare, complimenting Willie Hughes on the versatility of his acting, on his wide range of parts, a range extending, as we know, from Rosalind to Juliet, and from Beatrice to Ophelia, says to him:

> What is your substance, whereof are you made,
> That millions of strange shadows on you tend?
> Since every one hath, every one, one shade,
> And you, but one, can every shadow lend –

lines that would be unintelligible if they were not addressed to an actor, for the word 'shadow' had in Shakespeare's day a technical meaning connected with the stage. 'The best in this kind are but shadows,' says Theseus of the actors in the *Midsummer Night's Dream*;

> Life's but a walking shadow, a poor player
> That struts and frets his hour upon the stage,

cries Macbeth in the moment of his despair, and there are many similar allusions in the literature of the day. This sonnet evidently belonged to the series in which Shakespeare discusses the nature of the actor's art, and of the strange and rare temperament that is essential to the perfect stage-player. 'How is it,' says Shakespeare to Willie Hughes, 'that you have so many personalities?' and then he goes on to point out that his beauty is such that it seems to realize every form and phase of fancy, to embody each dream of the creative imagination – an idea that is still further expanded in the sonnet that immediately follows, where, beginning with the fine thought,

> O, how much more doth beauty beauteous seem
> By that sweet ornament which *truth* doth give!

Shakespeare invites us to notice how the truth of acting, the truth of visible presentation on the stage, adds to the wonder of poetry, giving life to its loveliness, and actual reality to its ideal form. And yet, in Sonnet LXVII, Shakespeare calls upon Willie Hughes to abandon the stage with its artificiality, its unreal life of painted face and mimic costume, its immoral influences and suggestions, its remoteness from the true world of noble action and sincere utterance.

> Ah! wherefore with infection should he live,
> And with his presence grace impiety,
> That sin by him advantage should receive,
> And lace itself with his society?
> Why should false painting imitate his cheek,
> And steal dead seeing of his living hue?
> Why should poor beauty indirectly seek
> Roses of shadow, since his rose is true?

It may seem strange that so great a dramatist as Shakespeare, who realized his own perfection as an artist and his full humanity as a man on the ideal plane of stage-writing and stage-playing, should have written in these terms about the theatre; but we must remember that in Sonnets CX and CXI, Shakespeare shows us that he too was wearied of the world of puppets, and full of shame at having made himself 'a motley to the view'. Sonnet CXI is especially bitter:

> O, for my sake do you with Fortune chide,
> The guilty goddess of my harmful deeds,
> That did not better for my life provide
> Than public means, which public manners breeds.
> Thence comes it that my name receives a brand;
> And almost thence my nature is subdued
> To what it works in, like the dyer's hand:
> Pity me then, and wish I were renewed –

and there are many signs of the same feeling elsewhere, signs familiar to all real students of Shakespeare.

One point puzzled me immensely as I read the Sonnets, and it was days before I struck on the true interpretation, which indeed Cyril Graham himself seemed to have missed. I could not understand how it was that Shakespeare set so high a value on his young friend marrying. He himself had married young and the result had been unhappiness, and it was not likely that he would have asked Willie Hughes to commit the same error. The boy-player of Rosalind had nothing to gain from marriage, or from the passions of real life. The early sonnets with their strange entreaties to love children seemed to be a jarring note.

The explanation of the mystery came on me quite suddenly and I found it in the curious dedication. It will be remembered that this dedication was as follows:

TO.THE.ONLIE.BEGETTER.OF.
THESE.INSUING.SONNETS.
MR.W.H.ALL.HAPPINESSE.
AND.THAT.ETERNITIE.
PROMISED.BY.
OUR.EVER-LIVING.POET.
WISHETH.
THE.WELL-WISHING.
ADVENTURER.IN.
SETTING.
FORTH.
T.T.

Some scholars have supposed that the word 'begetter' here means simply the procurer of the Sonnets for Thomas Thorpe the publisher; but this view is now generally abandoned, and the highest authorities are quite agreed that it is to be taken in the sense of inspirer, the metaphor being drawn from the analogy of physical life. Now I saw that the same metaphor was used by Shakespeare himself all through the poems, and this set me on the right track. Finally I made my great discovery. The marriage that Shakespeare proposes for Willie Hughes is the 'marriage with his Muse', an expression which is definitely put forward in Sonnet LXXXII where, in the bitterness of his heart at the defection of the boy-actor for whom he had written his greatest parts, and whose beauty had indeed suggested them, he opens his complaint by saying –

> I grant thou wert not married to my Muse.

The children he begs him to beget are no children of flesh and blood, but more immortal children of undying fame. The whole cycle of the early sonnets is simply Shakespeare's invitations to Willie Hughes to go upon the stage and become a player. How barren and profitless a thing, he says, is this beauty of yours if it be not used:

> When forty winters shall besiege thy brow,
> And dig deep trenches in thy beauty's field,
> Thy youth's proud livery, so gazed on now,
> Will be a tattered weed, of small worth held:
> Then, being asked where all thy beauty lies,
> Where all the treasure of thy lusty days;
> To say, within thine own deep-sunken eyes,
> Were an all-eating shame and thriftless praise.

You must create something in art: my verse 'is thine and *born* of thee'; only listen to me, and I will

> *bring forth* eternal numbers to outlive long date,

and you shall people with forms of your own image the imaginary world of the stage. These children that you beget, he continues, will not wither away, as mortal children do, but you shall live in them and in my plays: do but –

> Make thee another self, for love of me,
> That beauty still may live in thine or thee!

Be not afraid to surrender your personality, to give your 'semblance to some other':

> To give away yourself, keeps yourself still,
> And you must live, drawn by your own sweet skill.

I may not be learned in astrology, and yet, in those 'constant stars' your eyes,

> I read such art
> As truth and beauty shall together thrive,
> If from thyself to store thou wouldst convert.

What does it matter about others?

> Let those whom Nature hath not made for store,
> Harsh, featureless, and rude, barrenly perish:

With you it is different, Nature –

> ... carv'd thee for her seal, and meant thereby
> Thou shouldst print more, nor let that copy die.

Remember, too, how soon Beauty forsakes itself. Its action is no stronger than a flower, and like a flower it lives and dies. Think of 'the stormy gusts of winter's day', of the 'barren edge of Death's eternal cold', and –

> ere thou be distilled:
> Make sweet some vial; treasure thou some place
> With beauty's treasure, ere it be self-killed.

Why, even flowers do not altogether die. When roses wither,

> Of their sweet deaths are sweetest odours made:

and you who are 'my rose' should not pass away without leaving your form in Art. For Art has the very secret of joy.

> Ten times thyself were happier than thou art,
> If ten of thine ten times refigur'd thee.

You do not require the 'bastard signs of fair', the painted face, the fantastic disguises of other actors:

> . . . the golden tresses of the dead,
> The right of sepulchres,

need not be shorn away for you. In you –

> . . . those holy antique hours are seen,
> Without all ornament, itself and true,
> Making no summer of another's green.

All that is necessary is to 'copy what in you is writ'; to place you on the stage as you are in actual life. All those ancient poets who have written of 'ladies dead and lovely knights' have been dreaming of such a one as you, and:

> All their praises are but prophecies
> Of this our time, all you prefiguring.

For your beauty seems to belong to all ages and to all lands. Your shade comes to visit me at night, but, I want to look upon your 'shadow' in the living day, I want to see you upon the stage. Mere description of you will not suffice:

> If I could write the beauty of your eyes,
> And in fresh numbers number all your graces,
> The age to come would say, 'This poet lies;
> Such heavenly touches ne'er touched earthly faces.'

It is necessary that 'some child of yours', some artistic creation that embodies you, and to which your imagination gives life, shall present you to the world's wondering eyes. Your own thoughts are your children, offspring of sense and spirit; give some expression to them, and you shall find –

> Those children nursed, delivered from thy brain.

My thoughts, also, are my 'children'. They are of your begetting and my brain is:

> the womb wherein they grew.

For this great friendship of ours is indeed a marriage, it is the 'marriage of true minds'.

I collected together all the passages that seemed to me to corroborate this view, and they produced a strong impression on me, and showed me how complete Cyril Graham's theory really was. I also saw that it was quite easy to separate those lines in which Shakespeare speaks of the Sonnets themselves, from those in which he speaks of his great dramatic work. This was a point that had been entirely overlooked by all critics up to Cyril Graham's day. And yet it was one of the most important in the whole series of poems. To the Sonnets Shakespeare was more or less indifferent. He did not wish to rest his fame on them. They were to him his 'slight Muse', as he calls them, and intended, as Meres tells us, for private circulation only among a few, a very few, friends. Upon the other hand he was extremely conscious of the high artistic value of his plays, and shows a noble self-reliance upon his dramatic genius. When he says to Willie Hughes:

> But thy eternal summer shall not fade,
> Nor lose possession of that fair thou owest;
> Nor shall Death brag thou wander'st in his shade,
> When in *eternal lines* to time thou growest:
> So long as men can breathe, or eyes can see,
> So long lives this, and this gives life to thee –

the expression 'eternal lines' clearly alludes to one of his plays that he was sending him at the time, just as the concluding couplet points to his confidence in the probability of his plays being always acted. In his address to the Dramatic Muse (Sonnets C and CI) we find the same feeling:

> Where art thou, Muse, that thou forget'st so long
> To speak of that which gives thee all thy might?
> Spend'st thou thy fury on some worthless song,
> Darkening thy power, to lend base subjects light?

he cries, and he then proceeds to reproach the mistress of Tragedy and Comedy for her 'neglect of truth in beauty dyed', and says:

> Because he needs no praise, wilt thou be dumb?
> Excuse not silence so; for 't lies in thee
> To make him much outlive a gilded tomb,
> And to be praised of ages yet to be.
> Then do thy office, Muse, I teach thee how,
> To make him seem long hence, as he shows now.

It is, however, perhaps in Sonnet LV that Shakespeare gives to this idea its fullest expression. To imagine that the 'powerful rhyme' of the second line refers to the sonnet itself was entirely to mistake Shakespeare's meaning. It seemed to me that it was extremely likely, from the general character of the sonnet, that a particular play was meant, and that the play was none other but *Romeo and Juliet*.

> Not marble, nor the gilded monuments
> Of princes, shall outlive this powerful rhyme;
> But you shall shine more bright in these contents
> Than unswept stone, besmeared with sluttish time.
> When wasteful war shall statues overturn,
> And broils root out the work of masonry,
> Nor Mars his sword nor war's quick fire shall burn
> The living record of your memory.

'Gainst death and all-oblivious enmity
Shall you pace forth; your praise shall still find room
Even in the eyes of all posterity
That wears this world out to the ending doom.
So, till the judgement that yourself arise,
You live in this, and dwell in lovers' eyes.

It was also very suggestive to note how here as elsewhere Shakespeare promised Willie Hughes immortality in a form that appealed to men's eyes – that is to say, in a spectacular form, in a play that is to be looked at.

For two weeks I worked hard at the Sonnets, hardly ever going out, and refusing all invitations. Every day I seemed to be discovering something new, and Willie Hughes became to me a kind of spiritual presence, an ever-dominant personality. I could almost fancy that I saw him standing in the shadow of my room, so well had Shakespeare drawn him, with his golden hair, his tender flower-like grace, his dreamy deep-sunken eyes, his delicate mobile limbs, and his white lily hands. His very name fascinated me. Willie Hughes! Willie Hughes! How musically it sounded! Yes; who else but he could have been the master-mistress of Shakespeare's passion,[a] the lord of his love to whom he was bound in vassalage,[b] the delicate minion of pleasure,[c] the rose of the whole world,[d] the herald of the spring,[e] decked in the proud livery of youth,[f] the lovely boy whom it was sweet music to hear,[g] and whose beauty was the very raiment of Shakespeare's heart,[h] as it was the keystone of his dramatic power? How bitter now seemed the whole tragedy of his desertion and his shame! – shame that he made sweet and lovely[i] by the mere magic of his personality, but that was none the less shame. Yet as Shakespeare forgave him, should not we forgive him also? I did not care to pry into the mystery of his sin or of the sin, if such it was, of the great poet who had so dearly loved him. 'I am that I am,' said Shakespeare in a sonnet of noble scorn –

[a] Sonnet xx. 2   [b] Sonnet xxvi. 1.   [c] Sonnet cxxvi. 9.
[d] Sonnet cix. 14.   [e] Sonnet i. 10.   [f] Sonnet ii. 3.
[g] Sonnet viii. 1.   [h] Sonnet xxii. 6.   [i] Sonnet xcv. 1.

I am that I am, and they that level
At my abuses reckon up their own;
I may be straight, though they themselves be bevel;
By their rank thoughts my deeds must not be shown.

Willie Hughes's abandonment of Shakespeare's theatre was a different matter, and I investigated it at great length. Finally I came to the conclusion that Cyril Graham had been wrong in regarding the rival dramatist of Sonnet LXXX as Chapman. It was obviously Marlowe[19] who was alluded to. At the time the Sonnets were written, which must have been between 1590 and 1595, such an expression as 'the proud full sail of his great verse' could not possibly have been used of Chapman's work, however applicable it might have been to the style of his later Jacobean plays. No; Marlowe was clearly the rival poet of whom Shakespeare spoke in such laudatory terms; the hymn he wrote in Willie Hughes' honour was the unfinished 'Hero and Leander', and that

> Affable familiar ghost
> Which nightly gulls him with intelligence,

was the Mephistopheles of his Doctor Faustus. No doubt, Marlowe was fascinated by the beauty and grace of the boy-actor, and lured him away from the Blackfriars Theatre, that he might play the Gaveston of his *Edward II*. That Shakespeare had some legal right to retain Willie Hughes in his own company seems evident from Sonnet LXXXVII, where he says:

> Farewell! thou art too dear for my possessing,
> And like enough thou know'st thy estimate:
> The *charter of thy worth* gives thee releasing;
> My *bonds* in thee are all determinate.
> For how do I hold thee but by thy granting?
> And for that riches where is my deserving?
> The cause of this fair gift in me is wanting,
> *And so my patent back again is swerving.*

> Thyself thou gav'st, thy own worth then not knowing,
> Or me, to whom thou gav'st it, else mistaking;
> So thy great gift, upon misprision growing,
> Comes home again, on better judgment making.
> Thus have I had thee, as a dream doth flatter,
> In sleep a king, but waking no such matter.

But him whom he could not hold by love, he would not hold by force. Willie Hughes became a member of Lord Pembroke's company, and perhaps in the open yard of the Red Bull Tavern, played the part of King Edward's delicate minion. On Marlowe's death, he seems to have returned to Shakespeare, who, whatever his fellow-partners may have thought of the matter, was not slow to forgive the wilfulness and treachery of the young actor.

How well, too, had Shakespeare drawn the temperament of the stage-player! Willie Hughes was one of those –

> That do not do the thing they most do show,
> Who, moving others, are themselves as stone.

He could act love, but could not feel it, could mimic passion without realizing it.

> In many's looks the false heart's history
> Is writ in moods and frowns and wrinkles strange,

but with Willie Hughes it was not so. 'Heaven,' says Shakespeare, in a sonnet of mad idolatry –

> Heaven in thy creation did decree
> That in thy face sweet love should ever dwell;
> Whate'er thy thoughts or thy heart's workings be,
> Thy looks should nothing thence but sweetness tell.

In his 'inconstant mind' and his 'false heart' it was easy to recognize the insincerity that somehow seems inseparable from the artistic nature, as in his love of praise, that desire for immediate recognition that characterizes all actors. And yet, more fortunate in this than other actors, Willie Hughes was to know something of immortality. Intimately connected with Shakespeare's plays, he was to live in them, and by their production.

> Your name from hence immortal life shall have,
> Though I, once gone, to all the world must die:
> The earth can yield me but a common grave,
> When you entombed in men's eyes shall lie.
> Your monument shall be my gentle verse,
> Which eyes not yet created shall o'er-read;
> And tongues to be, your being shall rehearse,
> When all the breathers of this world are dead.

Nash with his venomous tongue had railed against Shakespeare for 'reposing eternity in the mouth of a player', the reference being obviously to the Sonnets.

But to Shakespeare, the actor was a deliberate and self-conscious fellow-worker who gave form and substance to a poet's fancy, and brought into Drama the elements of a noble realism. His silence could be as eloquent as words, and his gesture as expressive, and in those terrible moments of Titan agony or of god-like pain, when thought outstrips utterance, when the soul sick with excess of anguish stammers or is dumb, and the very raiment of speech is rent and torn by passion in its storm, then the actor could become, though it were but for a moment, a creative artist, and touch by his mere presence and person-ality those springs of terror and of pity to which tragedy appeals. This full recognition of the actor's art, and of the actor's power, was one of the things that distinguished the Romantic from the Classical Drama, and one of the things, consequently, that we owed to Shakespeare, who, fortunate in much, was fortunate also in this, that he was able to find Richard Burbage and to fashion Willie Hughes.

With what pleasure he dwelt upon Willie Hughes's influence over his audience – the 'gazers' as he calls them; with what charm of fancy did he analyse the whole art! Even in the 'Lover's Complaint' he speaks of his acting, and tells us that he was a nature so impressionable to the quality of dramatic situations that he could assume all 'strange forms' –

> Of burning blushes, or of weeping water,
> Or swooning paleness;

explaining his meaning more fully later on where he tells us how Willie Hughes was able to deceive others by his wonderful power to –

> Blush at speeches rank, to weep at woes,
> Or to turn white and swoon at tragic shows.

It had never been pointed out before that the shepherd of this lovely pastoral, whose 'youth in art and art in youth' are described with such subtlety of phrase and passion, was none other than the Mr W. H. of the Sonnets. And yet there was no doubt that he was so. Not merely in personal appearance are the two lads the same, but their natures and temperaments are identical. When the false shepherd whispers to the fickle maid –

> All my offences that abroad you see
> Are errors of the blood, none of the mind;
> Love made them not:

when he says of his lovers,

> Harm have I done to them, but ne'er was harmed;
> Kept hearts in liveries, but mine own was free,
> And reigned, commanding in his monarchy:

when he tells us of the 'deep-brained sonnets' that one of them had sent him, and cries out in boyish pride –

> The broken bosoms that to me belong
> Have emptied all their fountains in my well:

it is impossible not to feel that it is Willie Hughes who is speaking to us. 'Deep-brained sonnets', indeed, had Shakespeare brought him, 'jewels' that to his careless eyes were but as 'trifles', though –

> each several stone,
> With wit well blazoned, smiled or made some moan;

and into the well of beauty he had emptied the sweet fountain of his song. That in both places it was an actor who was alluded to, was also clear. The betrayed nymph tells us of the 'false fire' in her lover's cheek, of the 'forced thunder' of his sighs, and of his 'borrowed motion': of whom, indeed, but of an actor could it be said that to him 'thought, characters, and words' were 'merely Art', or that –

> To make the weeper laugh, the laugher weep,
> He had the dialect and different skill,
> Catching all passions in his craft of will?

The play on words in the last line is the same as that used in the punning sonnets, and is continued in the following stanza of the poem, where we are told of the youth who –

> did in the general bosom reign
> Of young, of old; and sexes both enchanted,

that there were those who –

> . . . dialogued for him what he would say,
> Asked their own wills, and made their Wills obey.

Yes: the 'rose-cheeked Adonis' of the Venus poem,[20] the false shepherd of the 'Lover's Complaint', the 'tender churl', the 'beauteous niggard' of the Sonnets, was none other but a young actor; and as I read through the various descriptions of him, I saw that the love that Shakespeare bore him was as the love of a musician for some delicate instrument on which he delights to play, as a sculptor's love for some rare and exquisite material that suggests a new form of plastic beauty, a new mode of plastic expression. For all Art has its medium, its material, be it that of rhythmical words, or of pleasurable colour, or of sweet and subtly-divided sound; and, as one of the most fascinating critics of our day has pointed out, it is to the qualities inherent in each material, and special to it, that we owe the sensuous element in Art, with it all that in Art is essentially artistic. What then shall we say of the material that the Drama requires for its perfect presentation? What of the Actor, who is the medium through which alone the Drama can truly reveal itself? Surely, in that strange mimicry of life by the living which is the mode and method of theatric art, there are sensuous elements of beauty that none of the other arts possess. Looked at from one point of view, the common players of the saffron-strewn stage[21] are Art's most complete, most satisfying instruments. There is no passion in bronze, nor motion in marble. The sculptor must surrender colour, and the painter fullness of form. The epos changes acts into words, and music changes words into tones. It is the Drama only that, to quote the fine saying of Gervinus,[22] uses all means at once, and, appealing both to eye and ear, has at its disposal, and in its service, form and colour, tone, look, and word, the swiftness of motion, the intense realism of visible action.

It may be that in this very completeness of the instrument lies the secret of some weakness in the art. Those arts are happiest that employ a material remote from reality, and there is a danger in the absolute identity of medium and matter, the danger of ignoble realism and unimaginative imitation. Yet Shakespeare himself was a player, and wrote for players. He saw the possibilities that lay hidden in an art that up to his time had expressed itself but in bombast or in clowning. He has left us the most perfect rules for acting that have ever been written. He created parts that can be only truly revealed to us on the stage, wrote plays that need the theatre for their full realization, and we cannot marvel that he so worshipped one who was the interpreter of his vision, as he was the incarnation of his dreams.

There was, however, more in his friendship than the mere delight of a dramatist in one who helps him to achieve his end. This was indeed a subtle element of pleasure, if not of passion, and a noble basis for an artistic comradeship. But it was not all that the Sonnets revealed to us. There was something beyond. There was the soul, as well as the language, of neo-Platonism.

'The fear of the Lord is the beginning of wisdom,' said the stern Hebrew prophet.[23] 'The beginning of wisdom is Love,' was the gracious message of the Greek. And the spirit of the Renaissance, which already touched Hellenism at so many points, catching the inner meaning of this phrase and divining its secret, sought to elevate friendship to the high dignity of the antique ideal, to make it a vital factor in the new culture, and a mode of self-conscious intellectual development. In 1492 appeared Marsilio Ficino's[24] translation of the *Symposium* of Plato, and this wonderful dialogue, of all the Platonic dialogues perhaps the most perfect, as it is the most poetical, began to exercise a strange influence over men, and to colour their words and thoughts, and manner of living. In its subtle suggestions of sex in soul, in the curious analogies it draws between intellectual enthusiasm and the physical passion of love, in its dream of the incarnation of the Idea in a beautiful and living form, and of a real spiritual conception with a travail and a bringing to birth, there was something that fascinated the poets and scholars of the sixteenth century. Shakespeare, certainly, was fascinated by it, and had read the dialogue, if not in Ficino's translation, of which many copies found their way to England, perhaps in that French translation by Leroy[25] to which Joachim du Bellay[26] contributed so many graceful metrical versions. When he says to Willie Hughes,

> he that calls on thee, let him bring forth
> Eternal numbers to outlive long date,

he is thinking of Diotima's[27] theory that Beauty is the goddess who presides over birth, and draws into the light of day the dim conceptions of the soul: when he tells us of the 'marriage of true minds', and exhorts his friend to beget children that time cannot destroy, he is but repeating the words in which the prophetess tells us that 'friends are married by a far nearer tie than those who beget mortal children, for fairer and more immortal are the children who are their common offspring'. So, also, Edward Blount[28] in his dedication of 'Hero and Leander' talks of Marlowe's works as his 'right children', being the 'issue of his brain'; and when Bacon[29] claims that 'the best works and of greatest merit for the public have proceeded from the un-married and childless men, which both in affection and means have married and endowed the public', he is paraphrasing a passage in the *Symposium.*

Friendship, indeed, could have desired no better warrant for its permanence or its ardours than the Platonic theory, or creed, as we might better call it, that the true world was the world of ideas, and that these ideas took visible form and became incarnate in man, and it is only when we realize the influence of neo-Platonism on the Renaissance that we can understand the true meaning of the amatory phrases and words with which friends were wont, at this time, to address each other. There was a kind of mystic transference of the expressions of the physical sphere to a sphere that was spiritual, that was removed from gross bodily appetite, and in which the soul was Lord. Love had, indeed, entered the olive garden of the new Acad-eme,[30] but he wore the same flame-coloured raiment, and had the same words of passion on his lips.

Michael Angelo, the 'haughtiest spirit in Italy' as he has been called, addresses the young Tommaso Cavalieri in such fervent and passionate terms that some have thought that the sonnets in question must have been intended for that noble lady, the widow of the Marchese di Pescara,[31] whose white hand, when she was dying, the great sculptor's lips had stooped to kiss. But that it was to Cavalieri that they were written, and that the literal interpretation is the right one, is evident not merely from the fact that Michael Angelo plays with his name, as Shakespeare plays with the name of Willie Hughes, but from the direct evidence of Varchi, who was well acquainted with the young man, and who, indeed, tells us that he possessed 'besides incomparable personal beauty, so much charm of nature, such excel-lent abilities, and such a graceful manner, that he deserved, and still deserves, to be the better loved the more he is known'. Strange as these sonnets may seem to us now, when rightly interpreted they merely serve to show with what intense and religious fervour Michael

Angelo addressed himself to the worship of intellectual beauty, and how, to borrow a fine phrase from Mr Symonds, he pierced through the veil of flesh and sought the divine idea it imprisoned. In the sonnet written for Luigi del Riccio on the death of his friend, Cecchino Bracci, we can also trace, as Mr Symonds points out, the Platonic conception of love as nothing if not spiritual, and of beauty as a form that finds its immortality within the lover's soul. Cecchino was a lad who died at the age of seventeen, and when Luigi asked Michael Angelo to make a portrait of him, Michael Angelo answered, 'I can only do so by drawing you in whom he still lives.'

> If the beloved in the lover shine,
> Since Art without him cannot work alone,
> Thee must I carve, to tell the world of him.

The same idea is also put forward in Montaigne's[32] noble essay on Friendship, a passion which he ranks higher than the love of brother for brother, or the love of man for woman. He tells us – I quote from Florio's[33] translation, one of the books with which Shakespeare was familiar – how 'perfect amitie' is indivisible, how it 'possesseth the soule, and swaies it in all soveraigntie', and how 'by the interposition of a spiritual beauty the desire of a spiritual conception is engendered in the beloved'. He writes of an 'internall beauty, of difficile knowledge, and abtruse discovery' that is revealed unto friends, and unto friends only. He mourns for the dead Étienne de la Boëtie,[34] in accents of wild grief and inconsolable love. The learned Hubert Languet,[35] the friend of Melanchthon[36] and of the leaders of the reformed church, tells the young Philip Sidney[37] how he kept his portrait by him some hours to feast his eyes upon it, and how his appetite was 'rather increased than diminished by the sight', and Sidney writes to him, 'the chief hope of my life, next to the everlasting blessedness of heaven, will always be the enjoyment of true friendship, and there you shall have the chiefest place'. Later on there came to Sidney's house in London, one – some day to be burned at Rome, for the sin of seeing God in all things – Giordano Bruno,[38] just fresh from his triumph before the University of Paris. 'A filosofia è necessario amore'[39] were the words ever upon

his lips, and there was something in his strange ardent personality
that made men feel that he had discovered the new secret of life.
Ben Jonson[40] writing to one of his friends subscribes himself 'your
true lover', and dedicates his noble eulogy on Shakespeare 'To the
memory of my Beloved'. Richard Barnfield[41] in his 'Affectionate
Shepherd' flutes on soft Virgilian reed the story of his attachment to
some young Elizabethan of the day. Out of all the Eclogues, Abraham
Fraunce[42] selects the second for translation, and Fletcher's[43] lines to
master W. C. show what fascination was hidden in the mere name of
Alexis.

It was no wonder then that Shakespeare had been stirred by a
spirit that so stirred his age. There had been critics, like Hallam,[44]
who had regretted that the Sonnets had ever been written, who had
seen in them something dangerous, something unlawful even. To
them it would have been sufficient to answer in Chapman's[45] noble
words:

> There is no danger to a man that knows
> What Life and Death is: there's not any law
> Exceeds his knowledge: neither is it lawful
> That he should stoop to any other law.

But it was evident that the Sonnets needed no such defence as this,
and that those who had talked of 'the folly of excessive and misplaced
affection'[46] had not been able to interpret either the language or the
spirit of these great poems, so intimately connected with the philosophy
and the art of their time. It is no doubt true that to be filled with an
absorbing passion is to surrender the security of one's lover life, and
yet in such surrender there may be gain, certainly there was for
Shakespeare. When Pico della Mirandola[47] crossed the threshold of
the villa of Careggi, and stood before Marsilio Ficino in all the grace
and comeliness of his wonderful youth, the aged scholar seemed to
see in him the realization of the Greek ideal, and determined to devote
his remaining years to the translation of Plotinus,[48] that new Plato, in
whom, as Mr Pater reminds us, 'the mystical element in the Platonic
philosophy had been worked out to the utmost limit of vision and

ecstasy'. A romantic friendship with a young Roman of his day initiated Winckelmann[49] into the secret of Greek art, taught him the mystery of its beauty and the meaning of its form. In Willie Hughes, Shakespeare found not merely a most delicate instrument for the presentation of his art, but the visible incarnation of his idea of beauty, and it is not too much to say that to this young actor, whose very name the dull writers of his age forgot to chronicle, the Romantic Movement of English Literature is largely indebted.

III

One evening I thought that I had really discovered Willie Hughes in Elizabethan literature. In a wonderfully graphic account of the last days of the great Earl of Essex, his chaplain, Thomas Knell, tells us that the night before the Earl died, 'he called William Hewes, which was his musician, to play upon the virginals[50] and to sing. "Play," said he, "my song, Will Hewes, and I will sing it myself." So he did it most joyfully, not as the howling swan, which, still looking down, waileth her end, but as a sweet lark, lifting up his hands and casting up his eyes to his God, with this mounted the crystal skies, and reached with his unwearied tongue the top of highest heavens.' Surely the boy who played on the virginals to the dying father of Sidney's Stella was none other than the Will Hews to whom Shakespeare dedicated the Sonnets, and who he tells us was himself sweet 'music to hear'. Yet Lord Essex died in 1576, when Shakespeare was but twelve years of age. It was impossible that his musician could have been the Mr W. H. of the Sonnets. Perhaps Shakespeare's young friend was the son of the player upon the virginals? It was at least something to have discovered that Will Hews was an Elizabethan name. Indeed the name Hews seemed to have been closely connected with music and the stage. The first English actress was the lovely Margaret Hews, whom Prince Rupert so madly adored. What more probable than that between her and Lord Essex's musician had come the boy-actor of Shakespeare's plays? In 1587 a certain Thomas Hews brought out at Gray's Inn[51] a Euripidean tragedy entitled *The Misfortunes of Arthur,* receiving much assistance in the arrangement of the dumb shows from one Francis Bacon,[52] then a student of law. Surely he was some near kinsman of the lad to whom Shakespeare said –

Take all my loves, my love, yea, take them all;

the 'profitless usurer' of 'unused beauty', as he describes him. But the proofs, the links – where were they? Alas! I could not find them. It seemed to me that I was always on the brink of absolute verification, but that I could never really attain to it. I thought it strange that no one had ever written a history of the English boy-actors of the sixteenth and seventeenth centuries, and determined to undertake the task myself, and to try to ascertain their true relations to the drama. The subject was, certainly, full of artistic interest. These lads had been the delicate reeds through which our poets had sounded their sweetest strains, the gracious vessels of honour into which they had poured the purple wine of their song. Foremost, naturally, among them all had been the youth to whom Shakespeare had intrusted the realization of his most exquisite creations. Beauty had been his, such as our age has never, or but rarely seen, a beauty that seemed to combine the charm of both sexes, and to have wedded, as the Sonnets tell us, the grace of Adonis and the loveliness of Helen. He had been quick-witted, too, and eloquent, and from those finely curved lips that the satirist had mocked at had come the passionate cry of Juliet, and the bright laughter of Beatrice, Perdita's flower-like words, and Ophelia's wandering songs. Yet as Shakespeare himself had been but as a god among giants, so Willie Hughes had only been one out of many marvellous lads to whom our English Renaissance owed something of the secret of its joy, and it appeared to me that they also were worthy of some study and record.

In a little book with fine vellum leaves and damask silk cover – a fancy of mine in those fanciful days – I accordingly collected such information as I could about them, and even now there is something in the scanty record of their lives, in the mere mention of their names, that attracts me. I seemed to know them all: Robin Armin,[53] the goldsmith's lad who was lured by Tarlton to go on the stage: Sandford, whose performance of the courtesan Flamantia Lord Burleigh witnessed at Gray's Inn: Cooke, who played Agríppina in the tragedy of *Sejanus*: Nat. Field, whose young and beardless portrait is still preserved for us at Dulwich, and who in *Cynthia's Revels* played the 'Queen and Huntress chaste and fair': Gil. Carie, who, attired as a mountain nymph, sang in the same lovely masque Echo's song of mourning for Narcissus: Parsons, the Salmacis of the strange pageant of *Tamburlaine*: Will. Ostler, who was one of 'The Children of the Queen's Chapel', and accompanied King James to Scotland: George Vernon, to whom the King sent a cloak of scarlet cloth, and a cape of crimson velvet: Alick Gough, who performed the part of Caenis, Vespasian's[54] concubine, in Massinger's[55] *Roman Actor*, and three years later that of Acanthe, in the same dramatist's *Picture*: Barrett, the heroine of Richards's tragedy of *Messalina*: Dicky Robinson, 'a very pretty fellow', Ben Jonson tells us, who was a member of Shakespeare's company, and was known for his exquisite taste in costume, as well as for his love of woman's apparel: Salathiel Pavy, whose early and tragic death Jonson mourned in one of the sweetest threnodies of our literature: Arthur Savile, who was one of 'the players of Prince Charles', and took a girl's part in a comedy by Marmion: Stephen Hammerton, 'a most noted and beautiful woman actor', whose pale oval face with its heavy-lidded eyes and somewhat sensuous mouth looks out at us from a curious miniature of the time: Hart, who made his first success by playing the Duchess in the tragedy of *The Cardinal*, and who in a poem that is clearly modelled upon some of Shakespeare's Sonnets is described by one who had seen him as 'beauty to the eye, and music to the ear': and Kynaston, of whom Betterton said that 'it has been disputed among the judicious, whether any woman could have more sensibly touched the passions', and whose white hands and amber-coloured hair seem to have retarded by some years the introduction of actresses upon our stage.

The Puritans, with their uncouth morals and ignoble minds, had of course railed against them, and dwelt on the impropriety of boys disguising as women, and learning to affect the manners and passions of the female sex. Gosson,[56] with his shrill voice, and Prynne,[57] soon to be made earless for many shameful slanders, and others to whom the rare and subtle sense of abstract beauty was denied, had from pulpit and through pamphlet said foul or foolish things to their dishonour. To Francis Lenton,[58] writing in 1629, what he speaks of as –

> loose action, mimic gesture
> By a poor boy clad in a princely vesture,

is but one of the many –

> tempting baits of hell
> Which draw more youth unto the damned cell
> Of furious lust, than all the devil could do
> Since he obtained his first overthrow.

Deuteronomy[59] was quoted and the ill-digested learning of the period laid under contribution. Even our own time had not appreciated the artistic conditions of the Elizabethan and Jacobean drama. One of the most brilliant and intellectual actresses[60] of this century had laughed at the idea of a lad of seventeen or eighteen playing Imogen, or Miranda, or Rosalind. 'How could any youth, however gifted and specially trained, even faintly suggest these fair and noble women to an audience? ... One quite pities Shakespeare, who had to put up with seeing his brightest creations marred, misrepresented, and spoiled.' In his book on *Shakespeare's Predecessors* Mr John Addington Symonds also had talked of 'hobbledehoys' trying to represent the pathos of Desdemona and Juliet's passion. Were they right? Are they right? I did not think so then. I do not think so now. Those who remember the Oxford production[61] of the *Agamemnon*, the fine utterance and marble dignity of the Clytemnestra, the romantic and imaginative rendering of the prophetic madness of Cassandra, will not agree with Lady Martin or Mr Symonds in their strictures on the conditions of the Elizabethan stage.

Of all the motives of dramatic curiosity used by our great playwrights, there is none more subtle or more fascinating than the ambiguity of the sexes. This idea, invented, as far as an artistic idea can be said to be invented, by Lyly,[62] perfected and made exquisite for us by Shakespeare, seems to me to owe its origin, as it certainly owes its possibility of life-like presentation, to the circumstance that the Elizabethan stage, like the stage of the Greeks, admitted the appearance of no female performers. It is because Lyly was writing for the boy-actors of St Paul's that we have the confused sexes and complicated loves of Phillida and Gallathea: it is because Shakespeare was writing for Willie Hughes that Rosalind dons doublet and hose, and calls herself Ganymede, that Viola and Julia put on pages' dress, that Imogen steals away in male attire. To say that only a woman can portray the passions of a woman, and that therefore no boy can play Rosalind, is to rob the art of acting of all claim to objectivity, and to assign to the mere accident of sex what properly belongs to imaginative insight and creative energy. Indeed, if sex be an element in artistic creation, it might rather be urged that the delightful combination of wit and romance which characterizes so many of Shakespeare's heroines was at least occasioned if it was not actually caused by the fact that the players of these parts were lads and young men, whose passionate purity, quick mobile fancy, and healthy freedom from sentimentality can hardly fail to have suggested a new and delightful type of girlhood or of womanhood. The very difference of sex between the player and the part he represented must also, as Professor Ward[63] points out, have constituted 'one more demand upon the imaginative capacities of the spectators', and must have kept them from that over-realistic identification of the actor with his *rôle*, which is one of the weak points in modern theatrical criticism.

This, too, must be granted, that it was to these boy-actors that we owe the introduction of those lovely lyrics that star the plays of Shakespeare, Dekker,[64] and so many of the dramatists of the period, those 'snatches of bird-like or god-like song', as Mr Swinburne[65] calls them. For it was out of the choirs of the cathedrals and royal chapels of England that most of these lads came, and from their earliest years they had been trained in the singing of anthems and madrigals, and in all that concerns the subtle art of music. Chosen at first for the beauty of their voices, as well as for a certain comeliness and freshness of appearance, they were then instructed in gesture, dancing, and elocution, and taught to play both tragedies and comedies in the

English as well as in the Latin language. Indeed, acting seems to have formed part of the ordinary education of the time, and to have been much studied not merely by the scholars of Eton and Westminster, but also by the students at the Universities of Oxford and Cambridge, some of whom went afterwards upon the public stage, as is becoming not uncommon in our own day. The great actors, too, had their pupils and apprentices, who were formally bound over to them by legal warrant, to whom they imparted the secrets of their craft, and who were so much valued that we read of Henslowe, one of the managers of the Rose Theatre, buying a trained boy of the name of James Bristowe for eight pieces of gold. The relations that existed between the masters and their pupils seem to have been of the most cordial and affectionate character. Robin Armin was looked upon by Tarlton as his adopted son, and in a will dated 'the fourth daie of Maie, anno Domini 1605', Augustine Phillips, Shakespeare's dear friend and fellow-actor, bequeathed to one of his apprentices his 'purple cloke, sword, and dagger', his 'base viall', and much rich apparel, and to another a sum of money and many beautiful instruments of music, 'to be delivered unto him at the expiration of his terme of yeres in his indenture[66] of apprenticehood'. Now and then, when some daring actor kidnapped a boy for the stage, there was an outcry or an investigation. In 1600, for instance, a certain Norfolk gentleman of the name of Henry Clifton came to live in London in order that his son, then about thirteen years of age, might have the opportunity of attending the Bluecoat School,[67] and from a petition which he presented to the Star Chamber,[68] and which has been recently brought to light by Mr Greenstreet, we learn that as the boy was walking quietly to Christ Church cloister one winter morning he was waylaid by James Robinson, Henry Evans, and Nathaniel Giles, and carried off to the Blackfriars Theatre, 'amongste a companie of lewde and dissolute mercenarie players', as his father calls them, in order that he might be trained 'in acting of parts in base playes and enterludes'. Hearing of his son's misadventure, Mr Clifton went down at once to the theatre, and demanded his surrender, but 'the sayd Nathaniel Giles, James Robinson and Henry Evans most arrogantlie then and there answered that they had authoritie sufficient soe to take any noble man's sonne in this land', and handing the young schoolboy 'a scrolle of paper, conteyning parte of one of their said playes and enterludes', commanded him to learn it by heart. Through a warrant issued by Sir John Fortescue, however, the boy was restored to his father the next day, and the Court of Star Chamber seems to have suspended or cancelled Evans's privileges.

The fact is that, following a precedent set by Richard III, Elizabeth had issued a commission authorizing certain persons to impress into her service all boys who had beautiful voices that they might sing for her in her Chapel Royal, and Nathaniel Giles, her Chief Commissioner, finding that he could deal profitably with the managers of the Globe Theatre, agreed to supply them with personable and graceful lads for the playing of female parts, under colour of taking them for the Queen's service. The actors, accordingly, had a certain amount of legal warrant on their side, and it is interesting to note that many of the boys whom they carried off from their schools or homes, such as Salathiel Pavy, Nat. Field, and Alvery Trussell, became so fascinated by their new art that they attached themselves permanently to the theatre, and would not leave it.

Once it seemed as if girls were to take the place of boys upon the stage, and among the christenings chronicled in the registers of St Giles', Cripplegate, occurs the following strange and suggestive entry: 'Comedia, base-born, daughter of Alice Bowker and William Johnson, one of the Queen's plaiers, 10 Feb. 1589.' But the child upon whom such high hopes had been built died at six years of age, and when, later on, some French actresses came over and played at Blackfriars, we learn that they were 'hissed, hooted, and pippin-pelted from the stage'. I think that, from what I have said above, we need not regret this in any way. The essentially male culture of the English Renaissance found its fullest and most perfect expression by its own method, and in its own manner.

I remember I used to wonder, at this time, what had been the social position and early life of Willie Hughes before Shakespeare had met with him. My investigations into the history of the boy-actors had made me curious of every detail about him. Had he stood in the carved stall of some gilded choir, reading out of a great book painted with square scarlet notes and long black key-lines? We know from the Sonnets how clear and pure his voice was, and what skill he had in the art of music. Noble gentlemen, such as the Earl of Leicester and Lord Oxford, had companies of boy-players in their service as part of their household. When Leicester went to the Netherlands in 1585 he brought with him a certain 'Will' described as a 'plaier'. Was this Willie Hughes? Had he acted for Leicester at Kenilworth, and was it there that Shakespeare had first known him? Or was he, like Robin Armin, simply a lad of low degree, but possessing some strange beauty and marvellous fascination? It was evident from the early sonnets that when Shakespeare first came across him he had no connection whatsoever with the stage, and that he was not of high birth has already been shewn. I began to think of him not as the delicate chorister of a Royal Chapel, not as a petted minion trained to sing and dance in Leicester's stately masque, but as some fair-haired English lad whom in one of London's hurrying streets, or on Windsor's green silent meadows, Shakespeare had seen and followed, recognizing the artistic possibilities that lay hidden in so comely and gracious a form, and divining by a quick and subtle instinct what an actor the lad would make could he be induced to go upon the stage. At this time Willie Hughes's father was dead, as we learn from Sonnet XIII, and his mother, whose remarkable beauty he is said to have inherited, may have been induced to allow him to become Shakespeare's apprentice by the fact that boys who played female characters were paid extremely large salaries, larger salaries, indeed, than were given to grown-up actors. Shakespeare's apprentice, at any rate, we know that he became, and we know what a vital factor he was in the development of Shakespeare's art. As a rule, a boy-actor's capacity for representing girlish parts on the stage lasted but for a few years at most. Such characters as Lady Macbeth, Queen Constance and Volumnia, remained of course always within the reach of those who had true dramatic genius and noble presence. Absolute youth was not necessary here, not desirable even. But with Imogen, and Perdita, and Juliet, it was different. 'Your beard has begun to grow, and I pray God your voice be not cracked,' says Hamlet mockingly to the boy-actor of the strolling company that came to visit him at Elsinore; and certainly when chins grew rough and voices harsh much of the charm and grace of the performance must have gone. Hence comes Shakespeare's passionate preoccupation with the youth of Willie Hughes, his terror of old age and wasting years, his wild appeal to time to spare the beauty of his friend:

> Make glad and sorry seasons as thou fleet'st,
> And do whate'er thou wilt, swift-footed time,
> To the wide world and all her fading sweets;
> But I forbid thee one most heinous crime:
> O carve not with thy hours my Love's fair brow
> Nor draw no lines there with thine antique pen;
> Him in thy course untainted do allow
> For beauty's pattern to succeeding men.

Time seems to have listened to Shakespeare's prayers, or perhaps Willie Hughes had the secret of perpetual youth. After three years he is quite unchanged:

> To me, fair friend, you never can be old,
> For as you were when first your eye I eyed,
> Such seems your beauty still. Three winters cold
> Have from the forests shook three summers' pride,
> Three beauteous springs to yellow autumn turned,
> In process of the seasons have I seen,
> Three April perfumes in three hot Junes burned,
> Since first I saw you fresh, which yet are green.

More years pass over, and the bloom of his boyhood seems to be still with him. When, in *The Tempest*, Shakespeare, through the lips of Prospero, flung away the wand of his imagination and gave his poetic sovereignty into the weak, graceful hands of Fletcher,[69] it may be that the Miranda who stood wondering by was none other than Willie Hughes himself, and in the last sonnet that his friend addressed to him, the enemy that is feared is not Time but Death.

O thou, my lovely boy, who in thy power
Dost hold time's fickle glass, his sickle hour;
Who hast by waning grown, and therein show'st
Thy lovers withering as thy sweet self grow'st;
If Nature, sovereign mistress over wrack,
As thou goest onwards, still will pluck thee back,
She keeps thee to this purpose, that her skill
May Time disgrace and wretched minutes kill.
Yet fear her, O thou minion of her pleasure!
She may detain, but not still keep, her treasure.
Her audit, though delay'd, answer'd must be,
And her quietus is to render thee.

IV

It was not for some weeks after I had begun my study of the subject that I ventured to approach the curious group of Sonnets (CXXVII–CLII) that deal with the dark woman who, like a shadow or thing of evil omen, came across Shakespeare's great romance, and for a season stood between him and Willie Hughes. They were obviously printed out of their proper place and should have been inserted between Sonnets XXXIII and XL. Psychological and artistic reasons necessitated this change, a change which I hope will be adopted by all future editors, as without it an entirely false impression is conveyed of the nature and final issue of this noble friendship.

Who was she, this black-browed, olive-skinned woman, with her amorous mouth 'that Love's own hand did make', her 'cruel eye', and her 'foul pride', her strange skill on the virginals and her false, fascinating nature? An over-curious scholar[70] of our day had seen in her a symbol of the Catholic Church, of that Bride of Christ who is 'black but comely'. Professor Minto,[71] following in the footsteps of Henry Brown,[72] had regarded the whole group of Sonnets as simply 'exercises of skill undertaken in a spirit of wanton defiance and derision of the commonplace'. Mr Gerald Massey,[73] without any historical proof or probability, had insisted that they were addressed to the celebrated Lady Rich,[74] the Stella of Sir Philip Sidney's sonnets, the Philoclea of his *Arcadia*,[75] and that they contained no personal revelation of Shakespeare's life and love, having been written in Lord Pembroke's name and at his request. Mr Tyler had suggested that they referred to one of Queen Elizabeth's maids-of-honour, by name Mary Fitton. But none of these explanations satisfied the conditions of the problem. The woman that came between Shakespeare and Willie Hughes was a real woman, black-haired, and married, and of evil repute. Lady Rich's fame was evil enough, it is true, but her hair was of –

> fine threads of finest gold,
> In curled knots man's thought to hold,

and her shoulders like 'white doves perching'. She was, as King James said to her lover, Lord Mountjoy, 'a fair woman with a black soul'. As for Mary Fitton, we know that she was unmarried in 1601, the time when her amour with Lord Pembroke was discovered, and besides, any theories that connected Lord Pembroke with the Sonnets were, as Cyril Graham has shewn, put entirely out of court by the fact that Lord Pembroke did not come to London till they had been actually written and read by Shakespeare to his friends.

It was not, however, her name that interested me. I was content to hold with Professor Dowden[76] that 'To the eyes of no diver among the wrecks of time will that curious talisman gleam.' What I wanted to discover was the nature of her influence over Shakespeare, as well as the characteristics of her personality. Two things were certain: she was much older than the poet, and the fascination that she exercised over him was at first purely intellectual. He began by feeling no physical passion for her. 'I do not love thee with mine eyes,' he says:

> Nor are mine ears with thy tongue's tune delighted;
> Nor tender feeling to base touches prone,
> Nor taste, nor smell, desire to be invited
> To any sensual feast with thee alone.

He did not even think her beautiful:

> My mistress' eyes are nothing like the sun;
> Coral is far more red than her lips' red:
> If snow be white, why then her breasts are dun;
> If hairs be wires, black wires grow on her head.

He had his moments of loathing for her, for, not content with enslaving the soul of Shakespeare, she seems to have sought to snare the senses of Willie Hughes. Then Shakespeare cries aloud –

> Two loves I have of comfort and despair,
> Which like two spirits do suggest me still:
> The better angel is a man right fair,
> The worser spirit a woman colour'd ill.
> To win me soon to hell, my female evil
> Tempteth my better angel from my side,
> And would corrupt my saint to be a devil,
> Wooing his purity with her foul pride.

Then he sees her as she really is, the 'bay where all men ride', the 'wide world's common place', the woman who is in the 'very refuse' of her evil deeds, and who is 'as black as hell, as dark as night'. Then it is that he pens that great sonnet upon Lust ('Th' expense of spirit in a waste of shame'), of which Mr Theodore Watts[77] says rightly that it is the greatest sonnet ever written. And it is then, also, that he offers to mortgage his very life and genius to her if she will but restore to him that 'sweetest friend' of whom she had robbed him.

To compass this end he abandons himself to her, feigns to be full of an absorbing and sensuous passion of possession, forges false words of love, lies to her, and tells her that he lies.

> My thoughts and my discourse as madmen's are,
> At random from the truth vainly express'd;
> For I have sworn thee fair, and thought thee bright,
> Who art as black as hell, as dark as night.

Rather than suffer his friend to be treacherous to him, he will himself be treacherous to his friend. To shield his purity, he will himself be vile. He knew the weakness of the boy-actor's nature, his susceptibility to praise, his inordinate love of admiration, and deliberately set himself to fascinate the woman who had come between them.

It is never with impunity that one's lips say Love's Litany. Words have their mystical power over the soul, and form can create the feeling from which it should have sprung. Sincerity itself, the ardent, momentary sincerity of the artist, is often the unconscious result of style, and in the case of those rare temperaments that are exquisitely susceptible to the influences of language, the use of certain phrases and modes of expression can stir the very pulse of passion, can send the red blood coursing through the veins, and can transform into a strange sensuous energy what in its origin had been mere aesthetic impulse, and desire of art. So, at least, it seems to have been with Shakespeare. He begins by pretending to love, wears a lover's apparel and has a lover's words upon his lips. What does it matter? It is only acting, only a comedy in real life. Suddenly he finds that what his tongue had spoken his soul had listened to, and that the raiment that he had put on for disguise is a plague-stricken and poisonous thing that eats into his flesh, and that he cannot throw away. Then comes Desire, with its many maladies, and Lust that makes one love all that one loathes, and Shame, with its ashen face and secret smile. He is enthralled by this dark woman, is for a season separated from his friend, and becomes the 'vassal-wretch' of one whom he knows to be evil and perverse and unworthy of his love, as of the love of Willie Hughes. 'O, from what power,' he says –

> hast thou this powerful might,
> With insufficiency my heart to sway?
> To make me give the lie to my true sight,
> And swear that brightness does not grace the day?
> Whence hast thou this becoming of things ill,
> That in the very refuse of thy deeds
> There is such strength and warranties of skill
> That, in my mind, thy worst all best exceeds?

He is keenly conscious of his own degradation, and finally, realizing that his genius is nothing to her compared to the physical beauty of the young actor, he cuts with a quick knife the bond that binds him to her, and in this bitter sonnet bids her farewell:

> In loving thee thou know'st I am forsworn,
> But thou art twice forsworn, to me love swearing;
> In act thy bed-vow broke, and new faith torn,
> In vowing new hate after new love bearing.
> But why of two oaths' breach do I accuse thee,
> When I break twenty? I am perjur'd most;
> For all my vows are oaths but to misuse thee,
> And all my honest faith in thee is lost:
> For I have sworn deep oaths of thy deep kindness,
> Oaths of thy love, thy truth, thy constancy;
> And, to enlighten thee, gave eyes to blindness,
> Or made them swear against the thing they see;
> For I have sworn thee fair; more perjur'd I,
> To swear against the truth so foul a lie!

His attitude towards Willie Hughes in the whole matter shews at once the fervour and the self-abnegation of the great love he bore him. There is a poignant touch of pathos in the close of this sonnet:

> Those pretty wrongs that liberty commits,
> When I am sometime absent from thy heart,
> Thy beauty and thy years full well befits,
> For still temptation follows where thou art.
> Gentle thou art, and therefore to be won,
> Beauteous thou art, therefore to be assailed;
> And when a woman woos, what woman's son
> Will sourly leave her till she have prevailed?
> Ah me! but yet thou mightst my seat forbear,
> And chide thy beauty and thy straying youth,
> Who lead thee in their riot even there
> Where thou art forc'd to break a two-fold truth;

> Hers, by thy beauty tempting her to thee,
> Thine, by thy beauty being false to me.

But here he makes it manifest that his forgiveness was full and complete:

> No more be griev'd at that which thou hast done:
> Roses have thorns, and silver fountains mud;
> Clouds and eclipses stain both moon and sun,
> And loathsome canker lives in sweetest bud.
> All men make faults, and even I in this,
> Authorizing thy trespass with compare,
> Myself corrupting, salving thy amiss,
> Excusing thy sins more than thy sins are;
> For to thy sensual fault I bring in sense, –
> Thy adverse party is thy advocate, –
> And 'gainst myself a lawful plea commence:
> Such civil war is in my love and hate,
> That I an accessary needs must be
> To that sweet thief which sourly robs from me.

Shortly afterwards Shakespeare left London for Stratford (Sonnets XLIII–LII), and when he returned Willie Hughes seems to have grown tired of the woman who for a little time had fascinated him. Her name is never mentioned again in the Sonnets, nor is there any allusion made to her. She had passed out of their lives.

But who was she? And, even if her name has not come down to us, were there any allusions to her in contemporary literature? It seems to me that although better educated than most of the women of her time, she was not nobly born, but was probably the profligate wife of some old and wealthy citizen. We know that women of this class, which was then first rising into social prominence, were strangely fascinated by the new art of stage playing. They were to be found almost every afternoon at the theatre, when dramatic performances were being given, and 'The Actors' Remonstrance'[78] is eloquent on the subject of their amours with the young actors.

Cranley[79] in his *Amanda* tells us of one who loved to mimic the actor's disguises, appearing one day 'embroidered, laced, perfumed, in glittering show . . . as brave as any Countess', and the next day, 'all in mourning, black and sad', now in the grey cloak of a country wench, and now 'in the neat habit of a citizen'. She was a curious woman, 'more changeable and wavering than the moon', and the books that she loved to read were Shakespeare's *Venus and Adonis*, Beaumont's *Salmacis and Hermaphroditus*, amorous pamphlets, and 'songs of love and sonnets exquisite'. These sonnets, that were to her the 'bookes of her devotion', were surely none other but Shakespeare's own, for the whole description reads like the portrait of the woman who fell in love with Willie Hughes, and, lest we should have any doubt on the subject, Cranley, borrowing Shakespeare's play on words, tells us that, in her 'proteus-like strange shapes', she is one who –

> Changes hews with the chameleon.

Manningham's Table-book,[80] also, contains a clear allusion to the same story. Manningham was a student at the Middle Temple with Sir Thomas Overbury and Edmund Curle,[81] whose chambers he seems to have shared; and his Diary is still preserved among the Harleian MSS. at the British Museum, a small duodecimo book written in a fair and tolerably legible hand, and containing many unpublished anecdotes about Shakespeare, Sir Walter Raleigh, Spenser, Ben Jonson and others. The dates, which are inserted with much care, extend from January 1600–1 to April 1603, and under the heading 'March 13, 1601', Manningham tells us that he heard from a member of Shakespeare's company that a certain citizen's wife being at the Globe Theatre one afternoon, fell in love with one of the actors, and 'grew so farre in liking with him, that before shee went from the play shee appointed him to come that night unto hir', but that Shakespeare 'overhearing their conclusion' anticipated his friend and came first to the lady's house, 'went before and was entertained', as Manningham puts it, with some added looseness of speech which it is unnecessary to quote.

It seemed to me that we had here a common and distorted version of the story that is revealed to us in the Sonnets, the story of the dark woman's love for Willie Hughes, and Shakespeare's mad attempt to make her love him in his friend's stead. It was not, of course, necessary to accept it as absolutely true in every detail. According to Manningham's informant, for instance, the name of the actor in question was not Willie Hughes, but Richard Burbage. Tavern gossip, however, is proverbially inaccurate, and Burbage was, no doubt, dragged into the story to give point to the foolish jest about William the Conqueror and Richard the Third, with which the entry in Manningham's Diary ends. Burbage was our first great tragic actor, but it needed all his genius to counterbalance the physical defects of low stature and corpulent figure under which he laboured, and he was not the sort of man who would have fascinated the dark woman of the Sonnets, or would have cared to be fascinated by her. There was no doubt that Willie Hughes was referred to, and the private diary of a young law student of the time thus curiously corroborated Cyril Graham's wonderful guess at the secret of Shakespeare's great romance. Indeed, when taken in conjunction with *Amanda*, Manningham's Table-book seemed to me to be an extremely strong link in the chain of evidence, and to place the new interpretation of the Sonnets on something like a secure historic basis, the fact that Cranley's poem was not published till after Shakespeare's death being really rather in favour of this view, as it was not likely that he would have ventured during the lifetime of the great dramatist to revive the memory of this tragic and bitter story.

This passion for the dark lady also enabled me to fix with still greater certainty the date of the Sonnets. From internal evidence, from the characteristics of language, style, and the like, it was evident that they belonged to Shakespeare's early period, the period of *Love's Labour's Lost* and *Venus and Adonis*. With the play, indeed, they are intimately connected. They display the same delicate euphuism,[82] the same delight in fanciful phrase and curious expression, the artistic wilfulness and studied graces of the same 'fair tongue, conceit's expositor', Rosaline, the –

> whitely wanton with a velvet brow,
> With two pitch-balls stuck in her face for eyes,

who is born 'to make black fair', and whose 'favour turns the fashion of the days', is the dark lady of the Sonnets who makes black 'beauty's successive heir'. In the comedy as well as in the poems we have that half-sensuous philosophy that exalts the judgement of the senses 'above all slower, more toilsome means of knowledge', and Berowne is perhaps, as Walter Pater suggests, a reflex of Shakespeare himself, 'when he has just become able to stand aside from and estimate the first period of his poetry'.

Now though *Love's Labour's Lost* was not published till 1598, when it was brought out 'newlie corrected and augmented' by Cuthbert Burby, there is no doubt that it was written and produced on the stage at a much earlier date, probably, as Professor Dowden points out, in 1588–9. If this be so, it is clear that Shakespeare's first meeting with Willie Hughes must have been in 1585, and it is just possible that this young actor may, after all, have been in his boyhood the musician of Lord Essex.

It is clear, at any rate, that Shakespeare's love for the dark lady must have passed away before 1594. In this year there appeared, under the editorship of Hadrian Dorell, that fascinating poem, or series of poems, *Willobie his Avisa*,[83] which is described by Mr Swinburne as the one contemporary book which has been supposed to throw any direct or indirect light on the mystic matter of the Sonnets. In it we learn how a young gentleman of St John's College, Oxford, by name Henry Willobie, fell in love with a woman so 'fair and chaste' that he called her Avisa, either because such beauty as hers had never been seen, or because she fled like a bird from the snare of his passion, and spread her wings for flight when he ventured but to touch her hand. Anxious to win his mistress, he consults his familiar friend W. S., 'who not long before had tried the curtesy of the like passion, and was now newly recovered of the like infection'. Shakespeare encouraged him in the siege that he is laying to the Castle of Beauty, telling him that every woman is to be wooed, and every woman to be won; views this 'loving comedy' from far off, in order to see 'whether it would sort to a happier end for this new actor than it did for the old player', and 'enlargeth the wound with the sharpe razor of a willing conceit', feeling the purely aesthetic interest of the artist in the moods and emotions of others. It is unnecessary, however, to enter more fully into this curious passage in Shakespeare's life, as all that I wanted to point out was that in 1594 he had been cured of his infatuation for the dark lady, and had already been acquainted for at least three years with Willie Hughes.

My whole scheme of the Sonnets was now complete, and, by placing those that refer to the dark lady in their proper order and position, I saw the perfect unity and completeness of the whole. The drama – for indeed they formed a drama and a soul's tragedy of fiery passion and of noble thought – is divided into four scenes or acts. In the first of these (Sonnets I–XXXII) Shakespeare invites Willie Hughes to go upon the stage as an actor, and to put to the service of Art his wonderful physical beauty, and his exquisite grace of youth, before passion has robbed him of the one, and time taken from him the other. Willie Hughes, after a time, consents to be a player in Shakespeare's company, and soon becomes the very centre and keynote of his inspiration. Suddenly, in one red-rose July (Sonnets XXXIII–LII, LXI, and CXXVII–CLII) there comes to the Globe Theatre a dark woman with wonderful eyes, who falls passionately in love with Willie Hughes. Shakespeare, sick with the malady of jealousy, and made mad by many doubts and fears, tries to fascinate the woman who had come between him and his friend. The love, that is at first feigned, becomes real, and he finds himself enthralled and dominated by a woman whom he knows to be evil and unworthy. To her the genius of a man is as nothing compared to a boy's beauty. Willie Hughes becomes for a time her slave and the toy of her fancy, and the second act ends with Shakespeare's departure from London. In the third act her influence has passed away. Shakespeare returns to London, and renews his friendship with Willie Hughes, to whom he promises immortality in his plays. Marlowe, hearing of the wonder and grace of the young actor, lures him away from the Globe Theatre to play Gaveston in the tragedy of *Edward II*, and for the second time Shakespeare is separated from his friend. The last act (Sonnets C–CXXVI) tells us of the return of Willie Hughes to Shakespeare's company. Evil rumour has now stained the white purity of his name, but Shakespeare's love still endures and is perfect. Of the mystery of this love, and of the mystery of passion, we are told strange and marvellous things, and the Sonnets conclude with an envoi of twelve lines, whose motive is the triumph of Beauty over Time, and of Death over Beauty.

And what had been the end of him who had been so dear to the soul of Shakespeare, and who by his presence and passion had given reality to Shakespeare's art? When the Civil War broke out, the English actors took the side of their king, and many of them, like Robinson foully slain by Major Harrison at the taking of Basing House, laid down their lives in the king's service. Perhaps on the trampled heath of Marston,[84] or on the bleak hills of Naseby, the dead body of Willie Hughes had been found by some of the rough peasants of the district, his gold hair 'dabbled with blood', and his breast pierced with many wounds. Or it may be that the Plague, which was very frequent in London at the beginning of the seventeenth century, and was indeed regarded by many of the Christians as a judgement sent on the city for its love of 'vaine plaies and idolatrous shewes', had touched the lad while he was acting, and he had crept home to his lodging to die there alone, Shakespeare being far away at Stratford, and those who had flocked in such numbers to see him, the 'gazers' whom, as the Sonnets tell us, he had 'led astray', being too much afraid of contagion to come near him. A story of this kind was current at the time about a young actor, and was made much use of by the Puritans in their attempts to stifle the free development of the English Renaissance. Yet, surely, had this actor been Willie Hughes, tidings of his tragic death would have been speedily brought to Shakespeare as he lay dreaming under the mulberry tree in his garden at New Place, and in an elegy as sweet as that written by Milton on Edward King,[85] he would have mourned for the lad who had brought such joy and sorrow into his life, and whose connection with his art had been of so vital and intimate a character. Something made me feel certain that Willie Hughes had survived Shakespeare, and had fulfilled in some measure the high prophecies the poet had made about him, and one evening the true secret of his end flashed across me.

He had been one of those English actors who in 1611, the year of Shakespeare's retirement from the stage, went across sea to Germany and played before the great Duke Henry Julius of Brunswick, himself a dramatist of no mean order, and at the Court of that strange Elector of Brandenburg, who was so enamoured of beauty that he was said to have bought for his weight in amber the young son of a travelling Greek merchant, and to have given pageants in honour of his slave, all through that dreadful famine year of 1606–7, when the people died of hunger in the very streets of the town, and for the space of seven months there was no rain. The Library at Cassel contains to the present day a copy of the first edition of Marlowe's *Edward II*, the only copy in existence, Mr Bullen[86] tells us. Who could have brought it to that town, but he who had created the part of the king's minion, and for whom indeed it had been written? Those stained and yellow pages had once been touched by his white hands. We also know that *Romeo and Juliet*, a play specially connected with Willie Hughes, was brought out at Dresden, in 1613, along with *Hamlet* and *King Lear*, and certain of Marlowe's plays, and it was surely to none other than Willie Hughes himself that in 1617 the death-mask of Shakespeare was brought by one of the suite of the English ambassador, pale token of the passing away of the great poet who had so dearly loved him. Indeed there was something peculiarly fitting in the idea that the boy-actor, whose beauty had been so vital an element in the realism and romance of Shakespeare's art, had been the first to have brought to Germany the seed of the new culture, and was in his way the precursor of the *Aufklärung* or Illumination of the eighteenth century, that splendid movement which, though begun by Lessing and Herder, and brought to its full and perfect issue by Goethe was in no small part helped on by a young actor – Friedrich Schroeder[87] – who awoke the popular consciousness, and by means of the feigned passions and mimetic methods of the stage showed the intimate, the vital, connection between life and literature. If this was so – and there was certainly no evidence against it – it was not improbable that Willie Hughes was one of those English comedians (*mimi quidam ex Britannia*,[88] as the old chronicle calls them), who were slain at Nuremberg in a sudden uprising of the people, and were secretly buried in a little vineyard outside the city by some young men 'who had found pleasure in their performances, and of whom some had sought to be instructed in the mysteries of the new art'. Certainly no more fitting place could there be for him to whom Shakespeare said 'thou art all my art', than this little vineyard outside the city walls. For was it not from the sorrows of Dionysos that Tragedy sprang? Was not the light laughter of Comedy, with its careless merriment and quick replies, first heard on the lips of the Sicilian vine-dressers? Nay, did not the purple and red stain of the wine-froth on face and limbs give the first suggestion of the charm and fascination of disguise? – the desire for self-concealment, the sense of the value of objectivity, thus showing itself in the rude beginnings of the art. At any rate, wherever he lay – whether in the little vineyard at the gate of the Gothic town, or in some dim London churchyard amidst the roar and bustle of our great city – no gorgeous monument marked his resting place. His true tomb, as Shakespeare saw, was the poet's verse, his true monument the permanence of the drama. So had it been with others whose beauty had given a new creative impulse to their age. The ivory body of the Bithynian slave[89] rots in the green ooze of the Nile, and on the yellow hills of the Cerameicus[90] is strewn the dust of the young Athenian; but Antinous lives in sculpture, and Charmides[91] in philosophy.

V

A young Elizabethan, who was enamoured of a girl so white that he named her Alba,[92] has left on record the impression produced on him by one of the first performances of *Love's Labour's Lost*. Admirable though the actors were, and they played 'in cunning wise', he tells us, especially those who took the lovers' parts, he was conscious that everything was 'feigned', that nothing came 'from the heart', that though they appeared to grieve they 'felt no care', and were merely presenting 'a show in jest'. Yet, suddenly, this fanciful comedy of unreal romance became to him, as he sat in the audience, the real tragedy of his life. The moods of his own soul seemed to have taken shape and substance, and to be moving before him. His grief had a mask that smiled, and his sorrow wore gay raiment. Behind the bright and quickly-changing pageant of the stage, he saw himself, as one sees one's image in a fantastic glass. The very words that came to the actors' lips were wrung out of his pain. Their false tears were of his shedding.

There are few of us who have not felt something akin to this. We become lovers when we see Romeo and Juliet, and Hamlet makes us students. The blood of Duncan is upon our hands, with Timon we rage against the world, and when Lear wanders out upon the heath the terror of madness touches us. Ours is the white sinlessness of Desdemona, and ours, also, the sin of Iago. Art, even the art of fullest scope and widest vision, can never really show us the external world. All that it shows us is our own soul, the one world of which we have any real cognizance. And the soul itself, the soul of each one of us, is to each one of us a mystery. It hides in the dark and broods, and consciousness cannot tell us of its workings. Consciousness, indeed, is quite inadequate to explain the contents of personality. It is Art, and Art only, that reveals us to ourselves.

We sit at the play with the woman we love, or listen to the music in some Oxford garden, or stroll with our friend through the cool galleries of the Pope's house at Rome, and suddenly we become aware that we have passions of which we have never dreamed, thoughts that make us afraid, pleasures whose secret has been denied to us, sorrows that have been hidden from our tears. The actor is unconscious of our presence: the musician is thinking of the subtlety of the fugue, of the tone of his instrument; the marble gods that smile so curiously at us are made of insensate stone. But they have given form and substance to what was within us; they have enabled us to realize our personality; and a sense of perilous joy, or some touch or thrill of pain, or that strange self-pity that man so often feels for himself, comes over us and leaves us different.

Some such impression the Sonnets of Shakespeare had certainly produced on me. As from opal dawns to sunsets of withered rose I read and re-read them in garden or chamber, it seemed to me that I was deciphering the story of a life that had once been mine, unrolling the record of a romance that, without my knowing it, had coloured the very texture of my nature, had dyed it with strange and subtle dyes. Art, as so often happens, had taken the place of personal experience. I felt as if I had been initiated into the secret of that passionate friendship, that love of beauty and beauty of love, of which Marsilio Ficino tells us, and of which the Sonnets, in their noblest and purest significance, may be held to be the perfect expression.

Yes: I had lived it all. I had stood in the round theatre with its open roof and fluttering banners, had seen the stage draped with black for a tragedy, or set with gay garlands for some brighter show. The young gallants came out with their pages, and took their seats in front of the tawny curtain that hung from the satyr-carved pillars of the inner scene. They were insolent and debonair in their fantastic dresses. Some of them wore French lovelocks,[93] and white doublets stiff with Italian embroidery of gold thread, and long hose of blue or pale yellow silk. Others were all in black, and carried huge plumed hats. These affected the Spanish fashion. As they played at cards, and blew thin wreaths of smoke from the tiny pipes that the pages lit for them, the truant prentices and idle schoolboys that thronged the yard mocked them. But they only smiled at each other. In the side boxes some masked women were sitting. One of them was waiting with hungry eyes and bitten lips for the drawing back of the curtain. As the trumpet sounded for the third time she leant forward, and I saw her olive skin and raven's-wing hair. I knew her. She had marred for a season the great friendship of my life. Yet there was something about her that fascinated me.

The play changed according to my mood. Sometimes it was *Hamlet*. Taylor[94] acted the Prince, and there were many who wept when Ophelia went mad. Sometimes it was *Romeo and Juliet*. Burbage was Romeo. He hardly looked the part of the young Italian, but there was a rich music in his voice, and passionate beauty in every gesture. I saw *As You Like It*, and *Cymbeline*, and *Twelfth Night*, and in each play there was some one whose life was bound up into mine, who realized for me every dream, and gave shape to every fancy. How gracefully he moved! The eyes of the audience were fixed on him.

And yet it was in this century that it had all happened. I had never seen my friend, but he had been with me for many years, and it was to his influence that I had owed my passion for Greek thought and art, and indeed all my sympathy with the Hellenic spirit. (Φιλοσοφεῖν μὲτ᾽ ἔρωτος!)[95] How that phrase had stirred me in my Oxford days! I did not understand then why it was so. But I knew now. There had been a presence beside me always. Its silver feet had trod night's shadowy meadows, and the white hands had moved aside the trembling curtains of the dawn. It had walked with me through the grey cloisters, and when I sat reading in my room, it was there also. What though I had been unconscious of it? The soul had a life of its own, and the brain its own sphere of action. There was something within us that knew nothing of sequence or extension, and yet, like the philosopher of the Ideal City, was the spectator of all time and of all existence.[96] It had senses that quickened, passions that came to birth, spiritual ecstasies of contemplation, ardours of fiery-coloured love. It was we who were unreal, and our conscious life was the least important part of our development. The soul, the secret soul, was the only reality.

How curiously it had all been revealed to me! A book of Sonnets, published nearly three hundred years ago, written by a dead hand and in honour of a dead youth, had suddenly explained to me the whole story of my soul's romance. I remembered how once in Egypt I had been present at the opening of a frescoed coffin that had been found in one of the basalt tombs at Thebes. Inside there was the body of a young girl swathed in tight bands of linen, and with a gilt mask over her face. As I stooped down to look at it, I had seen that one of the little withered hands held a scroll of yellow papyrus covered with strange characters. How I wished now that I had had it read to me! It might have told me something more about the soul that hid within me, and had its mysteries of passion of which I was kept in ignorance. Strange, that we knew so little about ourselves, and that our most intimate personality was concealed from us! Were we to look in tombs for our real life, and in art for the legend of our days?

Week after week, I pored over these poems, and each new form of knowledge seemed to me a mode of reminiscence. Finally, after two months had elapsed, I determined to make a strong appeal to Erskine to do justice to the memory of Cyril Graham, and to give to the world his marvellous interpretation of the Sonnets – the only interpretation that thoroughly explained the problem. I have not any copy of my letter, I regret to say, nor have I been able to lay my hand upon the original; but I remember that I went over the whole ground, and covered sheets of paper with passionate reiteration of the arguments and proofs that my study had suggested to me.

It seemed to me that I was not merely restoring Cyril Graham to his proper place in literary history, but rescuing the honour of Shakespeare himself from the tedious memory of a commonplace intrigue. I put into the letter all my enthusiasm. I put into the letter all my faith.

No sooner, in fact, had I sent it off than a curious reaction came over me. It seemed to me that I had given away my capacity for belief in the Willie Hughes theory of the Sonnets, that something had gone out of me, as it were, and that I was perfectly indifferent to the whole subject. What was it that had happened? It is difficult to say. Perhaps, by finding perfect expression for a passion, I had exhausted the passion itself. Emotional forces, like the forces of physical life, have their positive limitations. Perhaps the mere effort to convert any one to a theory involves some form of renunciation of the power of credence. Influence is simply a transference of personality, a mode of giving away what is most precious to one's self, and its exercise produces a sense, and, it may be, a reality of loss. Every disciple takes away something from his master. Or perhaps I had become tired of the whole thing, wearied of its fascination, and, my enthusiasm having burnt out, my reason was left to its own unimpassioned judgement. However it came about, and I cannot pretend to explain it, there was no doubt that Willie Hughes suddenly became to me a mere myth, an idle dream, the boyish fancy of a young man who, like most ardent spirits, was more anxious to convince others than to be himself convinced.

I must admit that this was a bitter disappointment to me. I had gone through every phase of this great romance. I had lived with it, and it had become part of my nature. How was it that it had left me? Had I touched upon some secret that my soul desired to conceal? Or was there no permanence in personality? Did things come and go through the brain, silently, swiftly, and without footprints, like shadows through a mirror? Were we at the mercy of such impressions as Art or Life chose to give us? It seemed to me to be so.

It was at night-time that this feeling first came to me. I had sent my servant out to post the letter to Erskine, and was seated at the window looking out at the blue and gold city. The moon had not yet risen, and there was only one star in the sky, but the streets were full of quick-moving and flashing lights, and the windows of Devonshire House were illuminated for a great dinner to be given to some of the foreign princes then visiting London. I saw the scarlet liveries of the royal carriages, and the crowd hustling about the sombre gates of the courtyard.

Suddenly, I said to myself: 'I have been dreaming, and all my life for these two months has been unreal. There was no such person as Willie Hughes.' Something like a faint cry of pain came to my lips as I began to realize how I had deceived myself, and I buried my face in my hands, struck with a sorrow greater than any I had felt since boyhood. After a few moments I rose, and going into the library took up the Sonnets, and began to read them. But it was all to no avail. They gave me back nothing of the feeling that I had brought to them; they revealed to me nothing of what I had found hidden in their lines. Had I merely been influenced by the beauty of the forged portrait, charmed by that Shelley-like face into faith and credence? Or, as Erskine had suggested, was it the pathetic tragedy of Cyril Graham's death that had so deeply stirred me? I could not tell. To the present day I cannot understand the beginning or the end of this strange passage in my life.

However, as I had said some very unjust and bitter things to Erskine in my letter, I determined to go and see him as soon as possible, and make my apologies to him for my behaviour. Accordingly, the next morning I drove down to Birdcage Walk, where I found him sitting in his library, with the forged picture of Willie Hughes in front of him.

'My dear Erskine!' I cried, 'I have come to apologize to you.'

'To apologize to me?' he said. 'What for?'

'For my letter,' I answered.

'You have nothing to regret in your letter,' he said. 'On the contrary, you have done me the greatest service in your power. You have shown me that Cyril Graham's theory is perfectly sound.'

I stared at him in blank wonder.

'You don't mean to say that you believe in Willie Hughes?' I exclaimed.

'Why not?' he rejoined. 'You have proved the thing to me. Do you think I cannot estimate the value of evidence?'

'But there is no evidence at all,' I groaned, sinking into a chair. 'When I wrote to you I was under the influence of a perfectly silly enthusiasm. I had been touched by the story of Cyril Graham's death, fascinated by his artistic theory, enthralled by the wonder and novelty of the whole idea. I see now that the theory is based on a delusion. The only evidence for the existence of Willie Hughes is that picture in front of you, and that picture is a forgery. Don't be carried away by mere sentiment in this matter. Whatever romance may have to say about the Willie Hughes theory, reason is dead against it.'

'I don't understand you,' said Erskine, looking at me in amazement. 'You have convinced me by your letter that Willie Hughes is an absolute reality. Why have you changed your mind? Or is all that you have been saying to me merely a joke?'

'I cannot explain it to you,' I rejoined, 'but I see now that there is really nothing to be said in favour of Cyril Graham's interpretation. The Sonnets may not be addressed to Lord Pembroke. They probably are not. But for heaven's sake don't waste your time in a foolish attempt to discover a young Elizabethan actor who never existed, and to make a phantom puppet the centre of the great cycle of Shakespeare's Sonnets.'

'I see that you don't understand the theory,' he replied.

'My dear Erskine,' I cried, 'not understand it! Why, I feel as if I had invented it. Surely my letter shows you that I not merely went into the whole matter, but that I contributed proofs of every kind. The one flaw in the theory is that it presupposes the existence of the person whose existence is the subject of dispute. If we grant that there was in Shakespeare's company a young actor of the name of Willie Hughes, it is not difficult to make him the object of the Sonnets. But as we know that there was no actor of this name in the company of the Globe Theatre, it is idle to pursue the investigation further.'

'But that is exactly what we don't know,' said Erskine. 'It is quite true that his name does not occur in the list given in the first folio; but, as Cyril pointed out, that is rather a proof in favour of the existence of Willie Hughes than against it, if we remember his treacherous desertion of Shakespeare for a rival dramatist. Besides,' and here I must admit that Erskine made what seems to me now a rather good point, though, at the time, I laughed at it, 'there is no reason at all why Willie Hughes should not have gone upon the stage under an assumed name. In fact it is extremely probable that he did so. We know that there was a very strong prejudice against the theatre in his day, and nothing is more likely than that his family insisted upon his adopting some *nom de plume*. The editors of the first folio would naturally put him down under his stage name, the name by which he was best known to the public, but the Sonnets were of course an entirely different matter, and in the dedication to them the publisher very properly addresses him under his real initials. If this be so, and it seems to me the most simple and rational explanation of the matter, I regard Cyril Graham's theory as absolutely proved.'

'But what evidence have you?' I exclaimed, laying my hand on his. 'You have no evidence at all. It is a mere hypothesis. And which of Shakespeare's actors do you think that Willie Hughes was? The "pretty fellow" Ben Jonson tells us of, who was so fond of dressing up in girls' clothes?'

'I don't know,' he answered rather irritably. 'I have not had time to investigate the point yet. But I feel quite sure that my theory is the true one. Of course it is a hypothesis, but then it is a hypothesis that explains everything, and if you had been sent to Cambridge to study science, instead of to Oxford to dawdle over literature, you would know that a hypothesis that explains everything is a certainty.'

'Yes, I am aware that Cambridge is a sort of educational institute,' I murmured. 'I am glad I was not there.'

'My dear fellow,' said Erskine, suddenly turning his keen grey eyes on me, 'you believe in Cyril Graham's theory, you believe in Willie Hughes, you know that the Sonnets are addressed to an actor, but for some reason or other you won't acknowledge it.'

'I wish I could believe it,' I rejoined. 'I would give anything to be able to do so. But I can't. It is a sort of moonbeam theory, very lovely, very fascinating, but intangible. When one thinks that one has got hold of it, it escapes one. No: Shakespeare's heart is still to us "a closet never pierc'd with crystal eyes", as he calls it in one of the sonnets. We shall never know the true secret of the passion of his life.'

Erskine sprang from the sofa, and paced up and down the room. 'We know it already,' he cried, 'and the world shall know it some day.'

I had never seen him so excited. He would not hear of my leaving him, and insisted on my stopping for the rest of the day.

We argued the matter over for hours, but nothing that I could say could make him surrender his faith in Cyril Graham's interpretation. He told me that he intended to devote his life to proving the theory, and that he was determined to do justice to Cyril Graham's memory. I entreated him, laughed at him, begged of him, but it was to no use. Finally we parted, not exactly in anger, but certainly with a shadow between us. He thought me shallow, I thought him foolish. When I called on him again, his servant told me that he had gone to Germany. The letters that I wrote to him remained unanswered.

Two years afterwards, as I was going into my club, the hall porter handed me a letter with a foreign postmark. It was from Erskine, and written at the Hôtel d'Angleterre, Cannes. When I had read it, I was filled with horror, though I did not quite believe that he would be so mad as to carry his resolve into execution. The gist of the letter was that he had tried in every way to verify the Willie Hughes theory, and had failed, and that as Cyril Graham had given his life for this theory, he himself had determined to give his own life also to the same cause. The concluding words of the letter were these: 'I still believe in Willie Hughes; and by the time you receive this I shall have died by my own hand for Willie Hughes' sake: for his sake, and for the sake of Cyril Graham, whom I drove to his death by my shallow scepticism and ignorant lack of faith. The truth was once revealed to you, and you rejected it. It comes to you now, stained with the blood of two lives – do not turn away from it.'

It was a horrible moment. I felt sick with misery, and yet I could not believe that he would really carry out his intention. To die for one's theological opinions is the worst use a man can make of his life; but to die for a literary theory! It seemed impossible.

I looked at the date. The letter was a week old. Some unfortunate chance had prevented my going to the club for several days, or I might have got it in time to save him. Perhaps it was not too late. I drove off to my rooms, packed up my things, and started by the night mail from Charing Cross.[97] The journey was intolerable. I thought I would never arrive.

As soon as I did, I drove to the Hôtel d'Angleterre. It was quite true. Erskine was dead. They told me that he had been buried two days before in the English cemetery. There was something horribly grotesque about the whole tragedy. I said all kinds of wild things, and the people in the hall looked curiously at me.

Suddenly Lady Erskine, in deep mourning, passed across the vestibule. When she saw me she came up to me, murmured something about her poor son, and burst into tears. I led her into her sitting room. An elderly gentleman was there, reading a newspaper. It was the English doctor.

We talked a great deal about Erskine, but I said nothing about his motive for committing suicide. It was evident that he had not told his mother anything about the reason that had driven him to so fatal, so mad an act. Finally Lady Erskine rose and said, 'George left you something as a memento. It was a thing he prized very much. I will get it for you.'

As soon as she had left the room I turned to the doctor and said, 'What a dreadful shock it must have been for Lady Erskine! I wonder that she bears it as well as she does.'

'Oh, she knew for months past that it was coming,' he answered.

'Knew it for months past!' I cried. 'But why didn't she stop him? Why didn't she have him watched? He must have been out of his mind.'

The doctor stared at me. 'I don't know what you mean,' he said.

'Well,' I cried, 'if a mother knows that her son is going to commit suicide –'

'Suicide!' he answered. 'Poor Erskine did not commit suicide. He died of consumption.[98] He came here to die. The moment I saw him

99

I knew that there was no chance. One lung was almost gone, and the other was very much affected. Three days before he died he asked me was there any hope. I told him frankly that there was none, and that he had only a few days to live. He wrote some letters, and was quite resigned, retaining his senses to the last.'

I got up from my seat, and going over to the open window I looked out on the crowded promenade. I remember that the brightly-coloured umbrellas and gay parasols seemed to me like huge fantastic butterflies fluttering by the shore of a blue-metal sea, and that the heavy odour of violets that came across the garden made me think of that wonderful sonnet[99] in which Shakespeare tells us that the scent of these flowers always reminded him of his friend. What did it all mean? Why had Erskine written me that extraordinary letter? Why when standing at the very gate of death had he turned back to tell me what was not true? Was Hugo[100] right? Is affectation the only thing that accompanies a man up the steps of the scaffold? Did Erskine merely want to produce a dramatic effect? That was not like him. It was more like something I might have done myself. No: he was simply actuated by a desire to reconvert me to Cyril Graham's theory, and he thought that if I could be made to believe that he too had given his life for it, I would be deceived by the pathetic fallacy of martyrdom. Poor Erskine! I had grown wiser since I had seen him. Martyrdom was to me merely a tragic form of scepticism, an attempt to realize by fire what one had failed to do by faith. No man dies for what he knows to be true. Men die for what they want to be true, for what some terror in their hearts tells them is not true. The very uselessness of Erskine's letter made me doubly sorry for him. I watched the people strolling in and out of the cafés, and wondered if any of them had known him. The white dust blew down the scorched sunlit road, and the feathery palms moved restlessly in the shaken air.

At that moment Lady Erskine returned to the room carrying the fatal portrait of Willie Hughes. 'When George was dying, he begged me to give you this,' she said. As I took it from her, her tears fell on my hand.

This curious work of art hangs now in my library, where it is very much admired by my artistic friends, one of whom has etched it for me. They have decided that it is not a Clouet, but an Ouvry.[101] I have never cared to tell them its true history, but sometimes, when I look at it, I think there is really a great deal to be said for the Willie Hughes theory of Shakespeare's Sonnets.

In Defence of Dorian Gray
(1890–91)

To the Editor of the *St James's Gazette*

25 June [1890]   *16 Tite Street*

Sir, I have read your criticism of my story, *The Picture of Dorian Gray*, and I need hardly say that I do not propose to discuss its merits or demerits, its personalities or its lack of personality. England is a free country, and ordinary English criticism is perfectly free and easy. Besides, I must admit that, either from temperament or from taste, or from both, I am quite incapable of understanding how any work of art can be criticized from a moral standpoint. The sphere of art and the sphere of ethics are absolutely distinct and separate; and it is to the confusion between the two that we owe the appearance of Mrs Grundy,[1] that amusing old lady who represents the only original form of humour that the middle classes of this country have been able to produce. What I do object to most strongly is that you should have placarded the town with posters on which was printed in large letters: MR OSCAR WILDE'S LATEST ADVERTISEMENT; A BAD CASE.

Whether the expression 'A Bad Case' refers to my book or to the present position of the Government, I cannot tell. What was silly and unnecessary was the use of the term 'advertisement'.

I think I may say without vanity – though I do not wish to appear to run vanity down – that of all men in England I am the one who requires least advertisement. I am tired to death of being advertised. I feel no thrill when I see my name in a paper. The chronicler does not interest me any more. I wrote this book entirely for my own pleasure, and it gave me very great pleasure to write it. Whether it becomes popular or not is a matter of absolute indifference to me. I am afraid, sir, that the real advertisement is your cleverly written article. The English public, as a mass, takes no interest in a work of art until it is told that the work in question is immoral, and your *réclame*[2] will, I have no doubt, largely increase the sale of the magazine; in which sale, I may mention with some regret, I have no pecuniary interest.

I remain, sir, your obedient servant

OSCAR WILDE

To the Editor of the *St James's Gazette*

26 June [*1890*]   *16 Tite Street*

In your issue of today you state that my brief letter published in your columns is the 'best reply' I can make to your article upon *Dorian Gray*. This is not so. I do not propose to fully discuss the matter here, but I feel bound to say that your article contains the most unjustifiable attack that has been made upon any man of letters for many years. The writer of it, who is quite incapable of concealing his personal malice, and so in some measure destroys the effect he wishes to produce, seems not to have the slightest idea of the temper in which a work of art should be approached. To say that such a book as mine should be 'chucked into the fire' is silly. That is what one does with newspapers.

Of the value of pseudo-ethical criticism in dealing with artistic work I have spoken already. But as your writer has ventured into the perilous grounds of literary criticism I ask you to allow me, in fairness not merely to myself but to all men to whom literature is a fine art, to say a few words about his critical method.

He begins by assailing me with much ridiculous virulence because the chief personages in my story are 'puppies'.[3] They *are* puppies. Does he think that literature went to the dogs when Thackeray wrote about puppydom? I think that puppies are extremely interesting from an artistic as well as from a psychological point of view. They seem to me to be certainly far more interesting than prigs; and I am of opinion that Lord Henry Wotton is an excellent corrective of the tedious ideal shadowed forth in the semi-theological novels of our age.

He then makes vague and fearful insinuations about my grammar and my erudition. Now, as regards grammar, I hold that, in prose at any rate, correctness should always be subordinate to artistic effect and musical cadence; and any peculiarities of syntax that may occur in *Dorian Gray* are deliberately intended, and are introduced to show the value of the artistic theory in question. Your writer gives no instance of any such peculiarity. This I regret, because I do not think that any such instances occur.

As regards erudition, it is always difficult, even for the most modest of us, to remember that other people do not know quite as much as one does oneself. I myself frankly admit I cannot imagine how a casual reference to Suetonius and Petronius Arbiter[4] can be construed into evidence of a desire to impress an unoffending and ill-educated public by an assumption of superior knowledge. I should fancy that the most ordinary of scholars is perfectly well acquainted with the *Lives of the Caesars* and with the *Satyricon*. The *Lives of the Caesars*, at any rate, forms part of the curriculum at Oxford for those who take the Honour School of *Literae Humaniores*;[5] and as for the *Satyricon*, it is popular even among passmen, though I suppose they are obliged to read it in translations.

The writer of the article then suggests that I, in common with that great and noble artist Count Tolstoi,[6] take pleasure in a subject because it is dangerous. About such a suggestion there is this to be said. Romantic art deals with the exception and with the individual. Good people, belonging as they do to the normal, and so, commonplace, type, are artistically uninteresting. Bad people are, from the point of view of art, fascinating studies. They represent colour, variety and strangeness. Good people exasperate one's reason; bad people stir one's imagination. Your critic, if I must give him so honourable a title, states that the people in my story have no counterpart in life; that they are, to use his vigorous if somewhat vulgar phrase, 'mere catchpenny revelations of the non-existent'. Quite so. If they existed they would not be worth writing about. The function of the artist is to invent, not to chronicle. There are no such people. If there were I would not write about them. Life by its realism is always spoiling the subject-matter of art. The supreme pleasure in literature is to realize the non-existent.

And finally, let me say this. You have reproduced, in a journalistic form, the comedy of *Much Ado About Nothing*, and have, of course, spoilt it in your reproduction. The poor public, hearing, from an authority so high as your own, that this is a wicked book that should be coerced and suppressed by a Tory Government, will, no doubt, rush to it and read it. But, alas! they will find that it is a story with a moral. And the moral is this: All excess, as well as all renunciation, brings its own punishment. The painter, Basil Hallward, worshipping physical beauty far too much, as most painters do, dies by the hand of one in whose soul he has created a monstrous and absurd vanity. Dorian Gray, having led a life of mere sensation and pleasure, tries to kill conscience, and at that moment kills himself. Lord Henry Wotton seeks to be merely the spectator of life. He finds that those who reject the battle are more deeply wounded than those who take part in it. Yes; there is a terrible moral in *Dorian Gray* – a moral which the prurient will not be able to find in it, but which will be revealed to all whose minds are healthy. Is this an artistic error? I fear it is. It is the only error in the book.

To the Editor of the *St James's Gazette*

27 June [1890]   *16 Tite Street*

Sir, As you still keep up, though in a somewhat milder form than before, your attacks on me and my book, you not merely confer on me the right, but you impose upon me the duty, of reply.

You state, in your issue of today, that I misrepresented you when I said that you suggested that a book so wicked as mine should be 'suppressed and coerced by a Tory Government'. Now you did not propose this, but you did suggest it. When you declare that you do not know whether or not the Government will take action about my book, and remark that the authors of books much less wicked have been proceeded against in law, the suggestion is quite obvious. In your complaint of misrepresentation you seem to me, sir, to have been not quite candid. However, as far as I am concerned, the suggestion is of no importance. What is of importance is that the editor of a paper like yours should appear to countenance the monstrous theory that the Government of a country should exercise a censorship over imaginative literature. This is a theory against which I, and all men of letters of my acquaintance, protest most strongly; and any critic who admits the reasonableness of such a theory shows at once that he is quite incapable of understanding what literature is, and what are the rights that literature possesses. A Government might just as well try to teach painters how to paint, or sculptors how to model, as attempt to interfere with the style, treatment and subject-matter of the literary artist; and no writer, however eminent or obscure, should ever give his sanction to a theory that would degrade literature far more than any didactic or so-called immoral book could possibly do.

You then express your surprise that 'so experienced a literary gentleman' as myself should imagine that your critic was animated by any feeling of personal malice towards him. The phrase 'literary gentleman' is a vile phrase; but let that pass. I accept quite readily your assurance that your critic was simply criticizing a work of art in the best way that he could; but I feel that I was fully justified in forming the opinion of him that I did. He opened his article by a gross personal attack on myself. This, I need hardly say, was an absolutely unpardonable error of critical taste. There is no excuse for it, except personal malice; and you, sir, should not have sanctioned it. A critic should be taught to criticize a work of art without making any reference to the personality of the author. This, in fact, is the beginning of criticism. However, it was not merely his personal attack on me that made me imagine that he was actuated by malice. What really confirmed me in my first impression was his reiterated assertion that my book was tedious and dull. Now, if I were criticizing my book, which I have some thoughts of doing, I think I would consider it my duty to point out that it is far too crowded with sensational incident, and far too paradoxical in style, as far, at any rate, as the dialogue goes. I feel that from a standpoint of art these are two defects in the book. But tedious and dull the book is not. Your critic has cleared himself of the charge of personal malice, his denial and yours being quite sufficient in the matter; but he has only done so by a tacit admission that he has really no critical instinct about literature and literary work, which, in one who writes about literature, is, I need hardly say, a much graver fault than malice of any kind.

Finally, sir, allow me to say this. Such an article as you have published really makes one despair of the possibility of any general culture in England. Were I a French author, and my book brought out in Paris, there is not a single literary critic in France, on any paper of high standing, who would think for a moment of criticizing it from an ethical standpoint. If he did so, he would stultify himself, not merely in the eyes of all men of letters, but in the eyes of the majority of the public. You have yourself often spoken against Puritanism. Believe me, sir, Puritanism is never so offensive and destructive as when it deals with art matters. It is there that its influence is radically wrong. It is this Puritanism, to which your critic has given expression, that is always marring the artistic instinct of the English. So far from encouraging it, you should set yourself against it, and should try to teach your critics to recognize the essential difference between art and life. The gentleman who criticized my book is in a perfectly hopeless confusion about it, and your attempt to help him out by proposing that the subject-matter of art should be limited does not mend matters. It is proper that limitations should be placed on action. It is not proper that limitations should be placed on art. To art belong all things that are and all things that are not, and even the editor of a London paper has no right to restrain the freedom of art in the selection of subject-matter.

I now trust, sir, that these attacks on me and on my book will cease. There are forms of advertisement that are unwarranted and unwarrantable.

I am, sir, your obedient servant,

OSCAR WILDE

To Ward, Lock & Co.

[*Circa 28 June 1890. Date of receipt 2 July 1890*]   *16 Tite Street*
Gentlemen, Kindly do not send out any more copies of Messrs Lippincott's puff of my book. It is really an insult to the critics. Also, will you
kindly let me know if I can have an interview with you on Thursday
morning at twelve o'clock. Yours truly

OSCAR WILDE

To the Editor of the *St James's Gazette*

28 June [*1890*]   *16 Tite Street*
Sir, In your issue of this evening you publish a letter from 'A London
Editor' which clearly insinuates in the last paragraph that I have in
some way sanctioned the circulation of an expression of opinion, on
the part of the proprietors of *Lippincott's Magazine*, of the literary and
artistic value of my story of *The Picture of Dorian Gray*.

Allow me, sir, to state that there are no grounds for this insinu-
ation. I was not aware that any such document was being circulated;
and I have written to the agents, Messrs Ward & Lock – who cannot, I feel sure, be primarily responsible for its appearance – to
ask them to withdraw it at once. No publisher should ever express
an opinion of the value of what he publishes. That is a matter entirely
for the literary critic to decide. I must admit, as one to whom contemporary literature is constantly submitted for criticism, that the only
thing that ever prejudices me against a book is the lack of literary style;
but I can quite understand how any ordinary critic would be strongly
prejudiced against a work that was accompanied by a premature and
unnecessary panegyric from the publisher. A publisher is simply a
useful middle-man. It is not for him to anticipate the verdict of
criticism.

I may, however, while expressing my thanks to the 'London Editor'
for drawing my attention to this, I trust, purely American method of
procedure, venture to differ from him in one of his criticisms. He states

that he regards the expression 'complete', as applied to a story, as a specimen of the 'adjectival exuberance of the puffer!' Here, it seems to me, he sadly exaggerates. What my story is, is an interesting problem. What my story is not, is a 'novelette', a term which you have more than once applied to it. There is no such word in the English language as novelette. It should never be used. It is merely part of the slang of Fleet Street.

In another part of your paper, sir, you state that I received your assurance of the lack of malice in your critic 'somewhat grudgingly'. This is not so. I frankly said that I accepted that assurance 'quite readily', and that your own denial and that of your own critic were 'sufficient'. Nothing more generous could have been said. What I did feel was that you saved your critic from the charge of malice by convicting him of the unpardonable crime of lack of literary instinct. I still feel that. To call my book an ineffective attempt at allegory that, in the hands of Mr Anstey,[7] might have been made striking, is absurd. Mr Anstey's sphere in literature and my sphere are different – very widely different.

You then gravely ask me what rights I imagine literature possesses. That is really an extraordinary question for the editor of a newspaper such as yours to ask. The rights of literature, sir, are the rights of intellect.

I remember once hearing M. Renan[8] say that he would sooner live under a military despotism than under the despotism of the Church, because the former merely limited the freedom of action, while the latter limited the freedom of mind. You say that a work of art is a form of action. It is not. It is the highest mode of thought.

In conclusion, sir, let me ask you not to force on me this continued correspondence, by daily attacks. It is a trouble and a nuisance. As you assailed me first, I have a right to the last word. Let that last word be the present letter, and leave my book, I beg you, to the immortality that it deserves.

I am, sir, your obedient servant,

OSCAR WILDE

To the Editor of the *Daily Chronicle*

30 June [1890]   *16 Tite Street*

Sir, Will you allow me to correct some errors into which your critic has fallen in his review of my story, *The Picture of Dorian Gray*, published in today's issue of your paper?

Your critic states, to begin with, that I make desperate attempts to 'vamp up'⁹ a moral in my story. Now, I must candidly confess that I do not know what 'vamping' is. I see, from time to time, mysterious advertisements in the newspapers about 'How to Vamp', but what vamping really means remains a mystery to me – a mystery that, like all other mysteries, I hope some day to explore.

However, I do not propose to discuss the absurd terms used by modern journalism. What I want to say is that, so far from wishing to emphasize any moral in my story, the real trouble I experienced in writing the story was that of keeping the extremely obvious moral subordinate to the artistic and dramatic effect.

When I first conceived the idea of a young man selling his soul in exchange for eternal youth – an idea that is old in the history of literature, but to which I have given new form – I felt that, from an aesthetic point of view, it would be difficult to keep the moral in its proper secondary place; and even now I do not feel quite sure that I have been able to do so. I think the moral too apparent. When the book is published in a volume I hope to correct this defect.

As for what the moral is, your critic states that it is this – that when a man feels himself becoming 'too angelic' he should rush out and make a 'beast of himself!' I cannot say that I consider this a moral. The real moral of the story is that all excess, as well as all renunciation, brings its punishment, and this moral is so far artistically and deliberately suppressed that it does not enunciate its law as a general principle, but realizes itself purely in the lives of individuals, and so becomes simply a dramatic element in a work of art, and not the object of the work of art itself.

Your critic also falls into error when he says that Dorian Gray, having a 'cool, calculating, conscienceless character', was inconsistent when he destroyed the picture of his own soul, on the ground that the picture did not become less hideous after he had done what, in his vanity, he had considered his first good action. Dorian Gray has not got a cool, calculating, conscienceless character at all. On the contrary, he is extremely impulsive, absurdly romantic, and is haunted all through his life by an exaggerated sense of conscience which mars his pleasures for him and warns him that youth and enjoyment are not everything in the world. It is finally to get rid of the conscience that had dogged his steps from year to year that he destroys the picture; and thus in his attempt to kill conscience Dorian Gray kills himself.

Your critic then talks about 'obtrusively cheap scholarship'. Now, whatever a scholar writes is sure to display scholarship in the distinction of style and the fine use of language; but my story contains no learned or pseudo-learned discussions, and the only literary books that it alludes to are books that any fairly educated reader may be supposed to be acquainted with, such as the *Satyricon* of Petronius Arbiter, or Gautier's *Émaux et Camées*.[10] Such books as Alphonso's *Clericalis Disciplina*[11] belong not to culture, but to curiosity. Anybody may be excused for not knowing them.

Finally, let me say this – the aesthetic movement produced certain colours, subtle in their loveliness and fascinating in their almost mystical tone. They were, and are, our reaction against the crude primaries of a doubtless more respectable but certainly less cultivated age. My story is an essay on decorative art. It reacts against the crude brutality of plain realism. It is poisonous if you like, but you cannot deny that it is also perfect, and perfection is what we artists aim at.

I remain, sir, your obedient servant

OSCAR WILDE

To the Editor of the *Scots Observer*

9 July 1890   *16 Tite Street, Chelsea*

Sir, You have published a review of my story, *The Picture of Dorian Gray*. As this review is grossly unjust to me as an artist, I ask you to allow me to exercise in your columns my right of reply.

Your reviewer, sir, while admitting that the story in question is 'plainly the work of a man of letters', the work of one who has 'brains, and art, and style', yet suggests, and apparently in all seriousness, that I have written it in order that it should be read by the most depraved members of the criminal and illiterate classes. Now, sir, I do not suppose that the criminal and illiterate classes ever read anything except newspapers. They are certainly not likely to be able to understand anything of mine. So let them pass, and on the broad question of why a man of letters writes at all let me say this. The pleasure that one has in creating a work of art is a purely personal pleasure, and it is for the sake of this pleasure that one creates. The artist works with his eye on the object. Nothing else interests him. What people are likely to say does not even occur to him. He is fascinated by what he has in hand. He is indifferent to others. I write because it gives me the greatest possible artistic pleasure to write. If my work pleases the few, I am gratified. If it does not, it causes me no pain. As for the mob, I have no desire to be a popular novelist. It is far too easy.

Your critic then, sir, commits the absolutely unpardonable crime of trying to confuse the artist with his subject-matter. For this, sir, there is no excuse at all. Of one who is the greatest figure[12] in the world's literature since Greek days Keats remarked that he had as much pleasure in conceiving the evil as he had in conceiving the good. Let your reviewer, sir, consider the bearings of Keats's fine criticism, for it is under these conditions that every artist works. One stands remote from one's subject-matter. One creates it, and one contemplates it. The further away the subject-matter is, the more freely can the artist work. Your reviewer suggests that I do not make it sufficiently clear whether I prefer virtue to wickedness or wickedness to virtue. An artist, sir, has no ethical sympathies at all. Virtue and wickedness are to him simply what the colours on his palette are to the painter. They are no more, and they are no less. He sees that by their means a certain artistic effect can be produced, and he produces it. Iago may be morally horrible and Imogen stainlessly pure. Shakespeare, as Keats said, had as much delight in creating the one as he had in creating the other.

It was necessary, sir, for the dramatic development of this story to surround Dorian Gray with an atmosphere of moral corruption. Otherwise the story would have had no meaning and the plot no issue. To keep this atmosphere vague and indeterminate and wonderful was the aim of the artist who wrote the story. I claim, sir, that he has succeeded. Each man sees his own sin in Dorian Gray. What Dorian Gray's sins are no one knows. He who finds them has brought them.

In conclusion, sir, let me say how really deeply I regret that you should have permitted such a notice as the one I feel constrained to write on to have appeared in your paper. That the editor of the *St James's Gazette* should have employed Caliban as his art-critic was possibly natural. The editor of the *Scots Observer* should not have allowed Thersites[13] to make mows in his review. It is unworthy of so distinguished a man of letters. I am, etc.

OSCAR WILDE

To the Editor of the *Scots Observer*

[? 31] *July 1890*   *16 Tite Street*

Sir, In a letter dealing with the relations of art to morals recently published in your columns – a letter which I may say seems to me in many respects admirable, especially in its insistence on the right of the artist to select his own subject-matter – Mr Charles Whibley[14] suggests that it must be peculiarly painful for me to find that the ethical import of *Dorian Gray* has been so strongly recognized by the foremost

Christian papers of England and America that I have been greeted by more than one of them as a moral reformer!

Allow me, sir, to reassure, on this point, not merely Mr Charles Whibley himself but also your no doubt anxious readers. I have no hesitation in saying that I regard such criticisms as a very gratifying tribute to my story. For if a work of art is rich, and vital, and complete, those who have artistic instincts will see its beauty, and those to whom ethics appeal more strongly than aesthetics will see its moral lesson. It will fill the cowardly with terror, and the unclean will see in it their own shame. It will be to each man what he is himself. It is the spectator, and not life, that art really mirrors.

And so, in the case of *Dorian Gray*, the purely literary critic, as in the *Speaker* and elsewhere, regards it as a 'serious and fascinating work of art': the critic who deals with art in its relation to conduct, as the *Christian Leader* and the *Christian World*, regards it as an ethical parable. *Light*, which I am told is the organ of the English mystics, regards it as 'a work of high spiritual import'. The *St James's Gazette*, which is seeking apparently to be the organ of the prurient, sees or pretends to see in it all kinds of dreadful things, and hints at Treasury prosecutions; and your Mr Charles Whibley genially says that he discovers in it 'lots of morality'. It is quite true that he goes on to say that he detects no art in it. But I do not think that it is fair to expect a critic to be able to see a work of art from every point of view. Even Gautier had his limitations just as much as Diderot had, and in modern England Goethes[15] are rare. I can only assure Mr Charles Whibley that no moral apotheosis to which he has added the most modest contribution could possibly be a source of unhappiness to an artist.

I remain, sir, your obedient servant

OSCAR WILDE

To the Editor of the *Scots Observer*

13 August 1890   *16 Tite Street*

Sir, I am afraid I cannot enter into any newspaper discussion on the subject of art with Mr Whibley, partly because the writing of letters is always a trouble to me, and partly because I regret to say that I do not know what qualifications Mr Whibley possesses for the discussion of so important a topic. I merely noticed his letter because, I am sure without in any way intending it, he made a suggestion about myself personally that was quite inaccurate. His suggestion was that it must have been painful to me to find that a certain section of the public, as represented by himself and the critics of some religious publications, had insisted on finding what he calls 'lots of morality' in my story of *The Picture of Dorian Gray*.

Being naturally desirous of setting your readers right on a question of such vital interest to the historian, I took the opportunity of pointing out in your columns that I regarded all such criticisms as a very gratifying tribute to the ethical beauty of the story, and I added that I was quite ready to recognize that it was not really fair to ask of any ordinary critic that he should be able to appreciate a work of art from every point of view. I still hold this opinion. If a man sees the artistic beauty of a thing, he will probably care very little for its ethical import. If his temperament is more susceptible to ethical than to aesthetic influences, he will be blind to questions of style, treatment, and the like. It takes a Goethe to see a work of art fully, completely, and perfectly, and I thoroughly agree with Mr Whibley when he says that it is a pity that Goethe never had an opportunity of reading *Dorian Gray*. I feel quite certain that he would have been delighted by it, and I only hope that some ghostly publisher is even now distributing shadowy copies in the Elysian fields, and that the cover of Gautier's copy is powdered with gilt asphodels.[16]

You may ask me, sir, why I should care to have the ethical beauty of my story recognized. I answer, simply because it exists, because the thing is there. The chief merit of *Madame Bovary* is not the moral lesson that can be found in it, any more than the chief merit of *Salammbô* is its archaeology; but Flaubert was perfectly right in exposing the ignorance of those who called the one immoral and the other inaccurate; and not merely was he right in the ordinary sense of the word, but he was artistically right, which is everything. The critic has to educate the public; the artist has to educate the critic.

Allow me to make one more correction, sir, and I will have done with Mr Whibley. He ends his letter with the statement that I have been indefatigable in my public appreciation of my own work. I have no doubt that in saying this he means to pay me a compliment, but he really overrates my capacity, as well as my inclination for work. I must frankly confess that, by nature and by choice, I am extremely indolent. Cultivated idleness[17] seems to me to be the proper occupation for man. I dislike newspaper controversies of any kind, and of the two hundred and sixteen criticisms of *Dorian Gray* that have passed from my library table into the waste-paper basket I have taken public notice of only three. One was that which appeared in the *Scots Observer*. I noticed it because it made a suggestion, about the intention of the author in writing the book, which needed correction. The second was an article in the *St James's Gazette*. It was offensively and vulgarly written, and seemed to me to require immediate and caustic censure. The tone of the article was an impertinence to any man of letters. The third was a meek attack in a paper called the *Daily Chronicle*. I think my writing to the *Daily Chronicle* was an act of pure wilfulness. In fact, I feel sure it was. I quite forget what they said. I believe they said that *Dorian Gray* was poisonous, and I thought that, on alliterative grounds, it would be kind to remind them that, however that may be, it is at any rate perfect. That was all. Of the other two hundred and thirteen criticisms I have taken no notice. Indeed, I have not read more than half of them. It is a sad thing, but one wearies even of praise.

As regards Mr Brown's letter, it is interesting only in so far as it exemplifies the truth of what I have said above on the question of the two obvious schools of critics. Mr Brown says frankly that he considers morality to be the 'strong point' of my story. Mr Brown means well, and has got hold of a half-truth, but when he proceeds to deal with the book from the artistic standpoint he, of course, goes sadly astray. To class *Dorian Gray* with M. Zola's *La Terre* is as silly as if one were to class Musset's *Fortunio*[18] with one of the Adelphi melodramas.[19] Mr Brown should be content with ethical appreciation. There he is impregnable.

Mr Cobban opens badly by describing my letter, setting Mr Whibley right on a matter of fact, as an 'impudent paradox'. The term 'impudent' is meaningless, and the word 'paradox' is misplaced. I am afraid that writing to newspapers has a deteriorating influence on style. People get violent, and abusive, and lose all sense of proportion, when they enter that curious journalistic arena in which the race is always to the noisiest. 'Impudent paradox' is neither violent nor abusive, but it is not an expression that should have been used about my letter. However, Mr Cobban makes full atonement afterwards for what was, no doubt, a mere error of manner, by adopting the impudent paradox in question as his own, and pointing out that, as I had previously said, the artist will always look at the work of art from the standpoint of beauty of style and beauty of treatment, and that those who have got the sense of beauty, or whose sense of beauty is dominated by ethical considerations, will always turn their attention to the subject-matter and make its moral import the test and touchstone of the poem, or novel, or picture, that is presented to them, while the newspaper critic will sometimes take one side and sometimes the other, according as he is cultured or uncultured. In fact, Mr Cobban converts the impudent paradox into a tedious truism, and, I dare say, in doing so does good service. The English public like tediousness, and like things to be explained to them in a tedious way. Mr Cobban has, I have no doubt, already repented of the unfortunate expression with which he has made his *début*, so I will say no more about it. As far as I am concerned he is quite forgiven.

And finally, sir, in taking leave of the *Scots Observer* I feel bound to make a candid confession to you. It has been suggested to me by a great friend of mine,[20] who is a charming and distinguished man of letters, and not unknown to you personally, that there have been really only two people engaged in this terrible controversy, and that those two people are the editor of the *Scots Observer* and the author of *Dorian*

Gray. At dinner this evening, over some excellent Chianti, my friend insisted that under assumed and mysterious names you had simply given dramatic expression to the views of some of the semi-educated classes in our community, and that the letters signed 'H' were your own skilful, if somewhat bitter, caricature of the Philistine as drawn by himself. I admit that something of the kind had occurred to me when I read 'H's' first letter – the one in which he proposed that the test of art should be the political opinions of the artist, and that if one differed from the artist on the question of the best way of misgoverning Ireland, one should always abuse his work. Still, there are such infinite varieties of Philistines, and North Britain[21] is so renowned for serious-ness, that I dismissed the idea as one unworthy of the editor of a Scotch paper. I now fear that I was wrong, and that you have been amusing yourself all the time by inventing little puppets and teaching them how to use big words. Well, sir, if it be so – and my friend is strong upon the point – allow me to congratulate you most sincerely on the cleverness with which you have reproduced that lack of literary style which is, I am told, essential for any dramatic and life-like characterization. I confess that I was completely taken in; but I bear no malice; and as you have no doubt been laughing at me in your sleeve, let me now join openly in the laugh, though it be a little against myself. A comedy ends when the secret is out. Drop your curtain, and put your dolls to bed. I love Don Quixote, but I do not wish to fight any longer with marionettes, however cunning may be the master-hand that works their wires. Let them go, sir, on the shelf. The shelf is the proper place for them. On some future occasion you can re-label them and bring them out for our amusement. They are an excellent company, and go well through their tricks, and if they are a little unreal, I am not the one to object to unreality in art. The jest was really a good one. The only thing that I cannot understand is why you gave your marionettes such extraordinary and improbable names. I remain, sir, your obedient servant

OSCAR WILDE

Preface to *The Picture of Dorian Gray*

The artist is the creator of beautiful things.

To reveal art and conceal the artist is art's aim.

The critic is he who can translate into another manner or a new material his impression of beautiful things.

The highest as the lowest form of criticism is a mode of autobiography.

Those who find ugly meanings in beautiful things are corrupt without being charming. This is a fault.

Those who find beautiful meanings in beautiful things are the cultivated. For these there is hope.

They are the elect to whom beautiful things mean only Beauty.

There is no such thing as a moral or an immoral book. Books are well written, or badly written. That is all.

The nineteenth-century dislike of Realism is the rage of Caliban seeing his own face in a glass.

The nineteenth-century dislike of Romanticism is the rage of Caliban not seeing his own face in a glass.

The moral life of man forms part of the subject-matter of the artist, but the morality of art consists in the perfect use of an imperfect medium.

No artist desires to prove anything. Even things that are true can be proved.

No artist has ethical sympathies. An ethical sympathy in an artist is an unpardonable mannerism of style.

No artist is ever morbid. The artist can express everything.

Thought and language are to the artist instruments of an art.

Vice and virtue are to the artist materials for an art.

From the point of view of form, the type of all the arts is the art of the musician. From the point of view of feeling, the actor's craft is the type.

All art is at once surface and symbol.

Those who go beneath the surface do so at their peril.

Those who read the symbol do so at their peril.

It is the spectator, and not life, that art really mirrors.

Diversity of opinion about a work of art shows that the work is new, complex, and vital.

When critics disagree the artist is in accord with himself.

We can forgive a man for making a useful thing as long as he does not admire it. The only excuse for making a useless thing is that one admires it intensely.

All art is quite useless.

The Soul of Man under Socialism
(1891)

The chief advantage that would result from the establishment of Socialism is, undoubtedly, the fact that Socialism would relieve us from that sordid necessity of living for others which, in the present condition of things, presses so hardly upon almost everybody. In fact, scarcely any one at all escapes.

Now and then, in the course of the century, a great man of science, like Darwin; a great poet, like Keats; a fine critical spirit, like M. Renan;[1] a supreme artist, like Flaubert,[2] has been able to isolate himself, to keep himself out of reach of the clamorous claims of others, to stand 'under the shelter of the wall', as Plato puts it, and so to realize the perfection of what was in him, to his own incomparable gain, and to the incomparable and lasting gain of the whole world. These, however, are exceptions. The majority of people spoil their lives by an unhealthy and exaggerated altruism – are forced, indeed, so to spoil them. They find themselves surrounded by hideous poverty, by hideous ugliness, by hideous starvation. It is inevitable that they should be strongly moved by all this. The emotions of man are stirred more quickly than man's intelligence; and, as I pointed out some time ago in an article on the function of criticism,[3] it is much more easy to have sympathy with suffering than it is to have sympathy with thought. Accordingly, with admirable though misdirected intentions, they very seriously and very sentimentally set themselves to the task of remedying the evils that they see. But their remedies do not cure the disease: they merely prolong it. Indeed, their remedies are part of the disease.

They try to solve the problem of poverty, for instance, by keeping the poor alive; or, in the case of a very advanced school, by amusing the poor.[4]

But this is not a solution: it is an aggravation of the difficulty. The proper aim is to try and reconstruct society on such a basis that poverty will be impossible. And the altruistic virtues have really prevented the carrying out of this aim. Just as the worst slave-owners were those who were kind to their slaves, and so prevented the horror of the system being realized by those who suffered from it, and understood by those who contemplated it, so, in the present state of things in England, the people who do most harm are the people who try to do most good; and at last we have had the spectacle of men who have really studied the problem and know the life – educated men who live in the East-End[5] – coming forward and imploring the community to restrain its altruistic impulses of charity, benevolence and the like. They do so on the ground that such charity degrades and demoralizes. They are perfectly right. Charity creates a multitude of sins.

There is also this to be said. It is immoral to use private property in order to alleviate the horrible evils that result from the institution of private property. It is both immoral and unfair.

Under Socialism all this will, of course, be altered. There will be no people living in fetid dens and fetid rags, and bringing up unhealthy, hunger-pinched children in the midst of impossible and absolutely repulsive surroundings. The security of society will not depend, as it does now, on the state of the weather. If a frost comes we shall not have a hundred thousand men out of work, tramping about the streets in a state of disgusting misery, or whining to their neighbours for alms, or crowding round the doors of loathsome shelters to try and secure a hunch[6] of bread and a night's unclean lodging. Each member of the society will share in the general prosperity and happiness of the society, and if a frost comes no one will practically be anything the worse.

Upon the other hand, Socialism itself will be of value simply because it will lead to Individualism.

Socialism, Communism, or whatever one chooses to call it, by converting private property into public wealth, and substituting cooperation for competition, will restore society to its proper condition of a thoroughly healthy organism, and ensure the material well-being of each member of the community. It will, in fact, give Life its proper basis and its proper environment. But for the full development of Life to its highest mode of perfection something more is needed. What is needed is Individualism. If the Socialism is Authoritarian; if there are

Governments armed with economic power as they are now with political power; if, in a word, we are to have Industrial Tyrannies, then the last state of man will be worse than the first. At present, in consequence of the existence of private property, a great many people are enabled to develop a certain very limited amount of Individualism. They are either under no necessity to work for their living, or are enabled to choose the sphere of activity that is really congenial to them and gives them pleasure. These are the poets, the philosophers, the men of science, the men of culture – in a word, the real men, the men who have realized themselves, and in whom all Humanity gains a partial realization. Upon the other hand, there are a great many people who, having no private property of their own, and being always on the brink of sheer starvation, are compelled to do the work of beasts of burden, to do work that is quite uncongenial to them, and to which they are forced by the peremptory, unreasonable, degrading Tyranny of want. These are the poor, and amongst them there is no grace of manner, or charm of speech, or civilization, or culture, or refinement in pleasures, or joy of life. From their collective force Humanity gains much in material prosperity. But it is only the material result that it gains, and the man who is poor is in himself absolutely of no impor-tance. He is merely the infinitesimal atom of a force that, so far from regarding him, crushes him: indeed, prefers him crushed, as in that case he is far more obedient.

Of course, it might be said that the Individualism generated under conditions of private property is not always, or even as a rule, of a fine or wonderful type, and that the poor, if they have not culture and charm, have still many virtues. Both these statements would be quite true. The possession of private property is very often extremely demoralizing, and that is, of course, one of the reasons why Socialism wants to get rid of the institution. In fact, property is really a nuisance. Some years ago people went about the country saying that property has duties. They said it so often and so tediously that, at last, the Church has begun to say it. One hears it now from every pulpit. It is perfectly true. Property not merely has duties, but has so many duties that its possession to any large extent is a bore. It involves endless claims upon one, endless attention to business, endless bother. If property had simply pleasures we could stand it; but its duties make it unbearable. In the interest of the rich we must get rid of it. The virtues of the poor may be readily admitted, and are much to be regretted. We are often told that the poor are grateful for charity. Some of them are, no doubt, but the best amongst the poor are never grateful. They are ungrateful, discontented, disobedient and rebellious. They are quite right to be so. Charity they feel to be a ridiculously inadequate mode of partial restitution, or a sentimental dole, usually accompanied by some impertinent attempt on the part of the sentimentalist to tyrannize over their private lives. Why should they be grateful for the crumbs that fall from the rich man's table? They should be seated at the board, and are beginning to know it. As for being discontented, a man who would not be discontented with such surroundings and such a low mode of life would be a perfect brute. Disobedience, in the eyes of any one who has read history, is man's original virtue. It is through disobedience that progress has been made, through disobedience and through rebellion. Sometimes the poor are praised for being thrifty. But to recommend thrift to the poor is both grotesque and insulting. It is like advising a man who is starving to eat less. For a town or country labourer to practise thrift would be absolutely immoral. Man should not be ready to show that he can live like a badly fed animal. He should decline to live like that, and should either steal or go on the rates,[7] which is considered by many to be a form of stealing. As for begging, it is safer to beg than to take, but it is finer to take than to beg. No: a poor man who is ungrateful, unthrifty, discontented and rebellious is probably a real personality, and has much in him. He is at any rate a healthy protest. As for the virtuous poor, one can pity them, of course, but one cannot possibly admire them. They have made private terms with the enemy, and sold their birthright for very bad pottage.[8] They must also be extraordinarily stupid. I can quite understand a man accepting laws that protect private property, and admit of its accumulation, as long as he himself is able under those conditions to realize some form of beautiful and intellectual life. But it is almost incredible to me how a man whose life is marred and made hideous by such laws can possibly acquiesce in their continuance.

However, the explanation is not really difficult to find. It is simply this. Misery and poverty are so absolutely degrading, and exercise such a paralysing effect over the nature of men, that no class is ever really conscious of its own suffering. They have to be told of it by other people, and they often entirely disbelieve them. What is said by great employers of labour against agitators is unquestionably true. Agitators are a set of interfering, meddling people, who come down to some perfectly contented class of the community and sow the seeds of discontent amongst them. That is the reason why agitators are so absolutely necessary. Without them, in our incomplete state, there would be no advance towards civilization. Slavery was put down in America, not in consequence of any action on the part of the slaves, or even any express desire on their part that they should be free. It was put down entirely through the grossly illegal conduct of certain agitators in Boston and elsewhere, who were not slaves themselves, nor owners of slaves, nor had anything to do with the question really. It was, undoubtedly, the Abolitionists who set the torch alight, who began the whole thing. And it is curious to note that from the slaves themselves they received, not merely very little assistance, but hardly any sympathy even; and when at the close of the war the slaves found themselves free, found themselves indeed so absolutely free that they were free to starve, many of them bitterly regretted the new state of things. To the thinker, the most tragic fact in the whole of the French Revolution is not that Marie Antoinette was killed for being a queen, but that the starved peasant of the Vendée[9] voluntarily went out to die for the hideous cause of feudalism.

It is clear, then, that no Authoritarian Socialism will do. For, while under the present system a very large number of people can lead lives of a certain amount of freedom and expression and happiness, under an industrial–barrack system,[10] or a system of economic tyranny, nobody would be able to have any such freedom at all. It is to be regretted that a portion of our community should be practically in slavery, but to propose to solve the problem by enslaving the entire community is childish. Every man must be left quite free to choose his own work. No form of compulsion must be exercised over him. If there is, his work will not be good for him, will not be good in itself, and will not be good for others. And by work I simply mean activity of any kind.

I hardly think that any Socialist, nowadays, would seriously propose that an inspector should call every morning at each house to see that each citizen rose up and did manual labour for eight hours. Humanity has got beyond that stage, and reserves such a form of life for the people whom, in a very arbitrary manner, it chooses to call criminals. But I confess that many of the socialistic views that I have come across seem to me to be tainted with ideas of authority, if not of actual compulsion. Of course authority and compulsion are out of the question. All association must be quite voluntary. It is only in voluntary association that man is fine.

But it may be asked how Individualism, which is now more or less dependent on the existence of private property for its development, will benefit by the abolition of such private property. The answer is very simple. It is true that, under existing conditions, a few men who have had private means of their own, such as Byron, Shelley, Browning, Victor Hugo, Baudelaire, and others, have been able to realize their personality more or less completely. Not one of these men ever did a single day's work for hire. They were relieved from poverty. They had an immense advantage. The question is whether it would be for the good of Individualism that such an advantage should be taken away. Let us suppose that it is taken away. What happens then to Individualism? How will it benefit?

It will benefit in this way. Under the new conditions Individualism will be far freer, far finer and far more intensified than it is now. I am not talking of the great imaginatively-realized Individualism of such poets as I have mentioned, but of the great actual Individualism latent and potential in mankind generally. For the recognition of private property has really harmed Individualism, and obscured it, by confusing a man with what he possesses. It has led Individualism entirely astray. It has made gain not growth its aim. So that man thought that the important thing was to have, and did not know that the important thing is to be. The true perfection of man lies, not in what man has, but in what man is. Private property has crushed true Individualism, and set up an Individualism that is false. It has debarred one part of the community from being individual by starving them. It has debarred the other part of the community from being individual, by putting them on the wrong road and encumbering them. Indeed, so completely has man's personality been absorbed by his possessions that the English law has always treated offences against a man's property with far more severity than offences against his person, and property is still the test of complete citizenship.[11] The industry necessary for the making of money is also very demoralizing. In a community like ours, where property confers immense distinction, social position, honour, respect, titles, and other pleasant things of the kind, man, being naturally ambitious, makes it his aim to accumulate this property, and goes on wearily and tediously accumulating it long after he has got far more than he wants, or can use, or enjoy, or perhaps even know of. Man will kill himself by overwork in order to secure property, and really, considering the enormous advantages that property brings, one is hardly surprised. One's regret is that society should be constructed on such a basis that man has been forced into a groove in which he cannot freely develop what is wonderful, and fascinating, and delightful in him – in which, in fact, he misses the true pleasure and joy of living. He is also, under existing conditions, very insecure. An enormously wealthy merchant may be – often is – at every moment of his life at the mercy of things that are not under his control. If the wind blows an extra point or so, or the weather suddenly changes, or some trivial thing happens, his ship may go down, his speculations may go wrong, and he finds himself a poor man, with his social position quite gone. Now, nothing should be able to harm a man except himself. Nothing should be able to rob a man at all. What a man really has, is what is in him. What is outside of him should be a matter of no importance.

With the abolition of private property, then, we shall have true beautiful, healthy Individualism. Nobody will waste his life in accumulating things and the symbols for things. One will live. To live is the rarest thing in the world. Most people exist, that is all.

It is a question whether we have ever seen the full expression of a personality, except on the imaginative plane of art. In action, we never have. Caesar, says Mommsen,[12] was the complete and perfect man.

But how tragically insecure was Caesar! Wherever there is a man who exercises authority, there is a man who resists authority. Caesar was very perfect, but his perfection travelled by too dangerous a road. Marcus Aurelius[13] was the perfect man, says Renan. Yes; the great emperor was a perfect man. But how intolerable were the endless claims upon him! He staggered under the burden of the empire. He was conscious how inadequate one man was to bear the weight of that Titan and too vast orb. What I mean by a perfect man is one who develops under perfect conditions; one who is not wounded, or worried, or maimed, or in danger. Most personalities have been obliged to be rebels. Half their strength has been wasted in friction. Byron's personality, for instance, was terribly wasted in its battle with the stupidity, and hypocrisy, and Philistinism of the English. Such battles do not always intensify strength: they often exaggerate weakness. Byron was never able to give us what he might have given us. Shelley escaped better. Like Byron, he got out of England as soon as possible. But he was not so well known. If the English had had any idea of what a great poet he really was, they would have fallen on him with tooth and nail, and made his life as unbearable to him as they possibly could. But he was not a remarkable figure in society, and consequently he escaped, to a certain degree. Still, even in Shelley the note of rebellion is sometimes too strong. The note of the perfect personality is not rebellion but peace.

It will be a marvellous thing – the true personality of man – when we see it. It will grow naturally and simply, flower-like, or as a tree grows. It will not be at discord. It will never argue or dispute. It will not prove things. It will know everything. And yet it will not busy itself about knowledge. It will have wisdom. Its value will not be measured by material things. It will have nothing. And yet it will have everything, and whatever one takes from it, it will still have, so rich will it be. It will not be always meddling with others, or asking them to be like itself. It will love them because they will be different. And yet while it will not meddle with others it will help all, as a beautiful thing helps us, by being what it is. The personality of man will be very wonderful. It will be as wonderful as the personality of a child.

In its development it will be assisted by Christianity, if men desire that; but if men do not desire that, it will develop none the less surely. For it will not worry itself about the past, nor care whether things happened or did not happen. Nor will it admit any laws but its own laws; nor any authority but its own authority. Yet it will love those who sought to intensify it, and speak often of them. And of these Christ was one.

'Know Thyself'[14] was written over the portal of the antique world. Over the portal of the new world, 'Be Thyself' shall be written. And the message of Christ to man was simply 'Be thyself'. That is the secret of Christ.

When Jesus talks about the poor he simply means personalities, just as when he talks about the rich he simply means people who have not developed their personalities. Jesus moved in a community that allowed the accumulation of private property just as ours does, and the gospel that he preached was not that in such a community it is an advantage for a man to live on scanty, unwholesome food, to wear ragged, unwholesome clothes, to sleep in horrid, unwholesome dwellings, and a disadvantage for a man to live under healthy, pleasant and decent conditions. Such a view would have been wrong there and then, and would of course be still more wrong now and in England; for as man moves northwards the material necessities of life become of more vital importance, and our society is infinitely more complex, and displays far greater extremes of luxury and pauperism than any society of the antique world. What Jesus meant was this. He said to man, 'You have a wonderful personality. Develop it. Be your self. Don't imagine that your perfection lies in accumulating or possessing external things. Your perfection is inside of you. If only you could realize that, you would not want to be rich. Ordinary riches can be stolen from a man. Real riches cannot. In the treasury-house of your soul, there are infinitely precious things, that may not be taken from you. And so, try so to shape your life that external things will not harm you. And try also to get rid of personal property. It involves sordid preoccupation, endless industry, continual wrong. Personal property hinders Individualism at every step.' It is to be noted that Jesus never says that impoverished people are necessarily good, or wealthy people necessarily bad. That would not have been true. Wealthy people are, as a class, better than impoverished people, more moral, more intellectual, more well-behaved. There is only one class in the community that thinks more about money than the rich, and that is the poor. The poor can think of nothing else. That is the misery of being poor. What Jesus does say is that man reaches his perfection, not through what he has, not even through what he does, but entirely through what he is. And so the wealthy young man who comes to Jesus is represented as a thoroughly good citizen, who has broken none of the laws of his state, none of the commandments of his religion. He is quite respectable, in the ordinary sense of that extraordinary word. Jesus says to him, 'You should give up private property. It hinders you from realizing your perfection. It is a drag upon you. It is a burden. Your personality does not need it. It is within you, and not outside of you, that you will find what you really are, and what you really want.' To his own friends he says the same thing. He tells them to be themselves, and not to be always worrying about other things. What do other things matter? Man is complete in himself. When they go into the world, the world will disagree with them. That is inevitable. The world hates Individualism. But that is not to trouble them. They are to be calm and self-centred. If a man takes their cloak, they are to give him their coat, just to show that material things are of no importance. If people abuse them, they are not to answer back. What does it signify? The things people say of a man do not alter a man. He is what he is. Public opinion is of no value whatsoever. Even if people employ actual violence, they are not to be violent in turn. That would be to fall to the same low level. After all, even in prison, a man can be quite free. His soul can be free. His personality can be untroubled. He can be at peace. And, above all things, they are not to interfere with other people or judge them in any way. Personality is a very mysterious thing. A man cannot always be estimated by what he does. He may keep the law, and yet be worthless. He may break the law, and yet be fine. He may be bad, without ever doing anything bad. He may commit a sin against society, and yet realize through that sin his true perfection.

There was a woman who was taken in adultery. We are not told the history of her love, but that love must have been very great; for

Jesus said that her sins were forgiven her, not because she repented, but because her love was so intense and wonderful. Later on, a short time before his death, as he sat at a feast, the woman came in and poured costly perfumes on his hair. His friends tried to interfere with her, and said that it was an extravagance, and that the money that the perfume cost should have been expended on charitable relief of people in want, or something of that kind. Jesus did not accept that view. He pointed out that the material needs of Man were great and very permanent, but that the spiritual needs of Man were greater still, and that in one divine moment, and by selecting its own mode of expression, a personality might make itself perfect. The world worships the woman, even now, as a saint.

Yes; there are suggestive things in Individualism. Socialism annihilates family life, for instance. With the abolition of private property, marriage in its present form must disappear. This is part of the programme. Individualism accepts this and makes it fine. It converts the abolition of legal restraint into a form of freedom that will help the full development of personality, and make the love of man and woman more wonderful, more beautiful, and more ennobling. Jesus knew this. He rejected the claims of family life, although they existed in his day and community in a very marked form. 'Who is my mother? Who are my brothers?' he said, when he was told that they wished to speak to him. When one of his followers asked leave to go and bury his father, 'Let the dead bury the dead,' was his terrible answer. He would allow no claim whatsoever to be made on personality.

And so he who would lead a Christlike life is he who is perfectly and absolutely himself. He may be a great poet, or a great man of science; or a young student at a University, or one who watches sheep upon a moor; or a maker of dramas, like Shakespeare, or a thinker about God, like Spinoza;[15] or a child who plays in a garden, or a fisherman who throws his nets into the sea. It does not matter what he is, as long as he realizes the perfection of the soul that is within him. All imitation in morals and in life is wrong. Through the streets of Jerusalem at the present day crawls one who is mad and carries a wooden cross on his shoulders. He is a symbol of the lives that are marred by imitation. Father Damien[16] was Christlike when he went out to live with the lepers, because in such service he realized fully what was best in him. But he was not more Christlike than Wagner,[17] when he realized his soul in music; or than Shelley, when he realized his soul in song. There is no one type for man. There are as many perfections as there are imperfect men. And while to the claims of charity a man may yield and yet be free, to the claims of conformity no man may yield and remain free at all.

Individualism, then, is what through Socialism we are to attain to. As a natural result the State must give up all idea of government. It must give it up because, as a wise man[18] once said many centuries before Christ, there is such a thing as leaving mankind alone; there is no such thing as governing mankind. All modes of government are failures. Despotism is unjust to everybody, including the despot, who was probably made for better things. Oligarchies are unjust to the many, and ochlocracies[19] are unjust to the few. High hopes were once formed of democracy; but democracy means simply the bludgeoning of the people by the people for the people.[20] It has been found out. I must say that it was high time, for all authority is quite degrading. It degrades those who exercise it, and degrades those over whom it is exercised. When it is violently, grossly and cruelly used, it produces a good effect, by creating, or at any rate bringing out, the spirit of revolt and Individualism that is to kill it. When it is used with a certain amount of kindness, and accompanied by prizes and rewards, it is dreadfully demoralizing. People, in that case, are less conscious of the horrible pressure that is being put on them, and so go through their lives in a sort of coarse comfort, like petted animals, without ever realizing that they are probably thinking other people's thoughts, living by other people's standards, wearing practically what one may call other people's second-hand clothes, and never being themselves for a single moment. 'He who would be free,' says a fine thinker,[21] 'must not conform.' And authority, by bribing people to conform, produces a very gross kind of over-fed barbarism amongst us.

With authority, punishment will pass away. This will be a great gain – a gain, in fact, of incalculable value. As one reads history, not in the expurgated editions written for schoolboys and passmen,[22] but in the original authorities of each time, one is absolutely sickened, not by the crimes that the wicked have committed, but by the punishments that the good have inflicted; and a community is infinitely more brutalized by the habitual employment of punishment, than it is by the occasional occurrence of crime. It obviously follows that the more punishment is inflicted the more crime is produced, and most modern legislation has clearly recognized this, and has made it its task to diminish punishment as far as it thinks it can. Wherever it has really diminished it, the results have always been extremely good. The less punishment, the less crime. When there is no punishment at all, crime will either cease to exist, or if it occurs, will be treated by physicians as a very distressing form of dementia, to be cured by care and kindness. For what are called criminals nowadays are not criminals at all. Starvation, and not sin, is the parent of modern crime. That indeed is the reason why our criminals are, as a class, so absolutely uninteresting from any psychological point of view. They are not marvellous Macbeths and terrible Vautrins.[23] They are merely what ordinary, respectable, commonplace people would be if they had not got enough to eat. When private property is abolished there will be no necessity for crime, no demand for it; it will cease to exist. Of course all crimes are not crimes against property, though such are the crimes that the English law, valuing what a man has more than what a man is, punishes with the harshest and most horrible severity, if we except the crime of murder, and regard death as worse than penal servitude, a point on which our criminals, I believe, disagree. But though a crime may not be against property, it may spring from the misery and rage and depression produced by our wrong system of property-holding, and so, when that system is abolished, will disappear. When each member of the community has sufficient for his wants, and is not interfered with by his neighbour, it will not be an object of any interest to him to interfere with any one else. Jealousy, which is an extraordinary source of crime in modern life, is an emotion closely bound up with our conceptions of property, and under Socialism and Individualism will die out. It is remarkable that in communistic tribes jealousy is entirely unknown.

Now as the State is not to govern, it may be asked what the State is to do. The State is to be a voluntary association that will organize labour, and be the manufacturer and distributor of necessary commodities. The State is to make what is useful. The individual is to make what is beautiful. And as I have mentioned the word labour, I cannot help saying that a great deal of nonsense is being written and talked nowadays about the dignity of manual labour. There is nothing necessarily dignified about manual labour at all, and most of it is absolutely degrading. It is mentally and morally injurious to man to do anything in which he does not find pleasure, and many forms of labour are quite pleasureless activities, and should be regarded as such. To sweep a slushy crossing for eight hours on a day when the east wind is blowing is a disgusting occupation. To sweep it with mental, moral or physical dignity seems to me to be impossible. To sweep it with joy would be appalling. Man is made for something better than disturbing dirt. All work of that kind should be done by a machine.

And I have no doubt that it will be so. Up to the present, man has been, to a certain extent, the slave of machinery, and there is something tragic in the fact that as soon as man had invented a machine to do his work he began to starve. This, however, is, of course, the result of our property system and our system of competition. One man owns a machine which does the work of five hundred men. Five hundred men are, in consequence, thrown out of employment, and having no work to do, become hungry and take to thieving. The one man secures the produce of the machine and keeps it, and has five hundred times as much as he should have, and probably, which is of much more importance, a great deal more than he really wants. Were that machine the property of all, every one would benefit by it. It would be an immense advantage to the community. All unintellectual labour, all monotonous, dull labour, all labour that deals with dreadful things, and involves unpleasant conditions, must be done by machinery. Machinery must work for us in coal mines, and do all sanitary services, and be the stoker of steamers, and clean the streets, and run messages on wet days, and do anything that is tedious or distressing. At present machinery competes against man. Under proper conditions machinery will serve man. There is no doubt at all that this is the future of machinery, and just as trees grow while the country gentleman is asleep, so while Humanity will be amusing itself, or enjoying cultivated leisure[24] – which, and not labour, is the aim of man – or making beautiful things, or reading beautiful things, or simply contemplating the world with admiration and delight, machinery will be doing all the necessary and unpleasant work. The fact is, that civilization requires slaves. The Greeks were quite right there. Unless there are slaves to do the ugly, horrible, uninteresting work, culture and contemplation become almost impossible. Human slavery is wrong, insecure and demoralizing. On mechanical slavery, on the slavery of the machine, the future of the world depends. And when scientific men are no longer called upon to go down to a depressing East-End and distribute bad cocoa and worse blankets to starving people, they will have delightful leisure in which to devise wonderful and marvellous things for their own joy and the joy of everyone else. There will be great storages of force[25] for every city, and for every house if required, and this force man will convert into heat, light or motion, according to his needs. Is this Utopian? A map of the world that does not include Utopia is not worth even glancing at, for it leaves out the one country at which Humanity is always landing. And when Humanity lands there, it looks out, and, seeing a better country, sets sail. Progress is the realization of Utopias.

Now, I have said that the community by means of organization of machinery will supply the useful things, and that the beautiful things will be made by the individual. This is not merely necessary, but it is the only possible way by which we can get either the one or the other. An individual who has to make things for the use of others, and with reference to their wants and their wishes, does not work with interest, and consequently cannot put into his work what is best in him. Upon the other hand, whenever a community or a powerful section of a community, or a government of any kind, attempts to dictate to the artist what he is to do, Art either entirely vanishes, or becomes stereotyped, or degenerates into a low and ignoble form of craft. A work of art is the unique result of a unique temperament. Its beauty comes from the fact that the author is what he is. It has nothing to do with the fact that other people want what they want. Indeed, the moment that an artist takes notice of what other people want, and tries to supply the demand, he ceases to be an artist, and becomes a dull or an amusing craftsman, an honest or a dishonest tradesman. He has no further claim to be considered as an artist. Art is the most intense mode of Individualism that the world has known. I am inclined to say that it is the only real mode of Individualism that the world has known. Crime, which, under certain conditions, may seem to have created Individualism, must take cognizance of other people and interfere with them. It belongs to the sphere of action. But alone, without any reference to his neighbours, without any interference, the artist can fashion a beautiful thing; and if he does not do it solely for his own pleasure, he is not an artist at all.

And it is to be noted that it is the fact that Art is this intense form of Individualism that makes the public try to exercise over it an authority that is as immoral as it is ridiculous, and as corrupting as it is contemptible. It is not quite their fault. The public has always, and in every age, been badly brought up. They are continually asking Art to be popular, to please their want of taste, to flatter their absurd vanity, to tell them what they have been told before, to show them what they ought to be tired of seeing, to amuse them when they feel heavy after eating too much, and to distract their thoughts when they are wearied of their own stupidity. Now Art should never try to be popular. The public should try to make itself artistic. There is a very wide difference. If a man of science were told that the results of his experiments, and the conclusions that he arrived at, should be of such a character that they would not upset the received popular notions on the subject, or disturb popular prejudice, or hurt the sensibilities of people who knew nothing about science; if a philosopher were told that he had a perfect right to speculate in the highest spheres of thought, provided that he arrived at the same conclusions as were held by those who had never thought in any sphere at all – well, nowadays the man of science and the philosopher would be considerably amused. Yet it is really a very few years since both philosophy and science were subjected to brutal popular control, to authority in fact – the authority of either the general ignorance of the community, or the terror and greed for power of an ecclesiastical or governmental class. Of course, we have to a very great extent got rid of any attempt on the part of the community, or the Church, or the Government, to interfere with the individualism of speculative thought, but the attempt to interfere with the individualism of imaginative art still lingers. In fact, it does more than linger: it is aggressive, offensive, and brutalizing.

In England, the arts that have escaped best are the arts in which the public takes no interest. Poetry is an instance of what I mean. We have been able to have fine poetry in England because the public does not read it, and consequently does not influence it. The public likes to insult poets because they are individual, but once they have insulted them they leave them alone. In the case of the novel and the drama, arts in which the public does take an interest, the result of the exercise of popular authority has been absolutely ridiculous. No country produces such badly written fiction, such tedious, common work in the novel-form, such silly, vulgar plays as in England. It must necessarily be so. The popular standard is of such a character that no artist can get to it. It is at once too easy and too difficult to be a popular novelist. It is too easy, because the requirements of the public as far as plot, style, psychology, treatment of life and treatment of literature are concerned, are within the reach of the very meanest capacity and the most uncultivated mind. It is too difficult, because to meet such requirements the artist would have to do violence to his temperament, would have to write not for the artistic joy of writing, but for the amusement of half-educated people, and so would have to suppress his individualism, forget his culture, annihilate his style, and surrender everything that is valuable in him. In the case of the drama, things are a little better: the theatre-going public likes the obvious, it is true, but it does not like the tedious; and burlesque and farcical comedy, the two most popular forms, are distinct forms of art. Delightful work may be produced under burlesque and farcical conditions, and in work of this kind the artist in England is allowed very great freedom. It is when one comes to the higher forms of the drama that the result of popular control is seen. The one thing that the public dislike is novelty. Any attempt to extend the subject-matter of art is extremely distasteful to the public; and yet the vitality and progress of art depend in a large measure on the continual extension of subject-matter. The public dislike novelty because they are afraid of it. It represents to them a mode of

Individualism, an assertion on the part of the artist that he selects his own subject, and treats it as he chooses. The public are quite right in their attitude. Art is Individualism, and Individualism is a disturbing and disintegrating force. Therein lies its immense value. For what it seeks to disturb is monotony of type, slavery of custom, tyranny of habit, and the reduction of man to the level of a machine. In Art, the public accept what has been, because they cannot alter it, not because they appreciate it. They swallow their classics whole, and never taste them. They endure them as the inevitable, and, as they cannot mar them, they mouth about them. Strangely enough, or not strangely, according to one's own views, this acceptance of the classics does a great deal of harm. The uncritical admiration of the Bible and Shakespeare in England is an instance of what I mean. With regard to the Bible, considerations of ecclesiastical authority enter into the matter, so that I need not dwell upon the point.

But in the case of Shakespeare it is quite obvious that the public really see neither the beauties nor the defects of his plays. If they saw the beauties, they would not object to the development of the drama; and if they saw the defects, they would not object to the development of the drama either. The fact is, the public makes use of the classics of a country as a means of checking the progress of Art. They degrade the classics into authorities. They use them as bludgeons for preventing the free expression of Beauty in new forms. They are always asking a writer why he does not write like somebody else, or a painter why he does not paint like somebody else, quite oblivious of the fact that if either of them did anything of the kind he would cease to be an artist. A fresh mode of Beauty is absolutely distasteful to them, and whenever it appears they get so angry and bewildered that they always use two stupid expressions – one is that the work of art is grossly unintelligible; the other, that the work of art is grossly immoral. What they mean by these words seems to me to be this. When they say a work is grossly unintelligible, they mean that the artist has said or made a beautiful thing that is new; when they describe a work as grossly immoral, they mean that the artist has said or made a beautiful thing that is true. The former expression has reference to style; the latter to subject-matter. But they probably use the words very vaguely, as an ordinary mob will use ready-made paving-stones. There is not a single real poet or prose-writer of this century, for instance, on whom the British public has not solemnly conferred diplomas of immorality,[26] and these diplomas practically take the place, with us, of what in France is the formal recognition of an Academy of Letters,[27] and fortunately make the establishment of such an institution quite unnecessary in England. Of course the public is very reckless in its use of the word. That they should have called Wordsworth an immoral poet, was only to be expected. Wordsworth was a poet. But that they should have called Charles Kingsley[28] an immoral novelist is extraordinary. Kingsley's prose was not of a very fine quality. Still, there is the word, and they use it as best they can. An artist is, of course, not disturbed by it. The true artist is a man who believes absolutely in himself, because he is absolutely himself. But I can fancy that if an artist produced a work of art in England that immediately on its appearance was recognized by the public, through its medium, which is the public press, as a work that was quite intelligible and highly moral, he would begin seriously to question whether in its creation he had really been himself at all, and consequently whether the work was not quite unworthy of him, and either of a thoroughly second-rate order, or of no artistic value whatsoever.

Perhaps, however, I have wronged the public in limiting them to such words as 'immoral', 'unintelligible', 'exotic', and 'unhealthy'. There is one other word that they use. That word is 'morbid'.[29] They do not use it often. The meaning of the word is so simple that they are afraid of using it. Still, they use it sometimes, and, now and then, one comes across it in popular newspapers. It is, of course, a ridiculous word to apply to a work of art. For what is morbidity but a mood of emotion or a mode of thought that one cannot express? The public are all morbid, because the public can never find expression for anything. The artist is never morbid. He expresses everything. He stands outside his subject, and through its medium produces incomparable and artistic effects. To call an artist morbid because he deals with morbidity as his subject-matter is as silly as if one called Shakespeare mad because he wrote *King Lear*.

On the whole, an artist in England gains something by being

attacked. His individuality is intensified. He becomes more completely himself. Of course the attacks are very gross, very impertinent, and very contemptible. But then no artist expects grace from the vulgar mind, or style from the suburban intellect. Vulgarity and stupidity are two very vivid facts in modern life. One regrets them, naturally. But there they are. They are subjects for study, like everything else. And it is only fair to state, with regard to modern journalists, that they always apologize to one in private for what they have written against one in public.

Within the last few years two other adjectives, it may be mentioned, have been added to the very limited vocabulary of art-abuse that is at the disposal of the public. One is the word 'unhealthy', the other is the word 'exotic'. The latter merely expresses the rage of the momentary mushroom against the immortal, entrancing, and exquisitely lovely orchid. It is a tribute, but a tribute of no importance. The word 'unhealthy', however, admits of analysis. It is a rather interesting word. In fact, it is so interesting that the people who use it do not know what it means.

What does it mean? What is a healthy, or an unhealthy work of art? All terms that one applies to a work of art, provided that one applies them rationally, have reference to either its style or its subject, or to both together. From the point of view of style, a healthy work of art is one whose style recognizes the beauty of the material it employs, be that material one of words or of bronze, of colour or of ivory, and uses that beauty as a factor in producing the aesthetic effect. From the point of view of subject, a healthy work of art is one the choice of whose subject is conditioned by the temperament of the artist, and comes directly out of it. In fine, a healthy work of art is one that has both perfection and personality. Of course, form and substance cannot be separated in a work of art; they are always one. But for purposes of analysis, and setting the wholeness of aesthetic impression aside for a moment, intellectually we can so separate them. An unhealthy work of art, on the other hand, is a work whose style is obvious, old-fashioned, and common, and whose subject is deliberately chosen, not because the artist has any pleasure in it, but because he thinks that the public will pay him for it. In fact, the popular novel that the public call healthy is always a thoroughly unhealthy production; and what the public call an unhealthy novel is always a beautiful and healthy work of art.

I need hardly say that I am not, for a single moment, complaining that the public and the public press misuse these words. I do not see how, with their lack of comprehension of what Art is, they could possibly use them in the proper sense. I am merely pointing out the misuse; and as for the origin of the misuse and the meaning that lies behind it all, the explanation is very simple. It comes from the barbarous conception of authority. It comes from the natural inability of a community corrupted by authority to understand or appreciate Individualism. In a word, it comes from that monstrous and ignorant thing that is called Public Opinion, which bad and well-meaning as it is when it tries to control action, is infamous and of evil meaning when it tries to control Thought or Art.

Indeed, there is much more to be said in favour of the physical force of the public than there is in favour of the public's opinion. The former may be fine. The latter must be foolish. It is often said that force is no argument. That, however, entirely depends on what one wants to prove. Many of the most important problems of the last few centuries, such as the continuance of personal government in England, or of feudalism in France, have been solved entirely by means of physical force. The very violence of a revolution may make the public grand and splendid for a moment. It was a fatal day when the public discovered that the pen is mightier than the paving-stone, and can be made as offensive as the brickbat. They at once sought for the journalist, found him, developed him, and made him their industrious and well-paid servant. It is greatly to be regretted, for both their sakes. Behind the barricade there may be much that is noble and heroic. But what is there behind the leading-article but prejudice, stupidity, cant and twaddle? And when these four are joined together they make a terrible force, and constitute the new authority.

In old days men had the rack.[30] Now they have the press. That is an improvement certainly. But still it is very bad, and wrong, and demoralizing. Somebody – was it Burke? – called journalism the fourth estate. That was true at the time, no doubt. But at the present moment it really is the only estate.[31] It has eaten up the other three. The Lords Temporal say nothing, the Lords Spiritual have nothing to say, and the House of Commons has nothing to say and says it. We are dominated by Journalism. In America the President reigns for four years, and Journalism governs for ever and ever. Fortunately in America journalism has carried its authority to the grossest and most brutal extreme. As a natural consequence it has begun to create a spirit of revolt. People are amused by it, or disgusted by it, according to their temperaments. But it is no longer the real force it was. It is not seriously treated. In England, Journalism, not, except in a few well-known instances, having been carried to such excesses of brutality, is still a great factor, a really remarkable power. The tyranny that it proposes to exercise over people's private lives seems to me to be quite extraordinary. The fact is, that the public have an insatiable curiosity to know everything, except what is worth knowing. Journalism, conscious of this, and having tradesmanlike habits, supplies their demands. In centuries before ours the public nailed the ears of journalists to the pump. That was quite hideous. In this century journalists have nailed their own ears to the keyhole. That is much worse. And what aggravates the mischief is that the journalists who are most to blame are not the amusing journalists who write for what are called Society papers. The harm is done by the serious, thoughtful, earnest journalists, who solemnly, as they are doing at present, will drag before the eyes of the public some incident in the private life of a great statesman, of a man who is a leader of political thought as he is a creator of political force, and invite the public to discuss the incident, to exercise authority in the matter, to give their views, and not merely to give their views, but to carry them into action, to dictate to the man upon all other points, to dictate to his party, to dictate to his country, in fact to make themselves ridiculous, offensive and harmful. The private lives of men and women[32] should not be told to the public. The public have nothing to do with them at all. In France they manage these things better. There they do not allow the details of the trials that take place in the divorce courts to be published for the amusement or criticism of the public. All that the public are allowed to know is that the divorce has taken place and was granted on petition of one or other or both of the married parties concerned. In France, in fact, they limit the journalist, and allow the artist almost perfect freedom. Here we allow absolute freedom to the journalist, and entirely limit the artist. English public opinion, that is to say, tries to constrain and impede and warp the man who makes things that are beautiful in effect, and compels the journalist to retail things that are ugly, or disgusting, or revolting in fact, so that we have the most serious journalists in the world and the most indecent newspapers. It is no exaggeration to talk of compulsion. There are possibly some journalists who take a real pleasure in publishing horrible things, or who, being poor, look to scandals as forming a sort of permanent basis for an income. But there are other journalists, I feel certain, men of education and cultivation, who really dislike publishing these things, who know that it is wrong to do so, and only do it because the unhealthy conditions under which their occupation is carried on oblige them to supply the public with what the public wants, and to compete with other journalists in making that supply as full and satisfying to the gross popular appetite as possible. It is a very degrading position for any body of educated men to be placed in, and I have no doubt that most of them feel it acutely.

However, let us leave what is really a very sordid side of the subject, and return to the question of popular control in the matter of Art, by which I mean Public Opinion dictating to the artist the form which he is to use, the mode in which he is to use it, and the materials with which he is to work. I have pointed out that the arts which have escaped best in England are the arts in which the public have not been interested. They are, however, interested in the drama, and as a certain advance has been made in the drama within the last ten or fifteen years, it is important to point out that this advance is entirely due to a few individual artists refusing to accept the popular want of taste as their standard, and refusing to regard Art as a mere matter of demand and supply. With his marvellous and vivid personality, with a style that has really a true colour-element in it, with his extraordinary power, not over mere mimicry but over imaginative and intellectual creation, Mr Irving,[33] had his sole object been to give the public what it wanted, could have produced the commonest plays in the commonest manner, and made as much success and money as a man could possibly desire. But his object was not that. His object was to realize his own perfection as an artist, under certain conditions, and in certain forms of Art. At first he appealed to the few: now he has educated the many. He has created in the public both taste and temperament. The public appreciate his artistic success immensely. I often wonder, however, whether the public understand that that success is entirely due to the fact that he did not accept their standard, but realized his own. With their standard the Lyceum would have been a sort of second-rate booth, as some of the popular theatres in London are at present. Whether they understand it or not the fact however remains, that taste and temperament have, to a certain extent, been created in the public, and that the public is capable of developing these qualities. The problem then is, why do not the public become more civilized? They have the capacity. What stops them?

The thing that stops them, it must be said again, is their desire to exercise authority over the artist and over works of art. To certain theatres, such as the Lyceum and the Haymarket,[34] the public seem to come in a proper mood. In both of these theatres there have been individual artists, who have succeeded in creating in their audiences – and every theatre in London has its own audience – the temperament to which Art appeals. And what is that temperament? It is the temperament of receptivity. That is all.

If a man approaches a work of art with any desire to exercise authority over it and the artist, he approaches it in such a spirit that he cannot receive any artistic impression from it at all. The work of art is to dominate the spectator: the spectator is not to dominate the work of art. The spectator is to be receptive. He is to be the violin on which the master is to play. And the more completely he can suppress his own silly views, his own foolish prejudices, his own absurd ideas of what Art should be or should not be, the more likely he is to understand and appreciate the work of art in question. This is, of course, quite obvious in the case of the vulgar theatre-going public of English men and women. But it is equally true of what are called educated people. For an educated person's ideas of Art are drawn naturally from what Art has been, whereas the new work of art is beautiful by being what

Art has never been; and to measure it by the standard of the past is to measure it by a standard on the rejection of which its real perfection depends. A temperament capable of receiving, through an imaginative medium, and under imaginative conditions, new and beautiful impressions is the only temperament that can appreciate a work of art. And true as this is in the case of the appreciation of sculpture and painting, it is still more true of the appreciation of such arts as the drama. For a picture and a statue are not at war with Time. They take no count of its succession. In one moment their unity may be apprehended. In the case of literature it is different. Time must be traversed before the unity of effect is realized. And so, in the drama, there may occur in the first act of the play something whose real artistic value may not be evident to the spectator till the third or fourth act is reached. Is the silly fellow to get angry and call out, and disturb the play, and annoy the artists? No. The honest man is to sit quietly, and know the delightful emotions of wonder, curiosity and suspense. He is not to go to the play to lose a vulgar temper. He is to go to the play to realize an artistic temperament. He is to go to the play to gain an artistic temperament. He is not the arbiter of the work of art. He is one who is admitted to contemplate the work of art, and, if the work be fine, to forget in its contemplation all the egotism that mars him – the egotism of his ignorance, or the egotism of his information. This point about the drama is hardly, I think, sufficiently recognized. I can quite understand that were *Macbeth* produced for the first time before a modern London audience, many of the people present would strongly and vigorously object to the introduction of the witches in the first act, with their grotesque phrases and their ridiculous words. But when the play is over one realizes that the laughter of the witches in *Macbeth* is as terrible as the laughter of madness in *Lear*, more terrible than the laughter of Iago in the tragedy of the Moor. No spectator of art needs a more perfect mood of receptivity than the spectator of a play. The moment he seeks to exercise authority he becomes the avowed enemy of Art and of himself. Art does not mind. It is he who suffers.

With the novel it is the same thing. Popular authority and the recognition of popular authority are fatal. Thackeray's *Esmond*[35] is a beautiful work of art because he wrote it to please himself. In his other novels, in *Pendennis*, in *Philip*, in *Vanity Fair* even, at times, he is too conscious of the public, and spoils his work by appealing directly to the sympathies of the public, or by directly mocking at them. A true artist takes no notice whatever of the public. The public are to him non-existent. He has no poppied or honeyed cakes through which to give the monster sleep or sustenance. He leaves that to the popular novelist. One incomparable novelist we have now in England, Mr George Meredith.[36] There are better artists in France, but France has no one whose view of life is so large, so varied, so imaginatively true. There are tellers of stories in Russia who have a more vivid sense of what pain in fiction may be. But to him belongs philosophy in fiction. His people not merely live, but they live in thought. One can see them from myriad points of view. They are suggestive. There is soul in them and around them. They are interpretative and symbolic. And he who made them, those wonderful quickly-moving figures, made them for his own pleasure, and has never asked the public what they wanted, has never cared to know what they wanted, has never allowed the public to dictate to him or influence him in any way, but has gone on intensifying his own personality, and producing his own individual work. At first none came to him. That did not matter. Then the few came to him. That did not change him. The many have come now. He is still the same. He is an incomparable novelist.

With the decorative arts it is not different. The public clung with really pathetic tenacity to what I believe were the direct traditions of the Great Exhibition[37] of international vulgarity, traditions that were so appalling that the houses in which people lived were only fit for blind people to live in. Beautiful things began to be made, beautiful colours came from the dyer's hand, beautiful patterns from the artist's brain, and the use of beautiful things and their value and importance were set forth. The public were really very indignant. They lost their temper. They said silly things. No one minded. No one was a whit the worse. No one accepted the authority of public opinion. And now it is almost impossible to enter any modern house without seeing some recognition of good taste. some recognition of the value of lovely surroundings, some sign of appreciation of beauty. In fact, people's houses are, as a rule, quite charming nowadays. People have been to a very great extent civilized. It is only fair to state, however, that the extraordinary success of the revolution in house-decoration[38] and furniture and the like has not really been due to the majority of the public developing a very fine taste in such matters. It has been chiefly due to the fact that the craftsmen of things so appreciated the pleasure of making what was beautiful, and woke to such a vivid consciousness of the hideousness and vulgarity of what the public had previously wanted, that they simply starved the public out. It would be quite impossible at the present moment to furnish a room as rooms were furnished a few years ago, without going for everything to an auction of second-hand furniture from some third-rate lodging-house. The things are no longer made. However they may object to it, people must nowadays have something charming in their surroundings. Fortunately for them, their assumption of authority in these art-matters came to entire grief.

It is evident, then, that all authority in such things is bad. People sometimes inquire what form of government is most suitable for an artist to live under. To this question there is only one answer. The form of government that is most suitable to the artist is no government at all. Authority over him and his art is ridiculous. It has been stated that under despotisms artists have produced lovely work. This is not quite so. Artists have visited despots, not as subjects to be tyrannized over, but as wandering wonder-makers, as fascinating vagrant personalities, to be entertained and charmed and suffered to be at peace, and allowed to create. There is this to be said in favour of the despot, that he, being an individual, may have culture, while the mob, being a monster, has none. One who is an Emperor and King may stoop down to pick up a brush for a painter, but when the democracy stoops down it is merely to throw mud. And yet the democracy have not so far to stoop as the emperor. In fact, when they want to throw mud they have not to stoop at all. But there is no necessity to separate the monarch from the mob; all authority is equally bad.

There are three kinds of despots. There is the despot who tyrannizes over the body. There is the despot who tyrannizes over the soul. There is the despot who tyrannizes over soul and body alike. The first is called the Prince. The second is called the Pope. The third is called the People. The Prince may be cultivated. Many Princes have been. Yet in the Prince there is danger. One thinks of Dante at the bitter feast in Verona,[39] of Tasso in Ferrara's madman's cell.[40] It is better for the artist not to live with Princes. The Pope may be cultivated. Many Popes have been; the bad Popes have been. The bad Popes loved Beauty, almost as passionately, nay, with as much passion as the good Popes hated Thought. To the wickedness of the Papacy humanity owes much. The goodness of the Papacy owes a terrible debt to humanity. Yet, though the Vatican has kept the rhetoric of its thunders and lost the rod of its lightning, it is better for the artist not to live with Popes. It was a Pope who said of Cellini[41] to a conclave of Cardinals that common laws and common authority were not made for men such as he; but it was a Pope who thrust Cellini into prison, and kept him there till he sickened with rage, and created unreal visions for himself, and saw the gilded sun enter his room, and grew so enamoured of it that he sought to escape, and crept out from tower to tower, and falling through dizzy air at dawn, maimed himself, and was by a vine-dresser covered with vine leaves, and carried in a cart to one who, loving beautiful things, had care of him. There is danger in Popes. And as for the People, what of them and their authority? Perhaps of them and their authority one has spoken enough. Their authority is a thing blind, deaf, hideous, grotesque, tragic, amusing, serious and obscene. It is impossible for the artist to live with the People. All despots bribe. The People bribe and brutalize. Who told them to exercise authority? They were made to live, to listen, and to love. They have marred themselves by imitation of their inferiors. They have taken the sceptre of the Prince. How should they use it? They have taken the triple tiara of the Pope. How should they carry its burden? They are as a clown whose heart is broken. They are as a priest whose soul is not yet born. Let all who love Beauty pity them. Though they themselves love not Beauty, yet let them pity themselves. Who taught them the trick of tyranny?

There are many other things that one might point out. One might point out how the Renaissance was great, because it sought to solve no social problem, and busied itself not about such things, but suffered the individual to develop freely, beautifully and naturally, and so had great and individual artists, and great and individual men. One might point out how Louis XIV,[42] by creating the modern state, destroyed the individualism of the artist, and made things monstrous in their monotony of repetition, and contemptible in their conformity to rule, and destroyed throughout all France all those fine freedoms of expression that had made tradition new in beauty, and new modes one with antique form. But the past is of no importance. The present is of no importance. It is with the future that we have to deal. For the past is what man should not have been. The present is what man ought not to be. The future is what artists are.

It will, of course, be said that such a scheme as is set forth here is quite unpractical, and goes against human nature. This is perfectly true. It is unpractical, and it goes against human nature. This is why it is worth carrying out, and that is why one proposes it. For what is a practical scheme? A practical scheme is either a scheme that is already in existence, or a scheme that could be carried out under existing conditions. But it is exactly the existing conditions that one objects to; and any scheme that could accept these conditions is wrong and foolish. The conditions will be done away with, and human nature will change. The only thing that one really knows about human nature is that it changes. Change is the one quality we can predicate of it. The systems that fail are those that rely on the permanency of human nature, and not on its growth and development. The error of Louis XIV was that he thought human nature would always be the same. The result of his error was the French Revolution. It was an admirable result. All the results of the mistakes of governments are quite admirable.

It is to be noted also that Individualism does not come to man with any sickly cant about duty, which merely means doing what other people want because they want it; or any hideous cant about self-sacrifice, which is merely a survival of savage mutilation. In fact, it does not come to man with any claims upon him at all. It comes naturally and inevitably out of man. It is the point to which all development tends. It is the differentiation[43] to which all organisms grow. It is the perfection that is inherent in every mode of life, and towards which every mode of life quickens. And so Individualism exercises no compulsion over man. On the contrary, it says to man that he should suffer no compulsion to be exercised over him. It does not try to force people to be good. It knows that people are good when they are let alone. Man will develop Individualism out of himself. Man is now so developing Individualism. To ask whether Individualism is practical is like asking whether Evolution is practical. Evolution is the law of life, and there is no evolution except towards Individualism. Where this tendency is not expressed, it is a case of artificially arrested growth, or of disease, or of death.

Individualism will also be unselfish and unaffected. It has been pointed out that one of the results of the extraordinary tyranny of authority is that words are absolutely distorted from their proper and simple meaning, and are used to express the obverse of their right signification. What is true about Art is true about Life. A man is called affected, nowadays, if he dresses as he likes to dress. But in doing that he is acting in a perfectly natural manner. Affectation, in such matters, consists in dressing according to the views of one's neighbour, whose views, as they are the views of the majority, will probably be extremely stupid. Or a man is called selfish if he lives in a manner that seems to him most suitable for the full realization of his own personality; if, in fact, the primary aim of his life is self-development. But this is the way in which every one should live. Selfishness is not living as one wishes to live, it is asking others to live as one wishes to live. And unselfishness is letting other people's lives alone, not interfering with them. Selfishness always aims at creating around it an absolute uniformity of type. Unselfishness recognizes infinite variety of type as a delightful thing, accepts it, acquiesces in it, enjoys it. It is not selfish to think for oneself. A man who does not think for himself does not think at all. It is grossly selfish to require of one's neighbour that he should think in the same way, and hold the same opinions. Why should he? If he can think, he will probably think differently. If he cannot think, it is monstrous to require thought of any kind from him. A red rose is not selfish because it wants to be a red rose. It would be horribly selfish if it wanted all the other flowers in the garden to be both red and roses. Under Individualism people will be quite natural and absolutely unselfish, and will know the meanings of the words, and realize them in their free, beautiful lives. Nor will men be egotistic as they are now. For the egotist is he who makes claims upon others, and the Individualist will not desire to do that. It will not give him pleasure. When man has realized Individualism, he will also realize sympathy and exercise it freely and spontaneously. Up to the present man has hardly cultivated sympathy at all. He has merely sympathy with pain, and sympathy with pain is not the highest form of sympathy. All sympathy is fine, but sympathy with suffering is the least fine mode. It is tainted with egotism. It is apt to become morbid. There is in it a certain element of terror for our own safety. We become afraid that we ourselves might be as the leper or as the blind, and that no man would have care of us. It is curiously limiting, too. One should sympathize with the entirety of life, not with life's sores and maladies merely, but with life's joy and beauty and energy and health and freedom. The wider sympathy is, of course, the more difficult. It requires more unselfishness. Anybody can sympathize with the sufferings of a friend, but it requires a very fine nature – it requires, in fact, the nature of a true Individualist – to sympathize with a friend's success. In the modern stress of competition and struggle for place, such sympathy is naturally rare, and is also very much stifled by the immoral ideal of uniformity of type and conformity to rule which is so prevalent everywhere, and is perhaps most obnoxious in England.

Sympathy with pain there will, of course, always be. It is one of the first instincts of man. The animals which are individual, the higher animals that is to say, share it with us. But it must be remembered that while sympathy with joy intensifies the sum of joy in the world, sympathy with pain does not really diminish the amount of pain. It may make man better able to endure evil, but the evil remains. Sympathy with consumption does not cure consumption; that is what Science does. And when Socialism has solved the problem of disease, the area of the sentimentalists will be lessened, and the sympathy of man will be large, healthy, and spontaneous. Man will have joy in the contemplation of the joyous lives of others.

For it is through joy that the Individualism of the future will develop itself. Christ made no attempt to reconstruct society, and consequently the Individualism that he preached to man could be realized only through pain or in solitude. The ideals that we owe to Christ are the ideals of the man who abandons society entirely, or of the man who resists society absolutely. But man is naturally social. Even the Thebaid[44] became peopled at last. And though the cenobite[45] realizes his personality, it is often an impoverished personality that he so realizes. Upon the other hand, the terrible truth that pain is a mode through which man may realize himself exercised a wonderful fascination over the world. Shallow speakers and shallow thinkers in pulpits and on platforms often talk about the world's worship of pleasure, and whine against it. But it is rarely in the world's history that its ideal has been one of joy and beauty. The worship of pain has far more often dominated the world. Medievalism, with its saints and martyrs, its love of self-torture, its wild passion for wounding itself, its gashing with knives and its whipping with rods – Medievalism is real Christianity, and the medieval Christ is the real Christ. When the Renaissance dawned upon the world, and brought with it the new ideals of the beauty of life and the joy of living, men could not understand Christ. Even Art shows us that. The painters of the Renaissance drew Christ as a little boy playing with another boy in a palace or a garden, or lying back in his mother's arms, smiling at her, or at a flower, or at a bright bird; or as a noble stately figure moving nobly through the world; or as a wonderful figure rising in a sort of ecstasy from death to life. Even when they drew him crucified they drew him as a beautiful God on whom evil men had inflicted suffering. But he did not preoccupy them much. What delighted them was to paint the men and women whom they admired, and to show the loveliness of this lovely earth. They painted many religious pictures – in fact, they painted far too many, and the monotony of type and motive is wearisome, and was bad for art. It was the result of the authority of the public in art-matters, and is to be deplored. But their soul was not in the subject. Raphael was a great artist when he painted his portrait of the Pope. When he painted his Madonnas and infant Christs, he is not a great artist at all. Christ had no message for the Renaissance, which was wonderful because it brought an ideal at variance with his, and to find the presentation of the real Christ we must go to medieval art. There, he is one maimed and marred; one who is not comely to look on, because Beauty is a joy; one who is not in fair raiment, because that may be a joy also: he is a beggar who has a marvellous soul; he is a leper whose soul is divine; he needs neither property nor health; he is a God realizing his perfection through pain.

The evolution of man is slow. The injustice of men is great. It was necessary that pain should be put forward as a mode of self-realization. Even now, in some places in the world, the message of Christ is necessary. No one who lived in modern Russia could possibly realize his perfection except by pain. A few Russian artists[46] have realized themselves in Art, in a fiction that is medieval in character, because its dominant note is the realization of men through suffering. But for those who are not artists, and to whom there is no mode of life but the actual life of fact, pain is the only door to perfection. A Russian who lives happily under the present system of government in Russia must either believe that man has no soul, or that, if he has, it is not worth developing. A Nihilist[47] who rejects all authority, because he knows authority to be evil, and who welcomes all pain, because through that he realizes his personality, is a real Christian. To him the Christian ideal is a true thing.

And yet, Christ did not revolt against authority. He accepted the imperial authority of the Roman Empire and paid tribute. He endured the ecclesiastical authority of the Jewish Church, and would not repel its violence by any violence of his own. He had, as I said before, no scheme for the reconstruction of society. But the modern world has schemes. It proposes to do away with poverty and the suffering that it entails. It desires to get rid of pain and the suffering that pain entails. It trusts to Socialism and to Science as its methods. What it aims at is an Individualism expressing itself through joy. This Individualism will be larger, fuller, lovelier than any Individualism has ever been. Pain is not the ultimate mode of perfection. It is merely provisional and a protest. It has reference to wrong, unhealthy, unjust surroundings. When the wrong, and the disease and the injustice are removed, it will have no further place. It will have done its work. It was a great work, but it is almost over. Its sphere lessens every day.

Nor will man miss it. For what man has sought for is, indeed, neither pain nor pleasure, but simply Life. Man has sought to live intensely, fully, perfectly. When he can do so without exercising restraint on others, or suffering it ever, and his activities are all pleasurable to him, he will be saner, healthier, more civilized, more himself. Pleasure is Nature's test, her sign of approval. When man is happy, he is in harmony with himself and his environment. The new Individualism, for whose service Socialism, whether it wills it or not, is working, will be perfect harmony. It will be what the Greeks sought for, but could not, except in Thought, realize completely, because they had slaves, and fed them; it will be what the Renaissance sought for, but could not realize completely, except in Art, because they had slaves, and starved them. It will be complete, and through it each man will attain to his perfection. The new Individualism is the new Hellenism.[48]

Intentions
(1891)

1. The Decay of Lying
An observation

A dialogue.

Persons: *Cyril and Vivian.*

Scene: *the library of a country house in Nottinghamshire.*

CYRIL (*coming in through the open window from the terrace*): My dear Vivian, don't coop yourself up all day in the library. It is a perfectly lovely afternoon. The air is exquisite. There is a mist upon the woods, like the purple bloom upon a plum. Let us go and lie on the grass and smoke cigarettes and enjoy Nature.

VIVIAN: Enjoy Nature! I am glad to say that I have entirely lost that faculty. People tell us that Art makes us love Nature more than we loved her before; that it reveals her secrets to us; and that after a careful study of Corot and Constable we see things in her that had escaped our observation. My own experience is that the more we study Art, the less we care for Nature. What Art really reveals to us is Nature's lack of design, her curious crudities, her extraordinary monotony, her absolutely unfinished condition. Nature has good intentions, of course, but, as Aristotle once said, she cannot carry them out. When I look at a landscape I cannot help seeing all its defects. It is fortunate for us, however, that Nature is so imperfect, as otherwise we should have had no art at all. Art is our spirited protest, our gallant attempt to teach Nature her proper place. As for the infinite variety of Nature, that is a pure myth. It is not to be found in Nature herself. It resides in the imagination, or fancy, or cultivated blindness of the man who looks at her.

CYRIL: Well, you need not look at the landscape. You can lie on the grass and smoke and talk.

VIVIAN: But Nature is so uncomfortable. Grass is hard and lumpy and damp, and full of dreadful black insects. Why, even Morris's poorest workman[1] could make you a more comfortable seat than the whole of Nature can. Nature pales before the furniture of 'the street which from Oxford has borrowed its name',[2] as the poet you love so much once vilely phrased it. I don't complain. If Nature had been comfortable, mankind would never have invented architecture, and I prefer houses to the open air. In a house we all feel of the proper proportions. Everything is subordinated to us, fashioned for our use and our pleasure. Egotism itself, which is so necessary to a proper sense of human dignity, is entirely the result of indoor life. Out of doors one becomes abstract and impersonal. One's individuality absolutely leaves one. And then Nature is so indifferent, so unappreciative. Whenever I am walking in the park here, I always feel that I am no more to her than the cattle that browse on the slope, or the burdock[3] that blooms in the ditch. Nothing is more evident than that Nature hates Mind. Thinking is the most unhealthy thing in the world, and people die of it just as they die of any other disease. Fortunately, in England at any rate, thought is not catching. Our splendid physique as a people is entirely due to our national stupidity. I only hope we shall be able to keep this great historic bulwark of our happiness for many years to come; but I am afraid that we are beginning to be over-educated; at least everybody who is incapable of learning has taken to teaching – that is really what our enthusiasm for education has come to. In the meantime, you had better go back to your wearisome uncomfortable Nature, and leave me to correct my proofs.

CYRIL: Writing an article! That is not very consistent after what you have just said.

VIVIAN: Who wants to be consistent? The dullard and the doctrinaire, the tedious people who carry out their principles to the bitter end of action, to the *reductio ad absurdum* of practice. Not I. Like Emerson, I write over the door of my library the word 'Whim'.[4] Besides, my article is really a most salutary and valuable warning. If it is attended to, there may be a new Renaissance of Art.

CYRIL: What is the subject?

VIVIAN: I intend to call it 'The Decay of Lying: A Protest'.

CYRIL: Lying! I should have thought that our politicians kept up that habit.

VIVIAN: I assure you that they do not. They never rise beyond the level of misrepresentation, and actually condescend to prove, to discuss, to argue. How different from the temper of the true liar, with his frank, fearless statements, his superb irresponsibility, his healthy, natural disdain of proof of any kind! After all, what is a fine lie? Simply that which is its own evidence. If a man is sufficiently unimaginative to produce evidence in support of a lie, he might just as well speak the truth at once. No, the politicians won't do. Something may, perhaps, be urged on behalf of the Bar. The mantle of the Sophist[5] has fallen on its members. Their feigned ardours and unreal rhetoric are delightful. They can make the worse appear the better cause, as though they were fresh from Leontine schools,[6] and have been known to wrest from reluctant juries triumphant verdicts of acquittal for their clients, even when those clients, as often happens, were clearly and unmistakably innocent. But they are briefed by the prosaic, and are not ashamed to appeal to precedent. In spite of their endeavours, the truth will out. Newspapers, even, have degenerated. They may now be absolutely relied upon. One feels it as one wades through their columns. It is always the unreadable that occurs. I am afraid that there is not much to be said in favour of either the lawyer or the journalist. Besides, what I am pleading for is Lying in art. Shall I read you what I have written? It might do you a great deal of good.

CYRIL: Certainly, if you give me a cigarette. Thanks. By the way, what magazine do you intend it for?

VIVIAN: For the *Retrospective Review*. I think I told you that the elect had revived it.

CYRIL: Whom do you mean by 'the elect'?

VIVIAN: Oh, The Tired Hedonists,[7] of course. It is a club to which I belong. We are supposed to wear faded roses in our button-holes when we meet, and to have a sort of cult for Domitian.[8] I am afraid you are not eligible. You are too fond of simple pleasures.

CYRIL: I should be black-balled on the ground of animal spirits, I suppose?

VIVIAN: Probably. Besides, you are a little too old. We don't admit anybody who is of the usual age.

CYRIL: Well, I should fancy you are all a good deal bored with each other.

VIVIAN: We are. That is one of the objects of the club. Now, if you promise not to interrupt too often, I will read you my article.

CYRIL: You will find me all attention.

VIVIAN (*reading in a very clear, musical voice*): 'THE DECAY OF LYING: A PROTEST. – One of the chief causes that can be assigned for the curiously commonplace character of most of the literature of our age is undoubtedly the decay of Lying as an art, a science and a social pleasure. The ancient historians gave us delightful fiction in the form of fact; the modern novelist presents us with dull facts under the guise of fiction. The Blue-Book[9] is rapidly becoming his ideal both for method and manner. He has his tedious *document humain*, his miserable little *coin de la création*,[10] into which he peers with his microscope. He is to be found at the Librairie Nationale, or at the British Museum, shamelessly reading up his subject. He has not even the courage of other people's ideas, but insists on going directly to life for everything, and ultimately, between encyclopaedias and personal experience, he comes to the ground, having drawn his types from the family circle or from the weekly washerwoman, and having acquired an amount of useful information from which never, even in his most meditative moments, can he thoroughly free himself.

'The loss that results to literature in general from this false ideal of our time can hardly be overestimated. People have a careless way of talking about a "born liar", just as they talk about a "born poet". But in both cases they are wrong. Lying and poetry are arts – arts, as Plato saw, not unconnected with each other – and they require the most careful study, the most disinterested devotion. Indeed, they have their technique, just as the more material arts of painting and sculpture have, their subtle secrets of form and colour, their craft-mysteries, their deliberate artistic methods. As one knows the poet by his fine music, so one can recognize the liar by his rich rhythmic utterance, and in neither case will the casual inspiration of the moment suffice. Here, as elsewhere, practice must precede perfection. But in modern days while the fashion of writing poetry has become far too common, and should, if possible, be discouraged, the fashion of lying has almost fallen into disrepute. Many a young man starts in life with a natural gift for exaggeration which, if nurtured in congenial and sympathetic surroundings, or by the imitation of the best models, might grow into something really great and wonderful. But, as a rule, he comes to nothing. He either falls into careless habits of accuracy –'

CYRIL: My dear fellow!

VIVIAN: Please don't interrupt in the middle of a sentence. 'He either falls into careless habits of accuracy, or takes to frequenting the society of the aged and the well-informed. Both things are equally fatal to his imagination, as indeed they would be fatal to the imagination of anybody, and in a short time he develops a morbid and unhealthy faculty of truth-telling, begins to verify all statements made in his presence, has no hesitation in contradicting people who are much younger than himself, and often ends by writing novels which are so lifelike that no one can possibly believe in their probability. This is no isolated instance that we are giving. It is simply one example out of many; and if something cannot be done to check, or at least to modify our monstrous worship of facts, Art will become sterile, and beauty will pass away from the land.

'Even Mr Robert Louis Stevenson,[11] that delightful master of delicate and fanciful prose, is tainted with this modern vice, for we know positively no other name for it. There is such a thing as robbing a story of its reality by trying to make it too true, and *The Black Arrow* is so inartistic as not to contain a single anachronism to boast of, while the transformation of Dr Jekyll reads dangerously like an experiment out of the *Lancet*.[12] As for Mr Rider Haggard,[13] who really has, or had once, the makings of a perfectly magnificent liar, he is now so afraid of being suspected of genius that when he does tell us anything marvellous, he feels bound to invent a personal reminiscence, and to put it into a footnote as a kind of cowardly corroboration. Nor are our other novelists much better. Mr Henry James[14] writes fiction as if it were a painful duty, and wastes upon mean motives and imperceptible "points of view" his neat literary style, his felicitous phrases, his swift and caustic satire. Mr Hall Caine,[15] it is true, aims at the grandiose, but then he writes at the top of his voice. He is so loud that one cannot hear what he says. Mr James Payn[16] is an adept in the art of concealing what is not worth finding. He hunts down the obvious with the enthusiasm of a short-sighted detective. As one turns over the pages, the suspense of the author becomes almost unbearable. The horses of Mr William Black's[17] phaeton do not soar towards the sun. They merely frighten the sky at evening into violent chromolithographic effects. On seeing them approach, the peasants take refuge in dialect. Mrs Oliphant[18] prattles pleasantly about curates, lawn-tennis parties, domesticity, and other wearisome things. Mr Marion Crawford[19] has immolated himself upon the altar of local colour. He is like the lady in the French comedy who keeps talking about *le beau ciel d'Italie*. Besides, he has fallen into the bad habit of uttering moral platitudes. He is always telling us that to be good is to be good, and that to be bad is to be wicked. At times he is almost edifying. *Robert Elsmere*[20] is of course a masterpiece – a masterpiece of the *genre ennuyeux*, the one form of literature that the English people seems thoroughly to enjoy. A thoughtful young friend of ours once told us that it reminded him of the sort of conversation that goes on at a meat tea in the house of a serious Nonconformist family, and we can quite believe it. Indeed it is only in England that such a book could be produced. England is the home of lost ideas. As for that great and daily increasing school of novelists for whom the sun always rises in the East-End,[21] the only thing that can be said about them is that they find life crude, and leave it raw.

'In France, though nothing so deliberately tedious as *Robert Elsmere* has been produced, things are not much better. M. Guy de Maupassant,[22] with his keen mordant irony and his hard vivid style, strips life of the few poor rags that still cover her, and shows us foul sore and festering wound. He writes lurid little tragedies in which everybody is ridiculous; bitter comedies at which one cannot laugh for very tears. M. Zola,[23] true to the lofty principle that he lays down in one of his pronunciamentos on literature, "L'homme de génie n'a jamais d'esprit," is determined to show that, if he has not got genius, he can at least be dull. And how well he succeeds! He is not without power. Indeed at times, as in *Germinal*, there is something almost epic in his work. But his work is entirely wrong from beginning to end, and wrong not on the ground of morals, but on the ground of art. From any ethical standpoint it is just what it should be. The author is perfectly truthful, and describes things exactly as they happen. What more can any moralist desire? We have no sympathy at all with the moral indignation of our time against M. Zola. It is simply the indignation of Tartuffe[24] on being exposed. But from the standpoint of art, what can be said in favour of the author of *L'Assommoir, Nana* and *Pot-Bouille*? Nothing. Mr Ruskin once described the characters in George Eliot's novels as being like the sweepings of a Pentonville omnibus,[25] but M. Zola's characters are much worse. They have their dreary vices, and their drearier virtues. The record of their lives is absolutely without interest. Who cares what happens to them? In literature we require distinction, charm, beauty and imaginative power. We don't want to be harrowed and disgusted with an account of the doings of the lower orders. M. Daudet[26] is better. He has wit, a light touch and an amusing style. But he has lately committed literary suicide. Nobody can possibly care for Delobelle with his "Il faut lutter pour l'art", or for Valmajour with his eternal refrain about the nightingale, or for the poet in *Jack* with his *mots cruels*, now that we have learned from *Vingt Ans de ma Vie littéraire* that these characters were taken directly from life. To us they seem to have suddenly lost all their vitality, all the few qualities they ever possessed. The only real people are the people who never existed, and if a novelist is base enough to go to life for his personages he should at least pretend that they are creations, and not boast of them as copies. The justification of a character in a novel is not that other persons are what they are, but that the author is what he is. Otherwise the novel is not a work of art. As for M. Paul Bourget,[27] the master of the *roman psychologique*, he commits the error of imagining that the men and women of modern life are capable of being infinitely analysed for an innumerable series of chapters. In point of fact what is interesting about people in good society – and M. Bourget rarely moves out of the Faubourg St Germain,[28] except to come to London – is the mask that each one of them wears, not the reality that lies behind the mask. It is a humiliating confession, but we are all of us made out of the same stuff. In Falstaff there is something of Hamlet, in Hamlet there is not a little of Falstaff. The fat knight has his moods of melancholy, and the young prince his moments of coarse humour. Where we differ from each other is purely in accidentals: in dress, manner, tone of voice, religious opinions, personal appearance, tricks of habit and the like. The more one analyses people, the more all reasons for analysis disappear. Sooner or later one comes to that dreadful universal thing called human nature. Indeed, as any one who has ever worked among the poor knows only too well, the brotherhood of man is no mere poet's dream, it is a most depressing and humiliating reality; and if a writer insists upon analysing the upper classes, he might just as well write of match-girls and costermongers at once.' However, my dear Cyril, I will not detain you any further just here. I quite admit that modern novels have many good points. All I insist on is that, as a class, they are quite unreadable.

CYRIL: That is certainly a very grave qualification, but I must say that I think you are rather unfair in some of your strictures. I like *The Deemster*, and *The Daughter of Heth*, and *Le Disciple*, and *Mr Isaacs*, and as for *Robert Elsmere*, I am quite devoted to it. Not that I can look upon it as a serious work. As a statement of the problems that confront the earnest Christian it is ridiculous and antiquated. It is simply Arnold's *Literature and Dogma*[29] with the literature left out. It is as much behind the age as Paley's *Evidences*,[30] or Colenso's method of Biblical exegesis.[31] Nor could anything be less impressive than the unfortunate hero gravely heralding a dawn that rose long ago, and so completely missing its true significance that he proposes to carry on the business of the old firm under the new name. On the other hand, it contains several clever caricatures, and a heap of delightful quotations, and Green's philosophy[32] very pleasantly sugars the somewhat bitter pill of the author's fiction. I also cannot help expressing my surprise that you have said nothing about two novelists whom you are always reading, Balzac[33] and George Meredith.[34] Surely they are realists, both of them?

VIVIAN: Ah! Meredith! Who can define him? His style is chaos illumined by flashes of lightning. As a writer he has mastered everything except language: as a novelist he can do everything, except tell a story: as an artist he is everything, except articulate. Somebody in Shakespeare – Touchstone, I think – talks about a man who is always breaking his shins over his own wit, and it seems to me that this might serve as the basis for a criticism of Meredith's method. But whatever he is, he is not a realist. Or rather I would say that he is a child of realism who is not on speaking terms with his father. By deliberate choice he has made himself a romanticist. He has refused to bow the knee to Baal,[35] and after all, even if the man's fine spirit did not revolt against the noisy assertions of realism, his style would be quite sufficient of itself to keep life at a respectful distance. By its means he has planted round his garden a hedge full of thorns, and red with wonderful roses. As for Balzac, he was a most remarkable combination of the artistic temperament with the scientific spirit. The latter he bequeathed to his disciples. The former was entirely his own. The difference between such a book as M. Zola's *L'Assommoir* and Balzac's *Illusions Perdues* is the difference between unimaginative realism and imaginative reality. 'All Balzac's characters,' said Baudelaire, 'are gifted with the same ardour of life that animated himself. All his fictions are as deeply coloured as dreams. Each mind is a weapon loaded to the muzzle with will. The very scullions have genius.' A steady course of Balzac reduces our living friends to shadows, and our acquaintances to the shadows of shades. His characters have a kind of fervent fiery-coloured existence. They dominate us, and defy scepticism. One of the greatest tragedies of my life is the death of Lucien de Rubempré.[36] It is a grief from which I have never been able completely to rid myself. It haunts me in my moments of pleasure. I remember it when I laugh. But Balzac is no more a realist than Holbein[37] was. He created life, he did not copy it. I admit, however, that he set far too high a value on modernity of form, and that, consequently, there is no book of his that, as an artistic masterpiece, can rank with *Salammbô* or *Esmond*, or *The Cloister and the Hearth*, or the *Vicomte de Bragelonne*.[38]

CYRIL: Do you object to modernity of form, then?

VIVIAN: Yes. It is a huge price to pay for a very poor result. Pure modernity of form is always somewhat vulgarizing. It cannot help being so. The public imagine that, because they are interested in their immediate surroundings, Art should be interested in them also, and should take them as her subject-matter. But the mere fact that they are interested in these things makes them unsuitable subjects for Art.

The only beautiful things, as somebody once said, are the things that do not concern us. As long as a thing is useful or necessary to us, or affects us in any way, either for pain or for pleasure, or appeals strongly to our sympathies, or is a vital part of the environment in which we live, it is outside the proper sphere of art. To art's subject-matter we should be more or less indifferent. We should, at any rate, have no preferences, no prejudices, no partisan feeling of any kind. It is exactly because Hecuba[39] is nothing to us that her sorrows are such an admirable motive for a tragedy. I do not know anything in the whole history of literature sadder than the artistic career of Charles Reade. He wrote one beautiful book, *The Cloister and the Hearth*, a book as much above *Romola* as *Romola* is above *Daniel Deronda*, and wasted the rest of his life in a foolish attempt to be modern, to draw public attention to the state of our convict prisons, and the management of our private lunatic asylums. Charles Dickens was depressing enough in all conscience when he tried to arouse our sympathy for the victims of the poor-law administration; but Charles Reade, an artist, a scholar, a man with a true sense of beauty, raging and roaring over the abuses of contemporary life like a common pamphleteer or a sensational journalist, is really a sight for the angels to weep over. Believe me, my dear Cyril, modernity of form and modernity of subject-matter are entirely and absolutely wrong. We have mistaken the common livery of the age for the vesture of the Muses, and spend our days in the sordid streets and hideous suburbs of our vile cities when we should be out on the hillside with Apollo. Certainly we are a degraded race, and have sold our birthright for a mess of facts.

CYRIL: There is something in what you say, and there is no doubt that whatever amusement we may find in reading a purely modern novel, we have rarely any artistic pleasure in re-reading it. And this is perhaps the best rough test of what is literature and what is not. If one cannot enjoy reading a book over and over again, there is no use reading it at all. But what do you say about the return to Life and Nature? This is the panacea that is always being recommended to us.

VIVIAN: I will read you what I say on that subject. The passage comes later on in the article, but I may as well give it to you now:

'The popular cry of our time is "Let us return to Life and Nature;

they will recreate Art for us, and send the red blood coursing through her veins; they will shoe her feet with swiftness and make her hand strong." But, alas! we are mistaken in our amiable and well-meaning efforts. Nature is always behind the age. And as for Life, she is the solvent that breaks up Art, the enemy that lays waste her house.'

CYRIL: What do you mean by saying that Nature is always behind the age?

VIVIAN: Well, perhaps that is rather cryptic. What I mean is this. If we take Nature to mean natural simple instinct as opposed to self-conscious culture, the work produced under this influence is always old-fashioned, antiquated, and out of date. One touch of Nature may make the whole world kin, but two touches of Nature will destroy any work of Art. If, on the other hand, we regard Nature as the collection of phenomena external to man, people only discover in her what they bring to her. She has no suggestions of her own. Wordsworth went to the lakes, but he was never a lake poet. He found in stones the sermons he had already hidden there. He went moralizing about the district, but his good work was produced when he returned, not to Nature but to poetry. Poetry gave him 'Laodamia', and the fine sonnets, and the great Ode,[40] such as it is. Nature gave him 'Martha Ray' and 'Peter Bell', and the address to Mr Wilkinson's spade.

CYRIL: I think that view might be questioned. I am rather inclined to believe in the 'impulse from a vernal wood',[41] though of course the artistic value of such an impulse depends entirely on the kind of temperament that receives it, so that the return to Nature would come to mean simply the advance to a great personality. You would agree with that, I fancy. However, proceed with your article.

VIVIAN (reading): 'Art begins with abstract decoration with purely imaginative and pleasurable work dealing with what is unreal and non-existent. This is the first stage. Then Life becomes fascinated with this new wonder, and asks to be admitted into the charmed circle. Art takes life as part of her rough material, recreates it, and refashions it in fresh forms, is absolutely indifferent to fact, invents, imagines, dreams, and keeps between herself and reality the impenetrable barrier of beautiful style, of decorative or ideal treatment. The third stage is when Life gets the upper hand, and drives Art out into the wilderness.

That is the true decadence,[42] and it is from this that we are now suffering.

'Take the case of the English drama. At first in the hands of the monks Dramatic Art was abstract, decorative and mythological. Then she enlisted Life in her service, and using some of life's external forms, she created an entirely new race of beings, whose sorrows were more terrible than any sorrow man has ever felt, whose joys were keener than lover's joys, who had the rage of the Titans[43] and the calm of the gods, who had monstrous and marvellous sins, monstrous and marvellous virtues. To them she gave a language different from that of actual use, a language full of resonant music and sweet rhythm, made stately by solemn cadence, or made delicate by fanciful rhyme, jewelled with wonderful words, and enriched with lofty diction. She clothed her children in strange raiment and gave them masks, and at her bidding the antique world rose from its marble tomb. A new Caesar stalked through the streets of risen Rome, and with purple sail and flute-led oars another Cleopatra passed up the river to Antioch. Old myth and legend and dream took shape and substance. History was entirely re-written, and there was hardly one of the dramatists who did not recognize that the object of Art is not simple truth but complex beauty. In this they were perfectly right. Art itself is really a form of exaggeration; and selection, which is the very spirit of art, is nothing more than an intensified mode of over-emphasis.

'But Life soon shattered the perfection of the form. Even in Shakespeare we can see the beginning of the end. It shows itself by the gradual breaking-up of the blank-verse in the later plays, by the predominance given to prose, and by the over-importance assigned to characterization. The passages in Shakespeare – and they are many – where the language is uncouth, vulgar, exaggerated, fantastic, obscene even, are entirely due to Life calling for an echo of her own voice, and rejecting the intervention of beautiful style, through which alone should life be suffered to find expression. Shakespeare is not by any means a flawless artist. He is too fond of going directly to life, and borrowing life's natural utterance. He forgets that when Art surrenders her imaginative medium she surrenders everything. Goethe says, somewhere –

In der Beschränkung zeigt sich erst der Meister,

"It is in working within limits that the master reveals himself," and the limitation, the very condition of any art is style. However, we need not linger any longer over Shakespeare's realism. *The Tempest* is the most perfect of palinodes.[44] All that we desired to point out was, that the magnificent work of the Elizabethan and Jacobean artists contained within itself the seeds of its own dissolution, and that, if it drew some of its strength from using life as rough material, it drew all its weakness from using life as an artistic method. As the inevitable result of this substitution of an imitative for a creative medium, this surrender of an imaginative form, we have the modern English melodrama. The characters in these plays talk on the stage exactly as they would talk off it; they have neither aspirations nor aspirates; they are taken directly from life and reproduce its vulgarity down to the smallest detail; they present the gait, manner, costume and accent of real people; they would pass unnoticed in a third-class railway carriage. And yet how wearisome the plays are! They do not succeed in producing even that impression of reality at which they aim, and which is their only reason for existing. As a method, realism is a complete failure.

'What is true about the drama and the novel is no less true about those arts that we call the decorative arts. The whole history of these arts in Europe is the record of the struggle between Orientalism, with its frank rejection of imitation, its love of artistic convention, its dislike to the actual representation of any object in Nature, and our own imitative spirit. Wherever the former has been paramount, as in Byzantium, Sicily and Spain, by actual contact, or in the rest of Europe by the influence of the Crusades, we have had beautiful and imaginative work in which the visible things of life are transmuted into artistic conventions, and the things that Life has not are invented and fashioned for her delight. But wherever we have returned to Life and Nature, our work has always become vulgar, common and uninteresting. Modern tapestry, with its aërial effects, its elaborate perspective, its broad expanses of waste sky, its faithful and laborious realism, has no beauty whatsoever. The pictorial glass of Germany is absolutely detestable. We are beginning to weave possible carpets in England, but only because we have returned to the method and spirit of the East. Our rugs and carpets of twenty years ago, with their solemn depressing truths, their inane worship of Nature, their sordid reproductions of visible objects, have become, even to the Philistine,[45] a source of laughter. A cultured Mahomedan once remarked to us, "You Christians are so occupied in misinterpreting the fourth commandment that you have never thought of making an artistic application of the second." He was perfectly right, and the whole truth of the matter is this: The proper school to learn art in is not Life but Art.'

And now let me read you a passage which seems to me to settle the question very completely.

'It was not always thus. We need not say anything about the poets, for they, with the unfortunate exception of Mr Wordsworth, have been really faithful to their high mission, and are universally recognized as being absolutely unreliable. But in the works of Herodotus,[46] who, in spite of the shallow and ungenerous attempts of modern sciolists to verify his history, may justly be called the "Father of Lies"; in the published speeches of Cicero[47] and the biographies of Suetonius;[48] in Tacitus[49] at his best; in Pliny's *Natural History*;[50] in Hanno's *Periplus*;[51] in all the early chronicles; in the Lives of the Saints; in Frossart[52] and Sir Thomas Mallory;[53] in the travels of Marco Polo;[54] in Olaus Magnus,[55] and Aldrovandus,[56] and Conrad Lycosthenes,[57] with his magnificent *Prodigiorum et Ostentorum Chronicon*; in the autobiography of Benvenuto Cellini;[58] in the memoirs of Casanuova;[59] in Defoe's *History of the Plague*;[60] in Boswell's *Life of Johnson*;[61] in Napoleon's despatches,[62] and in the works of our own Carlyle, whose *French Revolution*[63] is one of the most fascinating historical novels ever written, facts are either kept in their proper subordinate position, or else entirely excluded on the general ground of dulness. Now, everything is changed. Facts are not merely finding a footing-place in history, but they are usurping the domain of Fancy, and have invaded the kingdom of Romance. Their chilling touch is over everything. They are vulgarizing mankind. The crude commercialism of America, its materializing spirit, its indifference to the poetical side of things, and its lack of imagination and of high unattainable ideals, are entirely due to that country having adopted for its national hero a man, who according to his own confession, was incapable of telling a lie, and it is not too much to say that the story of George Washington[64] and the cherry-tree has done more harm, and in a shorter space of time, than any other moral tale in the whole of literature.'

CYRIL: My dear boy!

VIVIAN: I assure you it is the case, and the amusing part of the whole thing is that the story of the cherry-tree is an absolute myth. However, you must not think that I am too despondent about the artistic future either of America or of our own country. Listen to this:

'That some change will take place before this century has drawn to its close we have no doubt whatsoever. Bored by the tedious and improving conversation of those who have neither the wit to exaggerate nor the genius to romance, tired of the intelligent person whose reminiscences are always based upon memory, whose statements are invariably limited by probability, and who is at any time liable to be corroborated by the merest Philistine who happens to be present, Society sooner or later must return to its lost leader, the cultured and fascinating liar. Who he was who first, without ever having gone out to the rude chase, told the wondering cavemen at sunset how he had dragged the Megatherium[65] from the purple darkness of its jasper cave, or slain the Mammoth in single combat and brought back its gilded tusks, we cannot tell, and not one of our modern anthropologists, for all their much-boasted science, has had the ordinary courage to tell us. Whatever was his name or race, he certainly was the true founder of social intercourse. For the aim of the liar is simply to charm, to delight, to give pleasure. He is the very basis of civilized society, and without him a dinner party, even at the mansions of the great, is as dull as a lecture at the Royal Society,[66] or a debate at the Incorporated Authors,[67] or one of Mr Burnand's farcical comedies.[68]

'Nor will he be welcomed by society alone. Art, breaking from the prison-house of realism, will run to greet him, and will kiss his false, beautiful lips, knowing that he alone is in possession of the great secret of all her manifestations, the secret that Truth is entirely and absolutely a matter of style; while Life – poor, probable, uninteresting human life – tired of repeating herself for the benefit of Mr Herbert Spencer,[69] scientific historians, and the compilers of statistics in general, will follow meekly after him, and try to reproduce, in her own simple and untutored way, some of the marvels of which he talks.

'No doubt there will always be critics who, like a certain writer in the *Saturday Review*, will gravely censure the teller of fairy tales for his defective knowledge of natural history, who will measure imaginative work by their own lack of any imaginative faculty, and will hold up their ink-stained hands in horror if some honest gentleman, who has never been farther than the yew-trees of his own garden, pens a fascinating book of travels like Sir John Mandeville,[70] or, like great Raleigh,[71] writes a whole history of the world, without knowing anything whatsoever about the past. To excuse themselves they will try and shelter under the shield of him who made Prospero the magician, and gave him Caliban and Ariel as his servants, who heard the Tritons blowing their horns round the coral reefs of the Enchanted Isle, and the fairies singing to each other in a wood near Athens, who led the phantom kings in dim procession across the misty Scottish heath, and hid Hecate in a cave with the weird sisters. They will call upon Shakespeare – they always do – and will quote that hackneyed passage forgetting that this unfortunate aphorism about Art holding the mirror up to Nature, is deliberately said by Hamlet in order to convince the bystanders of his absolute insanity in all art-matters.'

CYRIL: Ahem! Another cigarette, please.

VIVIAN: My dear fellow, whatever you may say, it is merely a dramatic utterance, and no more represents Shakespeare's real views upon art than the speeches of Iago represent his real views upon morals. But let me get to the end of the passage:

'Art finds her own perfection within, and not outside of, herself. She is not to be judged by any external standard of resemblance. She is a veil, rather than a mirror. She has flowers that no forests know of, birds that no woodland possesses. She makes and unmakes many worlds, and can draw the moon from heaven with a scarlet thread. Hers are the "forms more real than living man", and hers the great archetypes of which things that have existence are but unfinished copies. Nature has, in her eyes, no laws, no uniformity. She can work miracles at her will, and when she calls monsters from the deep they come. She can bid the almond tree blossom in winter, and send the snow upon the ripe cornfield. At her word the frost lays its silver finger on the burning mouth of June, and the winged lions creep out from the hollows of the Lydian hills.[72] The dryads peer from the thicket as she passes by, and the brown fauns smile strangely at her when she comes near them. She has hawk-faced gods that worship her, and the centaurs gallop at her side.'

CYRIL: I like that. I can see it. Is that the end?

VIVIAN: No. There is one more passage, but it is purely practical. It simply suggests some methods by which we could revive this lost art of Lying.

CYRIL: Well, before you read it to me, I should like to ask you a question. What do you mean by saying that life, 'poor, probable, uninteresting human life', will try to reproduce the marvels of art? I can quite understand your objection to art being treated as a mirror. You think it would reduce genius to the position of a cracked looking glass. But you don't mean to say that you seriously believe that Life imitates Art, that Life in fact is the mirror, and Art the reality?

VIVIAN: Certainly I do. Paradox though it may seem – and paradoxes are always dangerous things – it is none the less true that Life imitates Art far more than Art imitates Life. We have all seen in our own day in England how a certain curious and fascinating type of beauty, invented and emphasized by two imaginative painters,[73] has so influenced Life that whenever one goes to a private view or to an artistic salon one sees, here the mystic eyes of Rossetti's dream, the long ivory throat, the strange square-cut jaw, the loosened shadowy hair that he so ardently loved, there the sweet maidenhood of 'The Golden Stair', the blossom-like mouth and weary loveliness of the 'Laus Amoris', the passion-pale face of Andromeda, the thin hands and lithe beauty of the Vivian in 'Merlin's Dream'. And it has always been so. A great artists invents a type, and Life tries to copy it, to reproduce it in a popular form, like an enterprising publisher. Neither Holbein nor Vandyck[74] found in England what they have given us. They brought their types with them, and Life with her keen imitative faculty set herself to supply the master with models. The Greeks, with their quick artistic instinct, understood this, and set in the bride's chamber the statue of Hermes or of Apollo, that she might bear children as lovely as the works of art that she looked at in her rapture or her pain. They knew that Life gains from Art not merely spirituality, depth of thought and feeling, soul-turmoil or soul-peace, but that she can form herself on the very lines and colours of art, and can reproduce the dignity of Pheidias as well as the grace of Praxiteles.[75] Hence came their objection to realism. They disliked it on purely social grounds. They felt that it inevitably makes people ugly, and they were perfectly right. We try to improve the conditions of the race by means of good air, free sunlight, wholesome water, and hideous bare buildings for the better housing of the lower orders. But these things merely produce health, they do not produce beauty. For this, Art is required, and the true disciples of the great artist are not his studio-imitators, but those who become like his works of art, be they plastic as in Greek days, or pictorial as in modern times; in a word, Life is Art's best, Art's only pupil.

As it is with the visible arts, so it is with literature. The most obvious and the vulgarest form in which this is shown is in the case of the silly boys who, after reading the adventures of Jack Sheppard or Dick Turpin,[76] pillage the stalls of unfortunate apple-women, break into sweet-shops at night, and alarm old gentlemen who are returning home from the city by leaping out on them in suburban lanes, with black masks and unloaded revolvers. This interesting phenomenon, which always occurs after the appearance of a new edition of either of the books I have alluded to, is usually attributed to the influence of literature on the imagination. But this is a mistake. The imagination is essentially creative, and always seeks for a new form. The boy-burglar is simply the inevitable result of life's imitative instinct. He is Fact, occupied as Fact usually is, with trying to reproduce Fiction, and what we see in him is repeated on an extended scale throughout the whole of life. Schopenhauer[77] has analysed the pessimism that characterizes modern thought, but Hamlet invented it. The world has become sad because a puppet was once melancholy. The Nihilist,[78] that strange martyr who has no faith, who goes to the stake without enthusiasm, and dies for what he does not believe in, is a purely literary product. He was invented by Tourgénieff, and completed by Dostoieffski.[79] Robespierre came out of the pages of Rousseau[80] as surely as the People's Palace[81] rose out of the *débris* of a novel. Literature always anticipates life. It does not copy it, but moulds it to its purpose. The nineteenth century, as we know it, is largely an invention of Balzac. Our Luciens de Rubempré, our Rastignacs, and De Marsays made their first appearance on the stage of the *Comédie Humaine*. We are merely carrying out, with footnotes and unnecessary additions, the whim or fancy or creative vision of a great novelist. I once asked a lady, who knew Thackeray intimately, whether he had had any model for Becky Sharp.[82] She told me that Becky was an invention, but that the idea of the character had been partly suggested by a governess who lived in the neighbourhood of Kensington Square, and was the companion of a very selfish and rich old woman. I inquired what became of the governess, and she replied that, oddly enough, some years after the appearance of *Vanity Fair*, she ran away with the nephew of the lady with whom she was living, and for a short time made a great splash in society, quite in Mrs Rawdon Crawley's style, and entirely by Mrs Rawdon Crawley's methods. Ultimately she came to grief, disappeared to the Continent, and used to be occasionally seen at Monte Carlo and other gambling places. The noble gentleman from whom the same great sentimentalist drew Colonel Newcome died, a few months after *The Newcomes* had reached a fourth edition, with the word '*Adsum*'[83] on his lips. Shortly after Mr Stevenson published his curious psychological story of transformation, a friend of mine, called Mr Hyde, was in the north of London, and being anxious to get to a railway station, took what he thought would be a short cut, lost his way, and found himself in a network of mean, evil-looking streets. Feeling rather nervous he began to walk extremely fast, when suddenly out of an archway ran a child right between his legs. It fell on the pavement, he tripped over it, and trampled upon it. Being of course very much frightened and a little hurt, it began to scream, and in a few seconds the whole street was full of rough people who came pouring out of the houses like ants. They surrounded him, and asked him his name. He was just about to give it when he suddenly remembered the opening incident in Mr Stevenson's story. He was so filled with horror at having realized in his own person that terrible and well-written scene, and at having done accidentally, though in fact, what the Mr Hyde of fiction had done with deliberate intent, that he ran away as hard as he could go. He was, however, very closely followed, and finally he took refuge in a surgery, the door of which happened to be open, where he explained to a young assistant, who happened to be there, exactly what had occurred. The humanitarian crowd were induced to go away on his giving them a small sum of money, and as soon as the coast was clear he left. As he passed out, the name on the brass door-plate of the surgery caught his eye. It was 'Jekyll'. At least it should have been.

Here the imitation, as far as it went, was of course accidental. In the following case the imitation was self-conscious. In the year 1879, just after I had left Oxford, I met at a reception at the house of one of the Foreign Ministers a woman of very curious exotic beauty. We became great friends, and were constantly together. And yet what interested me most in her was not her beauty, but her character, her entire vagueness of character. She seemed to have no personality at all, but simply the possibility of many types. Sometimes she would give herself up entirely to art, turn her drawing-room into a studio, and spend two or three days a week at picture galleries or museums. Then she would take to attending race-meetings, wear the most horsey clothes, and talk about nothing but betting. She abandoned religion for mesmerism, mesmerism for politics, and politics for the melodramatic excitements of philanthropy. In fact, she was a kind of Proteus, and as much a failure in all her transformations as was that wondrous sea-god when Odysseus[84] laid hold of him. One day a serial began in one of the French magazines. At that time I used to read serial stories, and I well remember the shock of surprise I felt when I came to the description of the heroine. She was so like my friend that I brought her the magazine, and she recognized herself in it immediately, and seemed fascinated by the resemblance. I should tell you, by the way, that the story was translated from some dead Russian writer, so that the author had not taken his type from my friend. Well, to put the matter briefly, some months afterwards I was in Venice, and finding the magazine in the reading-room of the hotel, I took it up casually to see what had become of the heroine. It was a most piteous tale, as the girl had ended by running away with a man absolutely inferior to her, not merely in social station, but in character and intellect also. I wrote to my friend that evening about my views on John Bellini,[85] and the admirable ices at Florio's,[86] and the artistic value of gondolas, but added a postscript to the effect that her double in the story had behaved in a very silly manner. I don't know why I added that, but I remember I had a sort of dread over me that she might do the same thing. Before my letter had reached her, she had run away with a man who deserted her in six months. I saw her in 1884 in Paris, where she was living with her mother, and I asked her whether the story had had anything to do with her action. She told me that she had felt an absolutely irresistible impulse to follow the heroine step by step in her strange and fatal progress, and that it was with a feeling of real terror that she had looked forward to the last few chapters of the story. When they appeared, it seemed to her that she was compelled to reproduce them in life, and she did so. It was a most clear example of this imitative instinct of which I was speaking, and an extremely tragic one.

However, I do not wish to dwell any further upon individual instances. Personal experience is a most vicious and limited circle. All that I desire to point out is the general principle that Life imitates Art far more than Art imitates Life, and I feel sure that if you think seriously about it you will find that it is true. Life holds the mirror up to Art, and either reproduces some strange type imagined by painter or sculptor, or realizes in fact what has been dreamed in fiction. Scientifically speaking, the basis of life – the energy of life, as Aristotle would call it – is simply the desire for expression, and Art is always presenting various forms through which this expression can be attained. Life seizes on them and uses them, even if they be to her own hurt. Young men have committed suicide because Rolla[87] did so, have died by their own hand because by his own hand Werther[88] died. Think of what we owe to the imitation of Christ, of what we owe to the imitation of Caesar.

CYRIL: The theory is certainly a very curious one, but to make it complete you must show that Nature, no less than Life, is an imitation of art. Are you prepared to prove that?

VIVIAN: My dear fellow, I am prepared to prove anything.

CYRIL: Nature follows the landscape painter, then, and takes her effects from him?

VIVIAN: Certainly. Where, if not from the Impressionists, do we get those wonderful brown fogs that come creeping down our streets, blurring the gas-lamps and changing the houses into monstrous shadows? To whom, if not to them and their master,[89] do we owe the lovely silver mists that brood over our river, and turn to faint forms of fading grace curved bridge and swaying barge? The extraordinary change that has taken place in the climate of London during the last ten years is entirely due to a particular school of Art. You smile. Consider the matter from a scientific or a metaphysical point of view, and you will find that I am right. For what is Nature? Nature is no great mother who has borne us. She is our creation. It is in our brain that she quickens to life. Things are because we see them, and what we see, and how we see it, depends on the arts that have influenced us. To look at a thing is very different from seeing a thing. One does not see anything until one sees its beauty. Then, and then only, does it come into existence. At present, people see fogs, not because there are fogs, but because poets and painters have taught them the mysterious loveliness of such effects. There may have been fogs for centuries in London. I dare say there were. But no one saw them, and so we do not know anything about them. They did not exist till Art had invented them. Now, it must be admitted, fogs are carried to excess. They have become the mere mannerism of a clique, and the exaggerated realism of their method gives dull people bronchitis. Where the cultured catch an effect, the uncultured catch cold. And so, let us be humane, and invite Art to turn her wonderful eyes elsewhere. She has done so already, indeed. That white quivering sunlight that one sees now in France, with its strange blotches of mauve, and its restless violet shadows, is her latest fancy, and, on the whole, Nature reproduces it quite admirably. Where she used to give us Corots and Daubignys, she gives us now exquisite Monets and entrancing Pisaros.[90] Indeed, there are moments, rare, it is true, but still to be observed from time to time, when Nature becomes absolutely modern. Of course she is not always to be relied upon. The fact is that she is in this unfortunate position. Art creates an incomparable and unique effect, and, having done so, passes on to other things. Nature, upon the other hand, forgetting that imitation can be made the sincerest form of insult, keeps on repeating this effect until we all become absolutely wearied of it. Nobody of any real culture, for instance, ever talks nowadays about the beauty of a sunset. Sunsets are quite old-fashioned. They belong to the time when Turner[91] was the last note in art. To admire them is a distinct sign of provincialism of temperament. Upon the other hand they go on. Yesterday evening Mrs Arundel insisted on my going to the window, and looking at the glorious sky, as she called it. Of course I had to look at it. She is one of those absurdly pretty Philistines to whom one can deny nothing. And what was it? It was simply a very second-rate Turner, a Turner of a bad period, with all the painter's worst faults exaggerated and over-emphasized. Of course, I am quite ready to admit that Life very often commits the same error. She produces her false Renés[92] and her sham Vautrins, just as Nature gives us, on one day a doubtful Cuyp, and on another a more than questionable Rousseau.[93] Still, Nature irritates one more when she does things of that kind. It seems so stupid, so obvious, so unnecessary. A false Vautrin might be delightful. A doubtful Cuyp is unbearable. However, I don't want to be too hard on Nature. I wish the Channel, especially at Hastings, did not look quite so often like a Henry Moore,[94] grey pearl with yellow lights, but then, when Art is more varied, Nature will, no doubt, be more varied also. That she imitates Art, I don't think even her worst enemy would deny now. It is the one thing that keeps her in touch with civilized man. But have I proved my theory to your satisfaction?

CYRIL: You have proved it to my dissatisfaction, which is better. But even admitting this strange imitative instinct in Life and Nature, surely you would acknowledge that Art expresses the temper of its age, the spirit of its time, the moral and social conditions that surround it, and under whose influence it is produced.

VIVIAN: Certainly not! Art never expresses anything but itself. This is the principle of my new aesthetics; and it is this, more than that vital connection between form and substance, on which Mr Pater dwells,[95] that makes music the type of all the arts. Of course, nations and individuals, with that healthy natural vanity which is the secret of existence, are always under the impression that it is of them that the Muses are talking, always trying to find in the calm dignity of imaginative art some mirror of their own turbid passions, always forgetting that the singer of life is not Apollo but Marsyas.[96] Remote from reality, and with her eyes turned away from the shadows of the cave,[97] Art reveals her own perfection, and the wondering crowd that watches the opening of the marvellous, many-petalled rose[98] fancies that it is its own history that is being told to it, its own spirit that is finding expression in a new form. But it is not so. The highest art rejects the burden of the human spirit, and gains more from a new medium or a fresh material than she does from any enthusiasm for art, or from any lofty passion, or from any great awakening of the human consciousness. She develops purely on her own lines. She is not symbolic of any age. It is the ages that are her symbols.

Even those who hold that Art is representative of time and place and people cannot help admitting that the more imitative an art is, the less it represents to us the spirit of its age. The evil faces of the Roman emperors look out at us from the foul porphyry and spotted jasper in which the realistic artists of the day delighted to work, and we fancy that in those cruel lips and heavy sensual jaws we can find the secret of the ruin of the Empire. But it was not so. The vices of Tiberius could not destroy that supreme civilization, any more than the virtues of the Antonines[99] could save it. It fell for other, for less interesting reasons. The sibyls and prophets of the Sistine[100] may indeed serve to interpret for some that new birth of the emancipated spirit that we call the Renaissance; but what do the drunken boors and brawling peasants of Dutch art tell us about the great soul of Holland? The more abstract, the more ideal an art is, the more it reveals to us the temper of its age. If we wish to understand a nation by means of its art, let us look at its architecture or its music.

CYRIL: I quite agree with you there. The spirit of an age may be best expressed in the abstract ideal arts, for the spirit itself is abstract and ideal. Upon the other hand, for the visible aspect of an age, for its look, as the phrase goes, we must of course go to the arts of imitation.

VIVIAN: I don't think so. After all, what the imitative arts really give us are merely the various styles of particular artists, or of certain schools of artists. Surely you don't imagine that the people of the Middle Ages bore any resemblance at all to the figures on medieval stained glass, or in medieval stone and wood carving, or on medieval metal-work, or tapestries, or illuminated MSS. They were probably very ordinary-looking people, with nothing grotesque, or remarkable, or fantastic in their appearance. The Middle Ages, as we know them in art, are simply a definite form of style, and there is no reason at all why an artist with this style should not be produced in the nineteenth century. No great artist ever sees things as they really are. If he did, he would cease to be an artist. Take an example from our own day. I know that you are fond of Japanese things. Now, do you really imagine that the Japanese people, as they are presented to us in art, have any existence? If you do, you have never understood Japanese art at all. The Japanese people are the deliberate self-conscious creation of certain individual artists. If you set a picture by Hokusai, or Hokkei,[101] or any of the great native painters, beside a real Japanese gentleman or lady, you will see that there is not the slightest resemblance between them. The actual people who live in Japan are not unlike the general run of English people; that is to say, they are extremely commonplace, and have nothing curious or extraordinary about them. In fact the whole of Japan is a pure invention. There is no such country, there are no such people. One of our most charming painters[102] went recently to the Land of the Chrysanthemum in the foolish hope of seeing the Japanese. All he saw, all he had the chance of painting, were a few lanterns and some fans. He was quite unable to discover the inhabitants, as his delightful exhibition at Messrs Dowdeswell's Gallery showed only too well. He did not know that the Japanese people are, as I have said, simply a mode of style, an exquisite fancy of art. And so, if you desire to see a Japanese effect, you will not behave like a tourist and go to Tokio. On the contrary, you will stay at home and steep yourself in the work of certain Japanese artists, and then, when you have absorbed the spirit of their style, and caught their imaginative manner of vision, you will go some afternoon and sit in the Park or stroll down Piccadilly, and if you cannot see an absolutely

Japanese effect there, you will not see it anywhere. Or, to return again to the past, take as another instance the ancient Greeks. Do you think that Greek art ever tells us what the Greek people were like? Do you believe that the Athenian women were like the stately dignified figures of the Parthenon frieze, or like those marvellous goddesses who sat in the triangular pediments of the same building? If you judge from the art, they certainly were so. But read an authority, like Aristophanes[103] for instance. You will find that the Athenian ladies laced tightly, wore high-heeled shoes, dyed their hair yellow, painted and rouged their faces, and were exactly like any silly fashionable or fallen creature of our own day. The fact is that we look back on the ages entirely through the medium of art, and Art, very fortunately, has never once told us the truth.

CYRIL: But modern portraits by English painters, what of them? Surely they are like the people they pretend to represent?

VIVIAN: Quite so. They are so like them that a hundred years from now no one will believe in them. The only portraits in which one believes are portraits where there is very little of the sitter, and a very great deal of the artist. Holbein's drawings of the men and women of his time impress us with a sense of their absolute reality. But this is simply because Holbein compelled life to accept his conditions, to restrain itself within his limitations, to reproduce his type, and to appear as he wished it to appear. It is style that makes us believe in a thing – nothing but style. Most of our modern portrait painters are doomed to absolute oblivion. They never paint what they see. They paint what the public sees, and the public never sees anything.

CYRIL: Well, after that I think I should like to hear the end of your article.

VIVIAN: With pleasure. Whether it will do any good I really cannot say. Ours is certainly the dullest and most prosaic century possible. Why, even Sleep has played us false, and has closed up the gates of ivory, and opened the gates of horn.[104] The dreams of the great middle classes of this country, as recorded in Mr Myers's two bulky volumes[105] on the subject, and in the Transactions of the Psychical Society, are the most depressing things that I have ever read. There is not even a fine nightmare among them. They are commonplace, sordid and tedious. As for the Church, I cannot conceive anything better for the culture of a country than the presence in it of a body of men whose duty it is to believe in the supernatural, to perform daily miracles, and to keep alive that mythopoeic faculty which is so essential for the imagination. But in the English Church a man succeeds, not through his capacity for belief, but through his capacity for disbelief. Ours is the only Church where the sceptic stands at the altar, and where St Thomas[106] is regarded as the ideal apostle. Many a worthy clergyman, who passes his life in admirable works of kindly charity, lives and dies unnoticed and unknown; but it is sufficient for some shallow uneducated passman[107] out of either University to get up in his pulpit and express his doubts about Noah's ark, or Balaam's ass, or Jonah and the whale, for half of London to flock to hear him, and to sit open-mouthed in rapt admiration at his superb intellect. The growth of common sense in the English Church is a thing very much to be regretted. It is really a degrading concession to a low form of realism. It is silly, too. It springs from an entire ignorance of psychology. Man can believe the impossible,[108] but man can never believe the improbable. However, I must read the end of my article:

'What we have to do, what at any rate it is our duty to do, is to revive this old art of Lying. Much of course may be done, in the way of educating the public, by amateurs in the domestic circle, at literary lunches, and at afternoon teas. But this is merely the light and graceful side of lying, such as was probably heard at Cretan dinner-parties.[109] There are many other forms. Lying for the sake of gaining some immediate personal advantage, for instance – lying with a moral purpose, as it is usually called – though of late it has been rather looked down upon, was extremely popular with the antique world. Athena laughs when Odysseus tells her "his words of sly devising", as Mr William Morris[110] phrases it, and the glory of mendacity illumines the pale brow of the stainless hero of Euripidean tragedy,[111] and sets among the noble women of the past the young bride of one of Horace's most exquisite odes. Later on, what at first had been merely a natural instinct was elevated into a self-conscious science. Elaborate rules were laid down for the guidance of mankind, and an important school of literature grew up round the subject. Indeed, when one remembers the excellent philosophical treatise of Sanchez[112] on the whole question, one cannot help regretting that no one has ever thought of publishing a cheap and condensed edition of the works of that great casuist. A short primer, "When To Lie and How", if brought out in an attractive and not too expensive a form, would no doubt command a large sale, and would prove of real practical service to many earnest and deep-thinking people. Lying for the sake of the improvement of the young, which is the basis of home education, still lingers amongst us, and its advantages are so admirably set forth in the early books of Plato's *Republic* that it is unnecessary to dwell upon them here. It is a mode of lying for which all good mothers have peculiar capabilities, but it is capable of still further development, and has been sadly overlooked by the School Board. Lying for the sake of a monthly salary is of course well known in Fleet Street, and the profession of a political leader-writer is not without its advantages. But it is said to be a somewhat dull occupation, and it certainly does not lead to much beyond a kind of ostentatious obscurity. The only form of lying that is absolutely beyond reproach is Lying for its own sake, and the highest development of this is, as we have already pointed out, Lying in Art. Just as those who do not love Plato more than Truth cannot pass beyond the threshold of the Academe,[113] so those who do not love Beauty more than Truth never know the inmost shrine of Art. The solid stolid British intellect lies in the desert sands like the Sphinx in Flaubert's marvellous tale,[114] and fantasy, *La Chimère*, dances round it, and calls to it with her false, flute-toned voice. It may not hear her now, but surely some day, when we are all bored to death with the commonplace character of modern fiction, it will hearken to her and try to borrow her wings.

'And when that day dawns, or sunset reddens, how joyous we shall all be! Facts will be regarded as discreditable, Truth will be found mourning over her fetters, and Romance, with her temper of wonder, will return to the land. The very aspect of the world will change to our startled eyes. Out of the sea will rise Behemoth and Leviathan, and sail round the high-pooped galleys, as they do on the delightful maps of those ages when books on geography were actually readable. Dragons will wander about the waste places, and the phoenix will soar from her nest of fire into the air. We shall lay our hands upon the basilisk, and see the jewel in the toad's head.[115] Champing his gilded oats, the Hippogriff[116] will stand in our stalls, and over our heads will float the Blue Bird singing of beautiful and impossible things, of things that are lovely and that never happen, of things that are not and that should be. But before this comes to pass we must cultivate the lost art of Lying.'

CYRIL: Then we must certainly cultivate it at once. But in order to avoid making any error I want you to tell me briefly the doctrines of the new aesthetics.

VIVIAN: Briefly, then, they are these. Art never expresses anything but itself. It has an independent life, just as Thought has, and develops purely on its own lines. It is not necessarily realistic in an age of realism, nor spiritual in an age of faith. So far from being the creation of its time, it is usually in direct opposition to it, and the only history that it preserves for us is the history of its own progress. Sometimes it returns upon its footsteps, and revives some antique form, as happened in the archaistic movement of late Greek art, and in the pre-Raphaelite movement of our own day.[117] At other times it entirely anticipates its age, and produces in one century work that it takes another century to understand, to appreciate and to enjoy. In no case does it reproduce its age. To pass from the art of a time to the time itself is the great mistake that all historians commit.

The second doctrine is this. All bad art comes from returning to Life and Nature, and elevating them into ideals. Life and Nature may sometimes be used as part of Art's rough material, but before they are of any real service to art they must be translated into artistic conventions. The moment art surrenders its imaginative medium it surrenders everything. As a method Realism is a complete failure, and the two things that every artist should avoid are modernity of form and modernity of subject-matter. To us, who live in the nineteenth century, any century is a suitable subject for art except our own. The only beautiful things are the things that do not concern us. It is, to have the pleasure of quoting myself, exactly because Hecuba is nothing to us that her sorrows are so suitable a motive for a tragedy. Besides, it is only the modern that ever becomes old-fashioned. M. Zola sits down to give us a picture of the Second Empire. Who cares for the Second Empire[118] now? It is out of date. Life goes faster than Realism, but Romanticism is always in front of Life.

The third doctrine is that Life imitates Art far more than Art imitates Life. This results not merely from Life's imitative instinct, but from the fact that the self-conscious aim of Life is to find expression, and that Art offers it certain beautiful forms through which it may realize that energy. It is a theory that has never been put forward before, but it is extremely fruitful, and throws an entirely new light upon the history of Art.

It follows, as a corollary from this, that external Nature also imitates Art. The only effects that she can show us are effects that we have already seen through poetry, or in paintings. This is the secret of Nature's charm, as well as the explanation of Nature's weakness.

The final revelation is that Lying, the telling of beautiful untrue things, is the proper aim of Art. But of this I think I have spoken at sufficient length. And now let us go out on the terrace, where 'droops the milk-white peacock like a ghost', while the evening star 'washes the dusk with silver'.[119] At twilight nature becomes a wonderfully suggestive effect, and is not without loveliness, though perhaps its chief use is to illustrate quotations from the poets. Come! We have talked long enough.

2. Pen, Pencil and Poison
A study in green

It has constantly been made a subject of reproach against artists and men of letters that they are lacking in wholeness and completeness of nature. As a rule this must necessarily be so. That very concentration of vision and intensity of purpose which is the characteristic of the artistic temperament is in itself a mode of limitation. To those who are preoccupied with the beauty of form nothing else seems of much importance. Yet there are many exceptions to this rule. Rubens served as ambassador, and Goethe as state councillor, and Milton as Latin secretary to Cromwell. Sophocles[1] held civic office in his own city; the humorists, essayists and novelists of modern America seem to desire nothing better than to become the diplomatic representatives of their country;[2] and Charles Lamb's friend, Thomas Griffiths Wainewright,[3] the subject of this brief memoir, though of an extremely artistic temperament, followed many masters other than art, being not merely a poet and a painter, an art-critic, an antiquarian, and a writer of prose, an amateur of beautiful things, and a dilettante of things delightful, but also a forger of no mean or ordinary capabilities, and as a subtle and secret poisoner almost without rival in this or any age.

This remarkable man, so powerful with 'pen, pencil and poison', as a great poet of our own day[4] has finely said of him, was born at Chiswick, in 1794. His father was the son of a distinguished solicitor of Gray's Inn and Hatton Garden. His mother was the daughter of the celebrated Dr Griffiths, the editor and founder of the *Monthly Review*, the partner in another literary speculation of Thomas Davies, that famous bookseller of whom Johnson said that he was not a bookseller, but 'a gentleman who dealt in books', the friend of Goldsmith and Wedgwood,[5] and one of the most well-known men of his day. Mrs Wainewright died, in giving him birth, at the early age of twenty-one, and an obituary notice in the *Gentleman's Magazine* tells us of her 'amiable disposition and numerous accomplishments', and adds somewhat quaintly that 'she is supposed to have understood the writings of Mr Locke[6] as well as perhaps any person of either sex now living'. His father did not long survive his young wife, and the little child seems to have been brought up by his grandfather, and, on the death of the latter in 1803, by his uncle George Edward Griffiths, whom he subsequently poisoned. His boyhood was passed at Linden House, Turnham Green, one of those many fine Georgian mansions that have unfortunately disappeared before the inroads of the suburban builder, and to its lovely gardens and well-timbered park he owed that simple and impassioned love of nature which never left him all through his life, and which made him so peculiarly susceptible to the spiritual influences of Wordsworth's poetry. He went to school at Charles Burney's academy at Hammersmith. Mr Burney was the son of the historian of music, and the near kinsman of the artistic lad who was destined to turn out his most remarkable pupil. He seems to have been a man of a good deal of culture, and in after years Mr Wainewright often spoke of him with much affection as a philosopher, an archaeologist and an admirable teacher who, while he valued the intellectual side of education, did not forget the importance of early moral training. It was under Mr Burney that he first developed his talent as an artist, and Mr Hazlitt[7] tells us that a drawing-book which he used at school is still extant, and displays great talent and natural feeling. Indeed, painting was the first art that fascinated him. It was not till much later that he sought to find expression by pen or poison.

Before this, however, he seems to have been carried away by boyish dreams of the romance and chivalry of a soldier's life, and to have become a young guardsman. But the reckless dissipated life of his companions failed to satisfy the refined artistic temperament of one who was made for other things. In a short time he wearied of the service. 'Art,' he tells us, in words that still move many by their ardent sincerity and strange fervour, 'Art touched her renegade; by her pure and high influence the noisome mists were purged; my feelings, parched, hot, and tarnished, were renovated with cool, fresh bloom, simple, beautiful to the simple-hearted.' But Art was not the only cause of the change. 'The writings of Wordsworth,' he goes on to say, 'did much towards calming the confusing whirl necessarily incident to sudden mutations. I wept over them tears of happiness and gratitude.' He accordingly left the army, with its rough barrack-life and coarse mess-room tittle-tattle, and returned to Linden House, full of his new-born enthusiasm for culture. A severe illness, in which, to use his own words, he was 'broken like a vessel of clay', prostrated him for a time. His delicately strung organization, however indifferent it might have been to inflicting pain on others, was itself most keenly sensitive to pain. He shrank from suffering as a thing that mars and maims human life, and seems to have wandered through that terrible valley of melancholia from which so many great, perhaps greater, spirits have never emerged. But he was young – only twenty-five years of age – and he soon passed out of the 'dead black waters', as he called them, into the larger air of humanistic culture. As he was recovering from the illness that had led him almost to the gates of death, he conceived the idea of taking up literature as an art. 'I said with John Woodvill,' he cries, 'it were a life of gods to dwell in such an element,' to see and hear and write brave things:

> These high and gusty relishes of life
> Have no allayings of mortality.

It is impossible not to feel that in this passage we have the utterance of a man who had a true passion for letters. 'To see and hear and write brave things,' this was his aim.

Scott, the editor of the *London Magazine*,[8] struck by the young man's genius, or under the influence of the strange fascination that he exercised on every one who knew him, invited him to write a series of articles on artistic subjects, and under a series of fanciful pseudonyms he began to contribute to the literature of his day. *Janus Weathercock*, *Egomet Bonmot*, and *Van Vinkvooms*, were some of the grotesque masks under which he chose to hide his seriousness or to reveal his levity. A mask tells us more than a face. These disguises intensified his personality. In an incredibly short time he seems to have made his mark. Charles Lamb speaks of 'kind, light-hearted Wainewright', whose prose is 'capital'. We hear of him entertaining Macready, John Forster,

Maginn, Talfourd, Sir Wentworth Dilke, the poet John Clare,[9] and others, at a *petit-dîner*. Like Disraeli,[10] he determined to startle the town as a dandy, and his beautiful rings, his antique cameo breast-pin and his pale lemon-coloured kid gloves, were well known, and indeed were regarded by Hazlitt as being the signs of a new manner in literature: while his rich curly hair, fine eyes and exquisite white hands gave him the dangerous and delightful distinction of being different from others. There was something in him of Balzac's Lucien de Rubempré.[11] At times he reminds us of Julien Sorel.[12] De Quincey[13] saw him once. It was at a dinner at Charles Lamb's. 'Amongst the company, all literary men, sat a murderer,' he tells us, and he goes on to describe how on that day he had been ill, and had hated the face of man and woman, and yet found himself looking with intellectual interest across the table at the young writer beneath whose affectations of manner there seemed to him to lie so much unaffected sensibility, and speculates on 'what sudden growth of another interest' would have changed his mood, had he known of what terrible sin the guest to whom Lamb paid so much attention was even then guilty.

His life-work falls naturally under the three heads suggested by Mr Swinburne, and it may be partly admitted that, if we set aside his achievements in the sphere of poison, what he has actually left to us hardly justifies his reputation.

But then it is only the Philistine who seeks to estimate a personality by the vulgar test of production. This young dandy sought to be somebody, rather than to do something. He recognized that Life itself is an art, and has its modes of style no less than the arts that seek to express it. Nor is his work without interest. We hear of William Blake[14] stopping in the Royal Academy before one of his pictures and pronouncing it to be 'very fine'. His essays are prefiguring of much that has since been realized. He seems to have anticipated some of those accidents of modern culture that are regarded by many as true essentials. He writes about La Gioconda,[15] and early French poets and the Italian Renaissance. He loves Greek gems, and Persian carpets, and Elizabethan translations of *Cupid and Psyche*,[16] and the *Hypnerotomachia*,[17] and book-bindings, and early editions, and wide-margined proofs. He is keenly sensitive to the value of beautiful surroundings, and never wearies of describing to us the rooms in which he lived, or would have liked to live. He had that curious love of green, which in individuals is always the sign of a subtle artistic temperament, and in nations is said to denote a laxity, if not a decadence of morals. Like Baudelaire[18] he was extremely fond of cats, and with Gautier,[19] he was fascinated by that 'sweet marble monster' of both sexes that we can still see at Florence and in the Louvre.[20]

There is of course much in his descriptions, and his suggestions for decoration, that shows that he did not entirely free himself from the false taste of his time. But it is clear that he was one of the first to recognize what is, indeed, the very keynote of aesthetic eclecticism, I mean the true harmony of all really beautiful things irrespective of age or place, of school or manner. He saw that in decorating a room, which is to be, not a room for show, but a room to live in, we should never aim at any archaeological reconstruction of the past, nor burden ourselves with any fanciful necessity for historical accuracy. In this artistic perception he was perfectly right. All beautiful things belong to the same age.

And so, in his own library, as he describes it, we find the delicate fictile[21] vase of the Greek, with its exquisitely painted figures and the faint ΚΑΛΟΣ[22] finely traced upon its side, and behind it hangs an engraving of the 'Delphic Sibyl' of Michael Angelo, or of the 'Pastoral' of Giorgione.[23] Here is a bit of Florentine majolica,[24] and here a rude lamp from some old Roman tomb. On the table lies a book of Hours,[25] 'cased in a cover of solid silver gilt, wrought with quaint devices and studded with small brilliants and rubies', and close by it 'squats a little ugly monster, a Lar,[26] perhaps, dug up in the sunny fields of corn-bearing Sicily'. Some dark antique bronzes contrast 'with the pale gleam of two noble *Christi Crucifixi*, one carved in ivory, the other moulded in wax'. He has his trays of Tassie's gems,[27] his tiny Louis-Quatorze *bonbonnière*[28] with a miniature by Petitot,[29] his highly prized 'brown-biscuit teapots,[30] filagree-worked', his citron morocco letter-case, and his 'pomona-green'[31] chair.

One can fancy him lying there in the midst of his books and casts and engravings, a true virtuoso, a subtle connoisseur, turning over his fine collection of Marc Antonios,[32] and his Turner's *Liber Studiorum*,[33] of which he was a warm admirer, or examining with a magnifier some of his antique gems and cameos, 'the head of Alexander on an onyx of two strata', or 'that superb *altissimo relievo* on cornelian,[34] Jupiter Ægiochus'. He was always a great amateur of engravings,[35] and gives some very useful suggestions as to the best means of forming a collection. Indeed, while fully appreciating modern art, he never lost sight of the importance of reproductions of the great masterpieces of the past, and all that he says about the value of plaster casts is quite admirable.

As an art-critic he concerned himself primarily with the complex impressions produced by a work of art, and certainly the first step in aesthetic criticism is to realize one's own impressions.[36] He cared nothing for abstract discussions on the nature of the Beautiful, and the historical method, which has since yielded such rich fruit, did not belong to his day, but he never lost sight of the great truth that Art's first appeal is neither to the intellect nor to the emotions, but purely to the artistic temperament, and he more than once points out that this temperament, this 'taste', as he calls it, being unconsciously guided and made perfect by frequent contact with the best work, becomes in the end a form of right judgement. Of course there are fashions in art just as there are fashions in dress, and perhaps none of us can ever quite free ourselves from the influence of custom and the influence of novelty. He certainly could not, and he frankly acknowledges how difficult it is to form any fair estimate of contemporary work. But, on the whole, his taste was good and sound. He admired Turner and Constable at a time when they were not so much thought of as they are now, and saw that for the highest landscape art we require more than 'mere industry and accurate transcription'. Of Crome's[37] 'Heath Scene near Norwich' he remarks that it shows 'how much a subtle observation of the elements, in their wild moods, does for a most uninteresting flat', and of the popular type of landscape of his day he says that it is 'simply an enumeration of hill and dale, stumps of trees, shrubs, water, meadows, cottages and houses; little more than topography, a kind of pictorial map-work; in which rainbows, showers, mists, haloes, large beams shooting through rifted clouds, storms, starlight, all the most valued materials of the real painter, are not'. He had a thorough dislike of what is obvious or commonplace in art, and while he was charmed to entertain Wilkie[38] at dinner, he cared as little for Sir David's pictures as he did for Mr Crabbe's poems.[39] With the imitative and realistic tendencies of his day he had no sympathy, and he tells us frankly that his great admiration for Fuseli[40] was largely due to the fact that the little Swiss did not consider it necessary that an artist should paint only what he sees. The qualities that he sought for in a picture were composition, beauty and dignity of line, richness of colour, and imaginative power. Upon the other hand, he was not a doctrinaire. 'I hold that no work of art can be tried otherwise than by laws deduced from itself: whether or not it be consistent with itself is the question.' This is one of his excellent aphorisms. And in criticizing painters so different as Landseer and Martin, Stothard and Etty,[41] he shows that, to use a phrase now classical, he is trying 'to see the object as in itself it really is'.[42]

However, as I pointed out before, he never feels quite at his ease in his criticisms of contemporary work. 'The present,' he says, 'is about as agreeable a confusion to me as Ariosto[43] on the first perusal . . . Modern things dazzle me. I must look at them through Time's telescope. Elia[44] complains that to him the merit of a MS. poem is uncertain; "print", as he excellently says, "settles it". Fifty years' toning does the same thing to a picture.' He is happier when he is writing about Watteau and Lancret, about Rubens and Giorgione, about Rembrandt, Corregio[45] and Michael Angelo; happiest of all when he is writing about Greek things. What is Gothic touched him very little, but classical art and the art of the Renaissance were always dear to him. He saw what our English school could gain from a study of Greek models, and never wearies of pointing out to the young student the artistic possibilities that lie dormant in Hellenic marbles and Hellenic methods of work. In his judgements on the great Italian Masters, says De Quincey, 'There seemed a tone of sincerity and of native sensibility, as in one who spoke for himself, and was not merely a copier from books.' The highest praise that we can give to him is that he tried to revive style as a conscious tradition. But he saw that no amount of art lectures or art congresses, or 'plans for advancing the fine arts', will ever produce this result. The people, he says very wisely, and in the true spirit of Toynbee Hall,[46] must always have 'the best models constantly before their eyes'.

As is to be expected from one who was a painter, he is often extremely technical in his art criticisms. Of Tintoret's 'St George delivering the Egyptian Princess from the Dragon',[47] he remarks:

The robe of Sabra, warmly glazed with Prussian blue, is relieved from the pale greenish background by a vermilion scarf; and the full hues of both are beautifully echoed, as it were, in a lower key by the purple-lake coloured stuffs and bluish iron armour of the saint, besides an ample balance to the vivid azure drapery on the foreground in the indigo shades of the wild wood surrounding the castle.

And elsewhere he talks learnedly of 'a delicate Schiavone,[48] various as a tulip-bed, with rich broken tints', of 'a glowing portrait, remarkable for *morbidezza*, by the scarce Moroni',[49] and of another picture being 'pulpy in the carnations'.

But, as a rule, he deals with his impressions of the work as an artistic whole, and tries to translate those impressions into words, to give, as it were, the literary equivalent for the imaginative and mental effect. He was one of the first to develop what has been called the art-literature of the nineteenth century, that form of literature which has found in Mr Ruskin and Mr Browning its two most perfect exponents. His description of Lancret's *Repas Italien*, in which 'a dark-haired girl, "amorous of mischief", lies on the daisy-powdered grass', is in some respects very charming. Here is his account of 'The Crucifixion', by Rembrandt. It is extremely characteristic of his style:

Darkness – sooty, portentous darkness – shrouds the whole scene: only above the accursed wood, as if through a horrid rift in the murky ceiling, a rainy deluge – 'sleety-flaw, discoloured water' – streams down amain, spreading a grisly spectral light, even more horrible than that palpable night. Already the Earth pants thick and fast! the darkened Cross trembles! the winds are dropt – the air is stagnant – a muttering rumble growls underneath their feet, and some of that miserable crowd begin to fly down the hill. The horses snuff the coming terror, and become unmanageable through fear. The moment rapidly

approaches when, nearly torn asunder by His own weight, fainting with loss
of blood, which now runs in narrower rivulets from His slit veins, His temples
and breast drowned in sweat, and His black tongue parched with the fiery
death-fever, Jesus cries, 'I thirst.' The deadly vinegar is elevated to Him.

His head sinks, and the sacred corpse 'swings senseless of the cross'. A sheet
of vermilion flame shoots sheer through the air and vanishes; the rocks of
Carmel and Lebanon cleave asunder; the sea rolls on high from the sands its
black weltering waves. Earth yawns, and the graves give up their dwellers.
The dead and the living are mingled together in unnatural conjunction and
hurry through the holy city. New prodigies await them there. The veil of the
temple – the unpierceable veil – is rent asunder from top to bottom, and that
dreaded recess containing the Hebrew mysteries – the fatal ark with the tables
and seven-branched candelabrum – is disclosed by the light of unearthly
flames to the God-deserted multitude.

Rembrandt never *painted* this sketch, and he was quite right. It would have
lost nearly all its charms in losing that perplexing veil of indistinctness which
affords such ample range wherein the doubting imagination may speculate.
At present it is like a thing in another world. A dark gulf is betwixt us. It is not
tangible by the body. We can only approach it in the spirit.

In this passage, written, the author tells us, 'in awe and reverence',
there is much that is terrible, and very much that is quite horrible, but
it is not without a certain crude form of power, or, at any rate, a
certain crude violence of words, a quality which this age should highly
appreciate, as it is its chief defect. It is pleasanter, however, to pass to
this description of Giulio Romano's [50] 'Cephalus and Procris': [51]

We should read Moschus's lament for Bion, [52] the sweet shepherd, before
looking at this picture, or study the picture as a preparation for the lament.
We have nearly the same images in both. For either victim the high groves
and forest dells murmur; the flowers exhale sad perfume from their buds; the
nightingale mourns on the craggy lands, and the swallow in the long-winding
vales; 'the satyrs, too, and fauns dark-veiled groan', and the fountain nymphs
within the wood melt into tearful waters. The sheep and goats leave their
pasture; and oreads, 'who love to scale the most accessible tops of all uprightest
rocks', hurry down from the song of their wind-courting pines; while the

dryads bend from the branches of the meeting trees, and the rivers moan for white Procris, 'with many-sobbing streams',

> Filling the far-seen ocean with a voice.

The golden bees are silent on the thymy Hymettus;[53] and the knelling horn of Aurora's love no more shall scatter away the cold twilight on the top of Hymettus. The foreground of our subject is a grassy sunburnt bank, broken into swells and hollows like waves (a sort of land-breakers), rendered more uneven by many foot-tripping roots and stumps of trees stocked untimely by the axe, which are again throwing out light-green shoots. This bank rises rather suddenly on the right to a clustering grove, penetrable to no star, at the entrance of which sits the stunned Thessalian king, holding between his knees that ivory-bright body which was, but an instant agone, parting the rough boughs with her smooth forehead, and treading alike on thorns and flowers with jealousy-stung foot – now helpless, heavy, void of all motion, save when the breeze lifts her thick hair in mockery.

From between the closely-neighboured boles astonished nymphs press forward with loud cries –

> And deerskin-vested satyrs, crowned with ivy twists, advance;
> And put strange pity in their horned countenance.

Laelaps lies beneath, and shows by his panting the rapid pace of death. On the other side of the group, Virtuous Love with 'vans dejected' holds forth the arrow to an approaching troop of sylvan people, fauns, rams, goats, satyrs, and satyr-mothers, pressing their children tighter with their fearful hands, who hurry along from the left in a sunken path between the foreground and a rocky wall, on whose lowest ridge a brook-guardian pours from her urn her grief-telling waters. Above and more remote than the Ephidryad, another female, rending her locks, appears among the vine-festooned pillars of an unshorn grove. The centre of the picture is filled by shady meadows, sinking down to a river-mouth; beyond is 'the vast strength of the ocean stream', from whose floor the extinguisher of stars, rosy Aurora,[54] drives furiously up her brine-washed steeds to behold the death-pangs of her rival.

Were this description carefully re-written, it would be quite admirable. The conception of making a prose poem out of paint is excellent. Much of the best modern literature springs from the same aim. In a very ugly and sensible age, the arts borrow, not from life, but from each other.

His sympathies, too, were wonderfully varied. In everything connected with the stage, for instance, he was always extremely interested, and strongly upheld the necessity for archaeological accuracy in costume and scene-painting. 'In art,' he says in one of his essays, 'whatever is worth doing at all is worth doing well'; and he points out that once we allow the intrusion of anachronisms, it becomes difficult to say where the line is to be drawn. In literature, again, like Lord Beaconsfield on a famous occasion, he was 'on the side of the angels'.[55] He was one of the first to admire Keats and Shelley – 'the tremulously-sensitive and poetical Shelley', as he calls him. His admiration for Wordsworth was sincere and profound. He thoroughly appreciated William Blake. One of the best copies of the *Songs of Innocence and Experience* that is now in existence was wrought specially for him. He loved Alain Chartier, and Ronsard,[56] and the Elizabethan dramatists, and Chaucer and Chapman, and Petrarch.[57] And to him all the arts were one. 'Our critics,' he remarks with much wisdom, 'seem hardly aware of the identity of the primal seeds of poetry and painting, nor that any true advancement in the serious study of one art co-generates a proportionate perfection in the other'; and he says elsewhere that if a man who does not admire Michael Angelo talks of his love for Milton, he is deceiving either himself or his listeners. To his fellow-contributors in the *London Magazine* he was always most generous, and praises Barry Cornwall, Allan Cunningham, Hazlitt, Elton and Leigh Hunt[58] without anything of the malice of a friend. Some of his sketches of Charles Lamb are admirable in their way, and, with the art of the true comedian, borrow their style from their subject:

What can I say of thee more than all know? that thou hadst the gaiety of a boy with the knowledge of a man: as gentle a heart as ever sent tears to the eyes.

How wittily would he mistake your meaning, and put in a conceit most seasonably out of season. His talk without affectation was compressed, like his beloved Elizabethans, even unto obscurity. Like grains of fine gold, his sentences would beat out into whole sheets. He had small mercy on spurious fame, and a caustic observation on the *fashion for men of genius* was a standing dish. Sir Thomas Browne was a 'bosom cronie' of his, so was Burton, and old Fuller.[59] In his amorous vein he dallied with that peerless Duchess of many-folio odour; and with the heyday comedies of Beaumont and Fletcher[60] he induced light dreams. He would deliver critical touches on these, like one inspired, but it was good to let him choose his own game; if another began even on the acknowledged pets he was liable to interrupt, or rather append, in a mode difficult to define whether as misapprehensive or mischievous. One night at C——'s, the above dramatic partners were the temporary subject of chat. Mr X. commended the passion and haughty style of a tragedy (I don't know which of them), but was instantly taken up by Elia, who told him '*That* was nothing; the lyrics were the high things – the lyrics!'

One side of his literary career deserves especial notice. Modern journalism may be said to owe almost as much to him as to any man of the early part of this century. He was the pioneer of Asiatic prose, and delighted in pictorial epithets and pompous exaggerations. To have a style so gorgeous that it conceals the subject is one of the highest achievements of an important and much admired school of Fleet Street leader-writers, and this school *Janus Weathercock* may be said to have invented. He also saw that it was quite easy by continued reiteration to make the public interested in his own personality, and in his purely journalistic articles this extraordinary young man tells the world what he had for dinner, where he gets his clothes, what wines he likes, and in what state of health he is, just as if he were writing weekly notes for some popular newspaper of our own time. This being the least valuable side of his work, is the one that has had the most obvious influence. A publicist, nowadays, is a man who bores the community with the details of the illegalities of his private life.

Like most artificial people, he had a great love of nature. 'I hold three things in high estimation,' he says somewhere: 'to sit lazily on an eminence that commands a rich prospect; to be shadowed by thick trees while the sun shines around me; and to enjoy solitude with the

consciousness of neighbourhood. The country gives them all to me.'
He writes about his wandering over fragrant furze and heath repeating
Collins's 'Ode to Evening',[61] just to catch the fine quality of the
moment; about smothering his face 'in a watery bed of cowslips, wet
with May dews'; and about the pleasure of seeing the sweet-breathed
kine 'pass slowly homeward through the twilight,' and hearing 'the
distant clank of the sheep-bell'. One phrase of his, 'the polyanthus
glowed in its cold bed of earth, like a solitary picture of Giorgione on
a dark oaken panel', is curiously characteristic of his temperament,
and this passage is rather pretty in its way:

The short tender grass was covered with marguerites – 'such that men called
daisies in our town' – thick as stars on a summer's night. The harsh caw of the
busy rooks came pleasantly mellowed from a high dusky grove of elms at some
distance off, and at intervals, was heard the voice of a boy scaring away the
birds from the newly-sown seeds. The blue depths were the colour of the
darkest ultramarine; not a cloud streaked the calm aether; only round
the horizon's edge streamed a light, warm film of misty vapour, against which
the near village with its ancient stone church showed sharply out with blinding
whiteness. I thought of Wordsworth's 'Lines written in March'.

However, we must not forget that the cultivated young man who
penned these lines, and who was so susceptible to Wordsworthian
influences, was also, as I said at the beginning of this memoir, one of
the most subtle and secret poisoners of this or any age. How he first
became fascinated by this strange sin he does not tell us, and the diary
in which he carefully noted the results of his terrible experiments and
the methods that he adopted, has unfortunately been lost to us. Even
in later days, too, he was always reticent on the matter, and preferred
to speak about 'The Excursion', and the 'Poems founded on the
Affections'. There is no doubt, however, that the poison that he used
was strychnine. In one of the beautiful rings of which he was so proud,
and which served to show off the fine modelling of his delicate ivory
hands, he used to carry crystals of the Indian *nux vomica*, a poison, one
of his biographers tells us, 'nearly tasteless, difficult of discovery, and
capable of almost infinite dilution'. His murders, says De Quincey,

were more than were ever made known judicially. This is no doubt so, and some of them are worthy of mention. His first victim was his uncle, Mr Thomas Griffiths. He poisoned him in 1829 to gain possession of Linden House, a place to which he had always been very much attached. In the August of the next year he poisoned Mrs Abercrombie, his wife's mother, and in the following December he poisoned the lovely Helen Abercrombie, his sister-in-law. Why he murdered Mrs Abercrombie is not ascertained. It may have been for a caprice, or to quicken some hideous sense of power that was in him, or because she suspected something, or for no reason. But the murder of Helen Abercrombie was carried out by himself and his wife for the sake of a sum of about £18,000, for which they had insured her life in various offices. The circumstances were as follows. On the 12th of December, he and his wife and child came up to London from Linden House, and took lodgings at No. 12 Conduit Street, Regent Street. With them were the two sisters, Helen and Madeleine Abercrombie. On the evening of the 14th they all went to the play, and at supper that night Helen sickened. The next day she was extremely ill, and Dr Locock, of Hanover Square, was called in to attend her. She lived till Monday, the 20th, when, after the doctor's morning visit, Mr and Mrs Wainewright brought her some poisoned jelly, and then went out for a walk. When they returned Helen Abercrombie was dead. She was about twenty years of age, a tall graceful girl with fair hair. A very charming red-chalk drawing of her by her brother-in-law is still in existence, and shows how much his style as an artist was influenced by Sir Thomas Lawrence,[62] a painter for whose work he had always entertained a great admiration. De Quincey says that Mrs Wainewright was not really privy to the murder. Let us hope that she was not. Sin should be solitary, and have no accomplices.

The insurance companies, suspecting the real facts of the case, declined to pay the policy on the technical ground of misrepresentation and want of interest, and, with curious courage, the poisoner entered an action in the Court of Chancery against the Imperial, it being agreed that one decision should govern all the cases. The trial, however, did not come on for five years, when, after one disagreement, a verdict was ultimately given in the companies' favour. The judge on the occasion was Lord Abinger. *Egomet Bonmot* was represented by Mr Erle and Sir William Follet, and the Attorney-General and Sir Frederick Pollock appeared for the other side. The plaintiff, unfortunately, was unable to be present at either of the trials. The refusal of the companies to give him the £18,000 had placed him in a position of most painful pecuniary embarrassment. Indeed, a few months after the murder of Helen Abercrombie, he had been actually arrested for debt in the streets of London while he was serenading the pretty daughter of one of his friends. This difficulty was got over at the time, but shortly afterwards he thought it better to go abroad till he could come to some practical arrangement with his creditors. He accordingly went to Boulogne on a visit to the father of the young lady in question, and while he was there induced him to insure his life with the Pelican Company for £3,000. As soon as the necessary formalities had been gone through and the policy executed, he dropped some crystals of strychnine into his coffee as they sat together one evening after dinner. He himself did not gain any monetary advantage by doing this. His aim was simply to revenge himself on the first office that had refused to pay him the price of his sin. His friend died the next day in his presence, and he left Boulogne at once for a sketching tour through the most picturesque parts of Brittany, and was for some time the guest of an old French gentleman, who had a beautiful country house at St Omer. From this he moved to Paris, where he remained for several years, living in luxury, some say, while others talk of his 'skulking with poison in his pocket, and being dreaded by all who knew him'. In 1837 he returned to England privately. Some strange mad fascination brought him back. He followed a woman whom he loved.

It was the month of June, and he was staying at one of the hotels in Covent Garden. His sitting-room was on the ground floor, and he prudently kept the blinds down for fear of being seen. Thirteen years before, when he was making his fine collection of majolica and Marc Antonios, he had forged the names of his trustees to a power of attorney, which enabled him to get possession of some of the money which he had inherited from his mother, and had brought into marriage settlement. He knew that this forgery had been discovered, and that by returning to England he was imperilling his life. Yet he returned. Should one wonder? It was said that the woman was very beautiful. Besides, she did not love him.

It was by a mere accident that he was discovered. A noise in the street attracted his attention, and, in his artistic interest in modern life, he pushed aside the blind for a moment. Some one outside called out, 'That's Wainewright, the Bank-forger.' It was Forrester, the Bow Street runner.[63]

On the 5th of July he was brought up at the Old Bailey. The following report of the proceedings appeared in the *Times*:

Before Mr Justice Vaughan and Mr Baron Alderson, Thomas Griffiths Waine-wright, aged forty-two, a man of gentlemanly appearance, wearing musta-chios, was indicted for forging and uttering a certain power of attorney for £2,259, with intent to defraud the Governor and Company of the Bank of England.

There were five indictments against the prisoner, to all of which he pleaded not guilty, when he was arraigned before Mr Serjeant Arabin in the course of the morning. On being brought before the judges, however, he begged to be allowed to withdraw the former plea, and then pleaded guilty to two of the indictments which were not of a capital nature.

The counsel for the Bank having explained that there were three other indictments, but that the Bank did not desire to shed blood, the plea of guilty on the two minor charges was recorded, and the prisoner at the close of the session sentenced by the Recorder to transportation for life.

He was taken back to Newgate, preparatory to his removal to the colonies. In a fanciful passage in one of his early essays he had fancied himself 'lying in Horsemonger Gaol under sentence of death' for having been unable to resist the temptation of stealing some Marc Antonios from the British Museum in order to complete his collection. The sentence now passed on him was to a man of his culture a form of death. He complained bitterly of it to his friends, and pointed out, with a good deal of reason, some people may fancy, that the money was practically his own, having come to him from his mother, and that the forgery, such as it was, had been committed thirteen years before, which, to use his own phrase, was at least a *circonstance attenuante*.[64] The permanence of personality is a very subtle metaphysical problem, and certainly the English law solves the question in an extremely rough-and-ready manner. There is, however, something dramatic in the fact that this heavy punishment was inflicted on him for what, if we remember his fatal influence on the prose of modern journalism, was certainly not the worst of all his sins.

While he was in gaol, Dickens, Macready and Hablot Browne[65] came across him by chance. They had been going over the prisons of London, searching for artistic effects, and in Newgate they suddenly caught sight of Wainewright. He met them with a defiant stare, Forster[66] tells us, but Macready was 'horrified to recognize a man familiarly known to him in former years, and at whose table he had dined'.

Others had more curiosity, and his cell was for some time a kind of fashionable lounge. Many men of letters went down to visit their old literary comrade. But he was no longer the kind light-hearted Janus whom Charles Lamb admired. He seems to have grown quite cynical.

To the agent of an insurance company who was visiting him one afternoon, and thought he would improve the occasion by pointing out that, after all, crime was a bad speculation, he replied: 'Sir, you City men enter on your speculations, and take the chances of them. Some of your speculations succeed, some fail. Mine happen to have failed, yours happen to have succeeded. That is the only difference, sir, between my visitor and me. But, sir, I will tell you one thing in which I have succeeded to the last. I have been determined through life to hold the position of a gentleman. I have always done so. I do so still. It is the custom of this place that each of the inmates of a cell shall take his morning's turn of sweeping it out. I occupy a cell with a bricklayer and a sweep, but they never offer me the broom!' When a friend reproached him with the murder of Helen Abercrombie he shrugged his shoulders and said, 'Yes; it was a dreadful thing to do, but she had very thick ankles.'

From Newgate he was brought to the hulks at Portsmouth,[67] and sent from there in the *Susan* to Van Diemen's Land[68] along with three hundred other convicts. The voyage seems to have been most distasteful to him, and in a letter written to a friend he spoke bitterly about the ignominy of 'the companion of poets and artists' being compelled to associate with 'country bumpkins'. The phrase that he applies to his companions need not surprise us. Crime in England is rarely the result of sin. It is nearly always the result of starvation. There was probably no one on board in whom he would have found a sympathetic listener, or even a psychologically interesting nature.

His love of art, however, never deserted him. At Hobart Town he started a studio, and returned to sketching and portrait-painting, and his conversation and manners seem not to have lost their charm. Nor did he give up his habit of poisoning, and there are two cases on record in which he tried to make away with people who had offended him. But his hand seems to have lost its cunning. Both of his attempts were complete failures, and in 1844, being thoroughly dissatisfied with Tasmanian society, he presented a memorial to the governor of the settlement, Sir John Eardley Wilmot, praying for a ticket-of-leave. In it he speaks of himself as being 'tormented by ideas struggling for outward form and realization, barred up from increase of knowledge, and deprived of the exercise of profitable or even of decorous speech'. His request, however, was refused, and the associate of Coleridge consoled himself by making those marvellous *Paradis Artificiels*[69] whose secret is only known to the eaters of opium. In 1852 he died of apoplexy, his sole living companion being a cat, for which he had evinced an extraordinary affection.

His crimes seem to have had an important effect upon his art. They gave a strong personality to his style, a quality that his early work certainly lacked. In a note to the *Life of Dickens*, Forster mentions that in 1847 Lady Blessington received from her brother, Major Power, who held a military appointment at Hobart Town, an oil portrait of a young lady from his clever brush; and it is said that 'he had contrived to put the expression of his own wickedness into the portrait of a nice, kind-hearted girl'. M. Zola, in one of his novels, tells us of a young man who, having committed a murder, takes to art, and paints greenish impressionist portraits of perfectly respectable people, all of which bear a curious resemblance to his victim. The development of Mr

Wainewright's style seems to me far more subtle and suggestive. One can fancy an intense personality being created out of sin.

This strange and fascinating figure that for a few years dazzled literary London, and made so brilliant a *début* in life and letters, is undoubtedly a most interesting study. Mr W. Carew Hazlitt, his latest biographer, to whom I am indebted for many of the facts contained in this memoir, and whose little book is, indeed, quite invaluable in its way, is of opinion that his love of art and nature was a mere pretence and assumption, and others have denied to him all literary power. This seems to me a shallow, or at least a mistaken, view. The fact of a man being a poisoner is nothing against his prose. The domestic virtues are not the true basis of art, though they may serve as an excellent advertisement for second-rate artists. It is possible that De Quincey exaggerated his critical powers, and I cannot help saying again that there is much in his published works that is too familiar, too common, too journalistic, in the bad sense of that bad word. Here and there he is distinctly vulgar in expression, and he is always lacking in the self-restraint of the true artist. But for some of his faults we must blame the time in which he lived, and, after all, prose that Charles Lamb thought 'capital' has no small historic interest. That he had a sincere love of art and nature seems to me quite certain. There is no essential incongruity between crime and culture. We cannot re-write the whole of history for the purpose of gratifying our moral sense of what should be.

Of course, he is far too close to our own time for us to be able to form any purely artistic judgement about him. It is impossible not to feel a strong prejudice against a man who might have poisoned Lord Tennyson, or Mr Gladstone, or the Master of Balliol.[70] But had the man worn a costume and spoken a language different from our own, had he lived in imperial Rome, or at the time of the Italian Renaissance, or in Spain in the seventeenth century, or in any land or any century but this century and this land, we would be quite able to arrive at a perfectly unprejudiced estimate of his position and value. I know that there are many historians, or at least writers on historical subjects, who still think it necessary to apply moral judgements to history, and who distribute their praise or blame with the solemn complacency of a successful schoolmaster. This, however, is a foolish habit, and merely shows that the moral instinct can be brought to such a pitch of perfection that it will make its appearance wherever it is not required. Nobody with the true historical sense ever dreams of blaming Nero, or scolding Tiberius, or censuring Caesar Borgia.[71] These personages have become like the puppets of a play. They may fill us with terror, or horror, or wonder, but they do not harm us. They are not in immediate relation to us. We have nothing to fear from them. They have passed into the sphere of art and science, and neither art nor science knows anything of moral approval or disapproval. And so it may be some day with Charles Lamb's friend. At present I feel that he is just a little too modern to be treated in that fine spirit of disinterested curiosity to which we owe so many charming studies of the great criminals of the Italian Renaissance from the pens of Mr John Addington Symonds, Miss A. Mary F. Robinson, Miss Vernon Lee[72] and other distinguished writers. However, Art has not forgotten him. He is the hero of Dickens's 'Hunted Down', the Varney of Bulwer's *Lucretia*;[73] and it is gratifying to note that fiction has paid some homage to one who was so powerful with 'pen, pencil and poison'. To be suggestive for fiction is to be of more importance than a fact.

3. The Critic as Artist
With some remarks on the importance
of doing nothing

A dialogue. Part I.
Persons: *Gilbert and Ernest.*
Scene: *the library of a house in Piccadilly, overlooking the Green Park.*

GILBERT (*at the piano*): My dear Ernest, what are you laughing at?

ERNEST (*looking up*): At a capital story that I have just come across in this volume of Reminiscences that I have found on your table.

GILBERT: What is the book? Ah! I see. I have not read it yet. Is it good?

ERNEST: Well, while you have been playing, I have been turning over the pages with some amusement, though, as a rule, I dislike modern memoirs. They are generally written by people who have either entirely lost their memories, or have never done anything worth remembering; which, however, is, no doubt, the true explanation of their popularity, as the English public always feels perfectly at its ease when a mediocrity is talking to it.

GILBERT: Yes: the public is wonderfully tolerant. It forgives everything except genius. But I must confess that I like all memoirs. I like them for their form, just as much as for their matter. In literature mere egotism is delightful. It is what fascinates us in the letters of personalities so different as Cicero and Balzac, Flaubert and Berlioz, Byron and Madame de Sévigné.[1] Whenever we come across it, and, strangely enough, it is rather rare, we cannot but welcome it, and do not easily forget it. Humanity will always love Rousseau[2] for having confessed his sins, not to a priest, but to the world, and the couchant nymphs that Cellini[3] wrought in bronze for the castle of King Francis, the green and gold Perseus, even, that in the open Loggia at Florence shows the moon the dead terror that once turned life to stone, have not given it more pleasure than has that autobiography in which the supreme scoundrel of the Renaissance relates the story of his splendour and his shame. The opinions, the character, the achievements of the man, matter very little. He may be a sceptic like the gentle Sieur de Montaigne,[4] or a saint like the bitter son of Monica,[5] but when he tells us his own secrets he can always charm our ears to listening and our lips to silence. The mode of thought that Cardinal Newman[6] represented – if that can be called a mode of thought which seeks to solve intellectual problems by a denial of the supremacy of the intellect – may not, cannot, I think, survive. But the world will never weary of watching that troubled soul in its progress from darkness to darkness. The lonely church at Littlemore,[7] where 'the breath of the morning is damp, and worshippers are few', will always be dear to it, and whenever men see the yellow snapdragon blossoming on the wall of Trinity they will think of that gracious undergraduate[8] who saw in the flower's sure recurrence a prophecy that he would abide for ever with the Benign Mother[9] of his days – a prophecy that Faith, in her wisdom or her folly, suffered not to be fulfilled. Yes; autobiography is irresistible. Poor, silly, conceited Mr Secretary Pepys[10] has chattered his way into the circle of the Immortals, and, conscious that indiscretion is the better part of valour, bustles about among them in that 'shaggy purple gown with gold buttons and looped lace' which he is so fond of describing to us, perfectly at his ease, and prattling, to his own and our infinite pleasure, of the Indian blue petticoat that he bought for his wife, of the 'good hog's harslet', and the 'pleasant French fricassee of veal' that he loved to eat, of his game of bowls with Will Joyce, and his 'gadding after beauties', and his reciting of *Hamlet* on a Sunday, and his playing of the viol on week days, and other wicked or trivial things. Even in actual life egotism is not without its attractions. When people talk to us about others they are usually dull. When they talk to us about themselves they are nearly always interesting, and if one could shut them up, when they become wearisome, as easily as one can shut up a book of which one has grown wearied, they would be perfect absolutely.

ERNEST: There is much virtue in that If, as Touchstone[11] would say. But do you seriously propose that every man should become his own

Boswell?[12] What would become of our industrious compilers of Lives and Recollections in that case?

GILBERT: What has become of them? They are the pest of the age, nothing more and nothing less. Every great man nowadays has his disciples, and it is always Judas who writes the biography.

ERNEST: My dear fellow!

GILBERT: I am afraid it is true. Formerly we used to canonize our heroes. The modern method is to vulgarize them. Cheap editions of great books may be delightful, but cheap editions of great men are absolutely detestable.

ERNEST: May I ask, Gilbert, to whom you allude?

GILBERT: Oh! to all our second-rate *littérateurs*. We are overrun by a set of people who, when poet or painter passes away, arrive at the house along with the undertaker, and forget that their one duty is to behave as mutes.[13] But we won't talk about them. They are the mere body-snatchers of literature. The dust is given to one, and the ashes to another, and the soul is out of their reach. And now let me play Chopin to you, or Dvorák?[14] Shall I play you a fantasy by Dvorák? He writes passionate, curiously-coloured things.

ERNEST: No; I don't want music just at present. It is far too indefinite. Besides, I took the Baroness Bernstein down to dinner last night, and, though absolutely charming in every other respect, she insisted on discussing music as if it were actually written in the German language. Now, whatever music sounds like, I am glad to say that it does not sound in the smallest degree like German. There are forms of patriotism that are really quite degrading. No; Gilbert, don't play any more. Turn round and talk to me. Talk to me till the white-horned day comes into the room. There is something in your voice that is wonderful.

GILBERT (*rising from the piano*): I am not in a mood for talking tonight. I really am not. How horrid of you to smile! Where are the cigarettes? Thanks. How exquisite these single daffodils are! They seem to be made of amber and cool ivory. They are like Greek things of the best period. What was the story in the confessions of the remorseful Academician[15] that made you laugh? Tell it to me. After playing Chopin, I feel as if I had been weeping over sins that I had never committed, and mourning over tragedies that were not my own. Music always seems to me to produce that effect. It creates for one a past of which one has been ignorant, and fills one with a sense of sorrows that have been hidden from one's tears. I can fancy a man who had led a perfectly commonplace life, hearing by chance some curious piece of music, and suddenly discovering that his soul, without his being conscious of it, had passed through terrible experiences, and known fearful joys, or wild romantic loves, or great renunciations. And so tell me this story, Ernest. I want to be amused.

ERNEST: Oh! I don't know that it is of any importance. But I thought it a really admirable illustration of the true value of ordinary art-criticism. It seems that a lady once gravely asked the remorseful Academician, as you call him, if his celebrated picture of 'A Spring-Day at Whiteley's', or 'Waiting for the Last Omnibus', or some subject of that kind, was all painted by hand?

GILBERT: And was it?

ERNEST: You are quite incorrigible. But, seriously speaking, what is the use of art-criticism? Why cannot the artist be left alone, to create a new world if he wishes it, or, if not, to shadow forth the world which we already know, and of which, I fancy, we would each one of us be wearied if Art, with her fine spirit of choice and delicate instinct of selection, did not, as it were, purify it for us, and give to it a momentary perfection. It seems to me that the imagination spreads, or should spread, a solitude around it, and works best in silence and in isolation. Why should the artist be troubled by the shrill clamour of criticism? Why should those who cannot create take upon themselves to estimate the value of creative work? What can they know about it? If a man's work is easy to understand, an explanation is unnecessary . . .

GILBERT: And if his work is incomprehensible, an explanation is wicked.

ERNEST: I did not say that.

GILBERT: Ah! but you should have. Nowadays, we have so few mysteries left to us that we cannot afford to part with one of them. The members of the Browning Society,[16] like the theologians of the Broad Church Party,[17] or the authors of Mr Walter Scott's Great Writers Series,[18] seem to me to spend their time in trying to explain their divinity away. Where one had hoped that Browning was a mystic, they have sought to show that he was simply inarticulate. Where one had fancied that he had something to conceal, they have proved that he had but little to reveal. But I speak merely of his incoherent work. Taken as a whole the man was great. He did not belong to the Olympians, and had all the incompleteness of the Titans.[19] He did not survey, and it was but rarely that he could sing. His work is marred by struggle, violence and effort, and he passed not from emotion to form, but from thought to chaos. Still, he was great. He has been called a thinker, and was certainly a man who was always thinking, and always thinking aloud; but it was not thought that fascinated him, but rather the processes by which thought moves. It was the machine he loved, not what the machine makes. The method by which the fool arrives at his folly was as dear to him as the ultimate wisdom of the wise. So much, indeed, did the subtle mechanism of mind fascinate him that he despised language, or looked upon it as an incomplete instrument of expression. Rhyme, that exquisite echo which in the Muse's hollow hill creates and answers its own voice; rhyme, which in the hands of the real artist becomes not merely a material element of metrical beauty, but a spiritual element of thought and passion also, waking a new mood, it may be, or stirring a fresh train of ideas, or opening by mere sweetness and suggestion of sound some golden door at which the Imagination itself had knocked in vain; rhyme, which can turn man's utterance to the speech of gods; rhyme, the one chord we have added to the Greek lyre,[20] became in Robert Browning's[21] hands a grotesque, misshapen thing, which at times made him masquerade in poetry as a low comedian, and ride Pegasus too often with his tongue in his cheek. There are moments when he wounds us by monstrous music. Nay, if he can only get his music by breaking the strings of his lute, he breaks them, and they snap in discord, and no Athenian tettix,[22] making melody from tremulous wings, lights on the ivory horn to make the movement perfect, or the interval less harsh. Yet, he was great: and though he turned language into ignoble clay, he made from it men and women that live. He is the most Shakespearean creature since Shakespeare. If Shakespeare could sing with myriad lips, Browning could stammer through a thousand mouths. Even now, as I am speaking, and speaking not against him but for him, there glides through the room the pageant of his persons. There, creeps Fra Lippo Lippi with his cheeks still burning from some girl's hot kiss. There, stands dread Saul with the lordly male sapphires gleaming in his turban. Mildred Tresham is there, and the Spanish monk, yellow with hatred, and Blougram, and Ben Ezra, and the Bishop of St Praxed's. The spawn of Setebos gibbers in the corner, and Sebald, hearing Pippa pass by, looks on Ottima's haggard face, and loathes her and his own sin, and himself. Pale as the white satin of his doublet, the melancholy king watches with dreamy treacherous eyes too loyal Strafford pass forth to his doom, and Andrea shudders as he hears the cousin's whistle in the garden, and bids his perfect wife go down. Yes, Browning was great. And as what will he be remembered? As a poet? Ah, not as a poet! He will be remembered as a writer of fiction, as the most supreme writer of fiction, it may be, that we have ever had. His sense of dramatic situation was unrivalled, and, if he could not answer his own problems, he could at least put problems forth, and what more should an artist do? Considered from the point of view of a creator of character he ranks next to him who made Hamlet. Had he been articulate, he might have sat beside him. The only man who can touch the hem of his garment is George Meredith.[23] Meredith is a prose Browning, and so is Browning. He used poetry as a medium for writing in prose.

ERNEST: There is something in what you say, but there is not everything in what you say. In many points you are unjust.

GILBERT: It is difficult not to be unjust to what one loves. But let us return to the particular point at issue. What was it that you said?

ERNEST: Simply this: that in the best days of art there were no art-critics.

GILBERT: I seem to have heard that observation before, Ernest. It has all the vitality of error and all the tediousness of an old friend.

ERNEST: It is true. Yes: there is no use your tossing your head in that petulant manner. It is quite true. In the best days of art there were no art-critics. The sculptor hewed from the marble block the great white-limbed Hermes[24] that slept within it. The waxers and gilders of images gave tone and texture to the statue, and the world, when it saw it, worshipped and was dumb. He poured the glowing bronze into the mould of sand, and the river of red metal cooled into noble curves and took the impress of the body of a god. With enamel or polished jewels he gave sight to the sightless eyes. The hyacinth-like curls grew crisp beneath his graver. And when, in some dim frescoed fane,[25] or pillared sunlit portico, the child of Leto[26] stood upon his pedestal, those who passed by, ἁβρῶς βαίνοντες διὰ λαμπροτάτου αἰθέρος,[27] became conscious of a new influence that had come across their lives, and dreamily, or with a sense of strange and quickening joy, went to their homes or daily labour, or wandered, it may be, through the city gates to that nymph-haunted meadow where young Phaedrus[28] bathed his feet, and, lying there on the soft grass, beneath the tall wind-whispering planes and flowering *agnus castus*,[29] began to think of the wonder of beauty, and grew silent with unaccustomed awe. In those days the artist was free. From the river valley he took the fine clay in his fingers, and with a little tool of wood or bone, fashioned it into forms so exquisite that the people gave them to the dead as their playthings, and we find them still in the dusty tombs on the yellow hillside by Tanagra,[30] with the faint gold and the fading crimson still lingering about hair and lips and raiment. On a wall of fresh plaster, stained with bright sandyx or mixed with milk and saffron, he pictured one who trod with tired feet the purple white-starred fields of asphodel,[31] one 'in whose eyelids lay the whole of the Trojan War', Polyxena,[32] the daughter of Priam; or figured Odysseus, the wise and cunning, bound by tight cords to the mast-step, that he might listen without hurt to the singing of the Sirens, or wandering by the clear river of Acheron,[33] where the ghosts of fishes flitted over the pebbly bed; or showed the Persian in trews and mitre[34] flying before the Greek at Marathon,[35] or the galleys clashing their beaks of brass in the little Salaminian bay.[36] He drew with silver-point and charcoal upon parchment and prepared cedar. Upon ivory and rose-coloured terracotta he painted with wax, making the wax fluid with juice of olives, and with heated irons making it firm. Panel and marble and linen canvas became wonderful as his brush swept across them; and life seeing her own image, was still, and dared not speak. All life, indeed, was his, from the merchants seated in the market-place to the cloaked shepherd lying on the hill; from the nymph hidden in the laurels and the faun that pipes at noon, to the king whom, in long green-curtained litter, slaves bore upon oil-bright shoulders, and fanned with peacock fans. Men and women, with pleasure or sorrow in their faces, passed before him. He watched them, and their secret became his. Through form and colour he re-created a world.

All subtle arts belonged to him also. He held the gem against the revolving disk, and the amethyst became the purple couch for Adonis, and across the veined sardonyx sped Artemis[37] with her hounds. He beat out the gold into roses, and strung them together for necklace or armlet. He beat out the gold into wreaths for the conqueror's helmet, or into palmates[38] for the Tyrian robe,[39] or into masks for the royal dead. On the back of the silver mirror he graved Thetis[40] borne by her Nereids, or love-sick Phaedra[41] with her nurse, or Persephone,[42] weary of memory, putting poppies in her hair. The potter sat in his shed, and, flower-like from the silent wheel, the vase rose up beneath his hands. He decorated the base and stem and ears with pattern of dainty olive-leaf, or foliated acanthus, or curved and crested wave. Then in black or red he painted lads wrestling, or in the race: knights in full armour, with strange heraldic shields and curious visors, leaning from shell-shaped chariot over rearing steeds: the gods seated at the feast or working their miracles: the heroes in their victory or in their pain. Sometimes he would etch in thin vermilion lines upon a ground of white the languid bridegroom and his bride, with Eros hovering round them – an Eros like one of Donatello's[43] angels, a little laughing thing with gilded or with azure wings. On the curved side he would write the name of his friend. ΚΑΛΟΣ ΑΛΚΙΒΙΑΔΗΣ or ΚΑΛΟΣ ΧΑΡΜΙΔΗΣ[44] tells us the story of his days. Again, on the rim of the wide flat cup he would draw the stag browsing, or the lion at rest, as his fancy willed it. From the tiny perfume-bottle laughed Aphrodite at her toilet, and, with bare-limbed Maenads[45] in his train, Dionysus danced round the wine-jar on naked must-stained feet,[46] while, satyr-like, the old Silenus[47] sprawled upon the bloated skins, or shook that magic spear which was tipped with a fretted fir-cone, and wreathed with dark ivy. And no one came to trouble the artist at his work. No irresponsible chatter disturbed him. He was not worried by opinions.

By the Ilyssus, says Arnold somewhere, there was no Higginbotham.[48] By the Ilyssus, my dear Gilbert, there were no silly art congresses bringing provincialism to the provinces and teaching the mediocrity how to mouth. By the Ilyssus there were no tedious magazines about art, in which the industrious prattle of what they do not understand. On the reed-grown banks of that little stream strutted no ridiculous journalism monopolizing the seat of judgement when it should be apologizing in the dock. The Greeks had no art-critics.

GILBERT: Ernest, you are quite delightful, but your views are terribly unsound. I am afraid that you have been listening to the conversation of someone older than yourself. That is always a dangerous thing to do, and if you allow it to degenerate into a habit you will find it absolutely fatal to any intellectual development. As for modern journalism, it is not my business to defend it. It justifies its own existence by the great Darwinian principle of the survival of the vulgarest. I have merely to do with literature.

ERNEST: But what is the difference between literature and journalism?

GILBERT: Oh! journalism is unreadable, and literature is not read. That is all. But with regard to your statement that the Greeks had no art-critics, I assure you that is quite absurd. It would be more just to say that the Greeks were a nation of art-critics.

ERNEST: Really?

GILBERT: Yes, a nation of art-critics. But I don't wish to destroy the delightfully unreal picture that you have drawn of the relation of the Hellenic artist to the intellectual spirit of his age. To give an accurate description of what has never occurred is not merely the proper occupation of the historian, but the inalienable privilege of any man of parts and culture. Still less do I desire to talk learnedly. Learned conversation is either the affectation of the ignorant or the profession of the mentally unemployed. And, as for what is called improving conversation, that is merely the foolish method by which the still more foolish philanthropist feebly tries to disarm the just rancour of the criminal classes. No: let me play to you some mad scarlet thing by Dvořák. The pallid figures on the tapestry are smiling at us, and the heavy eyelids of my bronze Narcissus[49] are folded in sleep. Don't let us discuss anything solemnly. I am but too conscious of the fact that we are born in an age when only the dull are treated seriously, and I live in terror of not being misunderstood. Don't degrade me into the position of giving you useful information. Education is an admirable thing, but it is well to remember from time to time that nothing that is worth knowing can be taught. Through the parted curtains of the window I see the moon like a clipped piece of silver. Like gilded bees the stars cluster round her. The sky is a hard hollow sapphire. Let us go out into the night. Thought is wonderful, but adventure is more wonderful still. Who knows but we may meet Prince Florizel of Bohemia,[50] and hear the fair Cuban tell us that she is not what she seems?

ERNEST: You are horribly wilful. I insist on your discussing this matter with me. You have said that the Greeks were a nation of art-critics. What art-criticism have they left us?

GILBERT: My dear Ernest, even if not a single fragment of art-criticism had come down to us from Hellenic or Hellenistic days, it would be none the less true that the Greeks were a nation of art-critics, and that they invented the criticism of art just as they invented the criticism of everything else. For, after all, what is our primary debt to the Greeks? Simply the critical spirit. And, this spirit, which they exercised on questions of religion and science, of ethics and metaphysics, of politics and education, they exercised on questions of art also, and, indeed, of the two supreme and highest arts, they have left us the most flawless system of criticism that the world has ever seen.

ERNEST: But what are the two supreme and highest arts?

GILBERT: Life and Literature, life and the perfect expression of life. The principles of the former, as laid down by the Greeks, we may not realize in an age so marred by false ideals as our own. The principles of the latter, as they laid them down, are, in many cases, so subtle that we can hardly understand them. Recognizing that the most perfect art is that which most fully mirrors man in all his infinite variety, they elaborated the criticism of language, considered in the light of the mere material of that art, to a point to which we, with our accentual system of reasonable or emotional emphasis, can barely if at all attain; studying, for instance, the metrical movements of a prose as scientifically as a modern musician studies harmony and counterpoint, and, I need hardly say, with much keener aesthetic instinct. In this they were right, as they were right in all things. Since the introduction of printing, and the fatal development of the habit of reading amongst the middle and lower classes of this country, there has been a tendency in literature to appeal more and more to the eye, and less and less to the ear which is really the sense which, from the standpoint of pure art, it should seek to please, and by whose canons of pleasure it should abide always. Even the work of Mr Pater, who is, on the whole, the most perfect master of English prose now creating amongst us, is often far more like a piece of mosaic than a passage in music, and seems, here and there, to lack the true rhythmical life of words and the fine freedom and richness of effect that such rhythmical life produces. We, in fact, have made writing a definite mode of composition, and have treated it as a form of elaborate design. The Greeks, upon the other hand, regarded writing simply as a method of chronicling. Their test was always the spoken word in its musical and metrical relations. The voice was the medium, and the ear the critic. I have sometimes thought that the story of Homer's blindness might be really an artistic myth, created in critical days, and serving to remind us, not merely that the great poet is always a seer, seeing less with the eyes of the body than he does with the eyes of the soul, but that he is a true singer also, building his song out of music, repeating each line over and over again to himself till he has caught the secret of its melody, chaunting in darkness the words that are winged with light. Certainly, whether this be so or not, it was to his blindness, as an occasion, if not as a cause, that England's great poet owed much of the majestic movement and sonorous splendour of his later verse. When Milton could no longer write he began to sing. Who would match the measures of *Comus* with the measures of *Samson Agonistes*, or of *Paradise Lost* or *Regained*? When Milton became blind he composed, as everyone should compose, with the voice purely, and so the pipe or reed of earlier days became that mighty many-stopped organ whose rich reverberant music has all the stateliness of Homeric verse, if it seeks not to have its swiftness, and is the one imperishable inheritance of English literature sweeping through all the ages, because above them, and abiding with us ever, being immortal in its form. Yes: writing has done much harm to writers. We must return to the voice. That must be our test, and perhaps then we shall be able to appreciate some of the subtleties of Greek art-criticism.

As it now is, we cannot do so. Sometimes, when I have written a piece of prose that I have been modest enough to consider absolutely free from fault, a dreadful thought comes over me that I may have been guilty of the immoral effeminacy of using trochaic and tribrachic movements,[51] a crime for which a learned critic of the Augustan age censures with most just severity the brilliant if somewhat paradoxical Hegesias.[52] I grow cold when I think of it, and wonder to myself if the admirable ethical effect of the prose of that charming writer, who once in a spirit of reckless generosity towards the uncultivated portion of our community proclaimed the monstrous doctrine that conduct is three-fourths of life,[53] will not some day be entirely annihilated by the discovery that the paeons[54] have been wrongly placed.

ERNEST: Ah! now you are flippant.

GILBERT: Who would not be flippant when he is gravely told that the Greeks had no art-critics? I can understand it being said that the constructive genius of the Greeks lost itself in criticism, but not that the race to whom we owe the critical spirit did not criticize. You will not ask me to give you a survey of Greek art-criticism from Plato to Plotinus. The night is too lovely for that, and the moon, if she heard us, would put more ashes on her face than are there already. But think merely of one perfect little work of aesthetic criticism, Aristotle's *Treatise on Poetry*. It is not perfect in form, for it is badly written, consisting perhaps of notes jotted down for an art lecture, or of isolated fragments destined for some larger book, but in temper and treatment it is perfect, absolutely. The ethical effect of art, its importance to culture, and its place in the formation of character, had been done once for all by Plato; but here we have art treated, not from the moral, but from the purely aesthetic point of view. Plato had, of course, dealt with many definitely artistic subjects, such as the importance of unity in a work of art, the necessity for tone and harmony, the aesthetic value of appearances, the relation of the visible arts to the external world, and the relation of fiction to fact. He first perhaps stirred in the soul of man that desire that we have not yet satisfied, the desire to know the connection between Beauty and Truth, and the place of Beauty in the moral and intellectual order of the Kosmos. The problems of idealism and realism, as he sets them forth, may seem to many to be somewhat barren of result in the metaphysical sphere of abstract being in which he places them, but transfer them to the sphere of art, and you will find that they are still vital and full of meaning. It may be that it is as a critic of Beauty that Plato is destined to live, and that by altering the name of the sphere of his speculation we shall find a new philosophy. But Aristotle, like Goethe, deals with art primarily in its concrete manifestations, taking Tragedy, for instance, and investigating the material it uses, which is language, its subject-matter, which is life, the method by which it works, which is action, the conditions under which it reveals itself, which are those of theatric presentation, its logical structure, which is plot, and its final aesthetic appeal, which is to the sense of beauty realized through the passions of pity and awe. That purification and spiritualizing of the nature which he calls κάθαρσις[55] is, as Goethe saw, essentially aesthetic, and is not moral, as Lessing[56] fancied. Concerning himself primarily with the impression that the work of art produces, Aristotle sets himself to analyse that impression, to investigate its source, to see how it is engendered. As a physiologist and psychologist, he knows that the health of a function resides in energy. To have a capacity for a passion and not to realize it, is to make oneself incomplete and limited. The mimic spectacle of life that Tragedy affords cleanses the bosom of much 'perilous stuff', and by presenting high and worthy objects for the exercise of the emotions purifies and spiritualizes the man; nay, not merely does it spiritualize him, but it initiates him also into noble feelings of which he might else have known nothing, the word κάθαρσις having, it has sometimes seemed to me, a definite allusion to the rite of initiation, if indeed that be not, as I am occasionally tempted to fancy, its true and only meaning here. This is of course a mere outline of the book. But you see what a perfect piece of aesthetic criticism it is. Who indeed but a Greek could have analysed art so well? After reading it, one does not wonder any longer that Alexandria[57] devoted itself so largely to art-criticism, and that we find the artistic temperaments of the day investigating every question of style and manner, discussing the great Academic schools of painting, for instance, such as the school of Sicyon,[58] that sought to preserve the dignified traditions of the antique mode, or the realistic and impressionist schools, that aimed at reproducing actual life, or the elements of ideality in portraiture, or the artistic value of the epic form in an age so modern as theirs, or the proper subject-matter for the artist. Indeed, I fear that the inartistic temperaments of the day busied themselves also in matters of literature and art, for the accusations of plagiarism were endless, and such accusations proceed either from the thin colourless lips of impotence, or from the grotesque mouths of those who, possessing nothing of their own, fancy that they can gain a reputation for wealth by crying out that they have been robbed. And I assure you, my dear Ernest, that the Greeks chattered about painters quite as much as people do nowadays, and had their private views, and shilling exhibitions, and Arts and Crafts guilds, and Pre-Raphaelite movements,[59] and movements towards realism, and lectured about art, and wrote essays on art, and produced their art-historians, and their archaeologists, and all the rest of it. Why, even the theatrical managers of travelling companies brought their dramatic critics with them when they went on tour, and paid them very handsome salaries for writing laudatory notices. Whatever, in fact, is modern in our life we owe to the Greeks. Whatever is an anachronism is due to medievalism. It is the Greeks who have given us the whole system of art-criticism, and how fine their critical instinct was, may be seen from the fact that the material they criticized with most care was, as I have already said, language. For the material that painter or sculptor uses is meagre in comparison with that of words. Words have not merely music as sweet as that of viol and lute, colour as rich and vivid as any that makes lovely for us the canvas of the Venetian or the Spaniard, and plastic form no less sure and certain than that which reveals itself in marble or in bronze, but thought and passion and spirituality are theirs also, are theirs indeed alone. If the Greeks had criticized nothing but language, they would still have been the great art-critics of the world. To know the principles of the highest art is to know the principles of all the arts.

But I see that the moon is hiding behind a sulphur-coloured cloud. Out of a tawny mane of drift she gleams like a lion's eye. She is afraid that I will talk to you of Lucian and Longinus, of Quinctilian and Dionysius, of Pliny and Fronto and Pausanias,[60] of all those who in the antique world wrote or lectured upon art matters. She need not be afraid. I am tired of my expedition into the dim, dull abyss of facts. There is nothing left for me now but the divine μονόχρονος ἡδονή[61] of another cigarette. Cigarettes have at least the charm of leaving one unsatisfied.

ERNEST: Try one of mine. They are rather good. I get them direct from Cairo. The only use of our *attachés*[62] is that they supply their friends with excellent tobacco. And as the moon has hidden herself, let us talk a little longer. I am quite ready to admit that I was wrong in what I said about the Greeks. They were, as you have pointed out, a nation of art-critics. I acknowledge it, and I feel a little sorry for them. For the creative faculty is higher than the critical. There is really no comparison between them.

GILBERT: The antithesis between them is entirely arbitrary. Without the critical faculty, there is no artistic creation at all, worthy of the name. You spoke a little while ago of that fine spirit of choice and delicate instinct of selection by which the artist realizes life for us, and gives to it a momentary perfection. Well, that spirit of choice, that subtle tact of omission, is really the critical faculty in one of its most characteristic moods, and no one who does not possess this critical faculty can create anything at all in art. Arnold's definition of literature as a criticism of life,[63] was not very felicitous in form, but it showed how keenly he recognized the importance of the critical element in all creative work.

ERNEST: I should have said that great artists worked unconsciously, that they were 'wiser than they knew',[64] as, I think, Emerson remarks somewhere.

GILBERT: It is really not so, Ernest. All fine imaginative work is self-conscious and deliberate. No poet sings because he must sing. At least, no great poet does. A great poet sings because he chooses to sing. It is so now, and it has always been so. We are sometimes apt to think that the voices that sounded at the dawn of poetry were simpler, fresher and more natural than ours, and that the world which the early poets looked at, and through which they walked, had a kind of poetical quality of its own, and almost without changing could pass into song. The snow lies thick now upon Olympus, and its steep scarped sides are bleak and barren, but once, we fancy, the white feet of the Muses brushed the dew from the anemones in the morning, and at evening came Apollo to sing to the shepherds in the vale. But in this we are merely lending to other ages what we desire, or think we desire, for our own. Our historical sense is at fault. Every century that produces poetry is, so far, an artificial century, and the work that seems to us to be the most natural and simple product of its time is always the result of the most self-conscious effort. Believe me, Ernest, there is no fine art without self-consciousness, and self-consciousness and the critical spirit are one.

ERNEST: I see what you mean, and there is much in it. But surely you would admit that the great poems of the early world, the primitive, anonymous collective poems, were the result of the imagination of races, rather than of the imagination of individuals?

GILBERT: Not when they became poetry. Not when they received a beautiful form. For there is no art where there is no style, and no style where there is no unity, and unity is of the individual. No doubt Homer had old ballads and stories to deal with, as Shakespeare had chronicles and plays and novels from which to work, but they were merely his rough material. He took them, and shaped them into song. They become his, because he made them lovely. They were built out of music,

> And so not built at all,
> And therefore built for ever.[65]

The longer one studies life and literature, the more strongly one feels that behind everything that is wonderful stands the individual, and that it is not the moment that makes the man, but the man who creates the age. Indeed, I am inclined to think that each myth and legend that seems to us to spring out of the wonder, or terror, or fancy of tribe and nation, was in its origin the invention of one single mind. The curiously limited number of the myths seems to me to point to this conclusion. But we must not go off into questions of comparative mythology. We must keep to criticism. And what I want to point out is this. An age that has no criticism is either an age in which art is immobile, hieratic, and confined to the reproduction of formal types, or an age that possesses no art at all. There have been critical ages that have not been creative, in the ordinary sense of the word, ages in which the spirit of man has sought to set in order the treasures of his treasure-house, to separate the gold from the silver, and the silver from the lead, to count over the jewels, and to give names to the pearls. But there has never been a creative age that has not been critical also. For it is the critical faculty that invents fresh forms. The tendency of creation is to repeat itself. It is to the critical instinct that we owe each new school that springs up, each new mould that art finds ready to its hand. There is really not a single form that art now uses that does not come to us from the critical spirit of Alexandria, where these forms were either stereotyped or invented or made perfect. I say Alexandria, not merely because it was there that the Greek spirit became most self-conscious, and indeed ultimately expired in scepticism and theology, but because it was to that city, and not to Athens, that Rome turned for her models, and it was through the survival, such as it was, of the Latin language that culture lived at all. When, at the Renaissance, Greek literature dawned upon Europe, the soil had been in some measure prepared for it. But, to get rid of the details of history, which are always wearisome and usually inaccurate, let us say generally, that the forms of art have been due to the Greek critical spirit. To it we owe the epic, the lyric, the entire drama in every one of its developments, including burlesque, the idyll, the romantic novel, the novel of adventure, the essay, the dialogue, the oration, the lecture, for which perhaps we should not forgive them, and the epigram, in all the wide meaning of that word. In fact, we owe it everything, except the sonnet, to which, however, some curious parallels of thought-movement may be traced in the Anthology,[66] American journalism, to which no parallel can be found anywhere, and the ballad in sham Scotch dialect, which one of our most industrious writers[67] has recently proposed should be made the basis for a final and unanimous effort on the part of our second-rate poets to make themselves really romantic. Each new school, as it appears, cries out against criticism, but it is to the critical faculty in man that it owes its origin. The mere creative instinct does not innovate, but reproduces.

ERNEST: You have been talking of criticism as an essential part of the creative spirit, and I now fully accept your theory. But what of criticism outside creation? I have a foolish habit of reading periodicals, and it seems to me that most modern criticism is perfectly valueless.

GILBERT: So is most modern creative work also. Mediocrity weighing mediocrity in the balance, and incompetence applauding its brother – that is the spectacle which the artistic activity of England affords us from time to time. And yet, I feel I am a little unfair in this matter. As a rule, the critics – I speak, of course, of the higher class, of those in fact who write for the sixpenny papers – are far more cultured than the people whose work they are called upon to review. This is, indeed, only what one would expect, for criticism demands infinitely more cultivation than creation does.

ERNEST: Really?

GILBERT: Certainly. Anybody can write a three-volumed novel.[68] It merely requires a complete ignorance of both life and literature. The difficulty that I should fancy the reviewer feels is the difficulty of sustaining any standard. Where there is no style a standard must be impossible. The poor reviewers are apparently reduced to be the reporters of the police-court of literature, the chroniclers of the doings of the habitual criminals of art. It is sometimes said of them that they do not read all through the works they are called upon to criticize. They do not. Or at least they should not. If they did so, they would become confirmed misanthropes, or if I may borrow a phrase from one of the pretty Newnham graduates,[69] confirmed womanthropes for the rest of their lives. Nor is it necessary. To know the vintage and quality of a wine one need not drink the whole cask. It must be perfectly easy in half an hour to say whether a book is worth anything or worth nothing. Ten minutes are really sufficient, if one has the instinct for form. Who wants to wade through a dull volume? One tastes it, and that is quite enough – more than enough, I should imagine. I am aware that there are many honest workers in painting as well as in literature who object to criticism entirely. They are quite right. Their work stands in no intellectual relation to their age. It brings us no new element of pleasure. It suggests no fresh departure of thought, or passion, or beauty. It should not be spoken of. It should be left to the oblivion that it deserves.

ERNEST: But, my dear fellow — excuse me for interrupting you — you seem to me to be allowing your passion for criticism to lead you a great deal too far. For, after all, even you must admit that it is much more difficult to do a thing than to talk about it.

GILBERT: More difficult to do a thing than to talk about it? Not at all. That is a gross popular error. It is very much more difficult to talk about a thing than to do it. In the sphere of actual life that is of course obvious. Anybody can make history. Only a great man can write it. There is no mode of action, no form of emotion, that we do not share with the lower animals. It is only by language that we rise above them, or above each other — by language, which is the parent, and not the child, of thought. Action, indeed, is always easy, and when presented to us in its most aggravated, because most continuous form, which I take to be that of real industry, becomes simply the refuge of people who have nothing whatsoever to do. No, Ernest, don't talk about action. It is a blind thing dependent on external influences, and moved by an impulse of whose nature it is unconscious. It is a thing incomplete in its essence, because limited by accident, and ignorant of its direction, being always at variance with its aim. Its basis is the lack of imagination. It is the last resource of those who know not how to dream.

ERNEST: Gilbert, you treat the world as if it were a crystal ball. You hold it in your hand, and reverse it to please a wilful fancy. You do nothing but re-write history.

GILBERT: The one duty we owe to history is to re-write it. That is not the least of the tasks in store for the critical spirit. When we have fully discovered the scientific laws that govern life, we shall realize that the one person who has more illusions than the dreamer is the man of action. He, indeed, knows neither the origin of his deeds nor their results. From the field in which he thought that he had sown thorns, we have gathered our vintage, and the fig-tree that he planted for our pleasure is as barren as the thistle, and more bitter. It is because

Humanity has never known where it was going that it has been able to find its way.

ERNEST: You think, then, that in the sphere of action a conscious aim is a delusion?

GILBERT: It is worse than a delusion. If we lived long enough to see the results of our actions it may be that those who call themselves good would be sickened with a dull remorse, and those whom the world calls evil stirred by a noble joy. Each little thing that we do passes into the great machine of life which may grind our virtues to powder and make them worthless, or transform our sins into elements of a new civilization, more marvellous and more splendid than any that has gone before. But men are the slaves of words. They rage against Materialism, as they call it, forgetting that there has been no material improvement that has not spiritualized the world, and that there have been few, if any, spiritual awakenings that have not wasted the world's faculties in barren hopes, and fruitless aspirations, and empty or trammelling creeds. What is termed Sin is an essential element of progress. Without it the world would stagnate, or grow old, or become colourless. By its curiosity Sin increases the experience of the race. Through its intensified assertion of individualism, it saves us from monotony of type. In its rejection of the current notions about morality, it is one with the higher ethics. And as for the virtues! What are the virtues? Nature, M. Renan[70] tells us, cares little about chastity, and it may be that it is to the shame of the Magdalen, and not to their own purity, that the Lucretias[71] of modern life owe their freedom from stain. Charity, as even those of whose religion it makes a formal part have been compelled to acknowledge, creates a multitude of evils. The mere existence of conscience, that faculty of which people prate so much nowadays, and are so ignorantly proud, is a sign of our imperfect development. It must be merged in instinct before we become fine. Self-denial is simply a method by which man arrests his progress, and self-sacrifice a survival of the mutilation of the savage, part of that old worship of pain which is so terrible a factor in the history of the world, and which even now makes its victims day by day, and has its altars in the land. Virtues! Who knows what the virtues are? Not you. Not I. Not any one. It is well for our vanity that we slay the criminal, for if we suffered him to live he might show us what we had gained by his crime. It is well for his peace that the saint goes to his martyrdom. He is spared the sight of the horror of his harvest.

ERNEST: Gilbert, you sound too harsh a note. Let us go back to the more gracious fields of literature. What was it you said? That it was more difficult to talk about a thing than to do it?

GILBERT (*after a pause*): Yes: I believe I ventured upon that simple truth. Surely you see now that I am right? When man acts he is a puppet. When he describes he is a poet. The whole secret lies in that. It was easy enough on the sandy plains by windy Ilion[72] to send the notched arrow from the painted bow, or to hurl against the shield of hide and flamelike brass the long ash-handled spear. It was easy for the adulterous queen to spread the Tyrian carpets for her lord, and then, as he lay couched in the marble bath, to throw over his head the purple net, and call to her smooth-faced lover to stab through the meshes at the heart that should have broken at Aulis.[73] For Antigone[74] even, with Death waiting for her as her bridegroom, it was easy to pass through the tainted air at noon, and climb the hill, and strew with kindly earth the wretched naked corse that had no tomb. But what of those who wrote about these things? What of those who gave them reality, and made them live for ever? Are they not greater than the men and women they sing of? 'Hector that sweet knight is dead,' and Lucian tells us how in the dim under-world Menippus[75] saw the bleaching skull of Helen, and marvelled that it was for so grim a favour that all those horned ships were launched, those beautiful mailed men laid low, those towered cities brought to dust. Yet, every day the swanlike daughter of Leda[76] comes out of the battlements, and looks down at the tide of war. The greybeards wonder at her loveliness, and she stands by the side of the king. In his chamber of stained ivory lies her leman.[77] He is polishing his dainty armour, and combing the scarlet plume. With squire and page, her husband passes from tent to tent. She can see his bright hair, and hears, or fancies that she hears, that clear cold voice. In the courtyard below, the son of Priam[78] is buckling on his brazen cuirass. The white arms of Andromache are around his neck. He sets his helmet on the ground, lest their babe should be frightened. Behind the embroidered curtains of his pavilion sits Achilles, in perfumed raiment, while in harness of gilt and silver the friend of his soul[79] arrays himself to go forth to the fight. From a curiously carven chest that his mother Thetis had brought to his ship-side, the Lord of the Myrmidons[80] takes out that mystic chalice that the lip of man had never touched, and cleanses it with brimstone, and with fresh water cools it, and, having washed his hands, fills with black wine its burnished hollow, and spills the thick grape-blood upon the ground in honour of Him whom at Dodona[81] barefooted prophets worshipped, and prays to Him, and knows not that he prays in vain, and that by the hands of two knights from Troy, Panthous' son, Euphorbus,[82] whose love-locks were looped with gold, and the Priamid, the lion-hearted, Patroklus, the comrade of comrades, must meet his doom. Phantoms, are they? Heroes of mist and mountain? Shadows in a song? No: they are real. Action! What is action? It dies at the moment of its energy. It is a base concession to fact. The world is made by the singer for the dreamer.

ERNEST: While you talk it seems to me to be so.

GILBERT: It is so in truth. On the mouldering citadel of Troy lies the lizard like a thing of green bronze. The owl has built her nest in the palace of Priam. Over the empty plain wander shepherd and goatherd with their flocks, and where, on the wine-surfaced, oily sea, οἶνοψ πόντος,[83] as Homer calls it, copper-prowed and streaked with vermilion, the great galleys of the Danaoi[84] came in their gleaming crescent, the lonely tunny-fisher sits in his little boat and watches the bobbing corks of his net. Yet, every morning the doors of the city are thrown open, and on foot, or in horse-drawn chariot, the warriors go forth to battle, and mock their enemies from behind their iron masks. All day long the fight rages, and when night comes the torches gleam by the tents, and the cresset[85] burns in the hall. Those who live in marble or on painted panel, know of life but a single exquisite instant, eternal indeed in its beauty, but limited to one note of passion or one mood of calm. Those whom the poet makes live have their myriad emotions of joy and terror, of courage and despair, of pleasure and of suffering. The seasons come and go in glad or saddening pageant, and with winged or leaden feet the years pass by before them. They have their youth and their manhood, they are children, and they grow old.

It is always dawn for St Helena, as Veronese saw her at the window. Through the still morning air the angels bring her the symbol of God's pain. The cool breezes of the morning lift the gilt threads from her brow. On that little hill by the city of Florence, where the lovers of Giorgione are lying, it is always the solstice of noon, of noon made so languorous by summer suns that hardly can the slim naked girl dip into the marble tank the round bubble of clear glass, and the long fingers of the lute-player rest idly upon the chords. It is twilight always for the dancing nymphs whom Corot[86] set free among the silver poplars of France. In eternal twilight they move, those frail diaphanous figures, whose tremulous white feet seem not to touch the dew-drenched grass they tread on. But those who walk in epos,[87] drama, or romance, see through the labouring months the young moons wax and wane, and watch the night from evening unto morning star, and from sunrise unto sunsetting, can note the shifting day with all its gold and shadow. For them, as for us, the flowers bloom and wither, and the Earth, that Green-tressed Goddess as Coleridge calls her, alters her raiment for their pleasure. The statue is concentrated[88] to one moment of perfection. The image stained upon the canvas possesses no spiritual element of growth or change. If they know nothing of death, it is because they know little of life, for the secrets of life and death belong to those, and those only, whom the sequence of time affects, and who possess not merely the present but the future, and can rise or fall from a past of glory or of shame. Movement, that problem of the visible arts, can be truly realized by Literature alone. It is Literature that shows us the body in its swiftness and the soul in its unrest.

ERNEST: Yes; I see now what you mean. But, surely, the higher you place the creative artist, the lower must the critic rank.

GILBERT: Why so?

ERNEST: Because the best that he can give us will be but an echo of rich music, a dim shadow of clear-outlined form. It may, indeed, be that life is chaos, as you tell me that it is; that its martyrdoms are mean and its heroisms ignoble; and that it is the function of Literature to create, from the rough material of actual existence, a new world that will be more marvellous, more enduring and more true than the world that common eyes look upon, and through which common natures seek to realize their perfection. But surely, if this new world has been made by the spirit and touch of a great artist, it will be a thing so complete and perfect that there will be nothing left for the critic to do. I quite understand now, and indeed admit most readily, that it is far more difficult to talk about a thing than to do it. But it seems to me that this sound and sensible maxim, which is really extremely soothing to one's feelings, and should be adopted as its motto by every Academy of Literature all over the world, applies only to the relations that exist between Art and Life, and not to any relations that there may be between Art and Criticism.

GILBERT: But, surely, Criticism is itself an art. And just as artistic creation implies the working of the critical faculty, and, indeed, without it cannot be said to exist at all, so Criticism is really creative in the highest sense of the word. Criticism is, in fact, both creative and independent.

ERNEST: Independent?

GILBERT: Yes; independent. Criticism is no more to be judged by any low standard of imitation or resemblance than is the work of poet or sculptor. The critic occupies the same relation to the work of art that he criticizes as the artist does to the visible world of form and colour, or the unseen world of passion and of thought. He does not even require for the perfection of his art the finest materials. Anything will serve his purpose. And just as out of the sordid and sentimental amours of the silly wife of a small country doctor in the squalid village of Yonville-l'Abbaye, near Rouen, Gustave Flaubert was able to create a classic, and make a masterpiece of style,[89] so, from subjects of little or of no importance, such as the pictures in this year's Royal Academy, or in any year's Royal Academy for that matter, Mr Lewis Morris's poems, M. Ohnet's novels, or the plays of Mr Henry Arthur Jones,[90] the true critic can, if it be his pleasure so to direct or waste his faculty of contemplation, produce work that will be flawless in beauty and instinct with intellectual subtlety. Why not? Dulness is always an irresistible temptation for brilliancy, and stupidity is the permanent *Bestia Trionfans*[91] that calls wisdom from its cave. To an artist so creative as the critic, what does subject-matter signify? No more and no less than it does to the novelist and the painter. Like them, he can find his motives everywhere. Treatment is the test. There is nothing that has not in it suggestion or challenge.

ERNEST: But is Criticism really a creative art?

GILBERT: Why should it not be? It works with materials, and puts them into a form that is at once new and delightful. What more can one say of poetry? Indeed, I would call criticism a creation within a creation. For just as the great artists, from Homer and Aeschylus, down to Shakespeare and Keats, did not go directly to life for their subject-matter, but sought for it in myth, and legend, and ancient tale, so the critic deals with materials that others have, as it were, purified for him, and to which imaginative form and colour have been already added. Nay, more, I would say that the highest Criticism, being the purest form of personal impression, is in its way more creative than creation, as it has least reference to any standard external to itself, and is, in fact, its own reason for existing, and, as the Greeks would put it, in itself, and to itself, an end. Certainly, it is never trammelled by any shackles of verisimilitude. No ignoble considerations of probability, that cowardly concession to the tedious repetitions of domestic or public life, affect it ever. One may appeal from fiction unto fact. But from the soul there is no appeal.

ERNEST: From the soul?

GILBERT: Yes, from the soul. That is what the highest Criticism really is, the record of one's own soul. It is more fascinating than history, as it is concerned simply with oneself. It is more delightful than philosophy, as its subject is concrete and not abstract, real and not vague. It is the only civilized form of autobiography, as it deals not with the events, but with the thoughts of one's life; not with life's physical accidents of deed or circumstance, but with the spiritual moods and imaginative passions of the mind. I am always amused by the silly vanity of those writers and artists of our day who seem to imagine that the primary function of the critic is to chatter about their second-rate work. The best that one can say of most modern creative art is that it is just a little less vulgar than reality, and so the critic, with his fine sense of distinction and sure instinct of delicate refinement, will prefer to look into the silver mirror or through the woven veil, and will turn his eyes away from the chaos and clamour of actual existence, though the mirror be tarnished and the veil be torn. His sole aim is to chronicle his own impressions. It is for him that pictures are painted, books written, and marble hewn into form.

ERNEST: I seem to have heard another theory of Criticism.

GILBERT: Yes: it has been said by one whose gracious memory we all revere,[92] and the music of whose pipe once lured Proserpina from her Sicilian fields, and made those white feet stir, and not in vain, the Cumnor cowslips, that the proper aim of Criticism is to see the object as in itself it really is. But this is a very serious error, and takes no cognizance of Criticism's most perfect form, which is in its essence purely subjective, and seeks to reveal its own secret and not the secret of another. For the highest Criticism deals with art not as expressive but as impressive purely.

ERNEST: But is that really so?

GILBERT: Of course it is. Who cares whether Mr Ruskin's views on Turner[93] are sound or not? What does it matter? That mighty and majestic prose of his, so fervid and so fiery-coloured in its noble eloquence, so rich in its elaborate symphonic music, so sure and certain, at its best, in subtle choice of word and epithet, is at least as great a work of art as any of those wonderful sunsets that bleach or rot on their corrupted canvases in England's Gallery; greater indeed, one is apt to think at times, not merely because its equal beauty is more enduring, but on account of the fuller variety of its appeal, soul speaking to soul in those long-cadenced lines, not through form and colour alone, though through these, indeed, completely and without loss, but with intellectual and emotional utterance, with lofty passion and with loftier thought, with imaginative insight, and with poetic aim; greater, I always think, even as Literature is the greater art. Who, again, cares whether Mr Pater has put into the portrait of Monna Lisa[94] something that Lionardo never dreamed of? The painter may have been merely the slave of an archaic smile, as some have fancied, but whenever I pass into the cool galleries of the Palace of the Louvre, and stand before that strange figure 'set in its marble chair in that cirque of fantastic rocks, as in some faint light under sea', I murmur to myself, 'She is older than the rocks among which she sits; like the vampire, she has been dead many times, and learned the secrets of the grave; and has been a diver in deep seas, and keeps their fallen day about her; and trafficked for strange webs with Eastern merchants; and, as Leda, was the mother of Helen of Troy, and, as St Anne, the mother of Mary; and all this has been to her but as the sound of lyres and flutes, and lives only in the delicacy with which it has moulded the changing lineaments, and tinged the eyelids and the hands.' And I say to my friend, 'The presence that thus so strangely rose beside the waters is expressive of what in the ways of a thousand years man had come to desire'; and he answers me, 'Hers is the head upon which all "the ends of the world are come", and the eyelids are a little weary.'

And so the picture becomes more wonderful to us than it really is, and reveals to us a secret of which, in truth, it knows nothing, and the music of the mystical prose is as sweet in our ears as was that flute-player's music that lent to the lips of La Gioconda those subtle and poisonous curves. Do you ask me what Lionardo would have said had any one told him of this picture that 'all the thoughts and experience of the world had etched and moulded there in that which they had of power to refine and make expressive the outward form, the animalism of Greece, the lust of Rome, the reverie of the Middle Age with its spiritual ambition and imaginative loves, the return of the Pagan world, the sins of the Borgias'? He would probably have answered that he had contemplated none of these things, but had concerned himself simply with certain arrangements of lines and masses, and with new and curious colour-harmonies of blue and green. And it is for this very reason that the criticism which I have quoted is criticism of the highest kind. It treats the work of art simply as a starting-point for a new creation. It does not confine itself – let us at least suppose so for the moment – to discovering the real intention of the artist and accepting that as final. And in this it is right, for the meaning of any beautiful created thing is, at least, as much in the soul of him who looks at it, as it was in his soul who wrought it. Nay, it is rather the beholder who lends to the beautiful thing its myriad meanings, and makes it marvellous for us, and sets it in some new relation to the age, so that it becomes a vital portion of our lives, and a symbol of what we pray for, or perhaps of what, having prayed for, we fear that we may receive. The longer I study, Ernest, the more clearly I see that the beauty of the visible arts is, as the beauty of music, impressive primarily, and that it may be marred, and indeed often is so, by any excess of intellectual intention on the part of the artist. For when the work is finished it has, as it were, an independent life of its own, and may deliver a message far other than that which was put into its lips to say. Sometimes, when I listen to the overture to *Tannhäuser*,[95] I seem indeed to see that comely knight treading delicately on the flower-strewn grass, and to hear the voice of Venus calling to him from the caverned hill. But at other times it speaks to me of a thousand different things, of myself, it may be, and my own life, or of the lives of others whom one has loved and grown weary of loving, or of the passions that man has known, or of the passions that man has not known, and so has sought for. Tonight it may fill one with that ΕΡΩΣ ΤΩΝ ΑΔΥΝΑΤΩΝ,[96] that *Amour de l'Impossible*, which falls like a madness on many who think they live securely and out of reach of harm, so that they sicken suddenly with the poison of unlimited desire, and, in the infinite pursuit of what they may not obtain, grow faint and swoon or stumble. Tomorrow, like the music of which Aristotle and Plato tell us, the noble Dorian music[97] of the Greek, it may perform the office of a physician, and give us an anodyne against pain, and heal the spirit that is wounded, and 'bring the soul into harmony with all right things'. And what is true about music is true about all the arts. Beauty has as many meanings as man has moods. Beauty is the symbol of symbols. Beauty reveals everything, because it expresses nothing. When it shows us itself, it shows us the whole fiery-coloured world.

ERNEST: But is such work as you have talked about really criticism?

GILBERT: It is the highest Criticism, for it criticizes not merely the individual work of art, but Beauty itself, and fills with wonder a form which the artist may have left void, or not understood, or understood incompletely.

ERNEST: The highest Criticism, then, is more creative than creation, and the primary aim of the critic is to see the object as in itself it really is not; that is your theory, I believe?

GILBERT: Yes, that is my theory. To the critic the work of art is simply a suggestion for a new work of his own, that need not necessarily bear any obvious resemblance to the thing it criticizes. The one characteristic of a beautiful form is that one can put into it whatever one wishes, and see in it whatever one chooses to see; and the Beauty, that gives to creation its universal and aesthetic element, makes the critic a creator in his turn, and whispers of a thousand different things which were not present in the mind of him who carved the statue or painted the panel or graved the gem.

It is sometimes said by those who understand neither the nature of the highest Criticism nor the charm of the highest Art, that the pictures that the critic loves most to write about are those that belong to the anecdotage of painting, and that deal with scenes taken out of literature or history. But this is not so. Indeed, pictures of this kind are far too intelligible. As a class, they rank with illustrations, and even considered from this point of view are failures, as they do not stir the imagination, but set definite bounds to it. For the domain of the painter is, as I suggested before, widely different from that of the poet. To the latter belongs life in its full and absolute entirety; not merely the beauty that men look at, but the beauty that men listen to also; not merely the momentary grace of form or the transient gladness of colour, but the whole sphere of feeling, the perfect cycle of thought. The painter is so far limited that it is only through the mask of the body that he can show us the mystery of the soul; only through conventional images that he can handle ideas; only through its physical equivalents that he can deal with psychology. And how inadequately does he do it then, asking us to accept the torn turban of the Moor for the noble rage of Othello, or a dotard in a storm for the wild madness of Lear! Yet it seems as if nothing could stop him. Most of our elderly English painters spend their wicked and wasted lives in poaching upon the domain of the poets, marring their motives by clumsy treatment, and striving to render, by visible form or colour, the marvel of what is invisible, the splendour of what is not seen. Their pictures are, as a natural consequence, insufferably tedious. They have degraded the invisible arts into the obvious arts, and the one thing not worth looking at is the obvious. I do not say that poet and painter may not treat of the same subject. They have always done so, and will always do so. But while the poet can be pictorial or not, as he chooses, the painter must be pictorial always. For a painter is limited, not to what he sees in nature, but to what upon canvas may be seen.

And so, my dear Ernest, pictures of this kind will not really fascinate the critic. He will turn from them to such works as make him brood and dream and fancy, to works that possess the subtle quality of suggestion, and seem to tell one that even from them there is an escape into a wider world. It is sometimes said that the tragedy of an artist's life is that he cannot realize his ideal. But the true tragedy that dogs the steps of most artists is that they realize their ideal too absolutely. For, when the ideal is realized, it is robbed of its wonder and its mystery, and becomes simply a new starting-point for an ideal that is other than itself. This is the reason why music is the perfect type of art. Music can never reveal its ultimate secret. This, also, is the explanation of the value of limitations in art. The sculptor gladly surrenders imitative colour, and the painter the actual dimensions of form, because by such renunciations they are able to avoid too definite a presentation of the Real, which would be mere imitation, and too definite a realization of the Ideal, which would be too purely intellectual. It is through its very incompleteness that Art becomes complete in beauty, and so addresses itself, not to the faculty of recognition nor to the faculty of reason, but to the aesthetic sense alone, which, while accepting both reason and recognition as stages of apprehension, subordinates them both to a pure synthetic impression of the work of art as a whole, and, taking whatever alien emotional elements the work may possess, uses their very complexity as a means by which a richer unity may be added to the ultimate impression itself. You see, then, how it is that the aesthetic critic rejects those obvious modes of art that have but one message to deliver, and having delivered it become dumb and sterile, and seeks rather for such modes as suggest reverie and mood, and by their imaginative beauty make all interpretations true, and no interpretation final. Some resemblance, no doubt, the creative work of the critic will have to the work that has stirred him to creation, but it will be such resemblance as exists, not between Nature and the mirror that the painter of landscape or figure may be supposed to hold up to her, but between Nature and the work of the decorative artist. Just as on the flowerless carpets of Persia, tulip and rose blossom indeed and are lovely to look on, though they are not reproduced in visible shape or line; just as the pearl and purple of the sea-shell is echoed in the church of St Mark at Venice; just as the vaulted ceiling of the wondrous chapel at Ravenna is made gorgeous by the gold and green and sapphire of the peacock's tail, though the birds of Juno fly not across it; so the critic reproduces the work that he criticizes in a mode that is never imitative, and part of whose charm may really consist in the rejection of resemblance, and shows us in this way not merely the meaning but also the mystery of Beauty, and, by transforming each art into literature, solves once and for all the problem of Art's unity.

But I see it is time for supper. After we have discussed some Chambertin and a few ortolans,[98] we will pass on to the question of the critic considered in the light of the interpreter.

ERNEST: Ah! you admit, then, that the critic may occasionally be allowed to see the object as in itself it really is.

GILBERT: I am not quite sure. Perhaps I may admit it after supper. There is a subtle influence in supper.

The Critic as Artist
With some remarks on the importance of discussing everything

A dialogue. Part II.
Persons: *the same.*
Scene: *the same.*

ERNEST: The ortolans were delightful, and the Chambertin perfect, and now let us return to the point at issue.

GILBERT: Ah! don't let us do that. Conversation should touch everything, but should concentrate itself on nothing. Let us talk about *Moral Indignation, its Cause and Cure*, a subject on which I think of writing:

or about *The Survival of Thersites*,[1] as shown by the English comic papers; or about any topic that may turn up.

ERNEST: No; I want to discuss the critic and criticism. You have told me that the highest criticism deals with art, not as expressive, but as impressive purely, and is consequently both creative and independent, is in fact an art by itself, occupying the same relation to creative work that creative work does to the visible world of form and colour, or the unseen world of passion and of thought. Well, now tell me, will not the critic be sometimes a real interpreter?

GILBERT: Yes; the critic will be an interpreter, if he chooses. He can pass from his synthetic impression of the work of art as a whole, to an analysis or exposition of the work itself, and in this lower sphere, as I hold it to be, there are many delightful things to be said and done. Yet his object will not always be to explain the work of art. He may seek rather to deepen its mystery, to raise round it, and round its maker, that mist of wonder which is dear to both gods and worshippers alike. Ordinary people are 'terribly at ease in Zion'.[2] They propose to walk arm in arm with the poets, and have a glib ignorant way of saying 'Why should we read what is written about Shakespeare and Milton? We can read the plays and the poems. That is enough.' But an appreciation of Milton is, as the late Rector of Lincoln[3] remarked once, the reward of consummate scholarship. And he who desires to understand Shakespeare truly must understand the relations in which Shakespeare stood to the Renaissance and the Reformation, to the age of Elizabeth and the age of James; he must be familiar with the history of the struggle for supremacy between the old classical forms and the new spirit of romance, between the school of Sidney, and Daniel, and Jonson, and the school of Marlowe and Marlowe's greater son;[4] he must know the materials that were at Shakespeare's disposal, and the method in which he used them, and the conditions of theatric presentation in the sixteenth and seventeenth century, their limitations and their opportunities for freedom, and the literary criticism of Shakespeare's day, its aims and modes and canons; he must study the English language in its progress, and blank or rhymed verse in its various developments; he must study the Greek drama, and the connection between the art of the creator of the Agamemnon[5] and the art of the creator of Macbeth; in a word, he must be able to bind Elizabethan London to the Athens of Pericles,[6] and to learn Shake-speare's true position in the history of European drama and the drama of the world. The critic will certainly be an interpreter, but he will not treat Art as a riddling Sphinx, whose shallow secret may be guessed and revealed by one whose feet are wounded[7] and who knows not his name. Rather, he will look upon Art as a goddess whose mystery it is his province to intensify, and whose majesty his privilege to make more marvellous in the eyes of men.

And here, Ernest, this strange thing happens. The critic will indeed be an interpreter, but he will not be an interpreter in the sense of one who simply repeats in another form a message that has been put into his lips to say. For, just as it is only by contact with the art of foreign nations that the art of a country gains that individual and separate life that we call nationality, so, by curious inversion, it is only by inten-sifying his own personality that the critic can interpret the personality and work of others, and the more strongly this personality enters into the interpretation the more real the interpretation becomes, the more satisfying, the more convincing, and the more true.

ERNEST: I would have said that personality would have been a disturbing element.

GILBERT: No; it is an element of revelation. If you wish to understand others you must intensify your own individualism.

ERNEST: What, then, is the result?

GILBERT: I will tell you, and perhaps I can tell you best by definite example. It seems to me that, while the literary critic stands of course first, as having the wider range, and larger vision, and nobler material, each of the arts has a critic, as it were, assigned to it. The actor is a critic of the drama. He shows the poet's work under new conditions, and by a method special to himself. He takes the written word, and action, gesture and voice become the media of revelation. The singer or the player on lute and viol, is the critic of music. The etcher of a picture robs the painting of its fair colours, but shows us by the use of a new material its true colour-quality, its tones and values, and the relations of its masses, and so is, in his way, a critic of it, for the critic is he who exhibits to us a work of art in a form different from that of the work itself, and the employment of a new material is a critical as well as a creative element. Sculpture, too, has its critic, who may be either the carver of a gem, as he was in Greek days, or some painter like Mantegna,[8] who sought to reproduce on canvas the beauty of plastic line and the symphonic dignity of processional bas-relief. And in the case of all these creative critics of art it is evident that personality is an absolute essential for any real interpretation. When Rubinstein[9] plays to us the *Sonata Appassionata* of Beethoven, he gives us not merely Beethoven, but also himself, and so gives us Beethoven absolutely – Beethoven re-interpreted through a rich artistic nature, and made vivid and wonderful to us by a new and intense personality. When a great actor plays Shakespeare we have the same experience. His own individuality becomes a vital part of the interpretation. People sometimes say that actors give us their own Hamlets, and not Shakespeare's; and this fallacy – for it is a fallacy – is, I regret to say, repeated by that charming and graceful writer who has lately deserted the turmoil of literature for the peace of the House of Commons, I mean the author of *Obiter Dicta*.[10] In point of fact, there is no such thing as Shakespeare's Hamlet. If Hamlet has something of the definiteness of a work of art, he has also all the obscurity that belongs to life. There are as many Hamlets as there are melancholies.

ERNEST: As many Hamlets as there are melancholies?

GILBERT: Yes: and as art springs from personality, so it is only to personality that it can be revealed, and from the meeting of the two comes right interpretative criticism.

ERNEST: The critic, then, considered as the interpreter, will give no less than he receives, and lend as much as he borrows?

GILBERT: He will be always showing us the work of art in some new relation to our age. He will always be reminding us that great works of art are living things – are, in fact, the only things that live. So much, indeed, will he feel this, that I am certain that, as civilization progresses and we become more highly organized, the elect spirits of each age, the critical and cultured spirits, will grow less and less interested in actual life, and will seek to gain their impressions almost entirely from what Art has touched. For Life is terribly deficient in form. Its catastrophes happen in the wrong way and to the wrong people. There is a grotesque horror about its comedies, and its tragedies seem to culminate in farce. One is always wounded when one approaches it. Things last either too long, or not long enough.

ERNEST: Poor life! Poor human life! Are you not even touched by the tears that the Roman poet[11] tells us are part of its essence?

GILBERT: Too quickly touched by them, I fear. For when one looks back upon the life that was so vivid in its emotional intensity, and filled with such fervent moments of ecstasy or of joy, it all seems to be a dream and an illusion. What are the unreal things, but the passions that once burned one like fire? What are the incredible things, but the things that one has faithfully believed? What are the improbable things? The things that one has done oneself. No, Ernest; life cheats us with shadows, like a puppet-master. We ask it for pleasure. It gives it to us, with bitterness and disappointment in its train. We come across some noble grief that we think will lend the purple dignity of tragedy to our days, but it passes away from us, and things less noble take its place, and on some grey windy dawn, or odorous eve of silence and of silver, we find ourselves looking with callous wonder, or dull heart of stone, at the tress of gold-flecked hair that we had once so wildly worshipped and so madly kissed.

ERNEST: Life then is a failure?

GILBERT: From the artistic point of view, certainly. And the chief thing that makes life a failure from this artistic point of view is the thing that lends to life its sordid security, the fact that one can never repeat exactly the same emotion. How different it is in the world of Art! On a shelf of the bookcase behind you stands the *Divine Comedy*,[12] and I know that, if I open it at a certain place, I shall be filled with a fierce hatred of someone who has never wronged me, or stirred by a great love for someone whom I shall never see. There is no mood or passion that Art cannot give us, and those of us who have discovered her secret can settle beforehand what our experiences are going to be. We can choose our day and select our hour. We can say to ourselves, 'Tomorrow, at dawn, we shall walk with grave Virgil through the valley of the shadow of death,' and lo! the dawn finds us in the obscure wood, and the Mantuan stands by our side. We pass through the gate of the legend fatal to hope, and with pity or with joy behold the horror of another world. The hypocrites go by, with their painted faces and their cowls of gilded lead. Out of the ceaseless winds that drive them, the carnal look at us, and we watch the heretic rending his flesh, and the glutton lashed by the rain. We break the withered branches from the tree in the grove of the Harpies, and each dull-hued poisonous twig bleeds with red blood before us, and cries aloud with bitter cries. Out of a horn of fire Odysseus speaks to us, and when from his sepulchre of flame the great Ghibelline rises, the pride that triumphs over the torture of that bed becomes ours for a moment. Through the dim purple air fly those who have stained the world with the beauty of their sin, and in the pit of loathsome disease, dropsy-stricken and swollen of body into the semblance of a monstrous lute, lies Adamo di Brescia, the coiner of false coin. He bids us listen to his misery; we stop, and with dry and gaping lips he tells us how he dreams day and night of the brooks of clear water that in cool dewy channels gush down the green Casentine hills. Sinon, the false Greek of Troy, mocks at him. He smites him in the face, and they wrangle. We are fascinated by their shame, and loiter, till Virgil chides us and leads us away to that city turreted by giants where great Nimrod blows his horn. Terrible things are in store for us, and we go to meet them in Dante's raiment and with Dante's heart. We traverse the marshes of the Styx, and Argenti swims to the boat through the slimy waves. He calls to us, and we reject him. When we hear the voice of his agony we are glad, and Virgil praises us for the bitterness of our scorn. We tread upon the cold crystal of Cocytus, in which traitors stick like straws in glass. Our foot strikes against the head of Bocca. He will not tell us his name, and we tear the hair in handfuls from the screaming skull. Alberigo prays us to break the ice upon his face that he may weep a little. We pledge our word to him, and when he has uttered his dolorous tale we deny the word that we have spoken, and pass from him; such cruelty being courtesy indeed, for who more base than he who has mercy for the condemned of God? In the jaws of Lucifer we see the man who sold Christ, and in the jaws of Lucifer the men who slew Caesar. We tremble, and come forth to re-behold the stars.

In the land of Purgation the air is freer, and the holy mountain rises into the pure light of day. There is peace for us, and for those who for a season abide in it there is some peace also, though, pale from the poison of the Maremma, Madonna Pia passes before us, and Ismene, with the sorrow of earth still lingering about her, is there. Soul after soul makes us share in some repentance or some joy. He whom the mourning of his widow taught to drink the sweet wormwood of pain, tells us of Nella praying in her lonely bed, and we learn from the mouth of Buonconte how a single tear may save a dying sinner from the fiend. Sordello, that noble and disdainful Lombard, eyes us from afar like a couchant lion. When he learns that Virgil is one of Mantua's citizens, he falls upon his neck, and when he learns that he is the singer of Rome he falls before his feet. In that valley whose grass and flowers are fairer than cleft emerald and Indian wood, and brighter than scarlet and silver, they are singing who in the world were kings; but the lips of Rudolph of Hapsburg do not move to the music of the others, and Philip of France beats his breast and Henry of England sits alone. On and on we go, climbing the marvellous stair, and the stars become larger than their wont, and the song of the kings grows faint, and at length we reach the seven trees of gold and the garden of the Earthly Paradise. In a griffin-drawn chariot appears one whose brows are bound with olive, who is veiled in white, and mantled in green, and robed in a vesture that is coloured like live fire. The ancient flame wakes within us. Our blood quickens through terrible pulses. We recognize her. It is Beatrice, the woman we have worshipped. The ice congealed about our heart melts. Wild tears of anguish break from us, and we bow our forehead to the ground, for we know that we have sinned. When we have done penance, and are purified, and have drunk of the fountain of Lethe and bathed in the fountain of Eunoe, the mistress of our soul raises us to the Paradise of Heaven. Out of that eternal pearl, the moon, the face of Piccarda Donati leans to us. Her beauty troubles us for a moment, and when, like a thing that falls through water, she passes away, we gaze after her with wistful eyes. The sweet planet of Venus is full of lovers. Cunizza, the sister of Ezzelin, the lady of Sordello's heart, is there, and Folco, the passionate singer of Provence, who in sorrow for Azalais forsook the world, and the Canaanitish harlot whose soul was the first that Christ redeemed. Joachim of Flora stands in the sun, and, in the sun, Aquinas recounts the story of St Francis and Bonaventure the story of St Dominic. Through the burning rubies of Mars, Cacciaguida approaches. He tells us of the arrow that is shot from the bow of exile, and how salt tastes the bread of another, and how steep are the stairs in the house of a stranger. In Saturn the soul sings not, and even she who guides us dare not smile. On a ladder of gold the flames rise and fall. At last, we see the pageant of the Mystical Rose. Beatrice fixes her eyes upon the face of God to turn them not again. The beatific vision is granted to us; we know the Love that moves the sun and all the stars.

Yes, we can put the earth back six hundred courses and make ourselves one with the great Florentine,[13] kneel at the same altar with him, and share his rapture and his scorn. And if we grow tired of an antique time, and desire to realize our own age in all its weariness and sin, are there not books that can make us live more in one single hour than life can make us live in a score of shameful years? Close to your hand lies a little volume, bound in some Nile-green skin that has been powdered with gilded nenuphars[14] and smoothed with hard ivory. It is the book that Gautier loved, it is Baudelaire's masterpiece.[15] Open it at that sad madrigal that begins

> Que m'importe que tu sois sage?
> Sois belle! et sois triste!

and you will find yourself worshipping sorrow as you have never worshipped joy. Pass on to the poem on the man who tortures himself, let its subtle music steal into your brain and colour your thoughts, and you will become for a moment what he was who wrote it; nay, not for a moment only, but for many barren moonlit nights and sunless sterile days will a despair that is not your own make its dwelling within you, and the misery of another gnaw your heart away. Read the whole book, suffer it to tell even one of its secrets to your soul, and your soul will grow eager to know more, and will feed upon poisonous honey,[16] and seek to repent of strange crimes of which it is guiltless, and to make atonement for terrible pleasures that it has never known. And then, when you are tired of these flowers of evil, turn to the flowers that grow in the garden of Perdita,[17] and in their dew-drenched chalices cool your fevered brow, and let their loveliness heal and restore your soul; or wake from his forgotten tomb the sweet Syrian, Meleager,[18] and bid the lover of Heliodore make you music, for he too has flowers in his song, red pomegranate blossoms, and irises that smell of myrrh, ringed daffodils and dark blue hyacinths, and marjoram and crinkled ox-eyes. Dear to him was the perfume of the bean-field at evening, and dear to him the odorous eared-spikenard that grew on the Syrian hills, and the fresh green thyme, the wine-cup's charm. The feet of his love as she walked in the garden were like lilies set upon lilies. Softer than sleep-laden poppy petals were her lips, softer than violets and as scented. The flame-like crocus sprang from the grass to look at her. For her the slim narcissus stored the cool rain; and for her the anemones forgot the Sicilian winds that wooed them. And neither crocus, nor anemone, nor narcissus was as fair as she was.

It is a strange thing, this transference of emotion. We sicken with the same maladies as the poets, and the singer lends us his pain. Dead lips have their message for us, and hearts that have fallen to dust can communicate their joy. We run to kiss the bleeding mouth of Fantine,[19] and we follow Manon Lescaut[20] over the whole world. Ours is the love-madness of the Tyrian,[21] and the terror of Orestes[22] is ours also. There is no passion that we cannot feel, no pleasure that we may not gratify, and we can choose the time of our initiation and the time of our freedom also. Life! Life! Don't let us go to life for our fulfilment or our experience. It is a thing narrowed by circumstances, incoherent in its utterance, and without that fine correspondence of form and spirit which is the only thing that can satisfy the artistic and critical temperament. It makes us pay too high a price for its wares, and we purchase the meanest of its secrets at a cost that is monstrous and infinite.

ERNEST: Must we go, then, to Art for everything?

GILBERT: For everything. Because Art does not hurt us. The tears that we shed at a play are a type of the exquisite sterile emotions that it is the function of Art to awaken. We weep, but we are not wounded. We grieve, but our grief is not bitter. In the actual life of man, sorrow, as Spinoza[23] says somewhere, is a passage to a lesser perfection. But the sorrow with which Art fills us both purifies and initiates, if I may quote once more from the great art-critic of the Greeks.[24] It is through Art, and through Art only, that we can realize our perfection; through Art, and through Art only, that we can shield ourselves from the sordid perils of actual existence. This results not merely from the fact that nothing that one can imagine is worth doing, and that one can imagine everything, but from the subtle law that emotional forces, like the forces of the physical sphere, are limited in extent and energy. One can feel so much, and no more. And how can it matter with what pleasure life tries to tempt one, or with what pain it seeks to maim and mar one's soul, if in the spectacle of the lives of those who have never existed one has found the true secret of joy, and wept away one's tears over their deaths who, like Cordelia and the daughter of Brabantio,[25] can never die?

ERNEST: Stop a moment. It seems to me that in everything that you have said there is something radically immoral.

GILBERT: All art is immoral.

ERNEST: All art?

GILBERT: Yes. For emotion for the sake of emotion is the aim of art, and emotion for the sake of action is the aim of life, and of that practical organization of life that we call society. Society, which is the beginning and basis of morals, exists simply for the concentration of human energy, and in order to ensure its own continuance and healthy stability it demands, and no doubt rightly demands, of each of its citizens that he should contribute some form of productive labour to the common weal, and toil and travail that the day's work may be done. Society often forgives the criminal; it never forgives the dreamer. The beautiful sterile emotions that art excites in us are hateful in its eyes, and so completely are people dominated by the tyranny of this dreadful social ideal that they are always coming shamelessly up to one at Private Views and other places that are open to the general public, and saying in a loud stentorian voice, 'What are you doing?' whereas 'What are you thinking?' is the only question that any single civilized being should ever be allowed to whisper to another. They mean well, no doubt, these honest beaming folk. Perhaps that is the reason why they are so excessively tedious. But some one should teach them that while, in the opinion of society, Contemplation is the gravest sin of which any citizen can be guilty, in the opinion of the highest culture it is the proper occupation of man.

ERNEST: Contemplation?

GILBERT: Contemplation. I said to you some time ago that it was far more difficult to talk about a thing than to do it. Let me say to you now that to do nothing at all is the most difficult thing in the world, the most difficult and the most intellectual. To Plato, with his passion for wisdom, this was the noblest form of energy. To Aristotle, with his passion for knowledge, this was the noblest form of energy also. It was to this that the passion for holiness led the saint and the mystic of medieval days.

ERNEST: We exist, then, to do nothing?

GILBERT: It is to do nothing that the elect exist. Action is limited and relative. Unlimited and absolute is the vision of him who sits at ease and watches, who walks in loneliness and dreams. But we who are born at the close of this wonderful age are at once too cultured and too critical, too intellectually subtle and too curious of exquisite pleasures, to accept any speculations about life in exchange for life itself. To us the *città divina* is colourless, and the *fruitio Dei*[26] without meaning. Metaphysics do not satisfy our temperaments, and religious ecstasy is out of date. The world through which the Academic philosopher[27] becomes 'the spectator of all time and of all existence' is not really an ideal world, but simply a world of abstract ideas. When we enter it, we starve amidst the chill mathematics of thought. The courts of the city of God are not open to us now. Its gates are guarded by Ignorance, and to pass them we have to surrender all that in our nature is most divine. It is enough that our fathers believed. They have exhausted the faith-faculty of the species. Their legacy to us is the scepticism of which they were afraid. Had they put it into words, it might not live within us as thought. No, Ernest, no. We cannot go back to the saint. There is far more to be learned from the sinner. We cannot go back to the philosopher, and the mystic leads us astray. Who, as Mr Pater[28] suggests somewhere, would exchange the curve of a single rose-leaf for that formless intangible Being which Plato rates so high? What to us is the Illumination of Philo, the Abyss of Eckhart, the Vision of Böhme, the monstrous Heaven itself that was revealed to Swedenborg's[29] blinded eyes? Such things are less than the yellow trumpet of one daffodil of the field, far less than the meanest of the visible arts; for, just as Nature is matter struggling into mind, so Art is mind expressing itself under the conditions of matter, and thus, even in the lowliest of her manifestations, she speaks to both sense and soul alike. To the aesthetic temperament the vague is always repellent. The Greeks were a nation of artists, because they were spared the sense of the infinite. Like Aristotle, like Goethe after he had read Kant, we desire the concrete, and nothing but the concrete can satisfy us.

ERNEST: What then do you propose?

GILBERT: It seems to me that with the development of the critical spirit we shall be able to realize, not merely our own lives, but the collective life of the race, and so to make ourselves absolutely modern, in the true meaning of the word modernity. For he to whom the present is the only thing that is present, knows nothing of the age in which he lives. To realize the nineteenth century, one must realize every century that has preceded it and that has contributed to its making. To know anything about oneself one must know all about others. There must be no mood with which one cannot sympathize, no dead mode of life that one cannot make alive. Is this impossible? I think not. By revealing to us the absolute mechanism of all action, and so freeing us from the self-imposed and trammelling burden of moral responsibility, the scientific principle of Heredity has become, as it were, the warrant for the contemplative life. It has shown us that we are never less free than when we try to act. It has hemmed us round with the nets of the hunter, and written upon the wall the prophecy of our doom. We may not watch it, for it is within us. We may not see it, save in a mirror that mirrors the soul. It is Nemesis[30] without her mask. It is the last of the Fates,[31] and the most terrible. It is the only one of the Gods whose real name we know.

And yet, while in the sphere of practical and external life it has robbed energy of its freedom and activity of its choice, in the subjective sphere, where the soul is at work, it comes to us, this terrible shadow, with many gifts in its hands, gifts of strange temperaments and subtle susceptibilities, gifts of wild ardours and chill moods of indifference, complex multiform gifts of thoughts that are at variance with each other, and passions that war against themselves. And so, it is not our own life that we live, but the lives of the dead, and the soul that dwells within us is no single spiritual entity, making us personal and individual, created for our service, and entering into us for our joy. It is something that has dwelt in fearful places, and in ancient sepulchres has made its abode. It is sick with many maladies, and has memories of curious sins. It is wiser than we are, and its wisdom is bitter. It fills us with impossible desires, and makes us follow what we know we cannot gain. One thing, however, Ernest, it can do for us. It can lead us away from surroundings whose beauty is dimmed to us by the mist of familiarity,,or whose ignoble ugliness and sordid claims are marring the perfection of our development. It can help us to leave the age in which we were born, and to pass into other ages, and find ourselves not exiled from their air. It can teach us how to escape from our experience, and to realize the experiences of those who are greater than we are. The pain of Leopardi[32] crying out against life becomes our pain. Theocritus[33] blows on his pipe, and we laugh with the lips of nymph and shepherd. In the wolfskin of Pierre Vidal[34] we flee before the hounds, and in the armour of Lancelot we ride from the bower of the Queen. We have whispered the secret of our love beneath the cowl of Abelard,[35] and in the stained raiment of Villon[36] have put our shame into song. We can see the dawn through Shelley's eyes, and when we wander with Endymion[37] the Moon grows amorous of our youth. Ours is the anguish of Atys,[38] and ours the weak rage and noble sorrows of the Dane.[39] Do you think that it is the imagination that enables us to live these countless lives? Yes: it is the imagination; and the imagination is the result of heredity. It is simply concentrated race-experience.

ERNEST: But where in this is the function of the critical spirit?

GILBERT: The culture that this transmission of racial experiences makes possible can be made perfect by the critical spirit alone, and indeed may be said to be one with it. For who is the true critic but he who bears within himself the dreams, and ideas, and feelings of myriad generations, and to whom no form of thought is alien, no emotional impulse obscure? And who the true man of culture, if not he who by fine scholarship and fastidious rejection has made instinct self-conscious and intelligent, and can separate the work that has distinction from the work that has it not, and so by contact and comparison makes himself master of the secrets of style and school, and understands their meanings, and listens to their voices, and develops that spirit of disinterested curiosity which is the real root, as it is the real flower, of the intellectual life, and thus attains to intellectual clarity, and, having learned 'the best that is known and thought in the world',[40] lives – it is not fanciful to say so – with those who are the Immortals.

Yes, Ernest: the contemplative life, the life that has for its aim not *doing* but *being*, and not *being* merely, but *becoming* – that is what the critical spirit can give us. The gods live thus: either brooding over their own perfection, as Aristotle tells us, or, as Epicurus[41] fancied, watching with the calm eyes of the spectator the tragi-comedy of the world that they have made. We, too, might live like them, and set ourselves to witness with appropriate emotions the varied scenes that man and nature afford. We might make ourselves spiritual by detaching ourselves from action, and become perfect by the rejection of energy. It has often seemed to me that Browning felt something of this. Shakespeare hurls Hamlet into active life, and makes him realize his mission by effort. Browning might have given us a Hamlet who would have realized his mission by thought. Incident and event were to him unreal or unmeaning. He made the soul the protagonist of life's tragedy, and looked on action as the one undramatic element of a play. To us, at any rate, the ΒΙΟΣ ΘΕΩΡΗΤΙΚΟΣ[42] is the true ideal. From the high tower of Thought we can look out at the world. Calm, and self-centred, and complete, the aesthetic critic contemplates life, and no arrow drawn at a venture can pierce between the joints of his harness.[43] He at least is safe. He has discovered how to live.

Is such a mode of life immoral? Yes: all the arts are immoral, except those baser forms of sensual or didactic art that seek to excite to action of evil or of good. For action of every kind belongs to the sphere of ethics. The aim of art is simply to create a mood. Is such a mode of life unpractical? Ah! it is not so easy to be unpractical as the ignorant Philistine[44] imagines. It were well for England if it were so. There is no country in the world so much in need of unpractical people as this country of ours. With us, Thought is degraded by its constant association with practice. Who that moves in the stress and turmoil of actual existence, noisy politician, or brawling social reformer, or poor narrow-minded priest blinded by the sufferings of that unimportant section of the community among whom he has cast his lot, can seriously claim to be able to form a disinterested intellectual judgement about any one thing? Each of the professions means a prejudice. The necessity for a career forces every one to take sides. We live in the age of the overworked, and the under-educated; the age in which people are so industrious that they become absolutely stupid. And, harsh though it may sound, I cannot help saying that such people deserve their doom. The sure way of knowing nothing about life is to try to make oneself useful.

ERNEST: A charming doctrine, Gilbert.

GILBERT: I am not sure about that, but it has at least the minor merit of being true. That the desire to do good to others produces a plentiful crop of prigs is the least of the evils of which it is the cause. The prig is a very interesting psychological study, and though of all poses a moral pose is the most offensive, still to have a pose at all is something. It is a formal recognition of the importance of treating life from a definite and reasoned standpoint. That Humanitarian Sympathy wars against Nature, by securing the survival of the failure, may make the man of science loathe its facile virtues. The political economist may cry out against it for putting the improvident on the same level as the provident, and so robbing life of the strongest, because most sordid, incentive to industry. But, in the eyes of the thinker, the real harm that emotional sympathy does is that it limits knowledge, and so prevents us from solving any single social problem. We are trying at present to stave off the coming crisis, the coming revolution as my friends the Fabianists[45] call it, by means of doles and alms. Well, when the revolution or crisis arrives, we shall be powerless, because we shall know nothing. And so, Ernest, let us not be deceived. England will never be civilized till she has added Utopia[46] to her dominions. There is more than one of her colonies that she might with advantage surrender for so fair a land. What we want are unpractical people who see beyond the moment, and think beyond the day. Those who try to lead the people can only do so by following the mob. It is through the voice of one crying in the wilderness that the ways of the gods must be prepared.

But perhaps you think that in beholding for the mere joy of beholding, and contemplating for the sake of contemplation, there is something that is egotistic. If you think so, do not say so. It takes a thoroughly selfish age, like our own, to deify self-sacrifice. It takes a thoroughly grasping age, such as that in which we live, to set above the fine intellectual virtues, those shallow and emotional virtues that are an immediate practical benefit to itself. They miss their aim, too, these philanthropists and sentimentalists of our day, who are always chattering to one about one's duty to one's neighbour. For the development of the race depends on the development of the individual, and where self-culture has ceased to be the ideal, the intellectual standard is instantly lowered, and, often, ultimately lost. If you meet at dinner a man who has spent his life in educating himself – a rare type in our time, I admit, but still one occasionally to be met with – you rise from table richer, and conscious that a high ideal has for a moment touched and sanctified your days. But oh! my dear Ernest, to sit next a man who has spent his life in trying to educate others! What a dreadful experience that is! How appalling is that ignorance which is the inevitable result of the fatal habit of imparting opinions! How limited in range the creature's mind proves to be! How it wearies us, and must weary himself, with its endless repetitions and sickly reiteration! How lacking it is in any element of intellectual growth! In what a vicious circle it always moves!

ERNEST: You speak with strange feeling, Gilbert. Have you had this dreadful experience, as you call it, lately?

GILBERT: Few of us escape it. People say that the schoolmaster is abroad. I wish to goodness he were. But the type of which, after all, he is only one, and certainly the least important, of the representatives, seems to me to be really dominating our lives; and just as the philanthropist is the nuisance of the ethical sphere, so the nuisance of the intellectual sphere is the man who is so occupied in trying to educate others, that he has never had any time to educate himself. No, Ernest, self-culture is the true ideal of man. Goethe saw it, and the immediate debt that we owe to Goethe is greater than the debt we owe to any man since Greek days. The Greeks saw it, and have left us, as their legacy to modern thought, the conception of the contemplative life as well as the critical method by which alone can that life be truly realized. It was the one thing that made the Renaissance great, and gave us Humanism. It is the one thing that could make our own age great also; for the real weakness of England lies, not in incomplete armaments or unfortified coasts, not in the poverty that creeps through sunless lanes, or the drunkenness that brawls in loathsome courts, but simply in the fact that her ideals are emotional and not intellectual.

I do not deny that the intellectual ideal is difficult of attainment, still less that it is, and perhaps will be for years to come, unpopular with the crowd. It is so easy for people to have sympathy with suffering. It is so difficult for them to have sympathy with thought. Indeed, so little do ordinary people understand what thought really is, that they seem to imagine that, when they have said that a theory is dangerous, they have pronounced its condemnation, whereas it is only such theories that have any true intellectual value. An idea that is not dangerous is unworthy of being called an idea at all.

ERNEST: Gilbert, you bewilder me. You have told me that all art is, in its essence, immoral. Are you going to tell me now that all thought is, in its essence, dangerous?

GILBERT: Yes, in the practical sphere it is so. The security of society lies in custom and unconscious instinct, and the basis of the stability of society, as a healthy organism, is the complete absence of any intelligence amongst its members. The great majority of people being fully aware of this, rank themselves naturally on the side of that splendid system that elevates them to the dignity of machines, and rage so wildly against the intrusion of the intellectual faculty into any question that concerns life, that one is tempted to define man as a rational animal who always loses his temper when he is called upon to act in accordance with the dictates of reason. But let us turn from the practical sphere, and say no more about the wicked philanthropists, who, indeed, may well be left to the mercy of the almond-eyed sage of the Yellow River, Chuang Tsŭ[47] the wise, who has proved that such well-meaning and offensive busybodies have destroyed the simple and spontaneous virtue that there is in man. They are a wearisome topic, and I am anxious to get back to the sphere in which criticism is free.

ERNEST: The sphere of the intellect?

GILBERT: Yes. You remember that I spoke of the critic as being in his own way as creative as the artist, whose work, indeed, may be merely of value in so far as it gives to the critic a suggestion for some new mood of thought and feeling which he can realize with equal, or perhaps greater, distinction of form, and, through the use of a fresh medium of expression, make differently beautiful and more perfect. Well, you seemed to be a little sceptical about the theory. But perhaps I wronged you?

ERNEST: I am not really sceptical about it, but I must admit that I feel very strongly that such work as you describe the critic producing – and creative such work must undoubtedly be admitted to be – is, of necessity, purely subjective, whereas the greatest work is objective always, objective and impersonal.

GILBERT: The difference between objective and subjective work is one of external form merely. It is accidental, not essential. All artistic creation is absolutely subjective. The very landscape that Corot looked at was, as he said himself, but a mood of his own mind; and those great figures of Greek or English drama that seem to us to possess an actual existence of their own, apart from the poets who shaped and fashioned them, are, in their ultimate analysis, simply the poets themselves, not as they thought they were, but as they thought they were not; and by such thinking came in strange manner, though but for a moment, really so to be. For out of ourselves we can never pass, nor can there be in creation what in the creator was not. Nay, I would say that the more objective a creation appears to be, the more subjective it really is. Shakespeare might have met Rosencrantz and Guildenstern in the white streets of London, or seen the serving-men of rival houses bite their thumbs at each other in the open square; but Hamlet came out of his soul, and Romeo out of his passion. They were elements of his nature to which he gave visible form, impulses that stirred so strongly within him that he had, as it were perforce, to suffer them to realize their energy, not on the lower plane of actual life, where they would have been trammelled and constrained and so made imperfect, but on that imaginative plane of art where Love can indeed find in Death its rich fulfilment, where one can stab the eavesdropper behind the arras, and wrestle in a new-made grave, and make a guilty king drink his own hurt, and see one's father's spirit, beneath the glimpses of the moon, stalking in complete steel from misty wall to wall. Action being limited would have left Shakespeare unsatisfied and unexpressed; and, just as it is because he did nothing that he has been able to achieve everything, so it is because he never speaks to us of himself in his plays that his plays reveal him to us absolutely, and show us his true nature and temperament far more completely than do those strange and exquisite sonnets, even, in which he bares to crystal eyes the secret closet of his heart. Yes, the objective form is the most subjective in matter. Man is least himself when he talks in his own person. Give him a mask, and he will tell you the truth.

ERNEST: The critic, then, being limited to the subjective form, will necessarily be less able fully to express himself than the artist, who has always at his disposal the forms that are impersonal and objective.

GILBERT: Not necessarily, and certainly not at all if he recognizes that each mode of criticism is, in its highest development, simply a mood, and that we are never more true to ourselves than when we are inconsistent. The aesthetic critic, constant only to the principle of beauty in all things, will ever be looking for fresh impressions, winning from the various schools the secret of their charm, bowing, it may be, before foreign altars, or smiling, if it be his fancy, at strange new gods. What other people call one's past has, no doubt, everything to do with them, but has absolutely nothing to do with oneself. The man who regards his past is a man who deserves to have no future to look forward to. When one has found expression for a mood, one has done with it. You laugh; but believe me it is so. Yesterday it was Realism that charmed one. One gained from it that *nouveau frisson*[48] which it was its aim to produce. One analysed it, explained it and wearied of it. At sunset came the *Luministe*[49] in painting, and the *Symboliste*[50] in poetry, and the spirit of medievalism, that spirit which belongs not to time but to temperament, woke suddenly in wounded Russia, and stirred us for a moment by the terrible fascination of pain. Today the cry is for Romance, and already the leaves are tremulous in the valley, and on the purple hill-tops walks Beauty with slim gilded feet. The old modes of creation linger, of course. The artists reproduce either themselves or each other, with wearisome iteration. But Criticism is always moving on, and the critic is always developing.

Nor, again, is the critic really limited to the subjective form of expression. The method of the drama in his, as well as the method of the epos. He may use dialogue, as he did who set Milton talking to Marvel[51] on the nature of comedy and tragedy, and made Sidney and Lord Brooke discourse on letters beneath the Penshurst oaks; or adopt narration, as Mr Pater is fond of doing, each of whose Imaginary Portraits[52] – is not that the title of the book? – presents to us, under the fanciful guise of fiction, some fine and exquisite piece of criticism, one on the painter Watteau, another on the philosophy of Spinoza, a third on the Pagan elements of the early Renaissance, and the last, and in some respects the most suggestive, on the source of that *Aufklärung*, that enlightening which dawned on Germany in the last century, and to which our own culture owes so great a debt. Dialogue, certainly, that wonderful literary form which, from Plato to Lucian,[53] and from Lucian to Giordano Bruno,[54] and from Bruno to that grand old Pagan[55] in whom Carlyle took such delight, the creative critics of the world have always employed, can never lose for the thinker its attraction as a mode of expression. By its means he can both reveal and conceal himself, and give form to every fancy, and reality to every mood. By its means he can exhibit the object from each point of view, and show it to us in the round, as a sculptor shows us things, gaining in this manner all the richness and reality of effect that comes from those side issues that are suddenly suggested by the central idea in its progress, and really illumine the idea more completely, or from those felicitous after-thoughts that give a fuller completeness to the central scheme, and yet convey something of the delicate charm of chance.

ERNEST: By its means, too, he can invent an imaginary antagonist, and convert him when he chooses by some absurdly sophistical argument.

GILBERT: Ah! it is so easy to convert others. It is so difficult to convert oneself. To arrive at what one really believes, one must speak through lips different from one's own. To know the truth one must imagine myriads of falsehoods. For what is Truth? In matters of religion, it is simply the opinion that has survived. In matters of science, it is the ultimate sensation. In matters of art, it is one's last mood. And you see now, Ernest, that the critic has at his disposal as many objective forms of expression as the artist has. Ruskin put his criticism into imaginative prose, and is superb in his changes and contradictions; and Browning put his into blank verse, and made painter and poet yield us their secret; and M. Renan uses dialogue, and Mr Pater fiction, and Rossetti[56] translated into sonnet-music the colour of Giorgione and the design of Ingres, and his own design and colour also, feeling, with the instinct of one who had many modes of utterance, that the ultimate art is literature, and the finest and fullest medium that of words.

ERNEST: Well, now that you have settled that the critic has at his disposal all objective forms, I wish you would tell me what are the qualities that should characterize the true critic.

GILBERT: What would you say they were?

ERNEST: Well, I should say that a critic should above all things be fair.

GILBERT: Ah! not fair. A critic cannot be fair in the ordinary sense of the word. It is only about things that do not interest one that one can give a really unbiased opinion, which is no doubt the reason why an unbiased opinion is always absolutely valueless. The man who sees both sides of a question, is a man who sees absolutely nothing at all. Art is a passion, and, in matters of art, Thought is inevitably coloured by emotion, and so is fluid rather than fixed, and, depending upon fine moods and exquisite moments, cannot be narrowed into the rigidity of a scientific formula or a theological dogma. It is to the soul that Art speaks, and the soul may be made the prisoner of the mind as well as of the body. One should, of course, have no prejudices; but, as a great Frenchman remarked a hundred years ago, it is one's business in such matters to have preferences, and when one has preferences one ceases to be fair. It is only an auctioneer who can equally and impartially admire all schools of Art. No: fairness is not one of the qualities of the true critic. It is not even a condition of criticism. Each form of Art with which we come in contact dominates us for the moment to the exclusion of every other form. We must surrender ourselves absolutely to the work in question, whatever it may be, if we wish to gain its secret. For the time, we must think of nothing else, can think of nothing else, indeed.

ERNEST: The true critic will be rational, at any rate, will he not?

GILBERT: Rational? There are two ways of disliking art, Ernest. One is to dislike it. The other, to like it rationally. For Art, as Plato saw, and not without regret, creates in listener and spectator a form of divine madness. It does not spring from inspiration, but it makes others inspired. Reason is not the faculty to which it appeals. If one loves Art at all, one must love it beyond all other things in the world, and against such love, the reason, if one listened to it, would cry out. There is nothing sane about the worship of beauty. It is too splendid to be sane. Those of whose lives it forms the dominant note will always seem to the world to be pure visionaries.

ERNEST: Well, at least, the critic will be sincere.

GILBERT: A little sincerity is a dangerous thing, and a great deal of it is absolutely fatal. The true critic will, indeed, always be sincere in his devotion to the principle of beauty, but he will seek for beauty in every age and in each school, and will never suffer himself to be limited to any settled custom of thought, or stereotyped mode of looking at things. He will realize himself in many forms, and by a thousand different ways, and will ever be curious of new sensations and fresh points of view. Through constant change, and through constant change alone, he will find his true unity. He will not consent to be the slave of his own opinions. For what is mind but motion in the intellectual sphere? The essence of thought, as the essence of life, is growth. You must not be frightened by words, Ernest. What people call insincerity is simply a method by which we can multiply our personalities.

ERNEST: I am afraid I have not been fortunate in my suggestions.

GILBERT: Of the three qualifications you mentioned, two, sincerity and fairness, were, if not actually moral, at least on the borderland of morals, and the first condition of criticism is that the critic should be able to recognize that the sphere of Art and the sphere of Ethics are absolutely distinct and separate. When they are confused, Chaos has come again. They are too often confused in England now, and though our modern Puritans cannot destroy a beautiful thing, yet, by means of their extraordinary prurience, they can almost taint beauty for a moment. It is chiefly, I regret to say, through journalism that such people find expression. I regret it because there is much to be said in favour of modern journalism. By giving us the opinions of the uneducated, it keeps us in touch with the ignorance of the community. By carefully chronicling the current events of contemporary life, it shows us of what very little importance such events really are. By invariably discussing the unnecessary, it makes us understand what things are requisite for culture, and what are not. But it should not allow poor Tartuffe[57] to write articles upon modern art. When it does this it stultifies itself. And yet Tartuffe's articles and Chadband's[58] notes do this good, at least. They serve to show how extremely limited is the area over which ethics, and ethical considerations, can claim to exercise influence. Science is out of the reach of morals, for her eyes are fixed upon eternal truths. Art is out of the reach of morals, for her eyes are fixed upon things beautiful and immortal and ever-changing. To morals belong the lower and less intellectual spheres. However, let these mouthing Puritans pass; they have their comic side. Who can help laughing when an ordinary journalist seriously proposes to limit the subject-matter at the disposal of the artist? Some limitation might well, and will soon, I hope, be placed upon some of our newspapers and newspaper writers. For they give us the bald, sordid, disgusting facts of life. They chronicle, with degrading avidity, the sins of the second-rate, and with the conscientiousness of the illiterate give us accurate and prosaic details of the doings of people of absolutely no interest whatsoever. But the artist, who accepts the facts of life, and yet transforms them into shapes of beauty, and makes them vehicles of pity or of awe, and shows their colour-element, and their wonder, and their true ethical import also, and builds out of them a world more real than reality itself, and of loftier and more noble import – who shall set limits to him? Not the apostles of that new Journalism which is but the old vulgarity 'writ large'. Not the apostles of that new

Puritanism, which is but the whine of the hypocrite, and is both writ and spoken badly. The mere suggestion is ridiculous. Let us leave these wicked people, and proceed to the discussion of the artistic qualifications necessary for the true critic.

ERNEST: And what are they? Tell me yourself.

GILBERT: Temperament[59] is the primary requisite for the critic – a temperament exquisitely susceptible to beauty, and to the various impressions that beauty gives us. Under what conditions, and by what means, this temperament is engendered in race or individual, we will not discuss at present. It is sufficient to note that it exists, and that there is in us a beauty-sense, separate from the other senses and above them, separate from the reason and of nobler import, separate from the soul and of equal value – a sense that leads some to create, and others, the finer spirits as I think, to contemplate merely. But to be purified and made perfect, this sense requires some form of exquisite environment. Without this it starves, or is dulled. You remember that lovely passage in which Plato describes how a young Greek should be educated, and with what insistence he dwells upon the importance of surroundings, telling us how the lad is to be brought up in the midst of fair sights and sounds, so that the beauty of material things may prepare his soul for the reception of the beauty that is spiritual. Insensibly, and without knowing the reason why, he is to develop that real love of beauty which, as Plato is never weary of reminding us, is the true aim of education. By slow degrees there is to be engendered in him such a temperament as will lead him naturally and simply to choose the good in preference to the bad, and, rejecting what is vulgar and discordant, to follow by fine instinctive taste all that possesses grace and charm and loveliness. Ultimately, in its due course, this taste is to become critical and self-conscious, but at first it is to exist purely as a cultivated instinct, and 'he who has received this true culture of the inner man will with clear and certain vision perceive the omissions and faults in art or nature, and with a taste that cannot err, while he praises, and finds his pleasure in what is good, and receives it into his soul, and so becomes good and noble, he will rightly blame and hate the bad, now in the days of his youth, even before he is able to know the reason why': and so, when, later on, the critical and self-conscious spirit develops in him, he 'will recognize and salute it as a friend with whom his education has made him long familiar'. I need hardly say, Ernest, how far we in England have fallen short of this ideal, and I can imagine the smile that would illuminate the glossy face of the Philistine if one ventured to suggest to him that the true aim of education was the love of beauty, and that the methods by which education should work were the development of temperament, the cultivation of taste and the creation of the critical spirit.

Yet, even for us, there is left some loveliness of environment, and the dulness of tutors and professors matters very little when one can loiter in the grey cloisters at Magdalen, and listen to some flute-like voice singing in Waynfleete's chapel,[60] or lie in the green meadow, among the strange snake-spotted fritillaries,[61] and watch the sunburnt noon smite to a finer gold the tower's gilded vanes, or wander up the Christ Church staircase beneath the vaulted ceiling's shadowy fans, or pass through the sculptured gateway of Laud's building[62] in the College of St John. Nor is it merely at Oxford, or Cambridge, that the sense of beauty can be formed and trained and perfected. All over England there is a renaissance of the decorative arts. Ugliness has had its day. Even in the houses of the rich there is taste, and the houses of those who are not rich have been made gracious and comely and sweet to live in. Caliban,[63] poor noisy Caliban, thinks that when he has ceased to make mows at a thing, the thing ceases to exist. But if he mocks no longer, it is because he has been met with mockery, swifter and keener than his own, and for a moment has been bitterly schooled into that silence which should seal for ever his uncouth distorted lips. What has been done up to now, has been chiefly in the clearing of the way. It is always more difficult to destroy than it is to create, and when what one has to destroy is vulgarity and stupidity, the task of destruction needs not merely courage but also contempt. Yet it seems to me to have been, in a measure, done. We have got rid of what was bad. We have now to make what is beautiful. And though the mission of the aesthetic movement is to lure people to contemplate, not to lead them to create, yet, as the creative instinct is strong in the Celt, and it is the Celt who leads in art, there is no reason why in future years this strange renaissance should not become almost as mighty in its way as was that new birth of art that woke many centuries ago in the cities of Italy.

Certainly, for the cultivation of temperament, we must turn to the decorative arts: to the arts that touch us, not to the arts that teach us. Modern pictures are, no doubt, delightful to look at. At least, some of them are. But they are quite impossible to live with; they are too clever, too assertive, too intellectual. Their meaning is too obvious, and their method too clearly defined. One exhausts what they have to say in a very short time, and then they become as tedious as one's relations. I am very fond of the work of many of the Impressionist painters of Paris and London. Subtlety and distinction have not yet left the school. Some of their arrangements and harmonies serve to remind one of the unapproachable beauty of Gautier's immortal *Symphonie en Blanc Majeur*,[64] that flawless masterpiece of colour and music which may have suggested the type as well as the titles of many of their best pictures. For a class that welcomes the incompetent with sympathetic eagerness, and that confuses the bizarre with the beautiful, and vulgarity with truth, they are extremely accomplished. They can do etchings that have the brilliancy of epigrams, pastels that are as fascinating as paradoxes, and as for their portraits, whatever the commonplace may say against them, no one can deny that they possess that unique and wonderful charm which belongs to works of pure fiction. But even the Impressionists, earnest and industrious as they are, will not do. I like them. Their white keynote, with its variations in lilac, was an era in colour. Though the moment does not make the man, the moment certainly makes the Impressionist, and for the moment in art, and the 'moment's monument'[65] as Rossetti phrased it, what may not be said? They are suggestive also. If they have not opened the eyes of the blind, they have at least given great encouragement to the short-sighted, and while their leaders may have all the inexperience of old age, their young men are far too wise to be ever sensible. Yet they will insist on treating painting as if it were a mode of autobiography invented for the use of the illiterate, and are always prating to us on their coarse gritty canvases of their unnecessary selves and their unnecessary opinions, and spoiling by a vulgar over-emphasis that fine contempt of nature which is the best and only modest thing about them. One tires, at the end, of the work of individuals whose individuality is always noisy, and generally uninteresting. There is far more to be said in favour of that newer school at Paris, the *Archaicistes*,[66] as they call themselves, who, refusing to leave the artist entirely at the mercy of the weather, do not find the ideal of art in mere atmospheric effect, but seek rather for the imaginative beauty of design and the loveliness of fair colour, and rejecting the tedious realism of those who merely paint what they see, try to see something worth seeing, and to see it not merely with actual and physical vision, but with that nobler vision of the soul which is as far wider in spiritual scope as it is far more splendid in artistic purpose. They, at any rate, work under those decorative conditions that each art requires for its perfection, and have sufficient aesthetic instinct to regret those sordid and stupid limitations of absolute modernity of form which have proved the ruin of so many of the Impressionists. Still, the art that is frankly decorative is the art to live with. It is, of all our visible arts, the one art that creates in us both mood and temperament. Mere colour, unspoiled by meaning, and unallied with definite form, can speak to the soul in a thousand different ways. The harmony that resides in the delicate proportions of lines and masses becomes mirrored in the mind. The repetitions of pattern give us rest. The marvels of design stir the imagination. In the mere loveliness of the materials employed there are latent elements of culture. Nor is this all. By its deliberate rejection of Nature as the ideal of beauty, as well as of the imitative method of the ordinary painter, decorative art not merely prepares the soul for the reception of true imaginative work, but develops in it that sense of form which is the basis of creative no less than of critical achievement. For the real artist is he who proceeds, not from feeling to form, but from form to thought and passion. He does not first conceive an idea, and then say to himself, 'I will put my idea into a complex metre of fourteen lines,' but, realizing the beauty of the sonnet-scheme, he conceives certain modes of music and methods of rhyme, and the mere form suggests what is to fill it and make it intellectually and emotionally complete. From time to time the world cries out against some charming artistic poet, because, to use its hackneyed and silly phrase, he has 'nothing to say'. But if he had something to say, he would probably say it, and the result would be tedious. It is just because he has no new message, that he can do beautiful work. He gains his inspiration from form, and from form purely, as an artist should. A real passion would ruin him. Whatever actually occurs is spoiled for art. All bad poetry springs from genuine feeling. To be natural is to be obvious, and to be obvious is to be inartistic.

ERNEST: I wonder do you really believe what you say?

GILBERT: Why should you wonder? It is not merely in art that the body is the soul. In every sphere of life Form is the beginning of things. The rhythmic harmonious gestures of dancing convey, Plato tells us, both rhythm and harmony into the mind. Forms are the food of faith, cried Newman in one of those great moments of sincerity that make us admire and know the man. He was right, though he may not have known how terribly right he was. The Creeds are believed, not because they are rational, but because they are repeated. Yes: Form is everything. It is the secret of life. Find expression for a sorrow, and it will become dear to you. Find expression for a joy, and you intensify its ecstasy. Do you wish to love? Use Love's Litany, and the words will create the yearning from which the world fancies that they spring. Have you a grief that corrodes your heart? Steep yourself in the language of grief, learn its utterance from Prince Hamlet and Queen Constance,[67] and you will find that mere expression is a mode of consolation, and that Form, which is the birth of passion, is also the death of pain. And so, to return to the sphere of Art, it is Form that creates not merely the critical temperament, but also the aesthetic instinct, that unerring instinct that reveals to one all things under their conditions of beauty. Start with the worship of form, and there is no secret in art that will not be revealed to you, and remember that in criticism, as in creation, temperament is everything, and that it is, not by the time of their production, but by the temperaments to which they appeal, that the schools of art should be historically grouped.

ERNEST: Your theory of education is delightful. But what influence will your critic, brought up in these exquisite surroundings, possess? Do you really think that any artist is ever affected by criticism?

GILBERT: The influence of the critic will be the mere fact of his own existence. He will represent the flawless type. In him the culture of the century will see itself realized. You must not ask of him to have any aim other than the perfecting of himself. The demand of the intellect, as has been well said,[68] is simply to feel itself alive. The critic may, indeed, desire to exercise influence; but, if so, he will concern himself not with the individual, but with the age, which he will seek to wake into consciousness, and to make responsive, creating in it new desires and appetites, and lending it his larger vision and his nobler moods. The actual art of today will occupy him less than the art of tomorrow, far less than the art of yesterday, and as for this or that person at present toiling away, what do the industrious matter? They do their best, no doubt, and consequently we get the worst from them. It is always with the best intentions that the worst work is done. And besides, my dear Ernest, when a man reaches the age of forty, or becomes a Royal Academician, or is elected a member of the Athenaeum Club,[69] or is recognized as a popular novelist, whose books are in great demand at suburban railway stations, one may have the amusement of exposing him, but one cannot have the pleasure of reforming him. And this is, I dare say, very fortunate for him; for I have no doubt that reformation is a much more painful process than punishment, is indeed punishment in its most aggravated and moral form – a fact which accounts for our entire failure as a community to reclaim that interesting phenomenon who is called the confirmed criminal.

ERNEST: But may it not be that the poet is the best judge of poetry, and the painter of painting? Each art must appeal primarily to the artist who works in it. His judgement will surely be the most valuable?

GILBERT: The appeal of all art is simply to the artistic temperament. Art does not address herself to the specialist. Her claim is that she is universal, and that in all her manifestations she is one. Indeed, so far from its being true that the artist is the best judge of art, a really great artist can never judge of other people's work at all, and can hardly, in fact, judge of his own. That very concentration of vision that makes a man an artist, limits by its sheer intensity his faculty of fine appreciation. The energy of creation hurries him blindly on to his own goal. The wheels of his chariot raise the dust as a cloud around him.

The gods are hidden from each other. They can recognize their worshippers. That is all.

ERNEST: You say that a great artist cannot recognize the beauty of work different from his own.

GILBERT: It is impossible for him to do so. Wordsworth saw in *Endymion* merely a pretty piece of Paganism, and Shelley, with his dislike of actuality, was deaf to Wordsworth's message, being repelled by its form, and Byron, that great passionate human incomplete creature, could appreciate neither the poet of the cloud nor the poet of the lake,[70] and the wonder of Keats was hidden from him. The realism of Euripides was hateful to Sophokles. Those droppings of warm tears had no music for him. Milton, with his sense of the grand style, could not understand the method of Shakespeare, any more than could Sir Joshua the method of Gainsborough.[71] Bad artists always admire each other's work. They call it being large-minded and free from prejudice. But a truly great artist cannot conceive of life being shown, or beauty fashioned, under any conditions other than those that he has selected. Creation employs all its critical faculty within its own sphere. It may not use it in the sphere that belongs to others. It is exactly because a man cannot do a thing that he is the proper judge of it.

ERNEST: Do you really mean that?

GILBERT: Yes, for creation limits, while contemplation widens, the vision.

ERNEST: But what about technique? Surely each art has its separate technique?

GILBERT: Certainly: each art has its grammar and its materials. There is no mystery about either, and the incompetent can always be correct. But, while the laws upon which Art rests may be fixed and certain, to find their true realization they must be touched by the imagination into such beauty that they will seem an exception, each one of them. Technique is really personality. That is the reason why the artist cannot teach it, why the pupil cannot learn it, and why the aesthetic critic can understand it. To the great poet, there is only one method of music – his own. To the great painter, there is only one manner of painting – that which he himself employs. The aesthetic critic, and the aesthetic critic alone, can appreciate all forms and modes. It is to him that Art makes her appeal.

ERNEST: Well, I think I have put all my questions to you. And now I must admit —

GILBERT: Ah! don't say that you agree with me. When people agree with me I always feel that I must be wrong.

ERNEST: In that case I certainly won't tell you whether I agree with you or not. But I will put another question. You have explained to me that criticism is a creative art. What future has it?

GILBERT: It is to criticism that the future belongs. The subject-matter at the disposal of creation becomes every day more limited in extent and variety. Providence and Mr Walter Besant[72] have exhausted the obvious. If creation is to last at all, it can only do so on the condition of becoming far more critical than it is at present. The old roads and dusty highways have been traversed too often. Their charm has been worn away by plodding feet, and they have lost that element of novelty or surprise which is so essential for romance. He who would stir us now by fiction must either give us an entirely new background, or reveal to us the soul of man in its innermost workings. The first is for the moment being done for us by Mr Rudyard Kipling. As one turns over the pages of his *Plain Tales from the Hills*, one feels as if one were seated under a palm-tree reading life by superb flashes of vulgarity. The bright colours of the bazaars dazzle one's eyes. The jaded, second-rate Anglo-Indians are in exquisite incongruity with their surroundings. The mere lack of style in the story-teller gives an odd journalistic realism to what he tells us. From the point of view of literature Mr Kipling is a genius who drops his aspirates. From the point of view of life, he is a reporter who knows vulgarity better than any one has ever known it. Dickens knew its clothes and its comedy. Mr Kipling knows its essence and its seriousness. He is our first authority on the second-rate, and has seen marvellous things through keyholes, and his backgrounds are real works of art. As for the second condition, we have had Browning, and Meredith is with us. But there is still much to be done in the sphere of introspection. People sometimes say that fiction is getting too morbid. As far as psychology is concerned, it has never been morbid enough. We have merely touched the surface of the soul, that is all. In one single ivory cell of the brain there are stored away things more marvellous and more terrible than even they have dreamed of, who, like the author of *Le Rouge et le noir*,[73] have sought to track the soul into its most secret places, and to make life confess its dearest sins. Still, there is a limit even to the number of untried backgrounds, and it is possible that a further development of the habit of introspection may prove fatal to that creative faculty to which it seeks to supply fresh material. I myself am inclined to think that creation is doomed. It springs from too primitive, too natural an impulse. However this may be, it is certain that the subject-matter at the disposal of creation is always diminishing, while the subject-matter of criticism increases daily. There are always new attitudes for the mind, and new points of view. The duty of imposing form upon chaos does not grow less as the world advances. There was never a time when Criticism was more needed than it is now. It is only by its means that Humanity can become conscious of the point at which it has arrived.

Hours ago, Ernest, you asked me the use of Criticism. You might just as well have asked me the use of thought. It is Criticism, as Arnold points out, that creates the intellectual atmosphere of the age. It is Criticism, as I hope to point out myself some day, that makes the mind a fine instrument. We, in our educational system, have burdened the memory with a load of unconnected facts, and laboriously striven to impart our laboriously-acquired knowledge. We teach people how to remember, we never teach them how to grow. It has never occurred to us to try and develop in the mind a more subtle quality of apprehension and discernment. The Greeks did this, and when we come in contact with the Greek critical intellect, we cannot but be conscious that, while our subject-matter is in every respect larger and more varied than theirs, theirs is the only method by which this subject-matter can be interpreted. England has done one thing; it has invented and established Public Opinion, which is an attempt to organize the ignorance of the community, and to elevate it to the dignity of physical force. But Wisdom has always been hidden from it. Considered as an instrument of thought, the English mind is coarse and undeveloped. The only thing that can purify it is the growth of the critical instinct.

It is Criticism, again, that, by concentration, makes culture possible. It takes the cumbersome mass of creative work, and distils it into a finer essence. Who that desires to retain any sense of form could struggle through the monstrous multitudinous books that the world has produced, books in which thought stammers or ignorance brawls? The thread that is to guide us across the wearisome labyrinth is in the hands of Criticism. Nay more, where there is no record, and history is either lost, or was never written, Criticism can re-create the past for us from the very smallest fragment of language or art, just as surely as the man of science can from some tiny bone, or the mere impress of a foot upon a rock, re-create for us the winged dragon or Titan lizard that once made the earth shake beneath its tread, can call Behemoth out of his cave, and make Leviathan swim once more across the startled sea. Prehistoric history belongs to the philological and archaeological critic. It is to him that the origins of things are revealed. The self-conscious deposits of an age are nearly always misleading. Through philological criticism alone we know more of the centuries of which no actual record has been preserved, than we do of the centuries that have left us their scrolls. It can do for us what can be done neither by physics nor metaphysics. It can give us the exact science of mind in the process of becoming. It can do for us what History cannot do. It can tell us what man thought before he learned how to write. You have asked me about the influence of Criticism. I think I have answered that question already; but there is this also to be said. It is Criticism that makes us cosmopolitan. The Manchester school[74] tried to make men realize the brotherhood of humanity, by pointing out the commercial advantages of peace. It sought to degrade the wonderful world into a common market-place for the buyer and the seller. It addressed itself to the lowest instincts, and it failed. War followed upon war, and the tradesman's creed did not prevent France and Germany from clashing together in blood-stained battle.[75] There are others of our own day who seek to appeal to mere emotional sympathies, or to the shallow dogmas of some vague system of abstract ethics. They have their Peace Societies, so dear to the sentimentalists, and their proposals for unarmed International Arbitration, so popular among those who have never read history. But mere emotional sympathy will not do. It is too variable, and too closely connected with the passions; and a board of arbitrators who, for the general welfare of the race, are to be deprived of the power of putting their decisions into execution, will not be of much avail. There is only one thing worse than Injustice, and that is Justice without her sword in her hand. When Right is not Might, it is Evil.

No: the emotions will not make us cosmopolitan, any more than the greed for gain could do so. It is only by the cultivation of the habit of intellectual criticism that we shall be able to rise superior to race-prejudices. Goethe – you will not misunderstand what I say – was a German of the Germans. He loved his country – no man more so. Its people were dear to him; and he led them. Yet, when the iron hoof of Napoleon trampled upon vineyard and cornfield, his lips were silent. 'How can one write songs of hatred without hating?' he said to Eckerman,[76] 'and how could I, to whom culture and barbarism are alone of importance, hate a nation which is among the most cultivated of the earth, and to which I owe so great a part of my own cultivation?' This note, sounded in the modern world by Goethe first, will become, I think, the starting point for the cosmopolitanism of the future. Criticism will annihilate race-prejudices, by insisting upon the unity of the human mind in the variety of its forms. If we are tempted to make war upon another nation, we shall remember that we are seeking to destroy an element of our own culture, and possibly its most important element. As long as war is regarded as wicked, it will always have its fascination. When it is looked upon as vulgar, it will cease to be popular. The change will of course be slow, and people will not be conscious of it. They will not say 'We will not war against France because her prose is perfect', but because the prose of France is perfect, they will not hate the land. Intellectual criticism will bind Europe together in bonds far closer than those that can be forged by shopman or sentimentalist. It will give us the peace that springs from understanding.

Nor is this all. It is Criticism that, recognizing no position as final, and refusing to bind itself by the shallow shibboleths of any sect or school, creates that serene philosophic temper which loves truth for its own sake, and loves it not the less because it knows it to be unattainable. How little we have of this temper in England, and how much we need it! The English mind is always in a rage. The intellect of the race is wasted in the sordid and stupid quarrels of second-rate politicians or third-rate theologians. It was reserved for a man of science to show us the supreme example of that 'sweet reasonableness' of which Arnold spoke so wisely, and alas! to so little effect. The author of the *Origin of Species*[77] had, at any rate, the philosophic temper. If one contemplates the ordinary pulpits and platforms of England, one can but feel the contempt of Julian, or the indifference of Montaigne.[78] We are dominated by the fanatic, whose worst vice is his sincerity. Anything approaching to the free play of the mind is practically unknown amongst us. People cry out against the sinner, yet it is not the sinful, but the stupid, who are our shame. There is no sin except stupidity.

ERNEST: Ah! what an antinomian[79] you are!

GILBERT: The artistic critic, like the mystic, is an antinomian always. To be good, according to the vulgar standard of goodness, is obviously quite easy. It merely requires a certain amount of sordid terror, a certain lack of imaginative thought and a certain low passion for middle-class respectability. Aesthetics are higher than ethics. They belong to a more spiritual sphere. To discern the beauty of a thing is the finest point to which we can arrive. Even a colour-sense is more important, in the development of the individual, than a sense of right and wrong. Aesthetics, in fact, are to Ethics in the sphere of conscious civilization, what, in the sphere of the external world, sexual is to natural selection. Ethics, like natural selection, make existence poss-ible. Aesthetics, like sexual selection, make life lovely and wonderful, fill it with new forms, and give it progress, and variety and change. And when we reach the true culture that is our aim, we attain to that perfection of which the saints have dreamed, the perfection of those to whom sin is impossible, not because they make the renunciations of the ascetic, but because they can do everything they wish without hurt to the soul, and can wish for nothing that can do the soul harm, the soul being an entity so divine that it is able to transform into elements of a richer experience, or a finer susceptibility, or a newer mode of thought, acts or passions that with the common would be commonplace, or with the uneducated ignoble, or with the shameful vile. Is this dangerous? Yes; it is dangerous – all ideas, as I told you, are so. But the night wearies, and the light flickers in the lamp. One more thing I cannot help saying to you. You have spoken against Criticism as being a sterile thing. The nineteenth century is a turning point in history simply on account of the work of two men, Darwin and Renan, the one the critic of the Book of Nature, the other the critic of the books of God. Not to recognize this is to miss the meaning of one of the most important eras in the progress of the world. Creation is always behind the age. It is Criticism that leads us. The Critical Spirit and the World-Spirit are one.

ERNEST: And he who is in possession of this spirit, or whom this spirit possesses, will, I suppose, do nothing?

GILBERT: Like the Persephone of whom Landor tells us, the sweet pensive Persephone around whose white feet the asphodel and amaranth are blooming, he will sit contented 'in that deep, motionless quiet which mortals pity, and which the gods enjoy'. He will look out upon the world and know its secret. By contact with divine things he will become divine. His will be the perfect life, and his only.

ERNEST: You have told me many strange things tonight, Gilbert. You have told me that it is more difficult to talk about a thing than to do it, and that to do nothing at all is the most difficult thing in the world; you have told me that all Art is immoral, and all thought dangerous; that criticism is more creative than creation, and that the highest criticism is that which reveals in the work of Art what the artist had not put there; that it is exactly because a man cannot do a thing that he is the proper judge of it; and that the true critic is unfair, insincere, and not rational. My friend, you are a dreamer.

GILBERT: Yes: I am a dreamer. For a dreamer is one who can only find his way by moonlight, and his punishment is that he sees the dawn before the rest of the world.

ERNEST: His punishment?

GILBERT: And his reward. But see, it is dawn already. Draw back the curtains and open the windows wide. How cool the morning air is! Piccadilly lies at our feet like a long riband of silver. A faint purple mist hangs over the Park, and the shadows of the white houses are purple. It is too late to sleep. Let us go down to Covent Garden and look at the roses. Come! I am tired of thought.

4. The Truth of Masks
A note on illusion

In many of the somewhat violent attacks that have recently been made on that splendour of mounting which now characterizes our Shakespearean revivals in England, it seems to have been tacitly assumed by the critics that Shakespeare himself was more or less indifferent to the costume of his actors, and that, could he see Mrs Langtry's[1] production of *Antony and Cleopatra*, he would probably say that the play, and the play only, is the thing, and that everything else is leather and prunella.[2] While, as regards any historical accuracy in dress, Lord Lytton,[3] in an article in the *Nineteenth Century*, has laid it down as a dogma of art that archaeology is entirely out of place in the presentation of any of Shakespeare's plays, and the attempt to introduce it one of the stupidest pedantries of an age of prigs.

Lord Lytton's position I shall examine later on; but, as regards the theory that Shakespeare did not busy himself much about the costume-wardrobe of his theatre, anybody who cares to study Shakespeare's method will see that there is absolutely no dramatist of the French, English or Athenian stage who relies so much for his illusionist effects on the dress of his actors as Shakespeare does himself.

Knowing how the artistic temperament is always fascinated by beauty of costume, he constantly introduces into his plays masques and dances, purely for the sake of the pleasure which they give the eye; and we have still his stage-directions for the three great processions in *Henry the Eighth*, directions which are characterized by the most extraordinary elaborateness of detail down to the collars of S.S.[4] and the pearls in Anne Boleyn's hair. Indeed it would be quite easy for a modern manager to reproduce these pageants absolutely as Shakespeare had them designed; and so accurate were they that one of the Court officials of the time, writing an account of the last performance of the play at the Globe Theatre to a friend, actually complains of their realistic character, notably of the production on the stage of the Knights of the Garter in the robes and insignia of the order, as being calculated to bring ridicule on the real ceremonies; much in the same spirit in which the French Government, some time ago, prohibited that delightful actor, M. Christian, from appearing in uniform, on the plea that it was prejudicial to the glory of the army that a colonel should be caricatured. And elsewhere the gorgeousness of apparel which distinguished the English stage under Shakespeare's influence was attacked by the contemporary critics, not as a rule, however, on the grounds of the democratic tendencies of realism, but usually on those moral grounds which are always the last refuge of people who have no sense of beauty.

The point, however, which I wish to emphasize is, not that Shakespeare appreciated the value of lovely costumes in adding picturesqueness to poetry, but that he saw how important costume is as a means of producing certain dramatic effects. Many of his plays, such as *Measure for Measure, Twelfth Night, The Two Gentlemen of Verona, All's Well that Ends Well, Cymbeline* and others, depend for their illusion on the character of the various dresses worn by the hero or the heroine; the delightful scene in *Henry the Sixth*,[5] on the modern miracles of healing by faith, loses all its point unless Gloster is in black and scarlet; and the *dénoument* of the *Merry Wives of Windsor* hinges on the colour of Anne Page's gown.[6] As for the uses Shakespeare makes of disguises the instances are almost numberless. Posthumus[7] hides his passion under a peasant's garb, and Edgar his pride beneath an idiot's rags; Portia wears the apparel of a lawyer, and Rosalind is attired in 'all points as a man'; the cloak-bag of Pisanio changes Imogen to the youth Fidele; Jessica flees from her father's house in boy's dress, and Julia ties up her yellow hair in fantastic love-knots, and dons hose and doublet; Henry the Eighth woos his lady as a shepherd, and Romeo his as a pilgrim; Prince Hal and Poins appear first as footpads in buckram suits, and then in white aprons and leather jerkins as the waiters in a tavern: and as for Falstaff, does he not come on as a highwayman, as an old woman, as Herne the Hunter, and as the clothes going to the laundry?

Nor are the examples of the employment of costume as a mode

of intensifying dramatic situation less numerous. After slaughter of Duncan, Macbeth appears in his night-gown as if aroused from sleep; Timon ends in rags the play he had begun in splendour; Richard flatters the London citizens in a suit of mean and shabby armour, and, as soon as he has stepped in blood to the throne, marches through the streets in crown and George and Garter; the climax of *The Tempest* is reached when Prospero, throwing off his enchanter's robes, sends Ariel for his hat and rapier, and reveals himself as the great Italian Duke; the very Ghost in *Hamlet* changes his mystical apparel to produce different effects; and as for Juliet, a modern playwright would probably have lain her out in her shroud, and made the scene a scene of horror merely, but Shakespeare arrays her in rich and gorgeous raiment, whose loveliness makes the vault 'a feasting presence full of light', turns the tomb into a bridal chamber, and gives the cue and motive for Romeo's speech of the triumph of Beauty over Death.

Even small details of dress, such as the colour of a major-domo's stockings, the pattern on a wife's handkerchief, the sleeve of a young soldier, and a fashionable woman's bonnets, become in Shakespeare's hands points of actual dramatic importance, and by some of them the action of the play in question is conditioned absolutely. Many other dramatists have availed themselves of costume as a method of expressing directly to the audience the character of a person on his entrance, though hardly so brilliantly as Shakespeare has done in the case of the dandy Parolles, whose dress, by the way, only an archaeologist can understand; the fun of a master and servant exchanging coats in presence of the audience, of shipwrecked sailors squabbling over the division of a lot of fine clothes, and of a tinker dressed up like a duke while he is in his cups, may be regarded as part of that great career which costume has always played in comedy from the time of Aristophanes down to Mr Gilbert;[8] but nobody from the mere details of apparel and adornment has ever drawn such irony of contrast, such immediate and tragic effect, such pity and such pathos, as Shakespeare himself. Armed cap-à-pie,[9] the dead King stalks on the battlements of Elsinore because all is not right with Denmark; Shylock's Jewish gaberdine is part of the stigma under which that wounded and embittered nature writhes; Arthur begging for his life can think of no better plea than the handkerchief he had given Hubert –

> Have you the heart? when your head did but ache,
> I knit my handkerchief about your brows,
> (The best I had, a princess wrought it me)
> And I did never ask it you again;

and Orlando's blood-stained napkin strikes the first sombre note in that exquisite woodland idyll, and shows us the depth of feeling that underlies Rosalind's fanciful wit and wilful jesting.

> Last night 'twas on my arm; I kissed it;
> I hope it be not gone to tell my lord
> That I kiss aught but he,

says Imogen, jesting on the loss of the bracelet which was already on its way to Rome to rob her of her husband's faith; the little Prince passing to the Tower plays with the dagger in his uncle's girdle; Duncan sends a ring to Lady Macbeth on the night of his own murder, and the ring of Portia turns the tragedy of the merchant into a wife's comedy. The great rebel York dies with a paper crown on his head; Hamlet's black suit is a kind of colour-motive in the piece, like the mourning of the Chimène[10] in the Cid; and the climax of Antony's speech is the production of Caesar's cloak:

> I remember
> The first time ever Caesar put it on.
> 'Twas on a summer's evening, in his tent,
> The day he overcame the Nervii: –
> Look, in this place ran Cassius' dagger through:
> See what a rent the envious Casca made:
> Through this the well-beloved Brutus stabbed . . .
> Kind souls, what, weep you when you but behold
> Our Caesar's vesture wounded?

The flowers which Ophelia carries with her in her madness are as pathetic as the violets that blossom on a grave; the effect of Lear's wandering on the heath is intensified beyond words by his fantastic attire; and when Cloten,[11] stung by the taunt of that simile which his sister draws from her husband's raiment, arrays himself in that husband's very garb to work upon her the deed of shame, we feel that there is nothing in the whole of modern French realism, nothing even in *Thérèse Raquin*,[12] that masterpiece of horror, which for terrible and tragic significance can compare with this strange scene in *Cymbeline*.

In the actual dialogue also some of the most vivid passages are those suggested by costume. Rosalind's

Dost thou think, though I am caparisoned like a man, I have a doublet and hose in my disposition?

Constance's

> Grief fills the place of my absent child,
> Stuffs out his vacant garments with his form;

and the quick sharp cry of Elizabeth –

> Ah! cut my lace asunder! –

are only a few of the many examples one might quote. One of the finest effects I have ever seen on the stage was Salvini,[13] in the last act of *Lear*, tearing the plume from Kent's cap and applying it to Cordelia's lips when he came to the line,

> This feather stirs; she lives!

Mr Booth, whose Lear had many noble qualities of passion, plucked, I remember, some fur from his archaeologically-incorrect ermine for the same business; but Salvini's was the finer effect of the two, as well as the truer. And those who saw Mr Irving in the last act of *Richard the Third* have not, I am sure, forgotten how much the agony and terror of his dream was intensified, by contrast, through the calm and quiet that preceded it, and the delivery of such lines as

> What, is my beaver[14] easier than it was?
> And all my armour laid into my tent?
> Look that my staves be sound and not too heavy –

lines which had a double meaning for the audience, remembering the last words which Richard's mother called after him as he was marching to Bosworth:

> Therefore take with thee my most grievous curse,
> Which in the day of battle tire thee more
> Than all the complete armour that thou wear'st.

As regards the resources which Shakespeare had at his disposal, it is to be remarked that, while he more than once complains of the smallness of the stage on which he has to produce big historical plays, and of the want of scenery which obliges him to cut out many effective open-air incidents, he always writes as a dramatist who had at his disposal a most elaborate theatrical wardrobe, and who could rely on the actors taking pains about their make-up. Even now it is difficult to produce such a play as the *Comedy of Errors*; and to the picturesque accident of Miss Ellen Terry's brother[15] resembling herself we owe the opportunity of seeing *Twelfth Night* adequately performed. Indeed, to put any play of Shakespeare's on the stage, absolutely as he himself wished it to be done, requires the services of a good property-man, a clever wig-maker, a costumier with a sense of colour and a knowledge of textures, a master of the methods of making-up, a fencing-master, a dancing-master, and an artist to direct personally the whole production. For he is most careful to tell us the dress and appearance of each character. 'Racine abhorre la réalité,' says Auguste Vacquerie[16] somewhere; 'il ne daigne pas s'occuper de son costume. Si l'on s'en rapportait aux indications du poète, Agamemnon serait vêtu d'un sceptre et Achille d'une épée.' But with Shakespeare it is very different. He gives us directions about the costumes of Perdita, Florizel,

Autolycus, the Witches in *Macbeth* and the apothecary in *Romeo and Juliet*, several elaborate descriptions of his fat knight, and a detailed account of the extraordinary garb in which Petruchio is to be married. Rosalind, he tells us, is tall, and is to carry a spear and a little dagger; Celia is smaller, and is to paint her face brown so as to look sunburnt. The children who play at fairies in Windsor Forest are to be dressed in white and green – a compliment, by the way, to Queen Elizabeth, whose favourite colours they were – and in white, with green garlands and gilded vizors, the angels are to come to Katharine in Kimbolton. Bottom is in home-spun, Lysander is distinguished from Oberon by his wearing an Athenian dress, and Launce has holes in his boots. The Duchess of Gloucester stands in a white sheet with her husband in mourning beside her. The motley of the Fool, the scarlet of the Cardinal and the French lilies broidered on the English coats, are all made occasion for jest or taunt in the dialogue. We know the patterns on the Dauphin's armour and the Pucelle's sword, the crest on Warwick's helmet and the colour of Bardolph's nose. Portia has golden hair, Phoebe is black-haired, Orlando has chestnut curls and Sir Andrew Aguecheek's hair hangs like flax on a distaff, and won't curl at all. Some of the characters are stout, some lean, some straight, some hunchbacked, some fair, some dark, and some are to blacken their faces. Lear has a white beard, Hamlet's father a grizzled, and Benedick is to shave his in the course of the play. Indeed, on the subject of stage beards Shakespeare is quite elaborate; tells us of the many different colours in use, and gives a hint to actors always to see that their own are properly tied on. There is a dance of reapers in rye-straw hats, and of rustics in hairy coats like satyrs; a masque of Amazons, a masque of Russians and a classical masque; several immortal scenes over a weaver in an ass's head, a riot over the colour of a coat which it takes the Lord Mayor of London to quell, and a scene between an infuriated husband and his wife's milliner about the slashing of a sleeve.

As for the metaphors Shakespeare draws from dress, and the aphorisms he makes on it, his hits at the costume of his age, particularly at the ridiculous size of the ladies' bonnets, and the many descriptions of the *mundus muliebris*,[17] from the song of Autolycus in the *Winter's Tale* down to the account of the Duchess of Milan's gown in *Much Ado About Nothing*, they are far too numerous to quote; though it may be worth while to remind people that the whole of the Philosophy of Clothes[18] is to be found in Lear's scene with Edgar – a passage which has the advantage of brevity and style over the grotesque wisdom and somewhat mouthing metaphysics of *Sartor Resartus*. But I think that from what I have already said it is quite clear that Shakespeare was very much interested in costume. I do not mean in that shallow sense by which it has been concluded from his knowledge of deeds and daffodils that he was the Blackstone[19] and Paxton[20] of the Elizabethan age; but that he saw that costume could be made at once impressive of a certain effect on the audience and expressive of certain types of character, and is one of the essential factors of the means which a true illusionist has at his disposal. Indeed to him the deformed figure of Richard was of as much value as Juliet's loveliness; he sets the serge[21] of the radical beside the silks of the lord, and sees the stage effects to be got from each: he has as much delight in Caliban as he has in Ariel,[22] in rags as he has in cloth of gold, and recognizes the artistic beauty of ugliness.

The difficulty Ducis[23] felt about translating *Othello* in consequence of the importance given to such a vulgar thing as a handkerchief, and his attempt to soften its grossness by making the Moor reiterate '*Le bandeau! le bandeau!*' may be taken as an example of the difference between *la tragédie philosophique* and the drama of real life; and the introduction for the first time of the word *mouchoir* at the Théâtre Français was an era in that romantic-realistic movement of which Hugo is the father and M. Zola the *enfant terrible*, just as the classicism of the earlier part of the century was emphasized by Talma's refusal to play Greek heroes any longer in a powdered periwig – one of the many instances, by the way, of that desire for archaeological accuracy in dress which has distinguished the great actors of our age.

In criticizing the importance given to money in *La Comédie Humaine*, Théophile Gautier says that Balzac may claim to have invented a new hero in fiction, *le héros métallique*.[24] Of Shakespeare it may be said that he was the first to see the dramatic value of doublets, and that a climax may depend on a crinoline.

The burning of the Globe Theatre[25] – an event due, by the way, to the results of the passion for illusion that distinguished Shakespeare's stage-management – has unfortunately robbed us of many important documents; but in the inventory, still in existence, of the costume-wardrobe of a London theatre in Shakespeare's time, there are mentioned particular costumes for cardinals, shepherds, kings, clowns, friars and fools; green coats for Robin Hood's men, and a green gown for Maid Marian; a white and gold doublet for Henry the Fifth, and a robe for Longshanks; besides surplices, copes, damask gowns, gowns of cloth of gold and of cloth of silver, taffeta gowns, calico gowns, velvet coats, satin coats, frieze coats, jerkins of yellow leather and of black leather, red suits, grey suits, French Pierrot suits, a robe 'for to goo invisibell', which seems inexpensive at £3, 10s., and four incomparable fardingales[26] – all of which show a desire to give every character an appropriate dress. There are also entries of Spanish, Moorish and Danish costumes, of helmets, lances, painted shields, imperial crowns and papal tiaras, as well as of costumes for Turkish Janissaries,[27] Roman Senators and all the gods and goddesses of Olympus, which evidence a good deal of archaeological research on the part of the manager of the theatre. It is true that there is a mention of a bodice for Eve, but probably the *donnée*[28] of the play was after the Fall.

Indeed, anybody who cares to examine the age of Shakespeare will see that archaeology was one of its special characteristics. After that revival of the classical forms of architecture which was one of the notes of the Renaissance, and the printing at Venice and elsewhere of the masterpieces of Greek and Latin literature, had come naturally an interest in the ornamentation and costume of the antique world. Nor was it for the learning that they could acquire, but rather for the loveliness that they might create, that the artists studied these things. The curious objects that were being constantly brought to light by excavations were not left to moulder in a museum, for the contemplation of a callous curator, and the *ennui* of a policeman bored by the absence of crime. They were used as motives for the production of a new art, which was to be not beautiful merely, but also strange.

Infessura[29] tells us that in 1485 some workmen digging on the

Appian Way came across an old Roman sarcophagus inscribed with the name 'Julia, daughter of Claudius'. On opening the coffer they found within its marble womb the body of a beautiful girl of about fifteen years of age, preserved by the embalmer's skill from corruption and the decay of time. Her eyes were half open, her hair rippled round her in crisp curling gold, and from her lips and cheek the bloom of maidenhood had not yet departed. Borne back to the Capitol, she became at once the centre of a new cult, and from all parts of the city crowded pilgrims to worship at the wonderful shrine, till the Pope fearing lest those who had found the secret of beauty in a Pagan tomb might forget what secrets Judaea's rough and rock-hewn sepulchre contained, had the body conveyed away by night, and in secret buried. Legend though it may be, yet the story is none the less valuable as showing us the attitude of the Renaissance towards the antique world. Archaeology to them was not a mere science for the antiquarian; it was a means by which they could touch the dry dust of antiquity into the very breath and beauty of life, and fill with the new wine of romanticism forms that else had been old and outworn. From the pulpit of Niccola Pisano[30] down to Mantegna's[31] 'Triumph of Caesar', and the service Cellini[32] designed for King Francis, the influence of this spirit can be traced; nor was it confined merely to the immobile arts – the arts of arrested movement – but its influence was to be seen also in the great Graeco-Roman masques which were the constant amusement of the gay courts of the time, and in the public pomps and processions with which the citizens of big commercial towns were wont to greet the princes that chanced to visit them; pageants, by the way, which were considered so important that large prints were made of them and published – a fact which is a proof of the general interest at the time in matters of such kind.

And this use of archaeology in shows, so far from being a bit of priggish pedantry, is in every way legitimate and beautiful. For the stage is not merely the meeting-place of all the arts, but is also the return of art to life. Sometimes in an archaeological novel the use of strange and obsolete terms seems to hide the reality beneath the learning, and I dare say that many of the readers of *Notre Dame de Paris* have been much puzzled over the meaning of such expressions as *la casaque à mahoitres, les voulgiers, le gallimard taché d'encre, les craaquiniers,*[33] and the like; but with the stage how different it is! The ancient world wakes from its sleep, and history moves as a pageant before our eyes, without obliging us to have recourse to a dictionary or an encyclopaedia for the perfection of our enjoyment. Indeed, there is not the slightest necessity that the public should know the authorities for the mounting of any piece. From such materials, for instance, as the disc of Theodosius,[34] materials with which the majority of people are probably not very familiar, Mr E. W. Godwin, one of the most artistic spirits of this century in England, created the marvellous loveliness of the first act of *Claudian*,[35] and showed us the life of Byzantium in the fourth century, not by a dreary lecture and a set of grimy casts, not by a novel which requires a glossary to explain it, but by the visible presentation before us of all the glory of that great town. And while the costumes were true to the smallest points of colour and design, yet the details were not assigned that abnormal importance which they must necessarily be given in a piecemeal lecture, but were subordinated to the rules of lofty composition and the unity of artistic effect. Mr Symonds, speaking of that great picture of Mantegna's, now in Hampton Court, says that the artist has converted an antiquarian motive into a theme for melodies of line. The same could have been said with equal justice of Mr Godwin's scene. Only the foolish called it pedantry, only those who would neither look nor listen spoke of the passion of the play being killed by its paint. It was in reality a scene not merely perfect in its picturesqueness, but absolutely dramatic also, getting rid of any necessity for tedious descriptions, and showing us, by the colour and character of Claudian's dress, and the dress of his attendants, the whole nature and life of the man, from what school of philosophy he affected, down to what horses he backed on the turf.

And indeed archaeology is only really delightful when transfused into some form of art. I have no desire to underrate the services of laborious scholars, but I feel that the use Keats made of Lemprière's Dictionary[36] is of far more value to us than Professor Max Müller's[37] treatment of the same mythology as a disease of language. Better *Endymion* than any theory, however sound, or, as in the present instance, unsound, of an epidemic among adjectives! And who does not feel that the chief glory of Piranesi's[38] book on Vases is that it gave Keats the suggestion for his 'Ode on a Grecian Urn'? Art, and art only, can make archaeology beautiful; and the theatric art can use it most directly and most vividly, for it can combine in one exquisite presentation the illusion of actual life with the wonder of the unreal world. But the sixteenth century was not merely the age of Vitruvius;[39] it was the age of Vecellio[40] also. Every nation seems suddenly to have become interested in the dress of its neighbours. Europe began to investigate its own clothes, and the amount of books published on national costumes is quite extraordinary. At the beginning of the century the *Nuremberg Chronicle*, with its two thousand illustrations, reached its fifth edition, and before the century was over seventeen editions were published of Munster's *Cosmography*.[41] Besides these two books there were also the works of Michael Colyns, of Hans Weigel, of Amman, and of Vecellio himself, all of them well illustrated, some of the drawings in Vecellio being probably from the hand of Titian.

Nor was it merely from books and treatises that they acquired their knowledge. The development of the habit of foreign travel, the increased commercial intercourse between countries, and the frequency of diplomatic missions, gave every nation many opportunities of studying the various forms of contemporary dress. After the departure from England, for instance, of the ambassadors from the Czar, the Sultan and the Prince of Morocco, Henry the Eighth and his friends gave several masques in the strange attire of their visitors. Later on London saw, perhaps too often, the sombre splendour of the Spanish Court, and to Elizabeth came envoys from all lands, whose dress, Shakespeare tells us, had an important influence on English costume.

And the interest was not confined merely to classical dress, or the dress of foreign nations; there was also a good deal of research, amongst theatrical people especially, into the ancient costume of England itself: and when Shakespeare, in the prologue to one of his plays, expresses his regret at being unable to produce helmets of the period, he is speaking as an Elizabethan manager and not merely as an Elizabethan poet. At Cambridge, for instance, during his day, a play of *Richard the Third* was performed, in which the actors were attired in real dresses of the time, procured from the great collection of historical costume in the Tower, which was always open to the inspection of managers, and sometimes placed at their disposal. And I cannot help thinking that this performance must have been far more artistic, as regards costume, than Garrick's mounting of Shakespeare's own play on the subject, in which he himself appeared in a nondescript fancy dress, and everybody else in the costume of the time of George the Third, Richmond especially being much admired in the uniform of a young guardsman.

For what is the use to the stage of that archaeology which has so strangely terrified the critics, but that it, and it alone, can give us the architecture and apparel suitable to the time in which the action of the play passes? It enables us to see a Greek dressed like a Greek, and an Italian like an Italian; to enjoy the arcades of Venice and the balconies of Verona; and, if the play deals with any of the great eras in our country's history, to contemplate the age in its proper attire, and the king in his habit as he lived. And I wonder, by the way, what Lord Lytton would have said some time ago, at the Princess's Theatre, had the curtain risen on his father's Brutus reclining in a Queen Anne chair, attired in a flowing wig and a flowered dressing-gown, a costume which in the last century was considered peculiarly appropriate to an antique Roman! For in those halcyon days of the drama no archaeology troubled the stage, or distressed the critics, and our inartistic grandfathers sat peaceably in a stifling atmosphere of anachronisms, and beheld with the calm complacency of the age of prose an Iachimo in powder and patches, a Lear in lace ruffles and a Lady Macbeth in a large crinoline. I can understand archaeology being attacked on the ground of its excessive realism, but to attack it as pedantic seems to be very much beside the mark. However, to attack it for any reason is foolish; one might just as well speak disrespectfully of the equator. For archaeology, being a science, is neither good nor bad, but a fact simply. Its value depends entirely on how it is used, and only an artist can use it. We look to the archaeologist for the materials, to the artist for the method.

In designing the scenery and costumes for any of Shakespeare's plays, the first thing the artist has to settle is the best date for the drama. This should be determined by the general spirit of the play, more than by any actual historical references which may occur in it. Most *Hamlets* I have seen were placed far too early. *Hamlet* is essentially a scholar of the Revival of Learning;[42] and if the allusion to the recent invasion of England by the Danes puts it back to the ninth century, the use of foils[43] brings it down much later. Once, however, that the date has been fixed, then the archaeologist is to supply us with the facts which the artist is to convert into effects.

It has been said that the anachronisms in the plays themselves show us that Shakespeare was indifferent to historical accuracy, and a great deal of capital has been made out of Hector's indiscreet quotation from Aristotle.[44] Upon the other hand, the anachronisms are really few in number, and not very important, and, had Shakespeare's attention been drawn to them by a brother artist, he would probably have corrected them. For, though they can hardly be called blemishes, they are certainly not the great beauties of his work; or, at least, if they are, their anachronistic charm cannot be emphasized unless the play is accurately mounted according to its proper date. In looking at Shakespeare's plays as a whole, however, what is really remarkable is their extraordinary fidelity as regards his personages and his plots. Many of his *dramatis personae*[45] are people who had actually existed, and some of them might have been seen in real life by a portion of his audience. Indeed the most violent attack that was made on Shakespeare in his time was for his supposed caricature of Lord Cobham.[46] As for his plots, Shakespeare constantly draws them either from authentic history, or from the old ballads and traditions which served as history to the Elizabethan public, and which even now no scientific historian would dismiss as absolutely untrue. And not merely did he select fact instead of fancy as the basis of much of his imaginative work, but he always gives to each play the general character, the social atmosphere in a word, of the age in question. Stupidity he recognizes as being one of the permanent characteristics of all European civilizations; so he sees no difference between a London mob of his own day and a Roman mob of pagan days, between a silly watchman in Messina and a silly Justice of the Peace in Windsor. But when he deals with higher characters, with those exceptions of each age which are so fine that they become its types, he gives them absolutely the stamp and seal of their time. Virgilia[47] is one of those Roman wives on whose tomb was written *Domi mansit, lanam fecit*, as surely as Juliet is the romantic girl of the Renaissance. He is even true to the characteristics of race. Hamlet has all the imagination and irresolution of the Northern nations, and the Princess Katharine[48] is as entirely French as the heroine of *Divorçons*. Harry the Fifth is a pure Englishman, and Othello a true Moor.

Again when Shakespeare treats of the history of England from the fourteenth to the sixteenth centuries, it is wonderful how careful he is to have his facts perfectly right – indeed he follows Holinshed[49] with curious fidelity. The incessant wars between France and England are described with extraordinary accuracy down to the names of the besieged towns, the ports of landing and embarkation, the sites and dates of the battles, the titles of the commanders on each side, and the lists of the killed and wounded. And as regards the Civil Wars of the Roses[50] we have many elaborate genealogies of the seven sons of Edward the Third; the claims of the rival Houses of York and Lancaster to the throne are discussed at length; and if the English aristocracy will not read Shakespeare as a poet, they should certainly read him as a sort of early Peerage. There is hardly a single title in the Upper House, with the exception of course of the uninteresting titles assumed by the law lords, which does not appear in Shakespeare along with many details of family history, creditable and discreditable. Indeed if it be really necessary that the School Board children[51] should know all about the Wars of the Roses, they could learn their lessons just as well out of Shakespeare as out of shilling primers, and learn them, I need not say, far more pleasurably. Even in Shakespeare's own day this use of his plays was recognized. 'The historical plays teach history to those who cannot read it in the chronicles,' says Heywood[52] in a tract about the stage, and yet I am sure that sixteenth-century chronicles were much more delightful reading than nineteenth-century primers are.

Of course the aesthetic value of Shakespeare's plays does not, in the slightest degree, depend on their facts, but on their Truth, and

Truth is independent of facts always, inventing or selecting them at pleasure. But still Shakespeare's use of facts is a most interesting part of his method of work, and shows us his attitude towards the stage, and his relations to the great art of illusion. Indeed he would have been very much surprised at anyone classing his plays with 'fairy tales', as Lord Lytton does; for one of his aims was to create for England a national historical drama, which should deal with incidents with which the public was well acquainted, and with heroes that lived in the memory of a people. Patriotism, I need hardly say, is not a necessary quality of art; but it means, for the artist, the substitution of a universal for an individual feeling, and for the public the presentation of a work of art in a most attractive and popular form. It is worth noticing that Shakespeare's first and last successes were both historical plays.

It may be asked, what has this to do with Shakespeare's attitude towards costume? I answer that a dramatist who laid such stress on historical accuracy of fact would have welcomed historical accuracy of costume as a most important adjunct to his illusionist method. And I have no hesitation in saying that he did so. The reference to helmets of the period in the prologue to *Henry the Fifth* may be considered fanciful, though Shakespeare must have often seen

The very casque
That did affright the air at Agincourt,

where it still hangs in the dusky gloom of Westminster Abbey, along with the saddle of that 'imp of fame',[53] and the dinted shield with its torn blue velvet lining and its tarnished lilies of gold; but the use of military tabards[54] in *Henry the Sixth* is a bit of pure archaeology, as they were not worn in the sixteenth century; and the King's own tabard, I may mention, was still suspended over his tomb in St George's Chapel, Windsor, in Shakespeare's day. For, up to the time of the unfortunate triumph of the Philistines in 1645,[55] the chapels and cathedrals of England were the great national museums of archaeology, and in them was kept the armour and attire of the heroes of English history. A good deal was of course preserved in the Tower, and even in Elizabeth's day tourists were brought there to see such curious relics of the past as Charles Brandon's[56] huge lance, which is still, I believe, the admiration of our country visitors; but the cathedrals and churches were, as a rule, selected as the most suitable shrines for the reception of the historic antiquities. Canterbury can still show us the helm of the Black Prince,[57] Westminster the robes of our kings, and in old St Paul's the very banner that had waved on Bosworth field[58] was hung up by Richmond himself.

In fact, everywhere that Shakespeare turned in London, he saw the apparel and appurtenances of past ages, and it is impossible to doubt that he made use of his opportunities. The employment of lance and shield, for instance, in actual warfare, which is so frequent in his plays, is drawn from archaeology, and not from the military accoutrements of his day; and his general use of armour in battle was not a characteristic of his age, a time when it was rapidly disappearing before firearms. Again, the crest on Warwick's helmet, of which such a point is made in *Henry the Sixth*, is absolutely correct in a fifteenth-century play when crests were generally worn, but would not have been so in a play of Shakespeare's own time, when feathers and plumes had taken their place – a fashion which, as he tells us in *Henry the Eighth*, was borrowed from France. For the historical plays, then, we may be sure that archaeology was employed, and as for the others I feel certain that it was the case also. The appearance of Jupiter on his eagle, thunderbolt in hand, of Juno with her peacocks, and of Iris with her many-coloured bow; the Amazon masque and the masque of the Five Worthies, may all be regarded as archaeological; and the vision which Posthumus sees in prison of Sicilius Leonatus – 'an old man, attired like a warrior, leading an ancient matron' – is clearly so. Of the 'Athenian dress' by which Lysander is distinguished from Oberon I have already spoken; but one of the most marked instances is in the case of the dress of Coriolanus, for which Shakespeare goes directly to Plutarch.[59] That historian, in his Life of the great Roman, tells us of the oak-wreath with which Caius Marcius was crowned, and of the curious kind of dress in which, according to ancient fashion, he had to canvass his electors; and on both of these points he enters into long disquisitions, investigating the origin and meaning of the old customs. Shakespeare, in the spirit of the true artist, accepts the facts of the antiquarian and converts them into dramatic and picturesque effects: indeed the gown of humility, the 'woolvish gown', as Shakespeare calls it, is the central note of the play. There are other cases I might quote, but this one is quite sufficient for my purpose; and it is evident from it at any rate that, in mounting a play in the accurate costume of the time, according to the best authorities, we are carrying out Shakespeare's own wishes and method.

Even if it were not so, there is no more reason that we should continue any imperfections which may be supposed to have characterized Shakespeare's stage-mounting than that we should have Juliet played by a young man, or give up the advantage of changeable scenery. A great work of dramatic art should not merely be made expressive of modern passion by means of the actor, but should be presented to us in the form most suitable to the modern spirit. Racine[60] produced his Roman plays in Louis Quatorze dress on a stage crowded with spectators; but we require different conditions for the enjoyment of his art. Perfect accuracy of detail, for the sake of perfect illusion, is necessary for us. What we have to see is that the details are not allowed to usurp the principal place. They must be subordinate always to the general motive of the play. But subordination in art does not mean disregard of truth; it means conversion of fact into effect, and assigning to each detail its proper relative value.

Les petits détails d'histoire et de vie domestique (says Hugo) doivent être scrupuleusement étudiés et reproduits par le poète, mais uniquement comme des moyens d'accroître la réalité de l'ensemble, et de faire pénétrer jusque dans les coins les plus obscurs de l'oeuvre cette vie générale et puissante au milieu de laquelle les personnages sont plus vrais, et les catastrophes, par conséquent, plus poignantes. Tout doit être subordonné à ce but. L'Homme sur le premier plan, le reste au fond.[61]

This passage is interesting as coming from the first great French dramatist who employed archaeology on the stage, and whose plays, though absolutely correct in detail, are known to all for their passion, not for their pedantry – for their life, not for their learning. It is true that he has made certain concessions in the case of the employment of curious or strange expressions. Ruy Blas[62] talks of M. de Priego as *sujet du roi* instead of *noble du roi*, and Angelo Malipieri speaks of *la croix rouge* instead of *la croix de gueules*.[63] But they are concessions made to the public, or rather to a section of it. 'J'en offre ici toute mes excuses aux spectateurs intelligents,' he says in a note to one of the plays; 'espérons qu'un jour un seigneur vénitien pourra dire tout bonnement sans péril son blason sur le théâtre. C'est un progrès qui viendra.' And, though the description of the crest is not couched in accurate language, still the crest itself was accurately right. It may, of course, be said that the public do not notice these things; upon the other hand, it should be remembered that Art has no other aim but her own perfection, and proceeds simply by her own laws, and that the play which Hamlet describes as being caviare to the general[64] is a play he highly praises. Besides, in England, at any rate, the public have undergone a transformation; there is far more appreciation of beauty now than there was a few years ago; and though they may not be familiar with the authorities and archaeological data for what is shown to them, still they enjoy whatever loveliness they look at. And this is the important thing. Better to take pleasure in a rose than to put its root under a microscope. Archaeological accuracy is merely a condition of illusionist stage effect; it is not its quality. And Lord Lytton's proposal that the dresses should merely be beautiful without being accurate is founded on a misapprehension of the nature of costume, and of its value on the stage. This value is twofold, picturesque and dramatic; the former depends on the colour of the dress, the latter on its design and character. But so interwoven are the two that, whenever in our own day historical accuracy has been disregarded, and the various dresses in a play taken from different ages, the result has been that the stage has been turned into that chaos of costume, that caricature of the centuries, the Fancy Dress Ball, to the entire ruin of all dramatic and picturesque effect. For the dresses of one age do not artistically harmonize with the dresses of another; and, as far as dramatic value goes, to confuse the costumes is to confuse the play. Costume is a growth, an evolution, and a most important, perhaps the most important, sign of the manners, customs and mode of life of each century. The Puritan dislike of colour, adornment and grace in apparel was part of the great revolt of the middle classes against Beauty in the seventeenth century. A historian who disregarded it would give us a most inaccurate picture of the time, and a dramatist who did not avail himself of it would miss a most vital element in producing an illusionist effect. The effeminacy of dress that characterized the reign of Richard the Second was a constant theme of contemporary authors. Shakespeare, writing two hundred years after, makes the king's fondness for gay apparel and foreign fashions a point in the play, from John of Gaunt's reproaches down to Richard's own speech in the third act on his deposition from the throne. And that Shakespeare examined Richard's tomb in Westminster Abbey seems to me certain from York's speech:

> See, see, King Richard doth himself appear
> As doth the blushing discontented sun
> From out the fiery portal of the east,
> When he perceives the envious clouds are bent
> To dim his glory.

For we can still discern on the King's robe his favourite badge – the sun issuing from a cloud. In fact, in every age the social conditions are so exemplified in costume, that to produce a sixteenth-century play in fourteenth-century attire, or *vice versa*, would make the performance seem unreal because untrue. And, valuable as beauty of effect on the stage is, the highest beauty is not merely comparable with absolute accuracy of detail, but really dependent on it. To invent an entirely new costume is almost impossible except in burlesque or extravaganza, and as for combining the dress of different centuries into one, the experiment would be dangerous, and Shakespeare's opinion of the artistic value of such a medley may be gathered from his incessant satire of the Elizabethan dandies for imagining that they were well dressed because they got their doublets in Italy, their hats in Germany and their hose in France. And it should be noted that the most lovely scenes that have been produced on our stage have been those that have been characterized by perfect accuracy, such as Mr and Mrs Bancroft's[65] eighteenth-century revivals at the Haymarket, Mr Irving's superb production of *Much Ado About Nothing*, and Mr Barrett's *Claudian*.[66] Besides, and this is perhaps the most complete answer to Lord Lytton's theory, it must be remembered that neither in costume nor in dialogue is beauty the dramatist's primary aim at all. The true dramatist aims first at what is characteristic, and no more desires that all his personages should be beautifully attired than he desires that they should all have beautiful natures or speak beautiful English. The true dramatist, in fact, shows us life under the conditions of art, not art in the form of life. The Greek dress was the loveliest dress the world has ever seen, and the English dress of the last century one of the most monstrous; yet we cannot costume a play by Sheridan as we would costume a play by Sophokles. For, as Polonius says in his excellent lecture, a lecture to which I am glad to have the opportunity of expressing my obligations, one of the first qualities of apparel is its expressiveness. And the affected style of dress in the last century was the natural characteristic of a society of affected manners and affected conversation – a characteristic which the realistic dramatist will highly value down to the smallest detail of accuracy, and the materials for which he can get only from archaeology.

But it is not enough that a dress should be accurate; it must be also appropriate to the stature and appearance of the actor, and to his supposed condition, as well as to his necessary action in the play. In Mr Hare's production of *As You Like It* at the St James's Theatre, for instance, the whole point of Orlando's complaint that he is brought up like a peasant, and not like a gentleman, was spoiled by the gorgeousness of his dress, and the splendid apparel worn by the banished Duke and his friends was quite out of place. Mr Lewis Wingfield's explanation that the sumptuary laws of the period necessitated their doing so, is, I am afraid, hardly sufficient. Outlaws, lurking in a forest and living by the chase, are not very likely to care much about ordinances of dress. They were probably attired like Robin Hood's men, to whom, indeed, they are compared in the course of the play. And that their dress was not that of wealthy noblemen may be seen by Orlando's words when he breaks in upon them. He mistakes them for robbers, and is amazed to find that they answer him in courteous and gentle terms. Lady Archibald Campbell's production,[67] under Mr E. W. Godwin's direction, of the same play in Coombe Wood was, as regards mounting, far more artistic. At least it seemed so to me. The Duke and his companions were dressed in serge tunics, leathern jerkins, high boots and gauntlets, and wore bycocket hats and hoods. And as they were playing in a real forest, they found, I am sure, their dresses extremely convenient. To every character in the play was given a perfectly appropriate attire, and the brown and green of their costumes harmonized exquisitely with the ferns through which they wandered, the trees beneath which they lay, and the lovely English landscape that surrounded the Pastoral Players. The perfect naturalness of the scene was due to the absolute accuracy and appropriateness of everything that was worn. Nor could archaeology have been put to a severer test, or come out of it more triumphantly. The whole production showed once for all that, unless a dress is archaeologically correct, and artistically appropriate, it always looks unreal, unnatural, and theatrical in the sense of artificial.

Nor, again, is it enough that there should be accurate and appropriate costumes of beautiful colours; there must be also beauty of colour on the stage as a whole, and as long as the background is painted by one artist, and the foreground figures independently designed by another, there is the danger of a want of harmony in the scene as a picture. For each scene the colour-scheme should be settled as absolutely as for the decoration of a room, and the textures which it is proposed to use should be mixed and re-mixed in every possible combination, and what is discordant removed. Then, as regards the particular kinds of colours, the stage is often made too glaring, partly through the excessive use of hot, violent reds, and partly through the costumes looking too new. Shabbiness, which in modern life is merely the tendency of the lower orders towards tone, is not without its artistic value, and modern colours are often much improved by being a little faded. Blue also is too frequently used: it is not merely a dangerous colour to wear by gaslight, but it is really difficult in England to get a thoroughly good blue. The fine Chinese blue, which we all so much admire, takes two years to dye, and the English public will not wait so long for a colour. Peacock blue, of course, has been employed on the stage, notably at the Lyceum, with great advantage; but all attempts at a good light blue, or good dark blue, which I have seen have been failures. The value of black is hardly appreciated; it was used effectively by Mr Irving in *Hamlet* as the central note of a composition, but as a tone-giving neutral its importance is not recognized. And this is curious, considering the general colour of the dress of a century in which, as Baudelaire says, 'Nous célébrons tous quelque enterrement.'[68] The archaeologist of the future will probably point to this age as a time when the beauty of black was understood; but I hardly think that, as regards stage-mounting or house decoration, it really is. Its decorative value is, of course, the same as that of white or gold; it can separate and harmonize colours. In modern plays the black frock coat of the hero becomes important in itself, and should be given a suitable background. But it rarely is. Indeed the only good background for a play in modern dress which I have ever seen was the dark grey and cream-white scene of the first act of the *Princesse Georges* in Mrs Langtry's[69] production. As a rule, the hero is smothered in *bric-à-brac* and palm-trees, lost in the gilded abyss of Louis Quatorze furniture, or reduced to a mere midge in the midst of marqueterie;[70] whereas the background should always be kept as a background, and colour subordinated to effect. This, of course, can only be done when there is one single mind directing the whole production. The facts of art are diverse, but the essence of artistic effect is unity. Monarchy, Anarchy and Republicanism may contend for the government of nations; but a theatre should be in the power of a cultured despot. There may be division of labour, but there must be no division of mind. Whoever understands the costume of an age understands of necessity its architecture and its surroundings also, and it is easy to see from the chairs of a century whether it was a century of crinolines or not. In fact, in art there is no specialism, and a really artistic production should bear the impress of one master, and one master only, who not merely should design and arrange everything, but should have complete control over the way in which each dress is to be worn.

Mademoiselle Mars,[71] in the first production of *Hernani*,[72] absolutely refused to call her lover '*Mon Lion!*' unless she was allowed to wear a little fashionable *toque*[73] then much in vogue on the Boulevards; and many young ladies on our own stage insist to the present day on wearing stiff starched petticoats under Greek dresses, to the entire ruin of all delicacy of line and fold; but these wicked things should not be allowed. And there should be far more dress rehearsals than there are now. Actors such as Mr Forbes-Robertson, Mr Conway, Mr George Alexander[74] and others, not to mention older artists, can move with ease and elegance in the attire of any century; but there are not a few who seem dreadfully embarrassed about their hands if they have no side pockets, and who always wear their dresses as if they were costumes. Costumes, of course, they are to the designer; but dresses they should be to those that wear them. And it is time that a stop should be put to the idea, very prevalent on the stage, that the Greeks and Romans always went about bareheaded in the open air – a mistake the Elizabethan managers did not fall into, for they gave hoods as well as gowns to their Roman senators.

More dress rehearsals would also be of value in explaining to the actors that there is a form of gesture and movement that is not merely appropriate to each style of dress, but really conditioned by it. The extravagant use of the arms in the eighteenth century, for instance, was the necessary result of the large hoop, and the solemn dignity of Burleigh[75] owed as much to his ruff as to his reason. Besides, until an actor is at home in his dress, he is not at home in his part.

Of the value of beautiful costume in creating an artistic temperament in the audience, and producing that joy in beauty for beauty's sake without which the great masterpieces of art can never be understood, I will not here speak; though it is worth while to notice how Shakespeare appreciated that side of the question in the production of his tragedies, acting them always by artificial light, and in a theatre hung with black; but what I have tried to point out is that archaeology is not a pedantic method, but a method of artistic illusion, and that costume is a means of displaying character without description, and of producing dramatic situations and dramatic effects. And I think it is a pity that so many critics should have set themselves to attack one of the most important movements on the modern stage before that movement has at all reached its proper perfection. That it will do so, however, I feel as certain as that we shall require from our dramatic critics in the future higher qualifications than that they can remember

Macready or have seen Benjamin Webster:[76] we shall require of them indeed, that they cultivate a sense of beauty. 'Pour être plus difficile, la tâche n'en est que plus glorieuse.'[77] And if they will not encourage, at least they must not oppose, a movement of which Shakespeare of all dramatists would have most approved, for it has the illusion of truth for its method, and the illusion of beauty for its result. Not that I agree with everything that I have said in this essay. There is much with which I entirely disagree. The essay simply represents an artistic standpoint, and in aesthetic criticism attitude is everything. For in art there is no such thing as a universal truth. A Truth in art is that whose contradictory is also true. And just as it is only in art-criticism, and through it, that we can apprehend the Platonic theory of ideas, so it is only in art-criticism, and through it, that we can realize Hegel's system of contraries.[78] The truths of metaphysics are the truths of masks.

NOTES

In preparing these notes I have profited from the work of earlier Wilde editors and scholars, in particular, Lawrence Danson's study of *Intentions* (see Further Reading), the late Sir Rupert Hart-Davis's editions of Wilde's letters (see Further Reading), Isobel Murray's *Oscar Wilde: A Critical Edition of the Major Works* and *Oscar Wilde: The Soul of Man and Prison Writings*, Horst Schroeder's two indispensable monographs on *The Portrait of Mr W. H.* (see Further Reading) and Ian Small's Penguin Classics edition of Wilde's *Complete Short Fiction*. Christopher Stray of the University of Wales, Swansea, has kindly given me much valuable help with Wilde's allusions to Greek and Roman literature.

Eight Reviews: 1885–90

1. Mr Whistler's Ten o'Clock

First published in the *Pall Mall Gazette* for 21 February 1885, the day after Whistler delivered his celebrated evening lecture. In it, the painter had protested on behalf of working artists against the intrusion by such 'middlemen in this matter of Art' as John Ruskin and Wilde himself, mere 'pretenders' to artistic knowledge, as Whistler considered them, who failed to see that 'Art seeks the Artist alone'.

1. *Mr Whistler*: James Abbott McNeill Whistler (1834–1903), American painter, engraver, author and controversialist, first made his reputation in France. His early patronizing friendship with Wilde later turned to bitter rivalry as the younger man became a more successful expositor of the art for art's sake doctrines that Whistler had himself taken from Théophile Gautier.
2. *diaper*: pattern of small constantly repeated figures, such as diamonds, originally used in medieval weaving.
3. *anthropophagous*: man-eating.
4. *private views*: a survey or inspection of art works, whether in artists' studios,

galleries or other venues, not open to the general public but available to invited guests. The private view of the Royal Academy of Arts, held every year in April before the opening of its annual exhibition, marked the official beginning of the Victorian social season. By the 1880s, the custom of private viewing had been widened through 'Show Sundays' – when artists invited members of the middle-class public to visit their studios instead of attending afternoon church services.

5. *Mephistopheles*: in medieval demonology, one of the seven chief devils. Whistler's moustache and beard gave him a devilish appearance, though Wilde's epithet is chosen for its alliteration.

6. *dilettanti . . . amateurs . . . dress reformers*: although to Whistler 'dilettante' and 'amateur' connoted mere dabblers in the fine arts, Wilde in this context intends the words to refer to those who cultivate or follow the arts for personal pleasure instead of doing so professionally or for gain. Wilde says '*O mea culpa!*' to confess his 'fault' (in Whistler's eyes) of being a dress reformer, although by 1885 Wilde had given up wearing 'Aesthetic' dress, noting that the celebrated knee-breeches and silken hose of his North American tour 'belonged to the Oscar Wilde of the first period'.

7. *Velásquez*: Diego Rodríguez de Silva y Velázquez (1599–1660), Spanish painter – Whistler's artistic hero.

8. *Crystal Palace*: see n. 20, p. 371 below.

9. *Corot*: Jean Baptiste Camille Corot (1796–1875), French landscape painter. Corot's later works are notable for their misty, translucent atmosphere. Wilde gives a word-picture of Corot's painting 'The Dance of the Nymphs' in 'The Critic as Artist, Part I' (see p. 235).

10. *Fusiyama*: more commonly, Fujiyama or Fuji, the highest mountain in Japan, celebrated for its perfect symmetry, and hence a frequent focus of Japanese art. In referring to Mount Fuji Whistler had concluded his lecture with a sentence rich in the alliteration Wilde loved, saying 'the story of the beautiful is already complete – hewn in the marbles of the Parthenon – and broidered, with the birds, upon the fan of Hokusai – at the foot of Fusiyama'.

11. *magenta . . . Albert blue*: among the earliest colours produced by the new coal-tar dyes first patented in 1856 by an English chemist, W. H. Perkin. The indiscriminate use in interior decorating and women's dress of such garish and unfading hues as Victoria Orange and Albert or Aniline Blue led to a reaction among advanced designers like William Morris and E. W. Godwin in favour of vegetal dyes and muted, 'low' colours – the 'greenery-yallery Grosvenor Gallery' colours associated with Aestheticism. Wilde regarded his own writing as part of this aesthetic revolution. In a letter defending *The Picture* *of Dorian Gray*, he declared that the novel 'is an essay on decorative art. It reacts against the crude brutality of plain realism.'

12. *mediums and megilp*: in painting, a medium is a liquid with which pigments are mixed for application; megilp is a specific kind of medium, usually consisting of linseed oil mixed with turpentine or mastic varnish. Wilde is twitting Whistler about the barbarous lingo used by professional artists in contrast to the wider culture of true aesthetic critics like himself.

13. *Benjamin West and Paul Delaroche*: West (1738–1820), American historical painter, lived in England almost sixty years, becoming President of the Royal Academy in 1792. His most famous painting is 'The Death of General Wolfe'. Delaroche (1797–1856), French historical painter; his best-known painting is perhaps 'The Princes in the Tower'. Both men were highly successful but relatively conventional painters.

2. The Relation of Dress to Art

First published in the *Pall Mall Gazette* for 28 February 1885, under the title 'The Relation of Dress to Art. A Note in Black and White on Mr Whistler's Lecture'.

1. *Sir Joshua Reynolds*: English painter (1723–92) best known for his brilliant portraits. The first president of the Royal Academy; also the author of celebrated *Discourses* on painting, which expressed the classical ideal in art.

2. *les grands coloristes savent faire de la couleur avec un habit noir, une cravate blanche, et un fond gris*: 'the great colourists know how to make colour out of a black suit, a white tie and a grey background'. The poet Charles Baudelaire (1821–67) makes the remark in the 'Heroism of Modern Life' section of his essay 'The Salon of 1846'.

3. *Piccadilly*: famous thoroughfare in London known for its clubs, shops and residences. Wilde is alluding to a song from *Patience* (1881), Gilbert and Sullivan's satire of Aestheticism, in which the aesthete Bunthorne recommends walking down 'Piccadilly with a poppy or a lily / In your medieval hand'. Although based on the painter and poet Dante Gabriel Rossetti (1828–82), Bunthorne was commonly taken as a caricature of Wilde.

4. chiaroscuro: the general distribution of light and shade in a painting or etching, frequently a focus of attention and judgement by connoisseurs.

5. *butterfly*: motif identified with Whistler because the artist reduced the letters of his signature on his paintings to a monogram in the shape of a butterfly – with a sting in its tail.

6. *Tite-street*: a street in Chelsea, where both Wilde (at Keats House, No. 16) and Whistler lived for a time during the 1880s. Bordering the Thames, Chelsea was at this time an inexpensive and artistic district. Thomas Carlyle lived there in Cheyne Walk, as did D. G. Rossetti in nearby Tudor House. Whistler commissioned the architect E. W. Godwin to build the strikingly simple and asymmetrical White House for him in Tite Street during 1877–8, but was forced to sell the house upon declaring bankruptcy in 1879.

7. *peplums . . . pastels*: a peplum was a short skirt or flounce covering the hips, a feature of the classicizing costumes depicted by such painters of the 1880s as Albert Moore, a close friend of Whistler's. Pastels are drawings made with crayons made of pigments ground with chalk.

8. *Burlington House . . . Grosvenor Gallery*: Burlington House was the home of the Royal Academy, hence the citadel of orthodox art. The Grosvenor Gallery was a new exhibition hall, established in 1877 by Sir Coutts Lindsay to display precisely those advanced painters – e.g. Whistler, Edward Burne-Jones – whose works were rejected for exhibition by the Royal Academy.

9. *Piazza di Spagna*: celebrated plaza in Rome, beside the even more famous Spanish Steps, where artists and models habitually congregated, posed or sketched. During the nineteenth century, the area was favoured by Anglo-American residents and travellers.

10. *Holland Park*: refers to the magnificent house and studio of Sir Frederick Leighton (later Baron Leighton of Stretton), neoclassical painter and President of the Royal Academy from 1878 until his death in 1896. One visitor to 2 Holland Park recalled that Leighton 'welcomed us at the terminus of a series of handsome rooms, each of which gave the impression of being the ante-room to another yet more handsome, culminating in the lofty spaciousness of the great studio'. In an 1887 review, Wilde mocked 'that wax-doll grace of treatment that is so characteristic of his best work, and is eminently suggestive of the President's earnest and continual struggles to discover the difference between chalk and colour'.

11. *Canaan . . . the Abruzzi*: in the Hebrew Bible, Canaan is the region between the Dead Sea and the Mediterranean. The Abruzzi, a remote and mountainous area in south central Italy, extending eastwards to the Adriatic coast, was known for its picturesque wolves, wild boars and bandits.

12. *the Pantechnicon*: an ambitious bazaar established early in the nineteenth century in Motcomb Street, Belgrave Square, at first devoted to displaying and selling all kinds of artistic work. When the enterprise failed, it was turned into a furniture depository, and the brightly hopeful term 'pantechnicon' (invented from Greek) dwindled to a merely utilitarian term for furniture van.

13. *Le milieu se renouvelant, l'art se renouvelle*: 'with the renewing of the [social and intellectual] environment, art revives' – an opinion deriving from the French critic Hippolyte Taine (1828–93), whose theoretical motto was *race, milieu, moment*. Author of the monumental *Histoire de la Littérature anglaise* (1863–4), Taine was at first a sociological critic, much influenced by Auguste Comte in attempting to understand the 'fixed laws' of artistic creation. Later, Taine's intense appreciation of the beautiful nude bodies depicted in Greek sculpture and Renaissance painting made him particularly congenial to such *fin de siècle* writers as John Addington Symonds and Wilde.

14. *Apocrypha*: in the Bible, fourteen books of the Old Testament not considered canonical. Included in the Greek and Latin versions of the Bible as an appendix, but usually omitted from Protestant editions.

15. *Philistine*: Matthew Arnold's celebrated term, taken over from Heinrich Heine, for those who are hostile or indifferent to beauty, culture, ideas and art. The epithet was particularly effective, noted Leslie Stephen, because it 'implies a healthy contempt for the public in general and therefore flatters it in particular'. Originally, the name referred to an ancient non-Semitic people on the coast of Palestine *c*.1200 BC.

16. *Ariel praising Caliban*: in Shakespeare's *The Tempest*, Ariel is a frolicsome airy spirit and Caliban a misshapen, evil-natured monster. Wilde will often use 'Caliban' as a type for human crudity and ill will.

17. *Commination Service*: in the liturgy of the Church of England, a penitential office proclaiming God's anger and judgements against sinners.

18. *Puck*: a mischievous sprite in Shakespeare's *A Midsummer Night's Dream*.

3. A Sentimental Journey through Literature

First published in the *Pall Mall Gazette* for 1 December 1886 as a review of *Essays on Poetry and Poets* by Roden Noel.

1. *Mr Robert Buchanan*: Scots poet, novelist and playwright (1841–1901), today remembered as a critic. In 1871 Buchanan's attack upon D. G. Rossetti and the Pre-Raphaelites in a magazine article entitled 'The Fleshly School of Poetry' began a celebrated controversy. The ratio of poetic worth implied by 'Keats is to Whitman as Tennyson is to Buchanan' suggests that Wilde found the chief value of the American poet's work, as he would say in an 1889 review, 'in its prophecy not in its performance'.

2. *Ruskin's 'pathetic fallacy of literature'*: in *Modern Painters*, vol. 5 (1860), Ruskin defined the 'pathetic fallacy' as the false impression of outward things produced by violent emotion, citing as example Charles Kingsley's poetic lines, 'They rowed her in across the rolling foam – / The cruel, crawling foam.' By the time Noel came to criticize the term, 'pathetic fallacy' had come to mean simply the attribution of a human response ('cruel') to non-human beings or objects ('foam'). Ruskin always maintained, however, that the pathetic fallacy, though false to appearances, told the truth about the world as subjectively experienced by someone under the influence of powerful emotion.

3. *Hugo*: Victor Hugo (1802–85), French poet, playwright, novelist and central figure of the Romantic movement in France. Wilde met Hugo in Paris in 1883.

4. *Chatterton*: Thomas Chatterton (1752–70), English poet whose brilliant pseudo-archaic poems arrested the attention of the Romantic poets who followed him. Alone and impoverished in London, he committed suicide at seventeen, thereby becoming an iconic figure of poetic genius undone by public indifference.

5. anlace *fell*: an anlace was a medieval dagger or short sword worn in front of the body. As used here, 'fell' is an adjective meaning 'deadly'.

6. *nineteenth-century restorations*: the Victorian neo-Gothic movement encouraged much research into and restoration of Britain's medieval Gothic buildings. Some of these restorations, however, involved a brutal defacing of old structures in which architectural detail and historical patina were lost. The vandalism of 'improvement' was so extreme that in 1877 William Morris formed the Society for the Protection of Ancient Buildings – nicknamed 'Anti-Scrape' – to combat it.

7. *Richard Hengist Horne*: English poet and critic (1803–84). Horne served in the Mexican navy during Mexico's war of independence, then turned epic poet in London and later became an Australian adventurer. His poem *Orion*, published to great acclaim in 1843, has been largely unread since.

8. *Sheridan ... Otway*: Richard Brinsley Sheridan (1751–1816), Anglo-Irish playwright and theatre manager, the author of *The Rivals* (1775) and *The School for Scandal* (1777). Thomas Otway (1652–85), best known for his verse tragedies, especially *Venice Preserv'd* (1682).

9. Sardanapalus: tragedy by Lord Byron (1821) which took as its hero the last king of Assyria, notorious in legend for his luxury and weakness, who lost his empire, his capital (Nineveh) and his life (by suicide).

10. *Thomson's 'Rule Britannia'*: the poet James Thomson (1700–48) is credited with writing the words to this famous song for the masque of *Alfred*, composed by him and David Mallet in 1740.

11. *Mr Alfred Austin*: editor and poet (1835–1913). Although Austin was eventually to be named Poet Laureate in 1896 (after an increasingly desperate search to replace Tennyson, who died in 1892), Wilde's suggestion that Austin was a negligible talent is strongly seconded by history.

12. *artists of note whom we may affiliate on Byron*: Wilde originally put inverted commas around this phrase, as if quoting from Noel. But Noel had actually written, 'I know not any artist of note, unless it be Edgar Poe, Bulwer Lytton, Disraeli, or Mr Alfred Austin whom we may affiliate to Byron.' Because of an earlier protest about using inverted commas around phrases that were not exact quotations, Wilde's anonymous review was printed by the editor without them.

13. *Sappho*: Greek lyric poet born about the middle of the seventh century BC on the island of Lesbos. She wrote about love with passionate fire.

14. *Marini*: Giambattista Marini (1569–1625), Italian poet, whose extravagant metaphors, forced antitheses and far-fetched conceits created around him a literary movement ('Marinism'), quickly identified both inside and outside Italy with literary decadence.

15. *Wilson*: John Wilson (1785–1854), Scottish critic and essayist, the 'Christopher North' of *Blackwood's Magazine*. Although Wilson came under the influence of Wordsworth, Coleridge and Southey, his own poetry is little more than interesting. Wilde's disdain for Wilson is doubtless heightened by the critic's participation in the notorious *Blackwood's* attack on Leigh Hunt and John Keats – Wilde's poetic idol.

16. Cain: verse drama by Byron (1821).

17. *Parnassus*: a high mountain in central Greece, associated by the ancient Greeks with the worship of Apollo and the Muses. Hence its use, as here, as a synonym for the world of art.

18. *Laura Bridgman*: the celebrated American blind deaf-mute (1829–89), who was taught to read by way of a system of raised letters by Dr Samuel Gridley Howe of Boston.

19. *Sentimental Journey through Literature*: Laurence Sterne's *A Sentimental Journey through France and Italy* (1768), an episodic and inconclusive account of the narrator's various sentimental adventures, was regarded as distinctly second rate compared to Sterne's great novel *Tristram Shandy* (1760–67).

4. Mr Pater's *Imaginary Portraits*

First published in the *Pall Mall Gazette* for 11 June 1887. Walter Pater (1839–94) was an Oxford don, essayist and fiction writer whose first book, *Studies in the History of the Renaissance* (1873), instantly became the bible of art and experience to Wilde's generation. *Imaginary Portraits* contained four fictional accounts of young men glimpsed at moments of psychic crisis in different historical periods: a younger associate of the French painter Antoine Watteau, Sebastian van Storck, Denys l'Auxerrois and Duke Carl of Rosenmold.

1. *him who saw Mona Lisa*: i.e. Pater himself, whose famous evocation of Leonardo da Vinci's Mona Lisa ('She is older than the rocks among which she sits . . .') had become one of the sacred texts of Aestheticism.

2. peintre des fêtes galantes: 'the painter of *fêtes galantes*' or romantic parties, a reference to Watteau, famous for his elegant and mysterious paintings of such gatherings.

3. *the Helder*: Den Helder, North Holland seaport situated on a peninsula opposite the island city of Ostend.

4. *Spinoza*: Baruch Spinoza (1632–77), Dutch philosopher and theologian.

5. *Dionysus*: Greek god of wine. Pater's Denys reincarnates the sensuous passion and violence characteristic of Dionysian followers.

6. *Mantegna*: see n. 8, p. 363 below.

7. *late King of Bavaria*: Louis II (1845–96), king of Bavaria – 'mad Ludwig' as he came to be known – succeeded to the throne in 1864, devoting himself to the arts rather than the army or diplomacy. Ludwig sought out the composer Richard Wagner, who became so intimate and influential a friend that the king, under pressure, was forced to give him up. Thereafter Ludwig craved solitude or inferior favourites, with whom he is rumoured to have engaged in cruel perversions. To house himself in a magnificence proportioned to his megalomania, the king built or altered such castles as Hohenschwangau and Neuschwanstein and these remain his most notable monument.

8. *the* Grand Monarque: Louis XIV of France, the 'Sun King', whose crushing magnificence, brilliant diplomacy and efficient centralization of power in his own person established the pattern for absolutist rule.

9. Aufklärung: German for 'enlightenment', referring to the intellectual and artistic renaissance in Germany taking place from 1770 to 1832 and centring in such writers and thinkers as J. G. Herder, Gotthold Lessing, Friedrich von Schiller and Johann Wolfgang von Goethe.

5. [The Actor as Critic]

First published as the opening section of 'Literary and Other Notes' in *Woman's World* for January 1888. Wilde became editor of *Woman's World* in November 1887 after insisting that its name be changed from the slightly vulgar *Lady's World*. Although he attracted a number of distinguished contributors to its pages, he quickly tired of editorial chores. In the face of faltering sales, the publisher, Cassell's, opted to cease publication in October 1889.

1. *Madame Ristori*: Adelaide Ristori (1822–1906), noted Italian actress, who contended with the celebrated French actress Rachel for dominion over the Paris stage in the 1850s. After many successful tours of the Continent and the US, Ristori retired from acting in 1885. Her *Studies and Memoirs* of 1888, the book Wilde is here reviewing, reveals her remarkable psychological and intellectual insight into the characters she portrayed.

2. *Lady Martin*: actress (1817–98) noted for her Shakespearean roles. See further n. 60, p. 323 below. Her volume *On Some of Shakespeare's Female Characters* was published in 1885.

3. *clever author of* Obiter Dicta: Augustine Birrell (1850–1933), barrister, essayist and politician, published three collections of urbanely amusing critical essays entitled *Obiter Dicta*, the first appearing in 1884. Originally a legal term, *obiter dictum* (Latin: '[something] said by the way') referred to an opinion rendered by a judge not essential to the decision and therefore not binding.

4. *Garrick*: David Garrick (1717–79), the greatest actor of his age in comedy and tragedy. He was a member of Dr Samuel Johnson's celebrated 'Club', as vividly described in James Boswell's *Life of Johnson* (1791).

5. *Talma*: François Joseph Talma, French actor (1763–1826), whose superb elocution and unrivalled portrayal of strong concentrated passion helped shape theatrical tradition at the Comédie Française.

6. *David*: Jacques-Louis David (1748–1825), celebrated French painter who had been both court painter to Louis XVI and later the virtual pope of art under Napoleon I. His demand that art return to the formal severity of classical Greek and Roman art, however, was antipathetic to later generations of artists.

7. *Kean*: Edmund Kean (1787–1833), actor celebrated for his portrayals of Shakespeare's tragic characters, beginning with a tumultuously received impersonation of Shylock in 1814. It was of Kean that Coleridge said, 'Seeing him act was like reading Shakespeare by flashes of lightning.'

8. *Hybla bees*: the bees of Hybla, a town in Sicily on the slopes of Mount Etna, were celebrated for their honey, accounted by Herodotus to be the very best available (beside that from Mount Hymettus in Attica).

9. *Salvini*: Tommaso Salvini (1829–1915), Italian actor.

10. *Sarah Bernhardt*: French actress (1844–1923). Her personal charisma and dramatic power enchanted Wilde from the first moment he saw her in 1879 to the last months of his life. He wrote *Salomé* in French for her, and it was planned as part of her 1892 London season but was banned by the Lord

Chamberlain's office. She produced it in Paris in 1896, by which time Wilde was in Reading Gaol.

11. Phèdre: tragedy by Racine, first produced 1677; became one of the showpieces in the classical French dramatic repertory. Sarah Bernhardt first achieved sensational success in *Phèdre* in 1874. When she re-created the role in London in 1879, Wilde attended the performance.

6. Poetical Socialists

First published in the *Pall Mall Gazette* for 15 February 1889 as a review of *Chants of Labour: A Song-Book of the People,* edited by Edward Carpenter, with designs by Walter Crane.

1. *Mr Stopford Brooke*: an Anglican divine (b. 1832) and chaplain in ordinary to Queen Victoria, who left the Church of England in 1880 to officiate as a Unitarian minister and pursue literary and artistic interests.

2. *Trafalgar Square*: on 'Bloody Sunday', 13 November 1887, a massive Socialist demonstration on behalf of free speech in Trafalgar Square was violently broken up by mounted police and Life Guards. In 1805 Trafalgar Bay was the scene of the great naval victory over the French and Spanish fleets by Lord Nelson, who lost his life during the engagement.

3. *'Vicar of Bray'*: celebrated eighteenth-century political song, satirizing an opportunistic Anglican churchman who so accommodates his beliefs to the successive – and religiously diverse – reigns of Charles II, James II, William, Anne and George I that he never loses his post.

4. *Mendelssohn ... Moody and Sankey*: Felix Mendelssohn (1808–47), distinguished German composer, pianist and conductor. Dwight Moody (1837–99) and Ira Sankey (1840–1908) were American evangelists whose collections of gospel hymns proved hugely popular in Britain and America. Mendelssohn's religious oratorios *St Paul* and *Elijah* were at the furthest remove imaginable from Moody and Sankey's thumping melodies.

5. *'Wacht am Rhein'* ... *'Marseillaise'*: 'The Watch on the Rhein' was a popular anthem in Germany during the Franco-Prussian war of 1870–71. The 'Marseillaise' was the battle song of the French Revolution which subsequently became the French national anthem.

6. *'Lillibulero'*, Norma, *'John Brown'*, Beethoven's Ninth: Wilde is here contrasting music as art (Bellini's opera *Norma*, Beethoven's Symphony No. 9) and music as an instrument of motivation ('Lillibulero' was sung by the English army during the suppression of Ireland in the seventeenth century; 'John Brown's

Body Lies a 'Mouldering in the Grave' was the marching song of the Union armies during the American Civil War).

7. *walls of Thebes*: in Greek legend, the walls of Thebes were raised by two brothers who became its rulers, Amphion and Zethus, offspring of a union between Antiope and Zeus. Amphion was a harper of such skill that the stones were said to have been drawn into their places by his music. Thebes was the principal city of Boeotia, a region proverbial for dullness.

7. Mr Swinburne's Last Volume

First published in the *Pall Mall Gazette* for 27 June 1889 as a review of Swinburne's *Poems and Ballads, Third Series*.

1. *very poisonous poetry*: *Poems and Ballads, First Series* (1866) made Swinburne an overnight sensation, as young people took to chanting his hypnotically melodious lines while older critics denounced him as the licentious laureate of a pack of satyrs. Swinburne became 'revolutionary and pantheistic' with *Songs before Sunrise* (1871). He 'invented Marie Stuart' in the tragedy *Bothwell* (1874) about the ill-fated Scottish queen and her wildly unscrupulous husband, James Hepburn, fourth earl of Bothwell (*c*.1536–1578). Swinburne 'returned to the nursery' with his many poems about babies and children published in *A Century of Roundels* (1883).

2. *Border dialect*: the language spoken in the territory on both sides of the boundary line between England and Scotland, but especially the Scottish side. At the beginning of the nineteenth century, Sir Walter Scott initiated literary interest in the Border ballads, most of them composed during the fifteenth century, and Swinburne continued it brilliantly with art ballads that achieved the simplicity and anonymity of the folk ballads he so admired. 'The Ballad,' Wilde told a correspondent in 1897, 'is the true origin of the romantic Drama, and the true predecessors of Shakespeare are not the tragic writers of the Greek or Latin stage, from Aeschylus to Seneca, but the ballad-writers of the Border.'

8. Mr Pater's Last Volume

First published in the *Speaker* for 22 March 1890 as a review of Pater's collection of essays, *Appreciations*.

1. *ballade ... villanelle ... triolet*: highly complex French fixed-verse forms, in which not only the rhyme scheme and metre are prescribed but also the use and sequence of repeated lines. The revival of these forms was begun in the 1870s by the Parnassians, a group of French poets (including Baudelaire) who sought to express the scientific and objective spirit of the age in appropriately formal and restrained verse. When translated to England in the 1880s, however, the vogue for fixed forms soon gave way to an empty virtuosity by second-rate poets (e.g. Austin Dobson, Edmund Gosse).

2. *Jacobean prose ... Queen Anne prose*: prose written during the reign of James I includes Robert Burton's *Anatomy of Melancholy*, the sermons of John Donne and Lancelot Andrewes and, most notably, the Authorized Version of the Bible. 'Queen Anne prose' (which Matthew Arnold also disliked) includes the essays of Joseph Addison and Richard Steele and the fiction and polemical writing of Jonathan Swift.

3. *'the golden book'*: cf. Swinburne's 'Sonnet (with a copy of Mademoiselle de Maupin)': 'This is the golden book of spirit and sense, / The holy writ of beauty.'

4. *Margaret Fuller*: American writer and journalist (1810–50). Although her forceful personality and wonderful power of inspiring others made her an important figure in the Transcendentalist circle, her self-dramatizing intensity frequently exposed her to ridicule. A famous example: Thomas Carlyle, when told that Fuller had declared that she 'accepted the universe', replied, 'Gad! she'd better!'

5. *Latin sense of the word*: the Latin verb *appretiare* means 'to set a value upon, to appraise'.

6. *to realize the nineteenth century*: a sense of history's organic continuity was characteristic of many post-Hegelian and post-Darwinian writers. Pater made the same point in 'Aesthetic Poetry', an essay in the volume Wilde is here reviewing: 'The composite experience of all the ages is part of each one of us; to deduct from that experience, to obliterate any part of it, to come face to face with the people of a past age, as if the middle age, the Renaissance, the eighteenth century had not been, is as impossible as to become a little child, or enter again into the womb and be born.'

7. *Charles Lamb*: English essayist (1775–1834). His contributions to the *London*

Magazine were later collected as the *Essays of Elia* (1823, 1833), after the pen-name he used in writing them.

8. *Sir Thomas Browne*: English physician and man of letters (1605–82). His *Religio Medici* (*The Religion of a Doctor*), a work notable for the beauty and rich complexity of its prose, appeared in 1643.

9. *the singer of the 'Defence of Guenevere'*: i.e. William Morris, whose collection of poems *The Defence of Guenevere and Other Poems* (1858) was reviewed by Pater in 1868. Pater later used the final section of this review for the 'Conclusion' to his *Studies in the History of the Renaissance* (1873), writing which immediately became notorious for its summons to pleasure and intense experience in the moment ('To burn always with this hard, gem-like flame, to maintain this ecstasy, is success in life').

10. *great sorrows*: in 1796, Charles Lamb's sister Mary, overcome by a fit of insanity, stabbed their mother to death. Lamb, then twenty-one, was able to secure her release from what would otherwise have been lifelong imprisonment on the express condition that he personally care for her.

11. purpurei panni: Latin for 'purple patches'. Deriving from a line in Horace's *Ars Poetica*, it became a conventional phrase for ornate writing. Here the reference is to Pater's description first of Leonardo's Mona Lisa and then of Botticelli's 'peevish-looking' madonnas and their strange attractiveness as figures in whom there seemed to be 'something mean or abject even, for the abstract lines of the face have little nobleness, and the colour is wan'. This latter passage scandalized many Victorians.

12. *Cardinal Newman*: John Henry Newman, poet, novelist and Anglican theologian (1801–90), whose conversion to Roman Catholicism in 1845 signalled the culmination of the Tractarian Movement of doctrinal and liturgical reform within the English Church. Newman's simple but eloquent style in his autobiography *Apologia pro Vita Sua* (1864) marked him as a master of English prose.

The Portrait of Mr W. H.

First published in the July 1889 number of *Blackwood's Edinburgh Magazine*, the story was almost immediately expanded by Wilde, who added the thematically important sections on Neoplatonism, the Dark Lady and Elizabethan boy actors. Initially Wilde hoped to publish the expanded version, as he told William Blackwood, 'in a special volume of essays and studies' which would include 'The Decay of Lying' and 'Pen, Pencil and Poison'. Later he decided that separate publication would be preferable and proposed the volume to his publishers Elkin Mathews and John Lane. In the event, however, the expanded version of *Mr W. H.* (almost twice as long as the original *Blackwood*'s story) was not published until after Wilde's death. The manuscript, disappearing in the chaotic aftermath of his arrest and bankruptcy, did not resurface until 1920, published in a limited edition by Mitchell Kennerley in 1921.

1. *Birdcage Walk*: fashionable promenade on the south side of St James's Park, London.

2. *Macpherson, Ireland, and Chatterton*: three notable literary forgers. James Macpherson (1736–96) claimed to be translating works of a Gaelic poet he had himself composed. William Henry Ireland (1777–1835) forged two pseudo-Shakespeare plays as well as other documents relating to the playwright. Thomas Chatterton (1752–70) achieved a brilliant if short-lived success fabricating the poems of an imaginary fifteenth-century Bristol poet, Thomas Rowley.

3. *François Clouet*: French court painter (*c.*1520–72) and son of Jean Clouet, himself a French court portraitist born in Flanders.

4. *Lord Pembroke*: William Herbert, third earl of Pembroke (1580–1630), long considered the most likely original for 'Mr W. H.'. Herbert was the patron of many poets, and Shakespeare dedicated his First Folio to him.

5. *Mrs Mary Fitton*: maid of honour to Queen Elizabeth and mistress of William Herbert, to whom she bore an illegitimate son. In 1886 the Shakespearean scholar Thomas Tyler proposed Fitton as the original for the Dark Lady of the Sonnets.

6. *costermonger*: a hawker of fruits and vegetables from a street barrow.

7. *A. D. C.*: the Amateur Dramatic Company at the University of Cambridge. Founded in 1855 by F. C. Burnand, it excluded women from membership until well into the twentieth century.

8. *read for the Diplomatic*: i.e. prepare for the competitive public examinations for entry into the colonial and foreign services.

9. *Lord Southampton*: Henry Wriothesley, third earl of Southampton (1573–1624), another frequently mentioned candidate for the original 'Mr W. H.'.

10. *Meres*: Francis Meres (1565–1647), Elizabethan literary historian whose *Palladis Tamia* (1598) surveyed works from Chaucer's time to his own.

11. *Drayton and John Davies of Hereford*: Michael Drayton (1563–1631) and John Davies (1565?–1618), talented poets and contemporaries of Shakespeare. The suggestion that Shakespeare was satirizing their work in his Sonnets was first put forward in 1870 by Henry Brown in *The Sonnets of Shakespeare Solved, and the Mystery of his Friendship, Love, and Rivalry Revealed.*

12. *Chapman*: George Chapman (1559?–1634?), English translator, poet and tragedian.

13. *Alleyne MSS. at Dulwich*: the Elizabethan actor Edward Alleyne (1566–1626), who acquired great wealth, founded Dulwich College and left his papers to it.

14. *Lord Chamberlain*: the Lord Chamberlain's office served as official censor of all theatrical performances in England until 1968. It was this office which refused a licence for the London performance of Wilde's *Salomé* on the ground that the play impermissibly represented biblical figures on stage.

15. *St Thomas*: the 'doubting' apostle who demanded ocular and palpable proof before he would believe Jesus had risen from the dead.

16. bleu de paon: French for 'peacock blue', a rich greenish-blue colour.

17. petit-pain: a bread-roll.

18. *Mr Tyler*: Thomas Tyler, author of the Mary Fitton theory (n. 5, p. 318 above), wrote an introduction to a facsimile edition of the Sonnets published in 1886.

19. *Marlowe*: Christopher Marlowe (1564–93), Elizabethan dramatist, whose *Tamburlaine* (*c.*1587) gave a new development to blank verse, opening the way to the achievements of Shakespeare.

20. *the Venus poem*: Shakespeare's *Venus and Adonis*, dedicated to the earl of Southampton, was published in 1593.

21. *saffron-strewn stage*: saffron is a colouring and flavouring agent made from the dried stigmas of the crocus. In ancient Greece, saffron, used as a perfume, was strewn in halls, courts and theatres.

22. *Gervinus*: Georg Gottfried Gervinus (1805–71), German scholar of Shakespeare who wrote that, 'Painting takes away the full form, sculpture the colour, both the motion; the epos changes acts into words, music changes words into tones, it is the drama only that uses all the means at once – form, colour, tone, word, look, motion, and action.' Wilde owned Gervinus's two-volume *Shakespeare Commentaries* (1863).

23. *stern Hebrew prophet*: see Psalms 111:10: 'The fear of the Lord is the beginning of wisdom.'

24. *Marsilio Ficino*: Renaissance philosopher and scholar (1433–99). Ficino's Latin translation of Plato, commissioned by Cosimo de Medici, was published in 1482 and gave a powerful impetus to the new learning in Europe.

25. *Leroy*: Louis Le Roy (1510–77), French humanist and translator, whose *Le Sympose de Platon, ou de l'amour et de beauté* appeared in 1559.

26. *Joachim du Bellay*: French poet (1522–60) and member of the Pléiade, the seven-member group around Pierre Ronsard who revolutionized French poetry by reviving classical models.

27. *Diotima*: character in Plato's *Symposium*, a wise woman who teaches Socrates the 'philosophy of love' that he in turn passes on to his listeners. Diotima says that unlike men who seek immortality through their children, men 'whose procreancy is of the spirit' seek to bring forth an immortal progeny in works of wisdom and beauty. Through an intellectual intercourse with other males, such men 'conceive and bear things of the spirit'. Wilde's narrator has expressed the same point earlier when he says that Shakespeare appeals to Willie Hughes to beget 'Immortal children of undying fame' by inspiring Shakespeare's own poetry.

28. *Edward Blount*: Elizabethan publisher, whose edition of Marlowe's narrative poem *Hero and Leander* was published in 1598.

29. *Bacon*: see n. 52, page 322 below. The quoted passage is from Bacon's essay 'Of Marriage and the Single Life'.

30. *the new Academe*: Cosimo de Medici founded a Platonic Academy outside Florence to spread knowledge of the Platonic philosophy.

31. *Tommaso Cavalieri . . . widow of the Marchese di Pescara*: until Cesare Guasti's edition was published in 1863, it had been assumed that Michelangelo's poems were addressed solely to Vittoria Colonna (1490–1547), the intellectual and nobly chaste widow of the Marchese di Pescara. Guasti, restoring masculine pronouns and terms of address which earlier editors had suppressed, suggested that a number of the poems were in fact addressed to Cavalieri, a Roman youth of remarkable beauty. In an 1871 essay on the poems, Pater had pointed out that 'Signior Guasti finds only four, or at most five' poems addressed to Vittoria Colonna. John Addington Symonds (1840–93), who translated Michelangelo's sonnets into English (1878), sent a copy of them to Wilde, then at Oxford. Symonds later discussed the artist's 'warm love for this young man' in vol. 3 of his *Renaissance in Italy*, from which Wilde largely draws his own account.

32. *Montaigne*: Michel de Montaigne (1533–92), French writer and the inventor of the familiar essay. The essay referred to is 'De l'amitié'.

33. *Florio*: John Florio (1553?–1625) translated Montaigne's *Essays* in 1603 in a version that was much admired and widely influential.

34. *Étienne de la Boëtie*: French poet, political philosopher and magistrate (1530–63), who served with Montaigne in the *parlement* of Bordeaux.

35. *Hubert Languet*: French Huguenot scholar (1518–81), who settled in Germany. His pioneering treatise of political philosophy *Vindiciae contra tyrannos* (1579) introduced the idea of a contract between ruler and people.

36. *Melanchthon*: pen-name of Philip Schwartzerd (1497–1560), German humanist and professor of Greek at Wittenberg University, where he was one of the leading partisans of the Reformation.

37. *Philip Sidney*: poet and courtier (1554–86), whose gallantry on the battlefield of Zutphen – the fatally stricken Sidney foregoing a drink of water that another wounded man might have it – endowed his life and works with an extraordinary influence upon his contemporaries.

38. *Giordano Bruno*: itinerant monk and Italian philosopher (1548?–1600). A vehement critic of the Catholic Church, Bruno lived in Switzerland, France, England and Germany before incautiously returning to Italy, where church officials burned him at the stake. His works had been much neglected before they were rediscovered in the second half of the nineteenth century. Swinburne published a notable poem about him entitled 'For the Feast of Giordano Bruno, Philosopher and Martyr'.

39. *'A filosofia è necessario amore'*: Italian for 'love is necessary for philosophy', a phrase Pater had quoted in an essay he wrote about Bruno published in the *Fortnightly Review* in 1889.

40. *Ben Jonson*: poet and dramatist (1572–1637), whose poem 'To the Memory of My Beloved Master, William Shakespeare' established the high terms of praise for that writer ever afterwards ('He was not of an age, but for all time!').

41. *Richard Barnfield*: minor Elizabethan poet (1574–1627), whose *The Affectionate Shepheard* of 1594 is a pastoral based on Virgil's second eclogue, in which the shepherd Corydon laments his unrequited love for the handsome youth Alexis.

42. *Abraham Fraunce*: English poet, lawyer and advocate of classical meters (*c.*1558–92/3), who published his version of Virgil's second eclogue as *The Lamentation of Corydon for the Love of Alexis* in 1591.

43. *Fletcher*: Phineas Fletcher (1582–1650), English poet of the Spenserian school and author of *The Purple Island* (1633).

44. *Hallam*: Henry Hallam (1777–1859), English historian who declared of the Sonnets in the third volume of his *Introduction to the Literature of Europe, in the Fifteenth, Sixteenth, and Seventeenth Centuries* (1837–9) that 'it is impossible not to wish that Shakespeare had never written them'.

45. *Chapman*: the lines quoted are from Chapman's *Conspiracy and Tragedy of Charles, Duke of Byron* (1608), although Wilde probably derived the quote second hand from Edward Dowden's introduction to his edition of Shakespeare's Sonnets (1881).

46. *'the folly of excessive and misplaced affection'*: another quote from Hallam's *Literature of Europe*.

47. *Pico della Mirandola*: Giovanni Pico della Mirandola (1463–94), Italian humanist and syncretic philosopher who joined in the Platonic Academy near Florence. In an essay on Pico, Pater declares that, at the moment of meeting, Pico and Ficino 'fell in to a conversation, deeper and more intimate than men usually fall into at first sight'.

48. *Plotinus*: Neoplatonic philosopher and mystic (born AD *c*.205), who held that the phenomenal world is the creation of the soul and has no real existence.

49. *Winckelmann*: Johann Joachim Winckelmann (1717–68), the first great German scholar of Greek sculpture and antiquities. Wilde knew Pater's essay on Winckelmann, which proposes that the German 'romantic, fervent friendships with young men' had 'perfected his reconciliation to the spirit of Greek sculpture'. In a letter of 1900 from Rome, Wilde says of an Italian youth he had met, 'He is so absurdly like the Apollo Belvedere that I feel always as if I was Winckelmann when I am with him.'

50. *the virginals*: a small harpsichord of rectangular shape, with the strings stretched parallel to the keyboard. In the sixteenth century, the instrument was compact enough to be placed on a table, where it was played chiefly by young women, hence its name.

51. *Gray's Inn*: one of the four Inns of Court, originally medieval legal institutions for the education, residence and regulation of barristers. By the nineteenth century, no law courses were offered at the Inns and only a minor residence requirement had to be satisfied. Bar examinations were instituted in England in 1872.

52. *Francis Bacon*: courtier, essayist and philosopher (1561–1626), whose works include *The Advancement of Learning* (1605), the *Novum Organon* (1620) and his celebrated *Essays* (1627).

53. *Robin Armin*: Robert Armin (*c*.1568–*c*.1611), a goldsmith's apprentice who was introduced to the stage by the famous clown Richard Tarleton, who took the boy as his 'adopted son'. Wilde's source for this probably apocryphal story is John Payne Collier's *English Dramatic Poetry to the Time of Shakespeare* (1879).

54. *Vespasian*: Roman emperor AD 70 to 79.

55. *Massinger*: Philip Massinger (1583–1640), poet and playwright who collaborated with Shakespeare on two plays. Wilde is deriving many of his details about Elizabethan theatrical history from Collier's *History of English Dramatic Poetry*.

56. *Gosson*: Stephen Gosson (1554–1624), Elizabethan playwright who under Puritan religious teachings soon turned against the stage, publishing a series of attacks upon players and poetry. Sir Philip Sidney answered him in his *Defence of Poesie* (written 1579–80, published 1595).

57. *Prynne*: William Prynne (1600–69), Puritan pamphleteer, whose massive attack against stage plays and the kings and emperors who supported them, *Histriomastix* (1633), won him imprisonment and lost him both ears as he stood in the pillory.

58. *Francis Lenton*: anti-theatrical partisan who published *The Young Gallant's Whirligig* in 1629.

59. *Deuteronomy*: cf. Deuteronomy 22:5: 'The woman shall not wear that which pertaineth unto a man, neither shall a man put on a woman's garment: for all that do so are abomination unto the Lord thy God.'

60. *one of the most brilliant and intellectual actresses*: i.e. Lady Martin (1817–98) in her book *On Some of Shakespeare's Female Characters* (1885). Before her marriage to Theodore, later Sir Theodore, Martin in 1851, she performed as Helena Faucit, appearing in Shakespearean roles under Charles Macready (see n. 9, p. 348 below) at the Covent Garden and Drury Lane theatres. Sir Theodore and Lady Martin were among those who sponsored Wilde's mother for a grant from the Royal Literary Fund in 1888.

61. *Oxford production*: Aeschylus' *Agamemnon* was performed by Oxford undergraduates in Greek at Balliol Hall in June 1880. When the production was offered in London for three days in December, Wilde attended the last performance, and later invited 'Clytemnestra' and 'Cassandra' and some of the other 'young Greeks' to his mother's house for tea. Wilde later told a New York newspaper that he had been the one to suggest performing a Greek play in Greek, but this claim is unconfirmed.

62. *Lyly*: John Lyly (1554?–1606), English prose writer and playwright. In his play of 1592, *Gallathea*, Phillida and Gallathea are disguised as boys. Wilde is gleaning a number of these details from a secondary source, John Addington Symonds's *Shakspere's Predecessors in the English Drama* (1884).

63. *Professor Ward*: Adolphus William Ward (1837–1924), professor of English language and literature at Owens College, Manchester, published a highly regarded history of English literature which Wilde owned.

64. *Dekker*: Thomas Dekker (1570?–1632), prolific English playwright of such comedies as *Patient Grissill* and *The Shoemaker's Holiday*, in the second of which is sung the famous song 'Troll the bowl, the jolly nut-brown bowl'.

65. *Mr Swinburne*: Algernon Charles Swinburne published the remark in his collection *Essays and Studies* (1875).

66. *indenture*: a contract by which a person is bound to service as an apprentice.

67. *Bluecoat School*: here, Christ's Hospital, the most famous of the charity schools whose students were required to wear distinctive attire.

68. *Star Chamber*: a former court of inquisitorial and criminal jurisdiction in England, which sat in secret without a jury, and was noted for its arbitrary methods and severe punishments. It was abolished in 1641.

69. *Fletcher*: John Fletcher (1579–1625), playwright and collaborator with Francis Beaumont. Fletcher is considered also to have had some hand in Shakespeare's *Two Noble Kinsmen* and *Henry VIII*.

70. *over-curious scholar*: i.e. John Abraham Heraud (1799–1887), poet, dramatist and critic who published *Shakspere, His Inner Life as Intimated in His Works* in 1865.

71. *Professor Minto*: William Minto (1845–93), professor of logic and literature at Aberdeen, published his *Secret Drama of Shakspeare's Sonnets* in 1888.

72. *Henry Brown*: yet another Victorian commentator on Shakespeare. His *The Sonnets of Shakespeare Solved, and the Mystery of his Friendship, Love, and Rivalry* appeared in 1870.

73. *Gerald Massey*: a minor Victorian littérateur who published a number of versions of this argument, one notably entitled *The Secret Drama of Shakespeare's Sonnets Unfolded, with the Characters Identified* (1872).

74. *Lady Rich*: Penelope Devereux (1562?–1607), daughter of the first earl of Essex. Married to Lord Rich against her will, she revenged herself by living openly with her lover, Lord Mountjoy, who later married her. She has traditionally been taken for the 'Stella' of Sidney's sonnet sequence *Astrophel and Stella*, although evidence suggests that from the first she found her 'Astrophel' in Mountjoy, not Sidney.

75. Arcadia: prose romance by Sidney, published in 1590 after his death.

76. *Professor Dowden*: Edward Dowden (1843–1913), Shakespeare scholar and from 1867 professor of English literature at Trinity College, Dublin. Wilde was grateful when Dowden signed a memorial requesting aid for Lady Wilde from the Royal Literary Fund, but considered him dull.

77. *Theodore Watts*: Walter Theodore Watts, later Watts-Dunton (1832–1914), solicitor, man of letters and author of the novel *Aylwin* (1898). Watts-Dunton is best remembered for rescuing Swinburne from alcoholism and becoming his tactful custodian from 1879 until the poet's death in 1909. Watts's high opinion of Sonnet 129 was quoted by William Sharp in his *William Shakespeare: The Songs, Poems, and Sonnets* (1885).

78. '*The Actors' Remonstrance*': a 1643 tract which complains about 'those Buxsome and Bountifull Lasses that usually were enamoured on the persons of the younger sort of Actors, for the good cloaths they wore upon the stage, believing them really to be the persons they did only represent'. Wilde found the reference to 'The Actors' Remonstrance' in Symonds's *Shakspere's Predecessors*.

79. *Cranley*: Thomas Cranley wrote *Amanda, or The Reformed Whore* in 1635. Wilde lifted some of the Cranley quotes from Symonds's *Shakspere's Predecessors*.

80. *Manningham's Table-book*: another detail Wilde appropriated from Collier, who mentions this valuable early seventeenth-century diary found in the Harleian manuscript collection of the British Museum.

81. *Sir Thomas Overbury . . . Edmund Curle*: Overbury (1581–1613), poet and essayist, is known for his *Characters* or succinct prose sketches of various human types. His notorious death sheds a curious light on the theme of love and sexual jealousy Wilde has just been discussing. When Overbury opposed the infatuation of his beloved friend Robert Carr with the infamous countess of Essex, he found himself imprisoned in the Tower of London on a pretext, and then slowly and painfully poisoned with sulphuric acid by the countess's agents. Edward Curle was the son of a retainer of the powerful noble, Robert Cecil (1563?–1612). Wilde has confused his first name with that of Edmund Curll, an eighteenth-century bookseller and satiric target of Alexander Pope.

82. *euphuism*: a highly elaborate mode of writing, characterized by abundant antitheses, frequent similes relating to fabulous natural history and alliteration, named after the hero of John Lyly's two-part prose romance *Euphues* (1578) and *Euphues and His England* (1580). Although long despised as an 'artificial' and over self-conscious style, euphuism returned to fashion among the Aesthetes, when Pater praised the mode at length in his novel *Marius the Epicurean* of 1885.

83. Avisa: in Latin, *avis* means 'bird', while *avisa* can be construed as 'not seen': *a* ('not') + *visa* ('seen').

84. *Marston*: the battle of Marston Moor, west of York, in 1644 saw the rout of the Royalist forces, with over 5,000 of them killed or taken prisoner.

85. *Edward King*: King (1612–37) was the college friend whose death by drowning at the age of twenty-five John Milton commemorated in his famous elegy *Lycidas* (1637).

86. *Mr Bullen*: Arthur Henry Bullen (1857–1920), editor of Elizabethan and Jacobean dramatists. Wilde owned his edition of Marlowe.

87. *Friedrich Schroeder*: German actor and theatre manager (1744–1816), who was the first to introduce Shakespeare to the German stage.

88. mimi quidam ex Britannia: Latin for 'certain actors from Britain'. Horst Schroeder has suggested that Wilde may have fabricated this quote from the 'old chronicle'.

89. *Bithynian slave*: Bithynia was an ancient district in what is now northwestern Turkey, first settled by Thracian tribes and later falling successively under the power of the Lydians, the Persians, the Macedonians and the Romans. The Greeks had established prosperous settlements in Bithynia, and from one of them came Antinous, the beautiful youth beloved by the Roman emperor Hadrian. When the boy drowned in the Nile (in AD 130), Hadrian commemorated him by building a city on the river bank.

90. *Cerameicus*: the potters' quarter in ancient Athens, lying partly inside and partly outside the city wall. The area beyond the wall was used as a burial ground.

91. *Charmides*: the beautiful youth and chief interlocutor of Socrates in the Platonic dialogue of the same name.

92. *Alba*: Robert Tofte's *Alba: The Month's Minde of a Melancholy Love* was published in 1598. Wilde's familiarity with the poem may have come from *Outlines of the Life of Shakespeare* (1884) by J. O. Halliwell-Phillipps, a leading Shakespearean scholar, who quotes it. *Alba* means 'white' in Latin.

93. *French lovelocks*: a lovelock was a long, flowing lock or curl, dressed separately from the rest of the hair, worn by courtiers and introduced from France.

94. *Taylor*: Joseph Taylor (*c*.1585–1652), actor who, upon the death of Richard Burbage, became the leading impersonator of Hamlet.

95. *Φιλοσοφεῖν μἐτ' ἔρωτος*: Greek for 'to do philosophy with love'. The phrase derives from Plato's *Republic*, Book 6. In Benjamin Jowett's translation it is rendered as to attain 'the knowledge of the true nature of every essence by a sympathetic and kindred power in the soul'. A version of the phrase is quoted in Pater's 'Winckelmann' essay, where it is used to emphasize the love of physical beauty as the portal to philosophic truth.

96. *spectator of all time and of all existence*: a favourite quotation of Wilde's, taken once again from Book 6 of *The Republic*, where Socrates describes the true philosopher as 'the spectator of all time and all existence'.

97. *night mail from Charing Cross*: Charing Cross Station, opened in 1864, became during the nineteenth century the chief point of departure for train passengers bound from London for the Continent.

98. *consumption*: name commonly given in the nineteenth century to the chronic pulmonary form of tuberculosis, then considered to be hereditary and incurable. Sufferers from the disease frequently sought relief from its symptoms in the warmer, dryer climate of the French Riviera.

99. *wonderful sonnet*: cf. Sonnet 99: 'The forward violet thus did I chide:/ Sweet thief, whence didst thou steal thy sweet that smells,/ If not from my love's breath? The purple pride/ Which on thy soft cheek for complexion dwells/ In my love's veins thou hast too grossly dyed.'

100. *Hugo*: Victor Hugo, in *Les Misérables*, notes on the occasion of a bishop's accompanying a condemned man up on to the scaffold that 'since the most sublime acts are often the least understood, there were people in the town who said it was all affectation'.

101. *Ouvry*: as the name 'Ouvry' is not known to art history, Horst Schroeder has made the intriguing suggestion that Wilde may have been referring to one P. Oudry, a French portrait painter belonging to the circle of Jean Clouet. Oudry's life-size portrait of Mary Queen of Scots was displayed in January 1889 at the 'Royal House of Stuart' Exhibition held at the New Gallery. The show attracted many viewers, including Wilde, who told a correspondent that the old paintings seemed 'rather dingy'.

In Defence of Dorian Gray

When *The Picture of Dorian Gray* was first published in *Lippincott's Monthly Magazine* for July 1890, it caused a storm of controversy. Wilde chose to respond to only three of the most offensive newspaper attacks, but his unrepentant responses did little to calm things. As his subsequent letters to the *St James's Gazette* and the *Scots Observer* indicate, Wilde's disdainful imperturbability inflamed his opponents to write further abuse. When Wilde came to publish an expanded version of *The Picture of Dorian Gray* as a separate volume in 1891, he prefaced the novel with a series of apophthegms about art and opinion which should be read as a further riposte to his opponents.

1. *Mrs Grundy*: the classic Victorian figure of prudery and propriety. The name derives from a character in Thomas Morton's comedy *Speed the Plough* (1798) who never actually appears on stage, though her opinions are constantly invoked and deferred to by the other characters.

2. réclame: French for advertising or publicity.

3. *puppy*: contemptuous term for a person, especially a vain, empty-headed, foppish young man. William Makepeace Thackeray in his novel *Pendennis* (1850) gives a classic account of the life history of one such puppy.

4. *Suetonius and Petronius Arbiter*: Suetonius (AD *c*.70–*c*.160), Roman historian and grammarian whose most famous work is *The Lives of the Caesars*, a gossipy, anecdotal account of Julius Caesar and the eleven emperors who followed him. Petronius Arbiter (died AD 65), an intimate of Nero's circle, served as the emperor's arbiter of taste. He is the putative author of the satiric and picaresque Latin novel known as the *Satyricon*. Wilde considered both men popular rather than scholarly authors.

5. *Honour School of* Literae Humaniores: at Oxford University, the course of reading and examination in Greek and Roman literature, history and philosophy that led to an honours degree. At this period, there were other honours schools (in modern history, mathematics and natural science), but *Literae humaniores* or 'Greats' was pre-eminent, attracting not only a majority of the undergraduates who read for honours (approximately one third of all undergraduates) but the ablest men as well. Achieving a first-class degree in 'Greats' was thus considered the crowning distinction in an Oxford classical career. Wilde achieved the rare triumph of a 'Double First' in 'Greats'. Hence his disdain, frequently expressed in his writing, for 'passmen', the less ambitious students who did not pursue an honours course.

6. *Count Tolstoi*: Leo Nikolaevich Tolstoy (1828–1910), Russian novelist and

social reformer. In the 1880s Tolstoy's intense sympathy with the plight of the Russian peasant, expressed in such works as 'John the Fool' and *The Power of Darkness*, aroused the hostility of the government and led to his censorship.

7. *Mr Anstey*: pen-name of Thomas Anstey Guthrie (1856–1934), author of *Vice Versa* and numerous other novels whose plots usually turned on some highly unlikely contingency. Anstey became a contributor to *Punch* in 1887.

8. *M. Renan*: Ernest Renan (1823–92), French philologist and historian who exerted a powerful influence upon Wilde. See also n. 1, page 330 below.

9. *vamp up*: to renovate or restore or furbish up. The phrase had been used to describe literary compositions since at least 1741. A 'vamp' was the part of a boot or shoe covering the front part of the foot, and 'vamp up' originally meant to provide with a new vamp or to repair as with patches.

10. *Gautier's* Émaux et Camées: Théophile Gautier (1811–72), French poet, novelist and journalist, expressed in the polemical preface to his novel *Mademoiselle de Maupin* (1835) the doctrines of art for art's sake (*l'art pour l'art*) which rallied such French writers as Charles Baudelaire and Gustave Flaubert to the cause and later proved so fruitful to Whistler and Wilde: the superiority of art to nature, the independence of the artist from all demands that he 'instruct' or 'elevate' his audience, the perfect unity of form and content in the art work and the achievement of formal beauty as art's sole purpose. Gautier's celebrated volume of poetry *Émaux et camées* (*Enamels and Cameos*, 1852) displayed the exquisite attention to the texture and colour of the visible world (Gautier famously said of himself, 'I am a man for whom the visible world exists') first developed in him when he was a Paris art student.

11. *Alphonso's* Clericalis Disciplina: Petrus Alphonsi, a Spanish Jew who compiled a collection of Jewish and Arabic fables entitled *Clericalis disciplina* early in the twelfth century, a work apparently intended, Rupert Hart-Davis suggested, to supply spice to medieval sermons.

12. *one who is the greatest figure*: i.e. Shakespeare, who possessed, according to Keats, the fullest measure of the true poetic character, which 'has as much delight in conceiving an Iago as an Imogen'.

13. *Thersites*: in the *Iliad*, a quarrelsome and deformed Greek soldier, killed by Achilles for laughing at Achilles' grief over the death of the beautiful queen of the Amazons; here used as a type for a brutish and rancorous scoffer.

14. *Mr Charles Whibley*: journalist (1860–1930) and one of a circle of younger writers devoted to the forceful editor and poet, W. E. Henley. Whibley, using the pseudonym of 'Thersites', had in fact written the review which Wilde objects to in his first letter to the *Scots Observer*.

15. *Diderot ... Goethe*: Denis Diderot (1713–84), French novelist, art critic and editor of the celebrated *Encyclopédie*, an encyclopaedic dictionary of the knowledge of the day. Diderot's accounts of nine contemporary art exhibitions (1759–81) inaugurated art criticism in France. Johann Wolfgang von Goethe (1749–1832), German poet, novelist, dramatist, administrator and amateur scientist, is here being invoked by Wilde as the ideally developed and rounded personality.

16. *powdered with gilt asphodels*: asphodels are pale lily-like flowers that Homer, in the *Odyssey*, describes as filling the great meadow of the underworld. 'Powdered' here means 'sprinkled or strewn as with powder', a formulation Wilde will use again in 'The Critic as Artist, Part II'. Wilde, who was deeply interested in the revival of printing led by William Morris and others, took great pains that his own books would approach the ideal of the 'Book Beautiful'.

17. *cultivated idleness*: here Wilde is giving a scandalous edge to the classical ideal of *otium* or learned leisure (see also n. 24, p. 332 below). In an age devoted to 'Work', 'Self-Help' and the 'Goddess of Getting-On', the notion of idleness as one's proper occupation was calculated to affront middle-class sensibilities.

18. *Musset's* Fortunio: *Fortunio*, published in 1837 by Gautier (*not* Musset, as readers hastened to point out), was an *Arabian Nights*-type tale, set in Paris. An English translation of Zola's *La Terre* was published in 1888 by Henry Vizetelly, who was charged with indecent publication by the Vigilance Society.

19. *Adelphi melodramas*: the Adelphi, a theatre in the Strand given that name in 1819, was notorious for popular melodramas so sensational in their effects that the plays were called 'Adelphi screamers'.

20. *a great friend of mine*: Robert Ross, according to Rupert Hart-Davis. Robert Baldwin Ross (1869–1918), who became one of Wilde's closest friends and later did more than anyone else to rescue Wilde's posthumous literary reputation, had worked for Henley on the *Scots Observer* in the later 1880s.

21. *North Britain*: i.e. Scotland.

The Soul of Man under Socialism

First published in the *Fortnightly Review* for February 1891. In a letter written to a French translator during the summer of 1891, Wilde remarked that the essay 'contains part of my aesthetic'. Indeed, there are a number of passages common to this essay and 'The Critic as Artist'. Wilde originally italicized some thirty-two epigrammatic sentences or passages in the *Fortnightly* version of *The Soul of Man*; these have been restored to roman type as consistent with Wilde's practice when reprinting his essays in *Intentions*.

1. *Renan*: Ernest Renan (1823–92), French philologist of Semitic languages and historian, whose brilliantly written and coolly sceptical *Vie de Jésus* (1863) became for Wilde a 'gracious Fifth Gospel, the Gospel according to St Thomas'. In 'The Critic as Artist, Part II' Gilbert says that the work of Renan, 'the critic of the books of God', marked an epoch in the progress of the world.

2. *Flaubert*: Gustave Flaubert (1821–80), French novelist, whose rigorous and scrupulous craftsmanship, with its self-denying pursuit of the exact or perfectly expressive word (*le mot juste*), made him the quintessential literary artist of Aestheticism.

3. *an article on the function of criticism*: Wilde published 'The True Function and Value of Criticism: with some Remarks on the Importance of Doing Nothing' in two parts in the *Nineteenth Century* (July and September 1890). He revised the essay extensively, retitling it 'The Critic as Artist', before republishing it in his volume of critical essays, *Intentions* (1891).

4. *amusing the poor*: the Kyrle Society, for example, founded by the philanthropists Octavia and Miranda Hill in the mid 1870s, sought to bring coloured prints and flower gardens to tenement dwellers. In a *Woman's World* article of January 1888, Wilde praised the Popular Musical Union for its plan of providing 'the inhabitants of the crowded districts of the East End with concerts and oratorios, to be performed as far as possible by trained members of the working classes'.

5. *educated men who live in the East-End*: Toynbee Hall, founded in the deeply impoverished Whitechapel district of London by Oxford university men, was a residence intended to bring together educated and poor people on terms of fellow feeling and practical help. It gave the model to innumerable other 'settlement houses' in Britain and America, including Jane Addams's famous Hull House in Chicago.

6. *hunch of bread*: a lump or thick piece.

7. *go on the rates*: i.e. to claim support from the fund raised by the 'poor rates', a tax assessed on property for the relief of the poor; cf. in the US, 'to go on welfare'.

8. *sold their birthright for very bad pottage*: in Genesis 25:29–34, Esau, overcome by hunger, sells his inheritance to his brother Jacob in exchange for food, and is given 'red pottage' or lentil soup. The phrase had become proverbial for making a bad bargain.

9. *starved peasant of the Vendée*: after the execution of King Louis XVI and his queen Marie Antoinette (1793), the Vendée, a coastal region in western France, became a centre of violent resistance to the Jacobin revolution. Initially successful as a result of their guerrilla tactics, the Vendéan peasants were eventually crushed with a loss of life greater than that brought by the Reign of Terror. The tragic significance of Marie Antoinette's downfall was the subject of a celebrated meditation in Edmund Burke's *Reflections on the Revolution in France* (1790).

10. *industrial–barrack system*: both Charles Fourier (1772–1837), French utopian socialist, and Edward Bellamy (1850–98), American author of the 1888 utopian novel *Looking Backward*, proposed social reforms upon a military model, Fourier calling his basic unit of socio-economic organization the 'phalanx' (*la phalange*) and Bellamy proposing to bring the efficiency and regimentation of the American Civil War years to the problems posed by urban labour.

11. *property is still the test of complete citizenship*: Britain had widened the franchise in 1832, 1867 and 1884, but even in the last and most liberal extension of the vote, male voters were still required to possess property – either directly or through rental – of at least ten pounds' value per year.

12. *Mommsen*: Theodor Mommsen (1817–1903), German historian and archae-ologist whose celebrated *History of Rome* (1854–6, translated 1868) inaugurated the era of 'scientific' or positivist history. Mommsen's *History*, as Wilde told the *Pall Mall Gazette* in 1889, was one of the few books which actually ought to be read. Indeed, it was one of the first titles he himself later requested and was permitted to receive in prison. Mommsen's account of Julius Caesar appears in vol. 5.

13. *Marcus Aurelius*: Roman emperor and philosopher (AD 121–80). Renan published *Marc-Aurèle et le fin de la monde antique* (*Marcus Aurelius and the End of the Ancient World*) in 1882.

14. *'Know Thyself'*: words inscribed over the doorway of the temple of Apollo at Delphi, and the central moral teaching of Socratic philosophy.

15. *Spinoza*: see n. 4, p. 312 above.

16. *Father Damien*: Belgian Catholic priest and missionary (1840–89) who volunteered to take spiritual charge of the lepers exiled by the Hawaiian government to the island of Molokai, where after sixteen years of service he himself contracted the disease and died.

17. *Wagner*: Richard Wagner (1813–83), the powerfully original German opera composer whose unification of song, poetry, symbol and myth in a 'total art work' (*Gesamtkunstwerk*) became widely influential in the latter half of the nineteenth century.

18. *a wise man*: Chuang Tsû (born 330 BC), sage of philosophical Taoism, a system which stood in relation to Confucianism much as Arnold and Wilde's ideal of 'criticism' did to Victorian middle-class values – prizing culture above possessions, individual autonomy above social conformity and rejecting such virtues as justice, reverence and sincerity as representing the first steps away from the harmony of life.

19. *ochlocracies*: government by mobs; mobocracies.

20. *bludgeoning of the people by the people for the people*: Wilde here implicitly contrasts the high hopes for American democracy expressed by Abraham Lincoln's celebrated phrase in the Gettysburg Address of 1863 with the new reality suggested by the Haymarket riots of 1886, which began when Chicago police attacked and killed half a dozen labour demonstrators.

21. *a fine thinker*: i.e., Ralph Waldo Emerson in his essay 'Self-Reliance'.

22. *passmen*: university students who sought merely to obtain a degree rather than, as Wilde himself had done, the distinction of an honours degree (which required a more demanding course of reading and examination). See also n. 5, p. 327 above.

23. *Vautrin*: master criminal in Balzac's *La Comédie humaine*.

24. *cultivated leisure*: Wilde here expresses the classical ideal of *otium*, or living a life retired from the corrupt world and devoted to learning and ethical friendship. The ideal derived from the thought of the Greek philosopher Epicurus (341–270 BC), especially as this philosophy came to be expressed by the Roman poet Lucretius (*c*.99–55 BC) in *De rerum natura*. See also n. 17, p. 329 above.

25. *great storages of force*: the transformation of mechanical energy was a common feature of contemporary utopian writing. In William Morris's *News from Nowhere* (1890), for example, powerful 'force barges' transport goods up and down the Thames.

26. *diplomas of immorality*: the writers whom Wilde most admired – in France, Gautier, Baudelaire and Flaubert, in England, Swinburne, Rossetti, Pater and Wilde himself – all had been either denounced or prosecuted for 'immorality'.

27. *Academy of Letters*: the Académie française, founded in 1635 with the encouragement of Cardinal Richelieu, was charged with defending the French language. Because its membership was limited to forty members, admission to *les Quarante* was considered the highest distinction in literature. Many of the great nineteenth-century writers were elected to the Academy, though hostility to Romanticism prevented the admission of Baudelaire and Flaubert.

28. *Charles Kingsley*: novelist, historian and liberal Anglican clergyman (1819–75). Kingsley's passionate sympathy for the plight of the working classes, expressed in his sermons and his early novels *Yeast* (1848) and *Alton Locke: Tailor and Poet* (1848–9), convinced ecclesiastical authorities that he was a dangerous man, and in 1851 he was forbidden to preach in London.

29. *'morbid'*: meaning 'unhealthy' or 'indicative of disease', the word had by the later nineteenth century come to be applied to mental states, at a time when fears of cultural, physiological and psychological degeneration in Britain had been heightened by Darwinian science, economic depression and social unrest.

30. *the rack*: an apparatus for torturing persons by stretching the body. Although Wilde here puns upon the modern meaning of the word, 'the press' was also an instrument of torture that worked by applying great weights to the body. Used upon persons accused of felonies who stood mute and refused to plead, the press was last employed in England in 1736.

31. *estate*: sociopolitical group or class. Traditionally in France and England, the nobles ('the Lords Temporal'), the clergy ('the Lords Spiritual') and the commons were understood to constitute the three estates of the realm. T. B. Macaulay, historian and Member of Parliament, made the famous remark that, 'The gallery [in the House of Commons] in which the reporters sit has become a fourth estate of the realm.'

32. *the private lives of men and women*: two notorious cases of trial by newspaper lie behind these remarks: in 1885 Sir Charles Dilke, perhaps the most talented among the radical MPs of his generation, was cited as co-respondent in a divorce case involving the sister-in-law of his brother, with Dilke as a result choosing to retire from public life. In 1887 Charles Stewart Parnell, the glamorous and enormously popular Irish Home Rule politician, was condemned by *The Times* of London for conniving with Fenian violence. Parnell vindicated himself only to be undone in 1890 by the widespread publicity given to his role as co-respondent in another divorce case.

33. *Irving*: Henry Irving (1838–1905), actor and theatre manager, who took over conduct of the Lyceum Theatre in 1878. As an actor, he was known for his Shakespearean roles; as a manager, Irving was famed for his spectacular productions, lavish costumes and sets – some of them designed by such artists as Edward Burne-Jones.

34. *Haymarket*: theatre managed from 1887 by Herbert Beerbohm Tree (1853–1917). Tree improved upon the tradition of theatre as highly commercial spectacle established by Irving. He produced Wilde's *A Woman of No Importance* at the Haymarket in 1893.

35. Esmond: *Henry Esmond*, published in 1852, a historical novel by W. M. Thackeray, dealing with such events as remote from Victorian middle-class preoccupations as the Battle of the Boyne (1690) and the War of the Spanish Succession (1701–13). Thackeray's *The Adventures of Philip* (1861–2), was his last complete novel.

36. *George Meredith*: English novelist and poet (1828–1909), whose complex and witty style severely limited his popularity to a narrow circle of admirers until the 1890s, when his work became the fashion for about twenty years. Thereafter, Meredith's novels slipped back into disregard.

37. *Great Exhibition*: the Great or Crystal Palace Exhibition, held in London in 1851, was the first world's fair, with over 13,000 exhibitors and more than 6 million visitors. Many of the decorative objects on view – and on sale – combined grotesque afunctionality with blinding polychromy.

38. *the revolution in house-decoration*: impelled by such innovators as Owen Jones, Christopher Dresser and the Pre-Raphaelite firm of Morris, Marshall, Faulkner & Co. (founded 1861), the decorative arts revolution, promoted by Wilde during his American tour, had by the 1890s deeply penetrated middle-class houses and buying habits. At the heart of its design principles lay respect for the materials and the workers employed.

39. *Verona*: city in northern Italy where the exiled poet Dante (1265–1321) sought refuge and, according to legend, was disdainfully treated by his host, Can Grande.

40. *Tasso*: Torquato Tasso (1544–95), Italian poet, whose extreme terror of persecution and adverse criticism led the Duke of Ferrara to confine him in a prison from 1579 to 1586, thereby fulfilling the poet's own worst fears.

41. *Cellini*: Benvenuto Cellini, Italian goldsmith, sculptor and autobiographer (1500–71).

42. *Louis XIV*: absolute ruler of France from 1643 to 1715. Louis's magnificent court at Versailles became the symbol of the supreme centralization of power enforced by his despotism and his personal cult as the 'Sun King'. The vast palace of Versailles with its huge grounds, magnified by mirrors, reflecting pools and tricks of perspective, was designed to express the utter insignificance of everyone apart from the monarch.

43. *differentiation*: a term from biology, meaning the change in cells or tissues from relatively generalized to specialized kinds during development, which the Darwinian publicist Herbert Spencer had invested with great if spurious significance, portraying it as the fundamental characteristic of all evolutionary change, in social and political as well as biological organisms.

44. *Thebaid*: the area around Thebes, the most important city of ancient Egypt for nearly a thousand years. Thebes was destroyed and largely emptied of population in the first century AD. Known today as Luxor, the site is famous for the magnificent remains of its great temples and royal tombs.

45. *cenobite*: a resident of a convent or religious community.

46. *a few Russian artists*: Wilde at various points in these essays declares his admiration for three great Russian novelists: 'Tolstoi', 'Tourgénieff' and 'Dostoieffski'. He prized Ivan Turgenev (1818–83) for his artistic unity of expression, Leo Tolstoy (1828–1910) for his epic grandeur and simplicity and Fyodor Dostoevsky (1821–81) for his powers of psychological penetration and human pity. Wilde's own work became in turn a powerful influence upon the Russian aesthetic renaissance of the 1890s.

47. *Nihilist*: member of the late-nineteenth-century Russian revolutionary group which urged the overthrow of existing social and political institutions, if necessary by violence and terror. Wilde's first play, *Vera: or, the Nihilists* (privately printed 1880, produced 1883), is set against the lurid backdrop of Russian oppression, desperate intrigue and political assassination.

48. *the new Hellenism*: the old Hellenism was made famous by Matthew Arnold in *Culture and Anarchy* (1869), where it is identified with aesthetic grace, intellectual flexibility and spontaneity of consciousness, Arnold proposing it as the redemptive power most needed in Victorian Britain. Walter Pater in *Studies in the History of the Renaissance* (1873) emphasized the deep sensuousness of Hellenism by describing in richly evocative prose the all-consuming love of beauty within Greek, Renaissance and Romantic Hellenism. Wilde brings the polemic on behalf of Hellenism up to date for a new generation by adapting Arnold's intellectual play and Pater's sensuous pleasure to the conditions of a world transformed by 'Socialism' and 'Science' – political democracy and Darwinian evolution.

Intentions

This collection of four essays was first published as a separate volume in May 1891 by Osgood, McIlvaine. Each of the individual essays had earlier appeared in periodicals, and then been much revised by Wilde.

1. The Decay of Lying

First published in the *Nineteenth Century* for January 1889. Writing to a woman friend just after the essay appeared, Wilde declared, 'It is meant to bewilder the masses by its fantastic form; *au fond* it is of course serious.' Much later, in *De Profundis*, he would call it 'the first and best of all my dialogues'.

1. *Morris's poorest workman*: William Morris's 'artistic' designs for furniture were based upon simple, traditional forms – e.g. the cane-bottomed 'Morris chair' – and buyers accustomed to conventional late-Victorian plush upholstery did not find them particularly comfortable.

2. *'the street from which Oxford has borrowed its name'*: a complicated joke: the reference is to Oxford Street, London's major shopping thoroughfare, and to the poem 'The Power of Music' by Wordsworth. Vivian says Wordsworth phrases things 'vilely' because the suggestion that Oxford university took its name from a Victorian shopping mall belittled that ancient institution, Wilde's own alma mater. In fact, however, Vivian misremembers the poem, which inoffensively refers to 'the street that from Oxford hath borrowed its name'.

3. *burdock*: a coarse, broad-leaved weed with prickly heads or burs which stick to the clothing.

4. *Whim*: in his 1841 essay 'Self-Reliance', Ralph Waldo Emerson declared, 'I shun father and mother and wife and brother when my genius calls me. I would write on the lintels of the doorpost, *Whim*.'

5. *the Sophist*: originally, a professional teacher of rhetoric and disputation in ancient Greece. Later, the term came to refer to a person more concerned with ingeniousness and specious effectiveness than soundness of argument.

6. *Leontine schools*: ancient schools of rhetoric located in Leontini, Sicily, which stressed beautiful ornament and poetic rhythm rather than dialectic and substantive content. Their most famous teacher was Gorgias (*c*.485–375 BC), who figures in a Platonic dialogue of the same name in which Socrates argues that rhetoric involves mere flattery rather than true statesmanship.

7. *The Tired Hedonists*: a hedonist is someone who believes that pleasure or happiness constitutes the highest good in life.

8. *cult for Domitian*: an enthusiasm for the more reprehensible Roman Emperors was characteristic of *fin de siècle* Decadence, first in France and later in England. While in Paris in 1883, for example, Wilde had his hair curled in imitation of a bust of Nero in the Louvre. Domitian, emperor (AD 81 to 96, began well, as lover of literature and the fine arts and the restorer of ancient religious cults – but ended badly. His extreme fear of assassination led to seven years of terror culminating in his own murder.

9. *Blue-Book*: official report or other document, typically bound in blue paper, printed by order of Parliament.

10. document humain . . . coin de la création: 'human document' . . . 'corner of the universe', phrases made famous by Émile Zola, theorist and leader of literary naturalism. Begun around 1865, naturalism sought to reproduce in fiction the documentary and experimental character of scientific observation. By 1890, however, the movement had come under attack for its predictability, monotony and pervasive dreariness.

11. *Robert Louis Stevenson*: poet, novelist and travel writer (1850–94) whose exquisitely self-conscious literary style appealed to Wilde even as the more famous adventure tales (*Treasure Island*, *Kidnapped*) did not. *The Black Arrow*

(1888) is set during the Wars of the Roses, the fifteenth-century struggle between the houses of York (whose emblem was a white rose) and Lancaster (red) for supremacy and the throne of England. Stevenson's enormously successful tale *The Strange Case of Dr Jekyll and Mr Hyde* (1886) was an important influence on Wilde's *The Picture of Dorian Gray*.

12. Lancet: the celebrated British medical journal.

13. *Rider Haggard*: Henry Rider Haggard (1856–1925), an immensely successful writer of exotic romances, achieved an instant bestseller with his first novel, *King Solomon's Mines* (1885), soon followed by the no less successful *She* and *Allan Quartermain* (both 1887). Such later works as *Jess* (1887) and *Swallow* (1889), however, drew in a more sober key upon Haggard's wide knowledge of Africa, where he had lived and worked.

14. *Henry James*: expatriate American novelist (1843–1916) who lived in England for many years. He and Wilde moved in many of the same circles, but were never friends. Instead, James developed his close observation of Wilde into the remarkable analyses of the artistic personality and the dilemmas of art found in such works as *The Tragic Muse* (1890). James's novels explored the complexities of consciousness with ever-increasing depth and subtlety.

15. *Hall Caine*: disciple of D. G. Rossetti and later a successful writer of melodramatic novels (1853–1921) who first achieved huge sales with his novel, *The Deemster* (1887).

16. *James Payn*: popular novelist (1830–98), powerful editor and London literary broker.

17. *William Black*: London newspaperman and Scottish novelist (1841–98) whose characteristic plots involved either introducing Scottish protagonists to the fleshpots of London or transplanting foreign-born maidens into Scottish homes – as happens in his vastly successful novel of 1871, *A Daughter of Heth*. Black's *The Strange Adventures of a Phaeton* (1872) followed the journey a phaeton or light carriage from London to Edinburgh according to what Wilde called in an 1887 review the 'chromo-lithographic method'. This was the favourite technique of those writers 'who have never yet fully realized the difference between colour and colours, and who imagine that by emptying a paint box over every page they can bring before us the magic of mist and mountain'. First developed in the 1830s, chromolithography employed separate stone plates for each colour, a process which encouraged the use of bright, hard colours with little gradation or subtlety.

18. *Mrs Oliphant*: highly productive and popular novelist (1828–97), whose seven-volume *Chronicles of Carlingford* novels, describing the comic religious feuding in a country town, made her Queen Victoria's favourite novelist.

19. *Marion Crawford*: prolific American expatriate novelist (1854–1909), who wrote fiction about the various countries he lived in and achieved his first success with *Mr Isaacs, A Tale of Modern India* (1882).

20. Robert Elsmere: the highly serious yet phenomenally successful novel of wrenching religious doubt and self-sacrificial devotion to the poor published by Mrs Humphry Ward in 1888. In a letter written to a friend immediately after the magazine version of this essay appeared, Wilde declared, 'I have blown my trumpet against the gate of dullness, and I hope some shaft has hit *Robert Elsmere* between the joints of his nineteenth edition.'

21. *school of novelists for whom the sun always rises in the East-End*: a category which would include Mrs Humphry Ward (whose hero in *Robert Elsmere* sets up a commune in the East End) as well as such others as George Gissing, and, especially, Walter Besant, whose *All Sorts and Conditions of Men* (1882) may be said to have begun the fashion for East End fiction. Besant's novel describes the founding of a 'People's Palace' for the recreation of the poor. Just five years later such an institution was actually built, rising in the Mile End Road, as Vivian will say, 'out of the *débris* of a novel'. Wilde declared, in an 1886 letter offering himself as a candidate for the secretaryship to the Beaumont Trust, 'this People's Palace will be to me the realization of much that I have long hoped for'. Wilde did not get the job.

22. *Guy de Maupassant*: Maupassant (1850–93), a novelist and short-story writer associated with the naturalist school of Zola, achieved an extraordinary literary success in the 1880s only to go mad in the early 1890s.

23. *Zola*: Émile Zola (1840–1902), French novelist and theorist of naturalism, the literary movement which sought to bring the methods and assumptions of contemporary science (i.e. observation, experimentation, the decisive influence of heredity and environment) to fiction. The Zola novels Wilde mentions here – *Germinal* (1885), *Nana* (1880), *L'Assommoir* (1877), *Pot-Bouille* (1882) – form part of the *Rougon-Macquart* cycle of novels, which traces the transmission of vicious characteristics over several generations. Zola was given to issuing literary manifestos, e.g. *Le Roman expérimental* (*The Experimental Novel*, 1880). Wilde deliberately mistranslates Zola's dictum as 'The man of genius is never witty' instead of as 'The man of genius has no need of wit'.

24. *Tartuffe*: protagonist of Molière's comedy of the same name, the quintessential hypocrite.

25. *sweepings of a Pentonville omnibus*: although Vivian seems disposed to apply the remark to George Eliot's *Romola* and *Daniel Deronda* as well, Ruskin in his *Fiction Fair and Foul* (1880–81) made the remark specifically about her novel *The Mill on the Floss*. Pentonville is a proverbially dreary London suburb, though Pentonville prison, where Wilde would spend the first six months of his sentence for gross indecency, is in another part of London.

26. *Daudet*: Delobelle with his 'It is necessary to struggle for art', Valmajour and the poet with his 'cruel words' are characters in works by Alphonse Daudet (1840–97), a novelist associated for a time with the school of French naturalism. As usual, Wilde does not hesitate to invent more suitable titles for authors he dislikes, here changing Daudet's two memoirs, *Souvenirs d'un homme de lettres* and *Trente ans de Paris* (both 1888), into '*Vingt Ans de ma Vie littéraire*'.

27. *Paul Bourget*: critic and psychological novelist (1852–1935) whose novel of 1889, *Le Disciple*, helped to undermine the prestige of positivist philosophy and literary naturalism.

28. *Faubourg St Germain*: the Paris residential neighbourhood of aristocratic and fashionable society.

29. *Arnold's* Literature and Dogma: published in 1873, *Literature and Dogma* attempted to lead Protestant believers away from an unwise reliance on biblical texts (undermined by German textual scholarship) and on natural 'fact' (undermined by Victorian discoveries in geology and biology) to a solider basis in human moral and spiritual experience.

30. *Paley's* Evidences: clergyman and philosopher William Paley published in 1794 his celebrated *View of the Evidences of Christianity*, a work which defended the credibility of revealed religion by presuming the existence of a benevolent deity. In *Natural Theology* (1802) Paley sought to prove the existence of such a deity by revealing the evidences of design in creatures, and especially in the miraculous complexity of the human body. In the aftermath of the Darwinian revolution, Paley's insistence that creatures did not adapt themselves to their circumstances made his work seem wholly outmoded.

31. *Colenso's method of Biblical exegesis*: John William Colenso (1814–83), undertaking to explain the meaning of the Old Testament to the native people of Natal, found that the numbers given in the first five books of the Bible quite literally did not add up. He published the results of his mathematical calculations in *The Pentateuch and Book of Joshua Critically Examined* (1862–3) and, because Colenso was Anglican bishop of Natal, the book provoked great scandal.

32. *Green's philosophy*: Thomas Hill Green (1836–82), Idealist philosopher and influential teacher at Oxford, stressed the importance of practical citizenship, encouraging his students to give help to the less fortunate. Green appears as the noble 'Mr Gray' in Mrs Ward's novel *Robert Elsmere*.

33. *Balzac*: Honoré de Balzac, French novelist (1799–1850), author of the panoramic series of novels known as *La Comédie humaine*. See also n. 36 below.

34. *George Meredith*: See n. 36, p. 333 above.

35. *Baal*: any one of a number of ancient pagan deities, usually represented as having been worshipped with much sensuality.

36. *Lucien de Rubempré*: a handsome and ambitious young poet in Balzac's vast fictional epic, *La Comédie humaine*, who seeks fame only to fall victim to the corruptions of Paris and the machinations of his evil counsellor, the master criminal Vautrin; Rastignac and De Marsay, mentioned later, are also characters from *La Comédie humaine*, a work Wilde considered 'the greatest monument that literature has produced in our century'.

37. *Holbein*: Hans Holbein (1497–1543), German painter who worked in England for many years, painting such notable figures as Sir Thomas More, Thomas Cromwell, Anne of Cleves and Henry VIII in portraits combining high finish with profound insight into character.

38. Salammbô *or* Esmond, *or* The Cloister and the Hearth, *or the* Vicomte de Bragelonne: historical novels by, respectively, Flaubert, Thackeray, Charles Reade and Alexandre Dumas the elder.

39. *Hecuba*: wife of Priam king of Troy. Vivian is alluding to the scene in *Hamlet* where Hamlet marvels at an actor's vivid portrayal of grief over a woman he never knew: 'What's Hecuba to him or he to Hecuba / That he should weep for her?' (II, ii.)

40. *great Ode*: Wordsworth's ode on 'Intimations of Immortality from Recollections of Early Childhood'.

41. *'impulse from a vernal wood'*: from Wordsworth's 'The Tables Turned': 'One impulse from a vernal wood / May teach you more of man / Of moral evil and of good / Than all the sages can.' Wilde copied this verse into his Oxford commonplace book.

42. *true decadence*: i.e. in contrast to the 'Decadence' proclaimed by or imputed to French and English avant-garde writers.

43. *Titans*: in Greek mythology, a race of superhuman beings who preceded and were overthrown by the Olympian gods.

44. *palinode*: poem in which the poet retracts something said in an earlier poem.

45. *Philistine*: See n. 15, p. 309 above.

46. *Herodotus*: Greek historian (*c.*480–*c.*425 BC). As the first historian to make the events of the past the subject of research and verification, he was called 'the father of history' by Cicero and others. Sciolists are people who possess merely superficial knowledge.

47. *Cicero*: Marcus Tullius Cicero (106–43 BC), a great Roman orator, author and statesman.

48. *Suetonius*: see n. 4, p. 327 above.

49. *Tacitus*: Publius Cornelius Tacitus (AD *c.*55–*c.*117), Roman historian.

50. *Pliny*: Gaius Plinius Secundus (AD *c.*23–79), called Pliny the Elder, Roman author, soldier and administrator. His *Natural History* contains much valuable information about the art, science and civilization of his day, along with much error and superstition.

51. *Hanno*: Carthaginian navigator who lived *c.*500 BC. His *Periplus* describes a coasting voyage taken along the African shore as far south as Cape Palmas (between present-day Liberia and the Ivory Coast), where Hanno encountered a race of hairy women he called 'Gorillas'.

52. *Froissart*: Jean Froissart (*c.*1337–*c.*1410), French chronicler whose writings are characterized by literary artistry more than historical accuracy.

53. *Mallory*: Sir Thomas Malory (d. 1471) was author of *Le Morte D'Arthur*, which rendered French Arthurian material into English.

54. *Marco Polo*: celebrated Venetian traveller (*c.*1254–*c.*1324) to Asia, and especially the court of Kublai Khan.

55. *Olaus Magnus*: Swedish ecclesiastic (1490–1558) whose famous *Historia de gentibus septentrionalibus* long remained the best source of curious information about Swedish life and folklore.

56. *Aldrovandus*: Ulissi Aldrovandi (1522–1605), whose *magnum opus* proposed to include everything known about natural history. Unfinished at his death, the work made no distinction between the fabulous and the true.

57. *Conrad Lycosthenes*: Swiss theologian (1518–61).

58. *Benvenuto Cellini*: see n. 41, p. 334 above. Cellini's famous *Autobiography* gives a vivid account of the personalities and events of his time.

59. *Casanuova*: Giacomo Casanova de Seingalt (1725–98), Italian adventurer notorious for his shamelessly frank and exaggerated accounts of his many amours.

60. *Defoe*: Daniel Defoe (1660–1731), highly prolific novelist, journalist and pamphleteer. His *Journal of the Plague Year* (1722) gives a vivid and not altogether fictional account of the great epidemic of 1664–5.

61. *Boswell*: Boswell's great biography of Samuel Johnson (1791) had long set the standard for literary biography.

62. *Napoleon*: Napoleon Bonaparte (1769–1821), military genius and emperor of France. He was a master of morale as well as of military strategy. When the English navy crushed the French in the naval battle of Trafalgar, the only official reference to the defeat was expressed in these terms: 'Storms caused us to lose some ships of the line after a fight imprudently engaged.'

63. *Carlyle*: Carlyle's *The French Revolution* made its author famous when it was published in 1837. Apart from being based on much primary research, the work swept readers away with its dramatic scenes and unforgettable portraiture.

64. *George Washington*: first president of the United States (1732–99). The story of Washington's cutting down a cherry tree with a hatchet and then piously confessing the crime to his father ('I cannot tell a lie') is now regarded as the invention of his popular early biographer, Mason Weems (d. 1825), an Episcopalian clergyman.

65. *Megatherium*: genus of huge extinct mammals, more or less resembling a ground sloth the size of an elephant, first discovered near Buenos Aires. The Megatherium became noteworthy to the Victorians because as a genus exclusively found in South America, its existence cast alarming doubts on the orthodox account of the Creation, which held that all species of animals had been uniformly dispersed throughout the globe.

66. *Royal Society*: learned society, chartered in 1662, which at first took all knowledge for its province but later narrowed its focus to science.

67. *Incorporated Authors*: an appropriately fictitious group resembling the Society of Authors (founded 1884) and the Author's Syndicate (founded 1890), both of which sought to protect the commercial interests of writers. Wilde was elected fellow of the Society of Authors in 1887. In his letter of acceptance he urged the membership secretary to invite 'the thinkers and the men of style, not merely the scribblers and the second-rate journalists'.

68. *Mr Burnand's farcical comedies*: F. C. Burnand (1836–1917) wrote many successful burlesques and, most notably, made over a French farce into a satire of Aestheticism and Wilde: *The Colonel* of 1881. As editor of *Punch* from 1880 to 1906, Burnand directed the magazine's unrelenting assault on the Aesthetes, making Wilde 'so annoyed at its offensive tone and horridness' that on one occasion he refused to attend a party where he believed Burnand would be present. See also n. 7, p. 318 above.

69. *Herbert Spencer*: self-taught philosopher and journalist (1820–1903), today largely unread, whose attempt to unify all thought and experience under the single principle of evolution deeply influenced Wilde and other later Victorians.

70. *Sir John Mandeville*: the ostensible author of a book of improbably romantic travels, composed in the middle of the fourteenth century but largely taken over from French sources.

71. *Raleigh*: Sir Walter Ralegh (1554–1618), soldier, explorer, poet. Only the first volume of his *History of the World* (1614) was completed.

72. *Lydian hills*: Lydia was an ancient kingdom in western Asia Minor, occupying the territory of modern Turkey, though the 'winged lions' mentioned here are more characteristic of the art of the Assyrian empire to the southeast.

73. *two imaginative painters*: Dante Gabriel Rossetti (1828–82) and Edward Burne-Jones (1833–98). 'The Golden Stair', 'Laus Amoris' and 'Merlin's Dream' are all paintings by Burne-Jones. Wilde was not alone in remarking how the mesmerizing women portrayed by both painters had seemingly persuaded a generation of late-Victorian women to change their looks and dress.

74. *Vandyke*: Sir Anthony Van Dyck (1599–1641), Flemish painter who lived and worked in England for many years.

75. *Pheidias . . . Praxiteles*: Phidias (*c*.500–*c*.432 BC), sculptor of the Parthenon frieze. Praxiteles (*fl. c*.350 BC), the second great sculptor among the ancient Greeks, is known for his 'Hermes with the Infant Dionysus'.

76. *Jack Sheppard . . . Dick Turpin*: Sheppard (1702–24), thief and highwayman, and Turpin (1706–39), horse-thief and highwayman, were both hanged, becoming heroes of popular ballads and romance.

77. *Schopenhauer*: Danish philosopher (1788–1860), whose extreme pessimism led him to recommend resignation, asceticism and chastity as the best means of eluding the evils of life.

78. *Nihilist*: member of a secret Russian revolutionary group devoting itself to the violent overthrow of existing political institutions.

79. *Tourgénieff . . . Dostoieffski*: see n. 46, p. 334 above.

80. *Robespierre . . . Rousseau*: Maximilien Robespierre (1756–94) was leader of the Jacobin faction during the French Revolution. He sought to justify his violent policies by appealing to the works of the philosopher and social reformer Jean-Jacques Rousseau (1712–78).

81. *People's Palace*: see n. 21, p. 338 above.

82. *Becky Sharp*: the brilliantly unscrupulous heroine of William Makepeace Thackeray's novel *Vanity Fair* (1847–8).

83. The Newcomes . . . 'Adsum': in Thackeray's novel *The Newcomes* (1855), Colonel Newcome, the hero's father, is a man who is financially ruined and ultimately forced to live as a pensioner at his son's old school. As Colonel Newcome lies dying, the school's attendance bell rings, and in a famous and pathetic scene, the old man murmurs, 'Adsum' – giving the schoolboy's ritual Latin answer of, 'Present'.

84. *Proteus . . . Odysseus*: in Greek mythology, Proteus was a sea god who possessed the power of changing into different shapes whenever he wished to avoid being questioned. In the *Odyssey*, it is Menelaus, not Odysseus, who lays hold of Proteus and compels him to answer.

85. *John Bellini*: Giovanni Bellini (1430/1–1516), Venetian painter whose work was particularly admired by Ruskin for combining the devotional gravity and worldly splendour of the Venice of his time. Bellini taught both Giorgione and Titian.

86. *admirable ices at Florio's*: in Venice, Florian's café on the Piazza San Marco was a fashionable watering place known for its scenic view and its ice cream.

87. *Rolla*: the hero of a Romantic narrative poem by Alfred de Musset published in 1833.

88. *Werther*: Goethe's *The Sorrows of Young Werther*, a romance in which the love-stricken hero commits suicide, was published in 1774.

89. *Impressionists . . . and their master*: group of French and English painters who sought to capture the effect of light and atmosphere on objects rather than the objects themselves. Although the group first earned its derisive name from an 1874 painting by Claude Monet ('Impression: soleil levant'), Vivian's account suggests that by 'master' he means J. A. M. Whistler, whose evocative Thames riverscapes were celebrated, not least of all by Whistler himself.

90. *Corots . . . Daubignys . . . Monets . . . Pisaros*: Corot (see p. 306 above) and Charles François Daubigny (1817–78) were landscape painters associated with the Barbizon School in France. Wilde preferred to view nature 'hanging on one's walls in the grey mists of Corot, or the opal mornings that Daubigny has given us'. Monet (1840–1926) and Camille Pissarro (1830–1903) were landscape painters of the newer Impressionist school.

91. *Turner*: the paintings of J. M. W. Turner (1775–1851) had been powerfully defended by Ruskin in the first volume of *Modern Painters* (1843) against a chorus of ignorant and prejudiced critics. By 1890, however, Turner's painted sunsets, which had once outraged critics, had been fully assimilated by middle-class taste, and thus seemed banal to the avant-garde.

92. *false Renés*: René, the yearning, melancholy hero of Chateaubriand's tale of the same name (1805), flees to darkest America, where he continues to be tortured by the forbidden love of his sister. For Vautrin, see n. 23, p. 332 above.

93. *doubtful Cuyp . . . questionable Rousseau*: Albert Cuyp (1620–91), Dutch painter, skilled in the depiction of herds and landscapes, especially the Meuse and Rhine rivers. Henri Rousseau (1844–1910), self-taught artist known as 'le Douanier' because of his job as a minor customs official before he became a professional painter. The naïve power of Rousseau's exotic landscapes made him posthumously famous.

94. *Henry Moore*: English painter (1831–95), noted for his seascapes.

95. *that vital connection between form and substance, on which Mr Pater dwells*: in 'The School of Giorgione', an essay added to the 1877 edition of *The Renaissance*, Pater put forward the famous dictum: '*All art constantly aspires to the condition of music*. For while in all other kinds of art it is possible to distinguish the matter from the form, and the understanding can always make this distinction, yet it is the constant effort of art to obliterate it.'

96. *Marsyas*: a Phrygian flute-player who imprudently challenged Apollo, god of music, to a contest of musical skill, the loser to be treated as the winner pleased. Apollo flayed him alive.

97. *the shadows of the cave*: Plato's parable of human knowledge in *The Republic*, Book 7, suggests that human beings, as if chained facing the wall of a cave where a fire burns brightly, can see only the flickering shadows of things, not the things themselves.

98. *many-petalled rose*: the concluding cantos of Dante's *Paradiso* culminate in his ecstatic vision of God and the heavenly host as a vast white rose.

99. *Tiberius . . . the Antonines*: Tiberius, a Roman emperor (AD 14–37) notable for his lust and cruelty. Antoninus Pius (AD 86–161) and his successor, Marcus Aurelius (AD 161–80), were by contrast moderate and moral men. The German historian Theodor Mommsen had shown that Rome failed, not because of moral decadence of its emperors, but through such 'less interesting' reasons as the decline in population, alteration of trade routes and injudicious tax policies. Mommsen's work became widely influential upon the late-Victorian historiography of Rome.

100. *sibyls and prophets of the Sistine*: colossal painted figures who punctuate Michelangelo's celebrated Sistine Chapel ceiling. Wilde had made the same point, contrasting the sibyls and prophets with the boors of Dutch art, in his American art lecture 'The English Renaissance of Art'.

101. *Hokusai . . . Hokkei*: Hokusai (1760–1849) Japanese painting master; Hokkei (1780–1850) was his student. Beginning in the 1860s, Whistler and Rossetti did much to spread admiration of Japanese art among Victorians.

102. *One of our most charming painters*: Mortimer Menpes, Australian painter (1860–1938), friend and admirer of Whistler.

103. *Aristophanes*: Greek comic dramatist and satirist (*c*.448–*c*.380 BC).

104. *the gates of ivory . . . the gates of horn*: the ancient belief, expressed most famously in Virgil's *Aeneid*, Book VI, that the gods send sleeping human beings dreams from the underworld, with false dreams passing through gates made of ivory and true dreams through gates of horn.

105. *Mr Myers's two bulky volumes*: F. W. H. Myers (1843–1901), a school inspector interested in mesmerism and spiritualism, helped to found the Society for Psychical Research and co-authored the first publication of its investigations, *Phantasms of the Living* (2 vols., 1886).

106. *St Thomas*: in John 20:25, the disciple Thomas, hearing from the other disciples that Jesus has risen from the dead, declares, 'Except I shall see in his hands the print of the nails, and put my finger into the print of the nails, and thrust my hand into his side, I will not believe.' As Cyril Graham says in *The Portrait of Mr W. H.*, 'The only apostle who did not deserve proof was St Thomas, and St Thomas was the only apostle who got it.'

107. *shallow uneducated passman out of either University*: as Wilde repeatedly emphasized (see also n. 5, p. 327, and n. 22, p. 332 above), a passman was a student who chose the softer option of merely taking a degree instead of undergoing the more rigorous course of reading and examination required for an honours degree. For Vivian, as for Wilde, only two universities counted – Oxford and Cambridge – and Wilde usually expressed grave doubts about Cambridge.

108. *Man can believe the impossible*: a remark deriving some of its verve from Tertullian's famous paradox about the incarnation of Christ: 'it's certain because it's impossible' *(certum est quia impossibile)*.

109. *Cretan dinner-parties*: Wilde appears to be alluding to the famous 'liar paradox' in philosophy, traditionally associated with Crete. Epimenides, a Cretan, said, 'The Cretans are always liars.' Is he telling the truth?

110. *William Morris*: Morris's verse translation of the *Odyssey* was published in 1887.

111. *stainless hero of Euripidean tragedy*: in Euripides' *Ion*, the hero conceals the truth about his birth and is rewarded by becoming the founder of the Ionian race.

112. *Sanchez*: Francisco Sánchez (1550–1623) published his *Treatise on the Noble and High Science of Ignorance (Quod nihil scitur)* in 1581.

113. *the Academe*: the olive grove near Athens where Plato and his successors taught philosophy.

114. *Flaubert's marvellous tale*: *La Tentation de Saint Antoine*, a prose poem of great imaginative power published in 1874. 'Flaubert is my master,' Wilde told W. E. Henley in 1888, 'and when I get on with my translation of the *Tentation* I shall be Flaubert II, *Roi par grâce de Dieu*, and I hope something else beyond.' Wilde always travelled with a copy of the *Tentation*, but his translation came to nothing.

115. *the jewel in the toad's head*: the belief in toadstones, i.e. that 'the foul toad hath a fair stone in his head', was a favourite conceit of Elizabethan writers, and derived from Pliny the Elder's description of a stone as 'of the colour of a frog'.

116. *Behemoth and Leviathan . . . basilisk . . . Hippogriff*: biblical and mythological beasts.

117. *the pre-Raphaelite movement of our own day*: founded in 1848, the Pre-Raphaelite Brotherhood, led by John Millais and D. G. Rossetti, sought to free British painting from the cold and mechanical formulas of the Royal Academy. The group turned instead to the pure, glowing colour and faithful transcription of natural detail of the Italian primitive painters who preceded Raphael. Gaining the adherence of Edward Burne-Jones and William Morris in the later 1850s, the movement began to exert a wide influence on church decoration, home décor, dress and architecture even as its impulse in painting gradually ebbed. In his American lecture tour of 1882, Wilde portrayed himself as part of the 'English Renaissance of Art' because he was extending the work of the Pre-Raphaelites into a younger generation.

118. *Second Empire*: France under the rule (1852–70) of Napoleon III, a period notable for its corruption and vulgar excess.

119. *'droops the milk-white peacock like a ghost'* . . . *'washes the dusk with silver'*: the first quotation is a line from a song ('Now sleeps the crimson petal, now the white') in Tennyson's narrative poem *The Princess* (1847); the second is from Blake's poem 'The Evening Star'. Blake and Tennyson were favourite poets among the Pre-Raphaelites and their followers.

2. Pen, Pencil and Poison

First published in the *Fortnightly Review* for January 1889.

1. *Rubens . . . Goethe . . . Milton . . . Sophocles*: Peter Paul Rubens, Flemish painter (1577–1640). For Goethe, see n. 15, p. 329 above. John Milton (1608–74), poet and Protestant controversialist, was Latin Secretary to the Council of State of the Commonwealth 1649–60; Sophocles, Greek tragic dramatist (496–406 BC).

2. *diplomatic representatives of their country*: the novelist Nathaniel Hawthorne was US Consul at Liverpool (1853–7); the novelist W. D. Howells was US Consul at Venice (1860–65); the poet, essayist and humorist James Russell Lowell (who wrote a letter of introduction for Wilde on his American tour) was US Minister first to Spain (1877–80) and later to England (1880–85).

3. *Thomas Griffiths Wainewright*: painter, forger, murderer (1794–1852). He wrote art criticism for the *London Magazine* (1820–23), where he was a colleague of Charles Lamb (see nn. 7 and 10, pp. 316, 317 above).

4. *a great poet of our own day*: i.e. A. C. Swinburne, who in *William Blake: A Critical Essay* (1866) had praised Wainewright's skilful ability 'with pen, with palette, or with poison'.

5. *Goldsmith and Wedgwood*: Oliver Goldsmith, poet, playwright, physician and hack writer (1730?–74), was a member of the celebrated circle around Samuel Johnson. Josiah Wedgwood (1730–95), the most distinguished English manufacturer of domestic as well as art pottery, was the friend of such eminent literary and scientific figures as Joseph Priestley.

6. *Mr Locke*: John Locke (1632–1704), pre-eminent English philosopher of empiricism, whose wide-ranging works treated the analytic philosophy of mind, education, government and religious toleration.

7. *Mr Hazlitt*: not the Romantic essayist William Hazlitt, but his grandson, W. Carew Hazlitt, from whose biographical essay to his edition of Wainewright's essays and criticism (1880) Wilde borrows heavily throughout this essay.

8. *Scott, the editor of the* London Magazine: John Scott (1783–1821), editor and author of successful travel books. He attracted many illustrious contributors to the *London Magazine* from 1820 until 1821, when he died as a result of gunshot wounds received in a duel with J. H. Christie.

9. *Macready . . . John Forster . . . Maginn . . . Talfourd . . . Sir Wentworth Dilke . . . John Clare*: William Charles Macready (1793–1873), eminent actor and theatre manager, was famous for his Shakespearean roles. John Forster (1812–76) editor, essayist and biographer, was most noted for his biography of his intimate friend Charles Dickens. William Maginn (1793–1842) was a humorous writer, essayist and contributor to *Blackwood's Edinburgh Magazine* and *Fraser's Magazine*. Thomas Noon Talfourd (1795–1854) was a judge, author and intimate friend of Charles Lamb. Charles Wentworth Dilke (1810–69) was a politician and promoter of the Great Exhibition of 1851, whose son (1843–1911) bore the same name and became a prominent Liberal politician until scandal prematurely ended his career (see n. 32, p. 333 above). John Clare (1793–1864), poet and unsuccessful farmer, wrote poems of rural life.

10. *Disraeli*: Benjamin Disraeli (1804–81), novelist, politician and Conservative prime minister (1868, 1874–80).

11. *Balzac's* Lucien de Rubempré: see n. 36, p. 340 above.

12. *Julien Sorel*: remorselessly ambitious hero of Stendahl's novel about post-Napoleonic France, *Le Rouge et le noir*, published in 1830.

13. *De Quincey*: Thomas De Quincey (1785–1859), essayist and critic, was a close observer of the Romantic writers.

14. *William Blake*: Romantic poet, engraver and seer (1757–1827). See also n. 119, p. 347 above.

15. *La Gioconda*: Leonardo's painting of the Mona Lisa, famously hymned by Pater in *Studies in the History of the Renaissance*, where Pater also praises early French poets and the Italian Renaissance.

16. Cupid and Psyche: an allegorical episode taken from Apuleius' *The Golden Ass* (second century AD). W. Adlington translated the work into English in the sixteenth century. William Morris makes the story of Cupid and Psyche part of his verse cycle *The Earthly Paradise* (1868–70). Pater gives a translation of the tale in his historical novel *Marius the Epicurean* (1885).

17. Hypnerotomachia: the *Hypnerotomachia Poliphili* (*The Strife of Love in a Dream*) by Poliphilus was reprinted in 1499 by the celebrated Venetian printer Aldus Manutius in an edition of great beauty set in the elegant type font that bears his name (Aldine).

18. *Baudelaire*: Charles Baudelaire (1821–67), French poet and art critic, whose work exerted a powerful influence over the generations of Swinburne and Wilde.

19. *Gautier*: see n. 10, p. 328 above.

20. *'sweet marble monster'* . . . *in the Louvre*: Hermaphroditus, a beautiful figure combining the characteristics of both sexes, was a favourite motif in late Greek sculpture. Gautier gave the figure modern prominence in his romance *Mademoiselle de Maupin* (1835). Swinburne published a notable poem about the statue of Hermaphroditus in the Louvre museum in his first volume of *Poems and Ballads* (1866).

21. *fictile*: moulded into form by art; made of earth, clay, etc., by a potter.

22. *KAΛOΣ*: Greek for 'beautiful'.

23. *Michael Angelo . . . Giorgione*: Michelangelo Buonarrotti (1475–1564), Italian painter, sculptor, architect and poet. Among the frescoes painted for the Sistine Chapel, his 'Delphic Sibyl' is the most beautiful of the large figures depicting the ancient prophets. Giorgione da Castelfranco (1478?–1511), Venetian painter whose 'Pastoral' or 'Fête Champêtre' (now usually attributed to Titian) had inspired both Rossetti ('For a Venetian Pastoral by Giorgione [In the Louvre]') and Pater ('The School of Giorgione').

24. *majolica*: a type of fine Italian pottery, coated in white enamel and painted in richly coloured decorative patterns.

25. *a book of Hours*: in medieval Christianity, a book containing the offices or services for the prayers and devotions offered by the worshipper at seven specific times during the day. Medieval books of hours were richly decorated in colours and gold.

26. *Lar*: a Roman household god or protective spirit.

27. *Tassie's gems*: James Tassie (1735–99), Scottish gem engraver, famous for his portrait medallions and his imitations of antique gems so exquisite they were sold by fraudulent dealers as originals.

28. *Louis-Quatorze* bonbonnière: a small box to hold sweets, made during the reign of Louis XIV (1643–1715).

29. *Petitot*: Jean Louis Petitot (1672–*c*.1730), French enamel painter, for a number of years resident in England, where he painted many portraits of Charles II.

30. *brown-biscuit teapots*: i.e. teapots of unglazed pottery, decorated with a lacy overlay design.

31. *'pomona-green'*: i.e. apple green.

32. *Marc Antonios*: engravings by the sixteenth-century master Marcantonio Raimondi, famous for his skilful renditions of Raphael's designs.

33. *Turner's* Liber Studiorum: a celebrated book of engraved drawings produced by J. M. W. Turner to vindicate his own mode of landscape painting against the practice of Claude Lorraine and other Old Masters. Because Claude had published his *Liber veritatis* (*Book of Truth*), Turner meant his 'book of studies' to demonstrate his own deep knowledge of the underlying structural principles in natural objects ignored by the older masters and only to be gained, as Turner believed, by unwearied study out of doors. Ruskin had put Turner's *Liber studiorum* at the centre of his art teaching at Oxford.

34. *'an onyx of two strata'* . . . *'altissimo relievo'* . . . *on cornelian*: terms relating to cameos or gems carved in relief from various sorts of quartzes, with onyx referring to stones with two or three strata or layers of colour (white, black, brown), sardonyx referring to those with additional bands of red (carnelian) and reddish brown (sard). The term *altissimo relievo*, Italian for 'highest relief', refers to the carving of a cameo or relief figure with utmost possible projection from its background.

35. *amateur of engravings*: as always with Wilde, the word 'amateur' is used in a positive sense, meaning 'someone who cultivates a study or art or other activity for personal pleasure or delight'.

36. *the first step in aesthetic criticism is to realize one's own impressions*: in his preface to *Studies in the History of the Renaissance* Pater had declared, 'in aesthetic criticism the first step towards seeing one's object as it really is, is to know one's own impression as it really is, to discriminate it, to realize it distinctly'.

37. *Crome*: John Crome (1768–1821), English landscape painter.

38. *Wilkie*: Sir David Wilkie (1785–1841), Scottish painter of rural scenes.

39. *Mr Crabbe's poems*: George Crabbe (1754–1832), Anglican vicar and poet. Crabbe's poetry and fiction did not shrink from describing life in its grimmer aspects.

40. *Fuseli*: John Henry Fuseli (1741–1825), Swiss painter who worked in England, becoming the greatest exponent of Michelangelesque and Mannerist motifs in Romantic painting, until the man he befriended, the genius poet-painter William Blake (see n. 14, p. 348 above), surpassed him.

41. *Landseer and Martin, Stothard and Etty*: Edwin Landseer (1802–73), a hugely successful English animal painter, whose later works tended to grow in both size and sentimentality. John Martin (1789–1854), an English painter of enormous and frequently apocalyptic canvases: e.g. 'Belshazzar's Feast' (1821), 'Destruction of Herculaneum' (1822), 'Eve of the Deluge' (1841). Thomas Stothard (1755–1834), an English subject painter and noted book illustrator. William Etty (1787–1849), an English painter, admired for his skill as a colourist.

42. *'to see the object as in itself it really is'*: a proposition about the goal of criticism which Matthew Arnold first made in 'On Translating Homer' (1861), and repeated with much polemical zest in 'The Function of Criticism at the Present Time' (1865). '

43. *Ariosto*: Ludovico Ariosto (1474–1533), Italian epic poet. His masterpiece *Orlando Furioso* (1532) centres less on the madness of Charlemagne's chief knight Roland than on the love between Ruggiero and Bradamante. The poem is filled with such apparently unconnected episodes as a voyage to the moon by hippogriff, a fabled beast half horse and half griffin.

44. *Elia*: pseudonym of Charles Lamb when publishing his first and second series of essays in the *London Magazine* (1820–23, 1833).

45. *Watteau...Lancret...Rubens...Giorgione...Rembrandt...Corregio*: Antoine Watteau (1684–1721), French painter. Nicolas Lancret (1660–1743), French painter. For Rubens, see n. 1, p. 347 above. For Giorgione, see n. 23, p. 349 above. Rembrandt van Ryn (1609–69), Dutch painter and etcher. Antonio Correggio (1494–1534), Italian painter.

46. *true spirit of Toynbee Hall*: i.e. a missionary spirit of outreach and uplift. Founded in 1884 by university graduates to honour the social reformer Arnold Toynbee (1852–83), Toynbee Hall was the first settlement house (see n. 5, p. 330 above). Wilde gave a copy of *The Happy Prince and Other Tales* to the library of Toynbee Hall in 1888.

47. *Tintoret's 'St George...'*: Jacopo Robusti (1518–94), Venetian painter nick-named 'the little dyer' (*Tintoretto*) because his father was a dyer. Ruskin, who celebrated the painter in vol. 2 of *Modern Painters* (1846), spread the fashion of calling him 'Tintoret'.

48. *Schiavone*: Giorgio Schiavone (1433?–1504), Dalmatian painter who worked in Padua, where he was known as 'the Slavonian' (*Schiavone*, in Italian). His mature paintings were known for their use of strong yellows, reds and dark greens.

49. *Moroni*: Italian portrait painter (*c*.1510–78) of the Venetian school. His portraits have a tendency to a violet tint in the flesh, here called *morbidezza* by Wilde.

50. *Giulio Romano*: Italian painter and architect (1499?–1546), trained by Raphael.

51. *Cephalus and Procris*: in Greek mythology, Cephalus was the husband of Procris, who became jealous when Eos (Aurora) fell in love with him. In an attempt at reconciliation, Procris gave Cephalus the two magical gifts Artemis had earlier given her: a hound named Laelaps that caught whatever it pursued and a spear that never missed its mark. Still tormented by jealousy, Procris, hidden, spies on Cephalus as he hunts. Thinking he hears an animal in the bush, Cephalus hurls his spear and kills his wife. 'Vans dejected' are drooping wings.

52. *Moschus's lament for Bion*: Moschus, a pastoral poet of Syracuse (*fl. c.*150 BC) is traditionally assumed to be the author of the beautiful 'Lament for Bion', an elegy for his friend and teacher.

53. *Hymettus*: a mountain in Attica famous for its bees and the thyme-scented honey they produced.

54. *Aurora*: in Roman mythology, the goddess of dawn.

55. *'on the side of the angels'*: the answer given by Benjamin Disraeli when he was asked at the Oxford Diocesan Conference in November 1864 whether he joined with the Darwinians and others arguing that man descended from the apes or with those who believe man's origin was spiritual, like that of the angels. Queen Victoria raised Disraeli to the peerage as first earl of Beaconsfield in 1876.

56. *Alain Chartier . . . Ronsard*: Chartier (*c.*1390–*c.*1440), French poet and prose writer. Pierre de Ronsard (1524–85), French poet and leader of the renaissance in French verse associated with the group known as the 'Pléiade'.

57. *Petrarch*: Francesco Petrarca (1304–74), Italian poet and humanist.

58. *Barry Cornwall, Allan Cunningham, Hazlitt, Elton . . . Leigh Hunt*: Barry Cornwall was the pen-name of Bryan Waller Procter (1787–1874), a minor writer associated with the circles around Leigh Hunt and, later, Charles Dickens. Allan Cunningham (1784–1842), a Scottish stonemason and poet, is best known for his imitations of ancient ballads. William Hazlitt (1778–1830), essayist and critic. Edward William Elton (1794–1843), an actor and writer. Leigh Hunt (1784–1859), editor, poet and essayist.

59. *Sir Thomas Browne . . . Burton . . . Fuller*: for Browne, see n. 8, p. 317 above; Robert Burton (1577–1640) was author of the *Anatomy of Melancholy* (1621), a work of rare and various learning. Thomas Fuller (1608–61), an Anglican divine best known for his *Worthies of England* (1662), a curious and amusing gazetteer. Lamb's delight in the long-neglected prose writers of the seventeenth century helped to revive the reputations of all these among the Victorians.

60. *Beaumont and Fletcher*: Francis Beaumont (1584–1616) collaborated with John Fletcher (1579–1625) to write approximately fifteen plays during the period 1606–16.

61. *Collins's 'Ode to Evening'*: William Collins, lyric poet (1721–59). His 'Ode to Evening' was published in 1747.

62. *Sir Thomas Lawrence*: painter (1769–1830), known for his elegant portraits.

63. *Bow Street runner*: i.e. a police officer. Bow Street, near Covent Garden, was the site of the principal metropolitan London police court.

64. circonstance attenuante: i.e. an extenuating circumstance which would make his crime seem less serious.

65. *Dickens, Macready and Hablot Browne*: Charles Dickens, the prodigiously talented and successful novelist (1812–70); for Macready, see n. 9, p. 348

above; Hablot Knight Browne (1815–82), gifted illustrator ('Phiz') of many of Dickens's novels.

66. *Forster*: see n. 9, p. 348.

67. *the hulks at Portsmouth*: decommissioned sailing vessels used as temporary prisons.

68. *Van Diemen's Land*: former name of Tasmania, the large island south of Melbourne, Australia, discovered by the Dutch explorer Abel Tasman (*c*.1603–*c*.1659) in 1642, and originally named for his patron. From 1840 to 1853, the island was the sole destination for convicts under sentence of transportation from Britain as well as from India and the colonies. Its capital city is Hobart.

69. Paradis Artificiels: 'artificial paradises', after the title of Baudelaire's collection of essays about opium and hashish (1860). Samuel Taylor Coleridge (1772–1834), who first took opium at Cambridge, became addicted to it. His poem 'Kubla Khan', written in 1797 under the residual effects of opium, became the quintessential expression of the Romantic quest for heightened consciousness and strange beauty.

70. *Lord Tennyson ... Mr Gladstone ... the Master of Balliol*: Alfred Tennyson (1809–92), who became Poet Laureate upon Wordsworth's death in 1850, was raised to the peerage in 1884; William Ewart Gladstone (1809–98), great Liberal statesman and prime minister four times between 1868 and 1894; Benjamin Jowett (1817–93) was the Master (senior academician) of Balliol College, Oxford, from 1870 to 1893.

71. *Nero ... Tiberius ... Caesar Borgia*: Nero, Roman emperor AD 54–68, was notorious for his cruelty and persecution of the Christians; Tiberius, Roman emperor AD 14–37, was feared for his cold determination and suspected of hideous debaucheries in later life; Cesare Borgia (1476–1507), the favourite son of Pope Alexander VI, became infamous for his violence, treachery and ruthlessness.

72. *Mr John Addington Symonds, Miss A. Mary F. Robinson, Miss Vernon Lee*: for Symonds, see n. 31, p. 320 above; A. Mary F. Robinson (1857–1944) published *The End of the Middle Ages: Essays and Questions in History* in 1889; Vernon Lee was the pen-name of Violet Paget, essayist and novelist (1856–1935). She published *Euphorion, being Studies of the Antique and Mediaeval in the Renaissance* in 1883, with a dedication to Pater. In a note to the 1888 edition of *The Renaissance*, Pater praised her book as 'abounding in knowledge and insight on the subjects of which it treats'.

73. *Dickens's 'Hunted Down' ... Bulwer's* Lucretia: Dickens's short tale 'Hunted Down' was first published in an American newspaper, the *New York Ledger*, in 1859. He was paid £1,000 for it. *Lucretia*, a novel by Edward Bulwer-Lytton

(1803–73) published in 1846, concerned itself with the scandalous career of a female poisoner who learns her craft from Varney's father and later conspires with Varney to murder a girl called Helen.

3. The Critic as Artist: Part I

First published under the title 'The True Function and Value of Criticism; with some Remarks on the Importance of Doing Nothing: A Dialogue' in the *Nineteenth Century* for July 1890. The editor, James Knowles, opted to publish the essay in two parts with a month intervening between them, a decision which, as Wilde wrote him in August 1890, 'is still a great source of regret to me'.

1. *Cicero . . . Balzac, Flaubert . . . Berlioz, Byron . . . Madame de Sévigné*: for Cicero, see above p. 340; the over 700 extant letters of Cicero are notable for their candour and charm. For Balzac, see n. 33, p. 339 above; his letters to various correspondents, including George Sand, are among the most remarkable in French literature. Hector Berlioz (1803–69), French composer; his *Mémoires* (1870) and *Lettres intimes* (1882) breathed the spirit of impetuous Romanticism. George Gordon, Lord Byron (1788–1824), Romantic poet. Marie de Rabutin-Chantal, Marquise de Sévigné (1626–96); her letters, which began to be published in 1725, were by turns amusing, picturesque and poignant.

2. *Rousseau*: see n. 80, p. 343. His autobiography, *Les Confessions* (1781, 1788), describes with astonishing candour the author's moral and emotional development.

3. *Cellini*: see n. 41, p. 334 above. Cellini worked in France from 1540 to 1544 at the invitation of Francis I. It was for this monarch that he created his famous sculpture of the Nymph of Fontainebleau, now in the Louvre. Cellini's 'Perseus Holding the Head of Medusa' (sculpted 1545–54) stood in the Loggia della Signoria in Florence. Boasting equally of murders committed as of art works created, Cellini's *Autobiography*, begun in 1553, was first published in 1730. J. A. Symonds's notable English translation appeared in 1888. Responding to a query from the *Pall Mall Gazette* in 1886, Wilde listed Cellini's *Autobiography* as one of the few books people ought actually to read.

4. *Sieur de Montaigne*: see n. 32, p. 320 above.

5. *the bitter son of Monica*: i.e. St Augustine (AD 345–430), bishop of Hippo, whose *Confessions* told the story of his conversion to Christianity. This was another book Wilde put on his *Pall Mall Gazette* list of books actually to be read.

6. *Cardinal Newman*: see n. 12, p. 317 above. Wilde's account of Newman's *Apologia* is notably unsympathetic, with Newman's assent to Catholic religious faith portrayed as his choice of intellectual darkness. Upon Newman's death in 1890, his work and thought came in for renewed scrutiny.

7. *Littlemore*: a village near Oxford to which Newman had retreated before resigning as vicar of the university church of St Mary's (1843) and converting to Roman Catholicism (1845).

8. *that gracious undergraduate*: Newman again, who wrote in his *Apologia* that, 'There used to be much snap-dragon growing on the walls opposite my freshman's rooms there [at Trinity College], and I had for years taken it as the emblem of my own perpetual residence even unto death in my University.'

9. *Benign Mother*: refers to Oxford, Newman's alma mater. While himself an Oxford undergraduate, Wilde toyed with the idea of consulting Newman about his spiritual difficulties but the interview never took place. Newman's *Apologia, Grammar of Assent, Two Essays on Miracles* and *The Idea of a University* were among the first fifteen books Wilde was permitted to receive in prison.

10. *Mr Secretary Pepys*: Samuel Pepys (1633–1703), diarist and administrator, became secretary to the Admiralty in 1672. His celebrated diary treats the years 1660 to 1669. Originally written in cipher, it was deciphered and published in 1825 to universal acclaim.

11. *Touchstone*: the clown in Shakespeare's *As You Like It* (v, iv) says, 'Your "if" is the only peace-maker; much virtue in "if".'

12. *Boswell*: see n. 61, p. 341 above.

13. *mutes*: professional mourners hired for funerals who silently mimicked grief.

14. *Chopin . . . Dvořák*: Frederic Chopin (1810–49), pianist and composer. Anton Dvořák (1841–1901), Czech composer. In *De Profundis* Wilde, who heard 'discontent' in Chopin's deferred resolutions, was to say that men and women of artistic temperament 'look with new eyes on modern life because they have listened to one of Chopin's nocturnes'.

15. *remorseful Academician*: William Powell Frith (1819–1909), celebrated painter of such panoramic and minutely detailed scenes of Victorian daily life as 'Ramsgate Sands' (1853) and 'The Railway Station' (1862). In *My Autobiography and Reminiscences* (1887), Frith had written, 'No artist who has arrived at mature age can look back at his early opportunities without a remorseful sense of his neglect of many of them. I can even accuse myself.' Frith's faithful depictions of ordinary Victorian domestic life are parodied in Ernest's title 'Waiting for the Last Omnibus'. As one of the first artists to use photographs as an aid in painting, Frith's work was notable for its elaborate realism. Hence the question as to whether it had all been painted 'by hand'. In 'The Private View of the

Royal Academy' (1883) Frith had depicted Wilde as a foolish fop surrounded by a crowd of absurdly worshipful 'Aesthetic' followers. The references here to Frith may thus be considered Wilde's revenge.

16. *Browning Society*: founded in London in 1881 to elucidate the difficulties in the poetry of Robert Browning (1812–89), the Browning Society expanded rapidly. The group and its offshoots in England and America quickly came to be associated with a solemnly reverential attitude towards poetry which many late Victorians found ridiculous.

17. *Broad Church Party*: the theologically liberal wing of the Anglican Church, known for its rationalism, doctrinal tolerance and acceptance of modern science and German biblical scholarship.

18. *Mr Walter Scott's Great Writers Series*: a series of biographical handbooks about literary figures published by the firm of Walter Scott and intended for readers desirous of 'self-improvement'.

19. *Olympians . . . Titan*: see n. 43, p. 340 above.

20. *the one chord we have added to the Greek lyre*: although the Greeks established the models for epic, lyric, elegiac, epigrammatic and pastoral poetry, their verse was unrhymed.

21. *Robert Browning*: Wilde admired Browning's earlier poetry for its acute psychological insight and dramatic portraiture. In the lines that follow, he describes some of the most famous characters from Browning's revolutionary volume of poetry, *Men and Women* (1855). But Wilde, who loved mellifluous language and considered the voice the ultimate measure of what might be attempted in verse, disliked Browning's later poetry, with its clashing consonants, erratic rhythms and indifference to formal beauty.

22. *tettix*: cicada.

23. *George Meredith*: n. 36, p. 333 above. cf. Charles Lamb's remark, 'Heywood is a sort of prose Shakespeare.'

24. *Hermes*: in Greek mythology, the messenger or herald of the gods. The fancy that the sculptor released or awakened by his carving a form already lodged within the block of stone was expressed by Michelangelo.

25. *fane*: temple.

26. *child of Leto*: Apollo, Greek god of poetry, was the child of Zeus and Leto, a goddess descended from the Titans.

27. ἀβρῶς βαίνοντες διὰ λαμπροτάτου αἰθέρος: Greek for 'passing gaily in that most brilliant air', a phrase describing the Athenians from the choral ode in Euripides' *Medea*. This was a favourite tag of Wilde's, who copied it into his Oxford commonplace book.

28. *Phaedrus*: the young interlocutor of Socrates in the Platonic dialogue of the same name, which discusses true and false rhetoric, giving examples of both kinds in speeches on the subject of love.

29. *agnus castus*: species of shrub, resembling verbena, which in pagan times was credited with the power to preserve chastity.

30. *Tanagra*: city in the Greek republic of Boeotia, the source of exquisitely moulded terracotta figurines produced from the late fourth to the first century BC. Used in religious rites and in daily life, the statuettes were frequently buried with the dead.

31. *asphodel*: a genus of perennial lily-like plants native to the Mediterranean region. In Greek legend, the asphodel was associated with the dead and the underworld, probably because the greyish colour of its leaves and the yellowish colour of its flowers suggested the gloom of the nether regions and the pallor of the dead.

32. *Polyxena*: daughter of Priam, king of Troy. In Homer's *Iliad*, after her brother Paris kills the Greek hero Achilles, Polyxena is claimed by Achilles' ghost as a prize, and she is slain on the tomb of her father.

33. *Acheron*: one of the rivers in Hades, visited by Odysseus in Book 10 of the *Odyssey*.

34. *trews and mitre*: the characteristic kilt and headdress worn by Persian warriors.

35. *Marathon*: crescent-shaped plain, 26.2 miles north-east of Athens, the site of the great Athenian victory over the invading Persians in 490 BC.

36. *Salaminian bay*: scene of the great naval battle of 480 BC in which the Persian fleet was destroyed by the Greeks.

37. *Adonis . . . Artemis*: in Greek mythology, Adonis is a beautiful youth loved by Aphrodite. When Adonis was killed by a boar, Aphrodite caused the rose to spring from his blood. Artemis was the Greek goddess of chastity, hunting and the moon.

38. *palmates*: stylized designs shaped like hands or palm leaves.

39. *Tyrian robe*: garment coloured with the rich purple dye extracted from shellfish, a technique first mastered by the Phoenicians of ancient Tyre.

40. *Thetis*: mother of Achilles, herself a Nereid or daughter of Nereus, Homer's old man of the sea.

41. *Phaedra*: wife of Theseus who falls in love with Hippolytus, and is scorned by him. In Euripides' play *Hippolytus*, Phaedra resists her own passion but her adulterous love is betrayed to Hippolytus by her nurse.

42. *Persephone*: in Greek mythology, the daughter of Zeus and Demeter, who is carried off by Hades to his kingdom in the lower world. Ultimately, Persephone is allowed to spend six months with her mother, and six with her captor. In the lower world she wreathes poppies, the symbol of forgetfulness, into her hair as the sign of her despair.

43. *Donatello*: Italian sculptor (1386–1466).

44. *ΚΑΛΟΣ ΑΛΚΙΒΙΑΔΗΣ or ΚΑΛΟΣ ΧΑΡΜΙΔΗΣ*: 'Beautiful Alcibiades or Beautiful Charmides' – two more characters from Plato's Socratic dialogues.

45. *Maenads*: female worshippers, usually drunken or otherwise ecstatic, of Dionysus, Greek god of wine.

46. *must-stained feet*: unfermented juice as pressed from the grape by the feet of peasants.

47. *Silenus*: in Greek mythology, an elderly drunken satyr.

48. *Ilyssus . . . Higginbotham*: in 'The Function of Criticism at the Present Time', Arnold contrasts the sonority of ancient Greek names with the repulsiveness of contemporary English ones by remarking 'by the Ilyssus there was no Wragg'.

49. *Narcissus*: in Greek mythology, a beautiful youth, the son of a river god and a nymph, who repulsed the love offered him by Echo. In revenge, Aphrodite makes him fall in love with his own reflection in a fountain. Unable to approach the beautiful creature he sees, Narcissus at length dies and is changed into the flower that bears his name.

50. *Prince Florizel of Bohemia*: character in Shakespeare's *The Winter's Tale* and also in R. L. Stevenson's *New Arabian Nights* (1882). The 'fair Cuban' is a character and narrator in the latter work.

51. *trochaic and tribrachic movements*: in prosody, a trochaic foot has a long syllable followed by a short; a tribrachic foot has three short syllables. Both measures were considered 'effeminate' in the nineteenth century because they ended with a light or weak stress.

52. *Hegesias*: Greek rhetorician who lived *c.*300 BC, considered by classical writers to have been the founder of the florid or 'Asiatic' style of composition. The learned critic referred to is Strabo (*c.*64 BC–AD 19).

53. *conduct is three-fourths of life*: Matthew Arnold made the remark in his preface to *Literature and Dogma* (1873), declaring, 'Conduct is three-fourths of our life and its largest concern.'

54. *paeons*: in prosody, a foot of four syllables, one long (in any position) and three short.

55. κάθαρσις: 'catharsis'; in Aristotle's theory of tragedy, the purgation of emotion in the audience by the experience of pity and terror. See also n. 24, p. 365 below.

56. *Goethe . . . Lessing*: for Goethe, see n. 15, p. 329 above. Gotthold Lessing (1729–81), critic and dramatist, was the author of *Laokoon* (1766), a treatise exploring the differences between the literary and the plastic arts.

57. *Alexandria*: city in Egypt founded by Alexander the Great (331 BC), later famous for its magnificent library and its schools of rhetoric and philosophy.

58. *Sicyon*: ancient Greek city on the Peloponnesus supposed to have invented painting, which flowered there during the fourth century BC.

59. *private views . . . Pre-Raphaelite movements*: for private views, see n. 4, pp. 305–6 above. Much influenced by the work of William Morris, the Arts and Crafts movement of the later 1880s and 1890s sought to raise the status of the handicrafts and the craftsmen and women who pursued them to the level achieved by the fine arts. Wilde, who promoted and consumed the products of this design revolution, did not fully endorse the claims for equal consideration made for such handicrafts as bookbinding. He considered there was a wide gulf set between such decorative arts and the fully expressive arts such as poetry and painting. For Pre-Raphaelitism, see n. 117, p. 346 above.

60. *Lucian . . . Longinus . . . Quinctilian . . . Dionysius . . . Pliny . . . Fronto . . . Pausanias . . .* : Lucian (AD *c*.115–*c*.200), Greek satirist, was the author of *Mortuorum dialogi* (*Dialogues of the Dead*). 'Longinus' was formerly thought to have been the author of an enormously influential Greek treatise on rhetoric and literary style, *On the Sublime* (first century AD); modern scholarship states the authorship is unknown. Quintilian (AD *c*.35–*c*.95), Roman writer on oratory and eloquence, whose work exerted a powerful influence on Renaissance humanism. Dionysius of Halicarnassus (*fl. c*.25 BC), a Greek historian and literary critic who lived in Rome, was one of the first writers to insist that 'the style is the man'. For Pliny, see n. 50, pp. 340–41 above. Chapters 35 and 36 of his *Natural History* are devoted to the history and reception of Greek painting and sculpture in Rome. Marcus Cornelius Fronto (AD *c*.100–*c*.176), was a Roman author who urged a reformation in style. Fronto figures as a minor character in Pater's historical novel *Marius the Epicurean*. Pausanias, Greek travel writer (*fl*. second century AD), has interesting remarks on Greek painting, sculpture and architecture.

61. μονόχρονος ἡδονή: a complicated joke; the Greek phrase can either mean 'momentary pleasure' or it can refer to the pleasure of the ideal present or mystic now, portrayed as the central philosophical ideal by Aristippus of Cyrene (fifth century BC). Pater, defending himself against the charge of having misled youth into a life of mere 'momentary pleasure' with the notorious 'Conclusion' to his *Studies in the History of the Renaissance*, spends much time in Chapter 9 of *Marius the Epicurean* (1885) insisting on this more philosophical meaning of the phrase. Wilde's Gilbert promptly undoes all Pater's careful qualifications by identifying μονόχρονος ἡδονή once again with fleeting pleasure.

62. attachés: persons connected with a diplomatic embassy or legation.

63. *criticism of life*: Arnold had declared in his essay 'The Study of Poetry' that poetry is 'a criticism of life under the conditions fixed for such a criticism by the laws of poetic truth and poetic beauty'.

64. *'wiser than they knew'*: cf. Emerson's poem 'The Problem', where artists from Phidias to Jeremy Taylor are portrayed as agents of divine powers in which they may no longer actively believe. Thus of Michelangelo it is said, 'He builded better than he knew/ The conscious stone to beauty grew.'

65. *And so not built at all,/ And therefore built for ever*: Wilde's approximation of Tennyson's description of the building of Camelot in *Idylls of the King* where the city is 'built/ To music, therefore never built at all/ And therefore built for ever.'

66. *the Anthology*: the Greek Anthology, a collection of over 6,000 short poems by various Greek authors ranging in time over seventeen centuries from the seventh century BC to the tenth century AD. Wilde told the *Pall Mall Gazette* to add the Greek Anthology to its list of '100 best books'.

67. *one of our most industrious writers*: William Sharp (1855–1905), Scots poet and prose writer, wrote many works in such a dialect. In *Romantic Ballads and Poems of Phantasy* (1888) Sharp had called for a rejection of French fixed poetic forms and a return to the rich dialectal tradition of the Border ballad. Reviewing Sharp's book, Wilde wondered aloud if such dialect words as 'drumly' and 'blawing' and 'snawing' could indeed supply an adequate basis for a new romantic movement.

68. *three-volumed novel*: the novel in three volumes was the format preferred by such commercial lending libraries as Mudie's. By the 1890s, however, as changes in book production made a one-volume format more profitable, the old 'triple-decker' came to seem lumbering and antique to younger writers.

69. *Newnham graduates*: Newnham was a women's college at Cambridge which opened in 1876. 'Womanthropes' was the sort of half-educated coinage females with no Latin and less Greek might be expected to come up with, according to opponents of women's education.

70. *M. Renan*: for Ernest Renan, see n. 1, p. 330 above. Renan's sceptical temper and distinguished prose style deeply influenced Matthew Arnold, Pater and Wilde.

71. *Magdalen . . . Lucretias*: Magdalen, after Mary Magdalen in the Christian Bible, was a common Victorian euphemism for reformed prostitute. In Roman legend, Lucretia was a virtuous wife who, upon being raped by a relative of her husband, took her own life. Gilbert is suggesting that respectable Victorian ladies maintained their chastity only at the price of consigning other women to a life of prostitution – a common argument in 'advanced' Victorian intellectual circles.

72. *Ilion*: ancient Troy.

73. *Aulis*: the place where Agamemnon, king of Argos, sacrificed his daughter Iphigenia in order to obtain favourable winds for sailing with his fleet to Troy. Upon his return from the Trojan war, Agamemnon's wife, Clytemnestra, intent on avenging Iphigenia's death, plotted with her lover to murder her husband in his bath.

74. *Antigone*: daughter of Oedipus, condemned to death by her uncle Creon, king of Thebes, for unlawfully burying the corpse of her brother, a rebel against the king.

75. *Lucian ... Menippus*: Menippus of Gadara, slave, satiric writer and Cynic philosopher, flourished *c*. third century BC. Menippus figures frequently as a character in the works of Lucian, Greek satirist (AD *c*.120–*c*.180).

76. *swanlike daughter of Leda*: Helen of Troy, the daughter of the nymph Leda and Jupiter, who for purposes of seduction had assumed the form of a swan.

77. *leman*: lover; here it refers to Paris, a younger son of Priam. Paris' abduction of Helen, wife of Menelaus, king of Sparta, began the Trojan War.

78. *son of Priam*: Hector, also called 'the Priamid' and 'the lionhearted', the greatest hero among the Trojans.

79. *the friend of his soul*: Patroclus, Achilles' beloved companion, who fights the Trojans when Achilles refuses to and is killed by Hector.

80. *Lord of the Myrmidons*: i.e. Achilles. In Greek mythology, the Myrmidons were a warlike people from ancient Thessaly, created by Zeus out of ants (*myrmēkes*) to re-people an island devastated by plague.

81. *Dodona*: site of a famous oracle of Zeus, mentioned in the *Iliad* and the *Odyssey*.

82. *Euphorbus*: Trojan warrior who first wounds Patroclus, beloved companion of Achilles.

83. οἶνοψ πόντος: 'wine-dark sea', the most famous of the Homeric epithets.

84. *Danaoi*: the Greeks.

85. *cresset*: a metal cup, mounted or hung, containing oil or pitch that is burned as a beacon.

86. *Veronese ... Giorgione ... Corot*: Gilbert paints word pictures of three canvases: Veronese's 'Vision of St Helen', the 'Fête Champêtre' (now usually attributed to Titian rather than to Giorgione) and Corot's 'The Dance of the Nymphs'.

87. *epos*: epic poetry.

88. *statue is concentrated*: Lessing contrasts sculpture and poetry in his famous treatise *Laokoon* (1766), a passage Wilde glossed as 'brilliant' in the commonplace book he kept at Oxford. Pater touched on the same theme in his essay on Winckelmann: 'at first sight sculpture, with its solidity of form, seems a thing more real and full than the faint, abstract world of poetry or painting. Still the fact is the reverse. Discourse and action show man as he is, more directly than the play of muscles and the moulding of the flesh; and over these poetry has command.'

89. *a masterpiece of style*: Flaubert's novel *Madame Bovary*, published 1857, followed the miserable fortunes in love of the hopelessly sentimental wife of a provincial doctor.

90. *Lewis Morris ... Ohnet ... Henry Arthur Jones*: Morris (1833–1907) wrote cheerful popular verse. Georges Ohnet (1848–1918) was a popular French writer whose novels combined sentimentality with snobbery. Jones (1851–1929) first achieved fame as a playwright in the 1880s with sentimental comedies and melodramas.

91. Bestia Trionfans: an allegorical figure, used by Giordano Bruno in his philosophical dialogue *Spaccio della Bestia Trionfante (The Expulsion of the Triumphant Beast*, 1584), to signify the vices which struggle to dominate over the moral virtues of Prudence, Wisdom, Law and Universal Judgement.

92. *one whose gracious memory we all revere*: Matthew Arnold, who died suddenly of a stroke in 1888. In his elegy *Thyrsis* (1867), Arnold complains that Proserpina precisely has not seen the 'Cumnor cowslips', that is, the primroses blooming in fields south-west of Oxford.

93. *Mr Ruskin's views on Turner*: in the beginning, Ruskin intended merely to write a pamphlet defending J. M. W. Turner against obtuse and hostile criticism. By the end, Ruskin had produced five thick volumes published over a period of seventeen years (1843–60). Turner left his paintings to the nation.

94. *Mr Pater has put into the portrait of Monna Lisa*: Pater's celebrated prose poem on the Mona Lisa – which Gilbert proceeds to quote – appeared in his essay on Leonardo da Vinci, first published in the *Fortnightly Review* in 1869 and later reprinted in *The Renaissance*.

95. Tannhäuser: Wagner's operatic version (1845) of the Tannhäuser legend, in which a poet follows Venus into a 'caverned hill' of sensual bliss. Roused at last by his conscience, Tannhäuser makes his way to Rome for absolution. The Pope denies him, saying that there is as little hope of Tannhäuser's being forgiven as of his own wooden staff bursting into bloom. Three days after the poet departs in despair, the Pope's staff miraculously blossoms. Although messengers are hurriedly sent out to bring Tannhäuser back, the poet has returned to the cave of Venus and is never found. The legend became a parable of accursed artist (*poète maudit*) among fin de siècle writers. In *The Picture of Dorian Gray* Wilde shows Dorian as repeatedly attending performances of *Tannhäuser*, 'seeing the prelude to that great work of art as a presentation of the tragedy of his own soul'.

96. ΕΡΩΣ ΤΩΝ ΑΔΨΝΑΤΩΝ: Greek for 'love of the impossible'. The phrase derives from a speech in Euripides' *Heracles* in which Hercules' father Amphitryon attempts to save his grandchildren from a sentence of death ('I am in love with what cannot be'). The expression subsequently became proverbial.

97. *Dorian music*: among the ancient Greeks, a mode of music that was simple and solemn, and hence believed to be conducive to military valour.

98. *Chambertin and a few ortolans*: Burgundy wine and a species of small bird like a bunting considered a rare culinary delicacy.

The Critic as Artist – Part II

First published under the title 'The True Function and Value of Criticism; with some Remarks on the Importance of Doing Nothing: A Dialogue' in the *Nineteenth Century* for September 1890.

1. *Thersites*: see n. 13, p. 328 above.

2. *'terribly at ease in Zion'*: a phrase Matthew Arnold in *Culture and Anarchy* attributes to Thomas Carlyle; here, it means to be obtusely complacent in a situation where awe or reverence is called for.

3. *Rector of Lincoln*: Mark Pattison (1813–84), who was elected Rector or head of Lincoln College, Oxford, in 1861, published a biographical study of Milton in 1879.

4. *Marlowe's greater son*: i.e. Shakespeare. Before his death in 1593, Marlowe wrote plays for the Earl of Pembroke's Men, the acting company Shakespeare is believed to have joined when he first came up to London.

5. *creator of the* Agamemnon: i.e. Aeschylus, earliest of the major Greek dramatists (525–456 BC). *Agamemnon* was the first play in his trilogy of the *Oresteia* (458 BC).

6. *Athens of Pericles*: Athens achieved its golden age under Pericles (490–429 BC).

7. *one whose feet are wounded*: i.e. Oedipus, who was exposed at birth and had his feet spiked to prevent him from fulfilling the terrible prophecy of the Delphic Oracle that he would kill his father and marry his mother. Surviving into adulthood, Oedipus is ignorant of his parentage when he confronts the Sphinx, a she-monster who demands – on penalty of death – correct answers to her riddles. Oedipus vanquishes the Sphinx only to fall victim to the dreadful prophecy.

8. *Mantegna*: Andrea Mantegna (1431–1506), early Renaissance artist whose close study of antique statues, reliefs and vases as a youth profoundly influenced his later painting and engraving.

9. *Rubenstein*: Anton Rubenstein (1829–94), Russian pianist and composer, who began performing as a child prodigy. Upon completing his musical education, Rubenstein began a series of concert tours through Europe, America and Russia which were by the 1880s attracting immense attention and acclaim.

10. *the author of* Obiter Dicta: Augustine Birrell (1850–1933), English author and politician who published the first of his witty collections of criticism in 1884. He became a Liberal MP in 1889.

11. *Roman poet*: i.e. Virgil, who in Book I of the *Aeneid* speaks of *Sunt lacrimae rerum et mentem mortalia tangunt* or, as Wilde himself would translate the line in *De Profundis*, 'one of the tears of which the world is made, and of the sadness of all human things'.

12. Divine Comedy: by Dante Alighieri (1265–1321). In this and the next paragraph, Gilbert paints word pictures of some of the notable scenes from the poem, though not strictly in the narrative order of the poem.

13. *great Florentine*: i.e. Dante. Born in Florence, he was exiled from the city by his political enemies in 1301, never to return.

14. *nenuphars*: water lilies.

15. *Baudelaire's masterpiece*: i.e. *Les Fleurs du mal (Flowers of Evil)*, a volume of poems dedicated to Gautier and published in 1857. Gilbert quotes the opening lines 'Que m'importe que tu sois sage?/ Sois belle! Et sois triste!' ('What do I care if you're good?/ Be beautiful and sad!') from 'Madrigal Triste', one of the poems added to the third edition of 1868.

16. *poisonous honey*: in 'To the Queen', a poem of 1872, Tennyson, thinking of Baudelaire's unwholesome influence upon Swinburne, had denounced, 'Art with poisonous honey stol'n from France.'

17. *Perdita*: the heroine of *The Winter's Tale*, raised as a shepherdess though of royal birth, who keeps a garden where grow the 'flowers/ Of middle summer': 'Hot lavender, mints, savory, marjoram;/ The marigold, that goes to bed wi' the sun.'

18. *Meleager*: Meleager of Gadara (present-day Syria), a gifted Greek poet who lived around 60 BC, writing exquisite short poems of love and death. These he collected with similar poems by other writers in an early anthology, now lost, which became the model for the later Greek Anthology (see n. 66, p. 360 above).

19. *Fantine*: character in Victor Hugo's novel *Les Misérables* (1862) who sacrifices her front teeth to save her infant daughter Cosette. Pater, in his Winckelmann essay, refers to 'the bleeding mouth of Fantine'.

20. *Manon Lescaut*: heroine of the abbé Prévost's celebrated tale of the same name (published 1731), who leads her noble but romantically besotted lover through a series of degrading adventures that ultimately end with exile in New Orleans and death in the American desert.

21. *Tyrian*: Adonis, a beautiful youth and prince of Syria beloved by both Aphrodite and Persephone, but later killed by a boar sent by Artemis. In the annual festival held in his honour at Alexandria, the image of Adonis was carried down to the shore and cast into the sea by women with dishevelled hair and bared breasts.

22. *Orestes*: son of Agamemnon, who avenges his father's murder by killing his mother and her guilty lover, and thereupon is pursued by the Furies.

23. *Spinoza*: see n. 4, p. 312 above.

24. *the great art-critic of the Greeks*: i.e. Aristotle, whom Wilde admired for his inductive method in aesthetics, proceeding from the individual artwork to more general principles. Here Gilbert outlines Aristotle's famous doctrine of catharsis or the purgation of the emotions through pity and terror brought about by tragic drama.

25. *Cordelia and the daughter of Brabantio*: Cordelia is Lear's youngest daughter, who is hanged at the end of *King Lear*. Brabantio's daughter is Desdemona, the innocent wife killed by her husband at the end of *Othello*.

26. città divina ... fruitio Dei: Italian for 'divine' or 'ideal city'; the phrase, which Wilde found in Pater's essay 'Sandro Botticelli', is an error for *La città di vita* ('The City of Life'), a fifteenth-century poem by Matteo Palmieri. The Latin words *fruitio Dei* mean 'enjoyment of God' – a medieval schoolman's phrase that Wilde had found in Benjamin Jowett's introduction to Plato's *Symposium*, and copied into his Oxford commonplace book.

27. *Academic philosopher*: i.e. the true philosopher as described by Socrates in Plato's *Republic*.

28. *Pater*: Pater asks in his essay 'Coleridge', 'Who would change the colour or curve of a rose-leaf for that ... colourless, formless, intangible, being – Plato put so high?'

29. *Philo ... Eckhart ... Böhme ... Swedenborg*: Philo Judeaus, who flourished around AD 39, was the most important philosopher of Hellenistic Judaism. In his effort to make the sacred text appeal to Greek readers, Philo stripped away all anthropomorphic references to God, a being he portrays as absolutely bare of qualities. Johannes, called Meister, Eckhart (1260?–1327), a German philosopher and mystic, was suspected of heresy by Church officials who mistrusted his homely and vivid mode of expression. Jakob Boehme (1575–1624) was a German mystical writer who 'saw' the root of all mysteries and the reconciliation of all contrasts in what he called the *Urgrund*, a word his

English translators rendered as 'Abyss'. Emanuel Swedenborg (1688–1772) was a Swedish scientist and philosopher whose life as a mystic began in 1745 when, he said, the Lord manifested Himself to him in person and permitted Swedenborg to see the heavens and the hells.

30. *Nemesis*: Greek goddess of vengeance.

31. *Fates*: in Greek mythology, the three old sisters who determined the span of human life – represented as a thread – with Clotho holding the spindle, Lachesis drawing off the thread and Atropos cutting it short.

32. *Leopardi*: Giacomo Leopardi (1798–1837), Italian poet and satirist, whose extraordinary gifts, thwarted ambition and miserable health helped to endow his writing with a pervasive pessimism.

33. *Theocritus*: *c*.310–*c*.250 BC, the creator of Greek pastoral poetry.

34. *Pierre Vidal*: Provençal troubadour (d. *c*.1200) who became the celebrated bard at the court of Alphonso III of Aragon.

35. *Abelard*: Peter Abelard (1079–1142), the brilliant disputant and founder of scholastic theology in Paris whose tragic love for Héloïse, a learned girl of noble rank, led to her pregnancy, his castration and their separation, with Héloïse entering a convent and Abelard becoming a monk.

36. *Villon*: François Villon (b. 1431), a French poet whose riotous life notoriously alternated between the tavern and the gaol.

37. *Endymion*: in Greek myth, a youth so handsome as to attract the love of the moon. Keats's poetic version of the tale was published in 1818. Here Wilde is using the poetic character as a synonym for the poet.

38. *Atys*: in Phrygian myth, a beautiful young man beloved by the earth goddess Cybele, who, upon finding that the youth preferred a mortal maiden, caused him to castrate himself. Violets later sprang from his blood.

39. *the Dane*: Hamlet.

40. *'the best that is known and thought in the world'*: Arnold's famous definition of Culture.

41. *Epicurus*: Greek philosopher (341–270 BC).

42. *ΒΙΟΣ ΘΕΟΡΗΤΙΚΟΣ*: Greek for 'the contemplative life'.

43. *harness*: i.e. no accident or lucky shot can pierce his defences. The metaphor is from 1 Kings 22:34: 'And a certain man drew a bow at a venture, and smote the king of Israel between the joints of the harness.'

44. *Philistine*: n. 15, p. 309 above.

45. *Fabianists*: i.e. Fabian socialists such as Beatrice and Sidney Webb and George Bernard Shaw who favoured a strategy of slow, incremental parliamentary gains over the violent revolution advocated by such Marxian socialists as William Morris.

46. *Utopia*: an ideal commonwealth existing nowhere, as first described in fiction by Sir Thomas More in 1516.

47. *Chuang Tsŭ*: fourth-century BC Taoist philosopher much admired by Wilde.

48. nouveau frisson: 'new sensation or thrill'. Victor Hugo famously said of Baudelaire that he had introduced a *nouveau frisson* into poetry.

49. Luministe: French school of painting stressing the effects of light and atmosphere.

50. Symboliste: French impulse in poetry deriving from Baudelaire, Mallarmé, Verlaine and Rimbaud.

51. *he who set Milton talking to Marvel*: Walter Savage Landor (1775–1864), poet and prose writer, whose *Imaginary Conversations* (1824–9) paired famous historical characters, as here, the seventeenth-century poets John Milton and Andrew Marvell and the sixteenth-century poets and courtiers Sir Philip Sidney and Fulke Greville (Lord Brooke), in dialogues of great wit and charm.

52. *Imaginary Portraits*: Pater's collection of four fictional portraits, depicting a French painter, a Dutch student of philosophy, a medieval organ-builder and a minor German prince, was published in 1887.

53. *Lucian*: see n. 60, p. 359 above.

54. *Giordano Bruno*: see n. 38, p. 321 above. During his many years of residence in England, he became acquainted with Sir Philip Sidney and published imaginatively vigorous but obscure allegorical dialogues.

55. *grand old Pagan*: i.e. Landor, see n. 51 above.

56. *Ruskin . . . Rossetti*: Wilde here names the pantheon of his literary heroes who have created the 'art-literature' of the nineteenth century. He refers here to two sonnets Rossetti wrote about art works: 'For a Venetian Pastoral, by Giorgione' and 'For Ruggiero and Angelica, by Ingres'. For Giorgione, see n. 23, p. 349 above. Jean August Dominique Ingres (1780–1867), French painter of Oriental scenes and supremely elegant portraits.

57. *Tartuffe*: see n. 24, p. 338 above.

58. *Chadband*: oily clergyman and canting hypocrite in Dickens's *Bleak House*.

59. *Temperament*: cf. Pater's preface to *Studies in the History of the Renaissance*: 'What is important, then, is not that the critic should possess a correct abstract definition of beauty for the intellect, but a certain kind of temperament, the power of being deeply moved by the presence of beautiful objects.'

60. *Waynfleete's chapel*: William of Waynfleete in 1458 founded Magdalen College, where Wilde was an undergraduate. Its chapel was noted for its fine boys' choir.

61. *fritillaries*: a species of lily-like bulbs, producing drooping, bell-shaped, spotted flowers, named after the Latin word for 'dice-box'.

62. *Laud's building*: William Laud (1573–1645), later archbishop of Canterbury, became in 1629 a vigorous and innovative chancellor of Oxford University, where he improved his own college of St John by building a magnificent back quadrangle after designs by Inigo Jones.

63. *Caliban*: see n. 16, p. 309 above.

64. *Gautier's immortal* Symphonie en Blanc Majeur: Gautier's poem ('Symphony in White Major') was published in *Émaux et camées*. Wilde is suggesting here that Whistler has not acknowledged the debt of his many 'Symphony in White' paintings to Gautier. The Impressionist painters were among the first to show that white light casts lavender – not black – shadows.

65. *'moment's monument'*: an allusion to D. G. Rossetti's sonnet on sonnets at the beginning of his sonnet sequence *The House of Life*: 'A sonnet is a moment's monument'. The French literary critic Hippolyte Taine had argued that 'the moment made the man', along with the two other determining influences of race and milieu.

66. Archaicistes: Gustave Moreau (1826–98) and his followers, a group later to be assimilated to the Symbolist painters.

67. *Queen Constance*: character in Shakespeare's *King John*, whose grief for her son Arthur is most eloquent while the youth still lives.

68. *the demand of the intellect, as has been well said*: said specifically by Pater, in his chapter on Winckelmann in *Studies in the History of the Renaissance* (1873).

69. *Royal Academician . . . Athenaeum Club*: founded in 1768, the Royal Academy of Arts had only forty full members, who thus tended to be older, more established painters. As the pre-eminent club for literary, artistic and intellectual men in London, the Athenaeum (founded 1824) also tended to draw a more settled and conservative membership.

70. *the poet of the cloud and the poet of the lake*: i.e. Shelley and Wordsworth.

71. *Sir Joshua . . . Gainsborough*: for Sir Joshua Reynolds, see n. 1, p. 307 above. Thomas Gainsborough (1727–88), landscape and portrait painter, a rival to Sir Joshua. His looser brushwork and turbulently Romantic backgrounds put his work at odds with Reynolds's, which was noted for its classical restraint and high finish.

72. *Walter Besant*: English novelist whose *All Sorts and Conditions of Men* (1882) began the fashion for East End fiction. (See n. 21, p. 338 above.) In October 1888, Besant was among a group of members who backed Wilde's admission to the Savile Club. His election was postponed indefinitely, however, apparently due to opposition.

73. Le Rouge et le noir: celebrated novel published by Stendhal, the pen-name of Henri Beyle, in 1830.

74. *Manchester school*: the economic and political theories of free trade, *laissez-*

faire and self-interest as promulgated by the Manchester politicians Richard Cobden and John Bright and their followers.

75. *blood-stained battle*: i.e. the Franco-Prussian War of 1870–71.

76. *Eckermann*: Johann Eckermann faithfully preserved a record of his conversations with Goethe from 1823 until the poet's death in 1832.

77. Origin of Species: Charles Darwin published his revolutionary work in 1859.

78. *Julian ... Montaigne*: Julian the Apostate (AD 331–63), Roman emperor whose contempt for Christianity prompted him to reintroduce paganism. For Michel de Montaigne, see n. 32, p. 320 above. His gaiety, irony and scepticism about all human claims to certainty exerted a gently corrosive influence on religious belief in succeeding centuries.

79. *antinomian*: one who believes the moral law is not binding upon himself. In *De Profundis* Wilde would declare, 'I am a born antinomian. I am one of those who are made for exceptions, not for laws.'

4. The Truth of Masks

A shorter version of this essay was first published under the title 'Shakespeare and Stage Costume' in the *Nineteenth Century* for May 1885. By the summer of 1891 Wilde had become dissatisfied with the essay, proposing that the French translation of *Intentions* substitute *The Soul of Man under Socialism* for it as the fourth essay of the collection.

1. *Mrs Langtry*: Lily Langtry, professional beauty and English actress (1853–1929) much celebrated by Wilde and patronized by the Prince of Wales. Wilde addressed his 1879 poem 'The New Helen' to her.

2. *leather and prunella*: a conventional expression, deriving from a line of Alexander Pope's, meaning something to which one is entirely indifferent.

3. *Lord Lytton*: Edward Robert Bulwer-Lytton, first earl of Lytton (1831–91), diplomat, poet (under the name of 'Owen Meredith') and son of the author of *The Last Days of Pompeii*. Lord Lytton published an essay on 'Miss Anderson's Juliet' in the December 1884 number of the *Nineteenth Century*, in which he declared, in a covert attack upon the brilliant stage designer E. W. Godwin, that 'the attempt to archaeologize the Shakespearean drama is one of the stupidest pedantries of this age of prigs'. Wilde was a friend of Godwin (1833–86), who decorated his Tite Street house. Wilde later became friendly with Lytton, visiting him in Paris a few days before his death, and dedicating *Lady Windermere's Fan* to his memory in 1893.

4. *collars of S. S.*: the collar is an ornamental chain consisting of a series of S's joined together, the mark of a knight and, originally, of an adherent of the House of Lancaster. In the coronation scene of *Henry the Eighth* (IV, i), the nobles Dorset, Surrey, Suffolk and Norfolk wear collars of S's.

5. Henry the Sixth: in *King Henry the Sixth, Part II* (II, i), the Duke of Gloucester tests the claim of a poor blind man that his sight has been miraculously restored by St Alban by asking him to name the colours of the duke's cloak and gown. When the fellow succeeds, Gloucester declares he is a fraud, because a truly blind man would be unable to associate the names 'red' and 'black' with the proper hues.

6. *Anne Page's gown*: Anne Page's father directs her to wear a white gown at a masquerade so his preferred suitor can elope with her. Meanwhile, Anne's mother arranges for the girl to wear a green gown so her own candidate can carry her off. Fenton, Anne's true lover, thwarts both plans by dressing two boys in white and green gowns to decoy the suitors, and escapes to marry Anne himself.

7. *Posthumus*: in this paragraph and the two that follow, Wilde demonstrates, as he does throughout the essay, both his deep knowledge of Shakespeare's plays and his acute sense of the expressive force of costume as an element in theatrical representation.

8. *Aristophanes ... Mr Gilbert*: for Aristophanes, see n. 103, p. 345 above. Sir William Schwenk Gilbert (1836–1911) was the brilliant satirist and comic-opera lyricist who collaborated so long and profitably with Sir Arthur Sullivan.

9. *cap-à-pie*: from head to foot.

10. *Chimène*: heroine of *Le Cid*, tragedy by Pierre Corneille (1606–84). Chimène wears mourning for her father, killed in a duel by her lover Rodrigue, who fights in order to vindicate the honour of his own father.

11. *Cloten*: in *Cymbeline* (II, iv) the widowed Imogen tells her villanous half-brother Cloten, who has declared his love, that she prefers her husband's 'meanest garment/ That ever hath but clipp'd his body' to Cloten himself. In revenge, Cloten plans to rape Imogen in the clothes her husband wore when she last saw him.

12. Thérèse Raquin: powerful novel by Émile Zola published in 1867. After Thérèse and her lover murder her husband, the pair are so haunted by terrors and visions of his corpse that they eventually commit suicide.

13. *Salvini*: Tommaso Salvini, Italian actor (1829–1915) noted for the emotional realism of his portrayals. Salvini performed frequently in England, retiring from the stage in 1890.

14. *beaver*: the lower part of a helmet protecting the mouth and chin.

15. *Miss Ellen Terry's brother*: Fred Terry (1863–1933) performed the role of

Gerald Arbuthnot in Wilde's *A Woman of No Importance* (1893). Ellen Terry (1848–1928) played Viola in *Twelfth Night* at Irving's Lyceum Theatre in 1884. It is essential to the plot of *Twelfth Night* that Viola and her brother Sebastian closely resemble each other. Separated in a shipwreck, brother and sister later encounter each other when Viola is disguised as a man. Upon seeing the pair together, their trusty servant exclaims, 'An apple, cleft in two, is not more twin/ Than these two creatures.'

16. *Auguste Vacquerie*: French author and critic (1819–95). The quotation reads, 'Racine abhors reality. He does not deign to concern himself with costume. If one were to follow the directions of the poet, Agamemnon would be dressed with nothing more than a sceptre and Achilles with only a sword.'

17. mundus muliebris: Latin for 'feminine world'.

18. *Philosophy of Clothes*: in his celebrated book *Sartor Resartus* ('the tailor re-patched'), Thomas Carlyle portrayed the vast nineteenth-century transformations in human life and institutions as changes merely in the external appearance of things ('old clothes'), while the divine reality immanent within continued as before – if only men and women would recognize it.

19. *Blackstone*: Sir William Blackstone's *Commentaries on the Laws of England* (1765–69) established him as the pre-eminent authority on the English common law and constitution.

20. *Paxton*: Joseph Paxton (1801–65), English gardener and designer, whose ingenious design for the Crystal Palace – made of prefabricated and modular glass and iron – at the great Exhibition of 1851 earned him a knighthood from the Queen.

21. *serge*: a type of rough cloth made from twilled worsted or woollen fabric.

22. *as much delight in Caliban as he has in Ariel*: cf. John Keats's famous description of the poetical character in one of his letters: 'It has as much delight in conceiving an Iago as an Imogen.'

23. *Ducis*: Jean-François Ducis (1733–1816), French dramatist and author of verse adaptations of Shakespeare's plays. Ducis hesitated at translating 'handkerchief' into French as *mouchoir* (handkerchief) because of its 'low' connotations: the verb *moucher* means 'to wipe or blow the nose of'. Instead Ducis chose *bandeau* (headband, fillet), in much the way a modern-day news commentator might say 'abdomen' rather than 'gut'.

24. le héros métallique: in an essay on Balzac published in *Portraits contemporains* (1874), Gautier says that the 'metallic hero' of *La Comédie humaine* was more interesting to modern readers than Werther or Lara or Waverley.

25. *Globe Theatre*: the theatre was set ablaze in 1613, when a cannon required by the stage directions in Shakespeare's *King John* misfired.

26. *fardingales*: the fardingale (more commonly, farthingale), was a hooped petticoat or elaborate framework for extending a woman's skirt worn in the sixteenth and seventeenth centuries.

27. *Janissaries*: a janissary was one of the élite corps in the Ottoman sultan's personal standing army.

28. donnée: the premise or given situation established at the beginning of a play, poem, etc.

29. *Infessura*: Stefano Infessura (1436–*c*.1500), Italian antipapal historian and jurist. His *Diario della città Roma* treated the period from 1294 to 1494. Wilde is paraphrasing from John Addington Symonds's *The Renaissance in Italy: The Age of the Despots* (1875).

30. *Niccola Pisano*: Nicola Pisano, Italian sculptor and architect (1206–78) whose rediscovery of classical sources in his art is much stressed by Vasari. The pulpit Wilde refers to is probably that of the Baptistery in Pisa (1260), considered the most beautiful of Pisano's works, although his pulpit for the Siena cathedral (1268) is larger and more magnificent.

31. *Mantegna*: see n. 8, pp. 363–4 above.

32. *Cellini*: see n. 41, p. 334 above.

33. la casaque à mahoitres, les voulgiers, le gallimard taché d'encre, les craaquiniers: In *Notre-Dame de Paris*, his novel of fifteenth-century Parisian life as it centred in the great cathedral, Victor Hugo made much use of Old French terms, here for military garments ('cassock with epaulettes') and two different kinds of soldiers (the *voulgier* was armed with a *vouge* or halberd, the *craaquinier* with an arbalest or crossbow). A *gallimard* was a case or compartment within a writing desk used for holding pens and penknives, and thus typically 'ink-stained' (*taché d'encre*).

34. disc of Theodosius: the universal sundial invented by the Greek geometer, astronomer and mathematician Theodosius of Tripolis (second or first century BC), which is praised by Vitruvius in *De architectura*.

35. *E. W. Godwin* . . . Claudian: for Godwin, see nn. 65–7, p. 375 below. For *Claudian*, see n. 66, p. 375 below.

36. *Lemprière's Dictionary*: John Lemprière (1765–1824), English classical scholar whose *Classical Dictionary* (1788) became a highly readable if not completely reliable reference work on classical history and mythology. Keats learned the book virtually by heart at his Enfield school, and drew upon it when he wrote *Endymion*.

37. *Professor Max Müller*: Friedrich Max Müller (1823–1900), German-born professor of comparative philology at Oxford, whose mastery of Sanskrit and other Indo-European languages led him to assert that myths derived from the corruption of names for divine powers. Summing up this shift from words to gods by fancifully calling myth a 'disease of language', Müller further posited that there was a single Indo-European solar myth at the root of all myths. Wilde attended Müller's lectures at Oxford.

38. *Piranesi*: Giovanni Battista Piranesi (d. 1778), Italian engraver of ancient architectural subjects.

39. *Vitruvius*: Marcus Vitruvius Pollio, Roman architect, engineer and author who lived in the first century BC. His great treatise on architecture, lost for centuries, was rediscovered in the fifteenth century and thereafter became the bible of the Renaissance classical revival.

40. *Vecellio*: Tiziano Vecellio (*c.*1485–1576), the artist currently known as Titian, hence Wilde's later joke about the drawings of Vecellio 'being probably from the hand of Titian'.

41. *Munster's* Cosmography: Sebastian Münster, German scholar and geographer (*c.*1489–1552), produced the *Cosmographia universalis* in 1544. Profusely illustrated with woodcuts, the work was repeatedly reprinted in the sixteenth and seventeenth centuries.

42. *Revival of learning*: the Renaissance in its relation to literature and scholarship, e.g. the rediscovery, translation and editing of Greek and Latin classical works.

43. *foils*: a foil is a light sword with a button at the tip used in fencing. The word is of obscure origin and, according to the *Oxford English Dictionary*, does not appear in English before 1594.

44. *Hector's indiscreet quotation from Aristotle*: in Shakespeare's *Troilus and Cressida* (II, ii), the Trojan hero Hector, rebuking Paris and Troilus for giving specious reasons for keeping Helen (instead of returning her to her Greek husband), says they have spoken superficially, 'not much/ Unlike young men, whom Aristotle thought/ Unfit to hear moral philosophy'. Aristotle, however, was born some 800 years after the Trojan War.

45. dramatis personae: Latin phrase referring to the list of characters in a play.

46. *Lord Cobham*: Henry Brooke, Lord Cobham (d. 1619). Accused as a conspirator in a Catholic plot against King James I, he in turn accused Sir Walter Ralegh of complicity in it. Though condemned to die, Cobham was allowed by the king to return to the Tower, where he proceeded to live for many years. He later died in poverty.

47. *Virgilia*: wife of Coriolanus in the Shakespeare play of the same name. The Latin phrase means, 'She stayed at home [and] made wool [cloth].'

48. *Princess Katharine*: Princess Katharine of France is wooed in English and broken French by King Henry at the end of Shakespeare's *Henry the Fifth*.

49. *Holinshed*: Raphael Holinshed (died 1580?), whose *Chronicles of England* (1577) became a source for Shakespeare and other Elizabethan dramatists.

50. *Wars of the Roses*: the thirty-year civil war between the houses of York and Lancaster began in 1455 in Henry VI's reign and ended with the defeat and death of Richard III at Bosworth Field in 1485. The victor, Henry VII, then married Elizabeth of York, uniting the two lines. Shakespeare's *Henry the Sixth*, Parts I, II, III, and *Richard the Third* are directly concerned with the struggle.

51. *School Board children*: pupils, generally from the poorer classes, who were taught in the government-sponsored elementary schools established by the Elementary Education Act of 1870.

52. *Heywood*: Thomas Heywood, prolific dramatist (1574?–1641), called by Charles Lamb a 'prose Shakespeare'. His tract *An Apology for Actors* (1612) was edited for the Shakespeare Society in 1841.

53. *'imp of fame'*: in Shakespeare's play (IV, i), King Henry is called this by one of his soldiers. 'Imp' here means son or offspring. Agincourt, a village near Calais in northern France, was the site of the decisive victory over the French in 1415 by Henry V and his English archers.

54. *tabards*: a tabard was a loose outer garment, with short sleeves or sleeveless, worn by knights over their armour and generally emblazoned with the arms of the wearer.

55. *triumph of the Philistines in 1645*: in 1645 Oliver Cromwell's New Model Army decisively defeated Charles I's soldiers at Naseby. Thereafter the monarchy and royalist partisans were in retreat before the forces of republicanism and religious dissent until the king's execution and the dissolution of the House of Lords in 1649.

56. *Charles Brandon*: Charles Brandon, first duke of Suffolk (1485–1545), brawling courtier and favourite of Henry VIII. In 1514 Brandon went to France to witness the marriage of Henry's daughter to Louis XII. While there, he participated in a joust as part of the wedding celebrations, and overthrew his opponent, horse and man.

57. *Black Prince*: the name given to Edward, prince of Wales (1330–76), eldest son of Edward III (1312–77), probably after the colour of his armour. The Black Prince was victor over the French in the great battle of Poitiers (1356). His helmet, shield and other equipment were displayed at his tomb in Canterbury cathedral.

58. *Bosworth field*: the battle of 1485 won by Henry, earl of Richmond, later Henry VII, ending the civil war between Lancaster and York. Henry VII hung the banner in 'old St Paul's', the medieval cathedral (built eleventh to thirteenth centuries) which was replaced by Christopher Wren's Baroque cathedral (built 1675–1710).

59. *Plutarch*: the Greek biographer Plutarch (AD *c*.46–*c*.120) tells the story of

Caius Marcius Coriolanus in *Parallel Lives*, a work Shakespeare knew in the famous translation of Sir Thomas North (1579).

60. *Racine*: Jean Racine, French tragic dramatist (1639–99). *Louis Quatorze* dress refers to clothing worn *c.*1650–1700.

61. *Les petits détails d'histoire . . . au fond*: 'The little details of history and domestic life ought to be scrupulously studied and reproduced by the poet, but solely as means of heightening the reality of the whole, and making penetrate into the darkest corners of the work this general and powerful life, in the middle of which characters are more true and, consequently, catastrophes more poignant. Everything should be subordinated to this purpose. Man in the foreground, the rest in the background.'

62. *Ruy Blas*: eponymous hero of Victor Hugo's verse drama (1838). Ruy Blas, a noble-minded valet, is coerced into disguising himself as a grandee and paying suit to the queen of Spain, a woman he has worshipped from afar.

63. la croix de gueules: both *la croix rouge* and *la croix de gueules* mean 'red cross', but *gueules* (English 'gules') is the heraldic term for the colour, and hence more appropriate to a seventeenth-century character. In the note quoted in French by Wilde, Hugo apologizes for such anachronism, saying, 'I offer all my excuses for it here to intelligent spectators; let us hope that some day a Venetian lord may safely show his coat of arms quite frankly on the stage. It is an improvement that will come.'

64. *caviare to the general*: a phrase meaning 'pleasures too rarefied for the multitude to appreciate'. In *Hamlet* (ii, ii), Hamlet praises and quotes from an 'excellent' play that failed because it 'pleased not the million; 'twas caviare to the general'.

65. *Mr and Mrs Bancroft*: Squire Bancroft (1841–1926) and his wife Marie Wilton (1839–1921), actor-managers who were admired for the 'cup and saucer' realism of their productions. E. W. Godwin served as historical adviser to the Bancrofts for their 1875 production of *The Merchant of Venice*.

66. *Mr Barrett's* Claudian: Wilson Barrett (1846–1904), actor-manager and author, produced *Claudian* by W. G. Wills in 1883. E. W. Godwin designed the sets for the production, lavishly praised by Wilde above.

67. *Lady Archibald Campbell's production*: in July 1884, a mixed troupe of amateur and professional actors, organized by the society hostess Lady Archibald Campbell, performed the forest scenes from *As You Like It* in an outdoors setting at Coombe Park, Surrey. The production was both designed and directed by the redoubtable E. W. Godwin. Wilde saw a revival of this *plein air* production in May 1885, reviewing it in the *Dramatic Review*.

68. *'Nous célébrons tous quelque enterrement'*: 'We are all of us celebrating some funeral' – a remark about the pervasive black of modern dress made by

Baudelaire in the 'Heroism of Modern Life' section of his essay 'The Salon of 1846'.

69. *Mrs Langtry*: see n. 1, p. 369 above. In London in 1885, Lily Langtry performed and produced *Princess George*, an English translation of a play by Alexandre Dumas the younger (1824–95), the most successful French playwright of his day.

70. *marqueterie*: inlaid work of variously coloured wood or other materials, especially in furniture. Wilde uses the word here, one suspects, for its alliterative possibilities – a characteristic feature of his early prose style.

71. *Mademoiselle Mars*: the stage name of Anne-Françoise-Hippolyte Boutet (1779–1847), a celebrated actress with the Comédie Française from around 1800 to 1841.

72. Hernani: the Romantic verse drama by Victor Hugo which provoked riots at the Comédie Française, so revolutionary was its departure from classical theatrical conventions.

73. toque: a hat with little or no brim and often with a soft or full crown.

74. *Mr Forbes-Robertson, Mr Conway, Mr George Alexander*: Johnston Forbes-Robertson, actor-manager (1853–1937). His first great success was in a play by W. S. Gilbert, *Dan'l Druce, Blacksmith* (1876). Wilde hoped that Forbes-Robertson would play a lead in *Vera* (1882) and later in *Mr and Mrs Daventry*. H. B. Conway was an actor descended from Lord Byron, who according to Ellen Terry in *The Story of My Life* 'had a look of the *handsomest* portraits of the poet', though she did not think so highly of his acting abilities. George Alexander (1858–1918), actor, was manager of the St James's Theatre from 1890 to 1918. He produced and acted with great success in two of Wilde's plays, *Lady Windermere's Fan* (1892) and *The Importance of Being Earnest* (1895).

75. *Burleigh*: William Cecil, Lord Burleigh (1520–98), lord treasurer and chief minister under Queen Elizabeth.

76. *Macready ... Benjamin Webster*: for Macready, see n. 9, p. 348 above. Webster (1797–1882) was an English actor, manager and dramatic writer. During the middle years of the nineteenth century, he was celebrated as a comic actor and as the patron of the best playwriting and acting then offered. Webster retired from the stage in 1874.

77. *Pour être plus difficile, la tâche n'en est que plus glorieuse*: 'The task is only the more glorious for being more difficult.' Baudelaire makes the remark in the 'Heroism of Modern Life' section of 'The Salon of 1846'.

78. *the Platonic theory of ideas ... Hegel's system of contraries*: in the metaphysical theory of Plato (427–348 BC), the *idea* or *form* of a thing, constituting something like our abstract conception of that thing, has a real existence outside the world of sense – the *idea* is the unchanging reality behind the changing appearance. According to the *Logic* of G. W. F. Hegel (1770–1831), thought, the basis of all reality whether material or mental, follows a triadic 'law' of thesis, antithesis and synthesis: the first stage involves a primary affirmation and unification, the second a negation and differentiation, while the third, preserving the contradictory elements of the first two phases, unifies them at a higher level. Wilde became familiar with Hegelian philosophy at Oxford, where a powerful school of English expositors of Hegel established itself by the 1870s under the leadership of Benjamin Jowett, T. H. Green and Edward Caird.

FURTHER READING

Bibliography

Fletcher, Ian, and John Stokes, 'Oscar Wilde', in *Anglo-Irish Literature: A Review of Research*, ed. Richard J. Finneran (New York, 1976), pp. 48–137.

Fletcher, Ian, and John Stokes, 'Oscar Wilde', in *Recent Research on Anglo-Irish Writers: A Supplement to Anglo-Irish Literature: A Review of Research*, ed. Richard J. Finneran (New York, 1983), pp. 21–47.

Mason, Stuart [C. S. Millard], *A Bibliography of Oscar Wilde* (London, 1914).

Mikhail, E. H., *Oscar Wilde: An Annotated Bibliography of Criticism* (London, 1978).

Small, Ian, *Oscar Wilde Revalued: An Essay on New Materials and Methods of Research* (Greensboro, North Carolina, 1993).

Letters

The Letters of Oscar Wilde, ed. Rupert Hart-Davis (New York, 1962).

More Letters of Oscar Wilde, ed. Rupert Hart-Davis (London, 1985).

Biography

Ellmann, Richard, *Oscar Wilde* (London, 1987).

Mikhail, E. H. (ed.), *Oscar Wilde: Interviews and Recollections*, 2 vols. (London, 1979).

Criticism

Beckson, Karl (ed.), *Oscar Wilde: The Critical Heritage* (London, 1970).

Brown, Julia Prewitt, *Cosmopolitan Criticism: Oscar Wilde's Philosophy of Art* (Charlottesville, Virginia, 1997).

Danson, Lawrence, *Wilde's Intentions: The Artist in His Criticism* (Oxford, 1997).

Dowling, Linda, *The Vulgarization of Art: the Victorians and Aesthetic Democracy* (Charlottesville, Virginia, 1996).

Gagnier, Regenia, *Idylls of the Marketplace: Oscar Wilde and the Victorian Public* (Stanford, California, 1986).

Hollander, Elizabeth, 'Oscar Wilde' in the *Oxford Encyclopedia of Aesthetics* (New York, 1998), vol. 4, pp. 447–53.

McCormack, Jerusha (ed.), *Wilde the Irishman* (New Haven, Connecticut, 1998).

Schroeder, Horst, *Annotations to Oscar Wilde, 'The Portrait of Mr W. H.'* (Braunschweig, 1986).

Schroeder, Horst, *Oscar Wilde, 'The Portrait of Mr W. H.': Its Composition, Publication and Reception* (Braunschweig, 1984).

Smith II, Philip E., and Michael S. Helfand, *Oscar Wilde's Oxford Notebooks: A Portrait of a Mind in the Making* (Oxford, 1989).

READ MORE IN PENGUIN

In every corner of the world, on every subject under the sun, Penguin represents quality and variety – the very best in publishing today.

For complete information about books available from Penguin – including Puffins, Penguin Classics and Arkana – and how to order them, write to us at the appropriate address below. Please note that for copyright reasons the selection of books varies from country to country.

In the United Kingdom: Please write to *Dept. EP, Penguin Books Ltd, Bath Road, Harmondsworth, West Drayton, Middlesex UB7 0DA*

In the United States: Please write to *Consumer Services, Penguin Putnam Inc., 405 Murray Hill Parkway, East Rutherford, New Jersey 07073-2136.* VISA and MasterCard holders call 1-800-631-8571 to order Penguin titles

In Canada: Please write to *Penguin Books Canada Ltd, 10 Alcorn Avenue, Suite 300, Toronto, Ontario M4V 3B2*

In Australia: Please write to *Penguin Books Australia Ltd, 487 Maroondah Highway, Ringwood, Victoria 3134*

In New Zealand: Please write to *Penguin Books (NZ) Ltd, Private Bag 102902, North Shore Mail Centre, Auckland 10*

In India: Please write to *Penguin Books India Pvt Ltd, 11 Community Centre, Panchsheel Park, New Delhi 110017*

In the Netherlands: Please write to *Penguin Books Netherlands bv, Postbus 3507, NL-1001 AH Amsterdam*

In Germany: Please write to *Penguin Books Deutschland GmbH, Metzlerstrasse 26, 60594 Frankfurt am Main*

In Spain: Please write to *Penguin Books S. A., Bravo Murillo 19, 1°B, 28015 Madrid*

In Italy: Please write to *Penguin Italia s.r.l., Via Vittorio Emanuele 45/a, 20094 Corsico, Milano*

In France: Please write to *Penguin France, 12, Rue Prosper Ferradou, 31700 Blagnac*

In Japan: Please write to *Penguin Books Japan Ltd, Iidabashi KM-Bldg, 2-23-9 Koraku, Bunkyo-Ku, Tokyo 112-0004*

In South Africa: Please write to *Penguin Books South Africa (Pty) Ltd, P.O. Box 751093, Gardenview, 2047 Johannesburg*

A CHOICE OF CLASSICS

Matthew Arnold	**Selected Prose**
Jane Austen	**Emma**
	Lady Susan/The Watsons/Sanditon
	Mansfield Park
	Northanger Abbey
	Persuasion
	Pride and Prejudice
	Sense and Sensibility
William Barnes	**Selected Poems**
Mary Braddon	**Lady Audley's Secret**
Anne Brontë	**Agnes Grey**
	The Tenant of Wildfell Hall
Charlotte Brontë	**Jane Eyre**
	Juvenilia: 1829–35
	The Professor
	Shirley
	Villette
Emily Brontë	**Complete Poems**
	Wuthering Heights
Samuel Butler	**Erewhon**
	The Way of All Flesh
Lord Byron	**Don Juan**
	Selected Poems
Lewis Carroll	**Alice's Adventures in Wonderland**
	The Hunting of the Snark
Thomas Carlyle	**Selected Writings**
Arthur Hugh Clough	**Selected Poems**
Wilkie Collins	**Armadale**
	The Law and the Lady
	The Moonstone
	No Name
	The Woman in White
Charles Darwin	**The Origin of Species**
	Voyage of the Beagle
Benjamin Disraeli	**Coningsby**
	Sybil

READ MORE IN PENGUIN

A CHOICE OF CLASSICS

Edward Gibbon	**The Decline and Fall of the Roman Empire** (in three volumes)
	Memoirs of My Life
George Gissing	**New Grub Street**
	The Odd Women
William Godwin	**Caleb Williams**
	Concerning Political Justice
Thomas Hardy	**Desperate Remedies**
	The Distracted Preacher and Other Tales
	Far from the Madding Crowd
	Jude the Obscure
	The Hand of Ethelberta
	A Laodicean
	The Mayor of Casterbridge
	A Pair of Blue Eyes
	The Return of the Native
	Selected Poems
	Tess of the d'Urbervilles
	The Trumpet-Major
	Two on a Tower
	Under the Greenwood Tree
	The Well-Beloved
	The Woodlanders
George Lyell	**Principles of Geology**
Lord Macaulay	**The History of England**
Henry Mayhew	**London Labour and the London Poor**
George Meredith	**The Egoist**
	The Ordeal of Richard Feverel
John Stuart Mill	**The Autobiography**
	On Liberty
	Principles of Political Economy
William Morris	**News from Nowhere and Other Writings**
John Henry Newman	**Apologia Pro Vita Sua**
Margaret Oliphant	**Miss Marjoribanks**
Robert Owen	**A New View of Society and Other Writings**
Walter Pater	**Marius the Epicurean**
John Ruskin	**Unto This Last and Other Writings**

READ MORE IN PENGUIN

A CHOICE OF CLASSICS

Walter Scott	**The Antiquary**
	Heart of Mid-Lothian
	Ivanhoe
	Kenilworth
	The Tale of Old Mortality
	Rob Roy
	Waverley
Robert Louis Stevenson	**Kidnapped**
	Dr Jekyll and Mr Hyde and Other Stories
	In the South Seas
	The Master of Ballantrae
	Selected Poems
	Weir of Hermiston
William Makepeace Thackeray	**The History of Henry Esmond**
	The History of Pendennis
	The Newcomes
	Vanity Fair
Anthony Trollope	**Barchester Towers**
	Can You Forgive Her?
	Doctor Thorne
	The Eustace Diamonds
	Framley Parsonage
	He Knew He Was Right
	The Last Chronicle of Barset
	Phineas Finn
	The Prime Minister
	The Small House at Allington
	The Warden
	The Way We Live Now
Oscar Wilde	**Complete Short Fiction**
Mary Wollstonecraft	**A Vindication of the Rights of Woman**
	Mary and Maria (includes Mary Shelley's Matilda)
Dorothy and William Wordsworth	**Home at Grasmere**